BLOOD TIES

GORDON ANTHONY

For Stuart,
With thanks for his help, suggestions and patience

Britain
c. 78 A.D.

Smertae

Cereni

Decantae

Vacomagi

Creones

Taexali

Caledones

Boresti

Tava

Venicones

Bodotria

Damnonii

Votadini

Clota

Selgovae

Novantae

*Dun Brigantia

Carvetii

Brigantes

* Isuria

*Eboracum

Parisi

Cornovii

*

* Lindum

Deceangli

*

Deva

Coritani

Ordovices

*Viraconium

Iceni

*

Durobrivae

Demetae

Silures

Dobunni

Catuvellauni

Trinovantes

*

*

Camulodunum

* Glevum

Verulamium

*

Atrebates

*

Londinium

*

Calleva

Regni

Dumnonii

Isca

*

Note on Place Names

The following list provides details of the places mentioned in this story, along with other principal places in First Century Britain. Most of these are marked on the accompanying map.

Bodotria
The River Forth.

Calleva
A Roman town built close to modern Silchester in Hampshire. Once the capital of the tribe of the Atrebates, its full Latin name was Calleva Atrebatum

Camulodunon / Camulodunum
The Celtic / Roman forms respectively of a settlement which occupied the site of modern Colchester. The name means, "The fort of Camulos". Camulos was the war god of the Catuvellauni. The original, Iron Age settlement was reputedly founded by King Cunobelinos (Shakespeare's "Cymbeline") when he conquered, subdued or assimilated the neighbouring tribe of the Trinovantes. The Romans regarded it as the "Capital" of the Catuvellauni and established their own colony there soon after the invasion.

Clota
The River Clyde.

Deva
Deva commonly denotes the Roman fort and settlement on the site of modern Chester but is also applied to the River Dee in north Wales and Cheshire.

Dun Brigantia
There is a major Iron Age settlement at Stanwick, near Scotch Corner. The ancient name of this place has been lost, but it is commonly accepted that it was the home of a powerful leader among the Brigantes. In the absence of any evidence suggesting what this place might have been called, I have used the invented name of Dun Brigantia.

Durobrivae
A Roman fortified camp on the site of modern Water Newton in Cambridgeshire. The fort guarded a crossing of the River Neane and was located in a strategic position on the borders of several of the major Iron Age British tribes. Confusingly, the name Durobrivae can also refer to the town of Rochester in Kent.

Eboracum
A Roman fort and settlement on the site of modern York.

Gesoriacum
The Roman name for the port of Boulogne in modern France. Gesoriacum was the principal port used by the Romans for cross-Channel voyages.

Glevum
A Roman military fort established on the site of modern Gloucester.

Hafren
The Celtic name for the River Severn.

Iova
The island of Iona, off the west coast of modern Scotland. There is some evidence that suggests the island was home to a druidical sect long before the arrival of Columba and Christianity.

Isca
The name Isca is attached to several Roman towns in Britain. The one marked on my map is more properly known as Isca Dumnoniorum, a fort and later settlement on the site of modern Exeter.

Ister
The River Danube.

Isuria
The Romans established a town they called "Isurium Brigantum" which was built on the site of the modern village of Aldborough in North Yorkshire. The settlement of Isuria in the Calgacus stories is a fictional Iron Age town set in roughly the same location.

Lindum
A Roman fort built on the site of modern Lincoln.

Londinium
A Roman port and trading settlement built on the site of modern London.

Mona
The Roman name for the island of Anglesey.

Rhenus
The River Rhine

Sabrina
The Roman name for the River Severn.

Tamesas / Tamesis
The Celtic / Roman names respectively for the River Thames.

Tava
The River Tay.

Verlamion / Verulamium
The Celtic / Roman names respectively for a settlement built on the site of modern St. Albans. Verlamion was once the principal settlement of the powerful tribe of the Catuvellauni until Cunobelinos moved the royal residence to Camulodunon.

Viroconium
A Roman fort and settlement on the site of the modern village of Wroxeter, Shropshire.

Ynis Mon
The Celtic name for the island of Anglesey - the druids' spiritual home.

Part I – Ordovices

Chapter I

"Are they going to fight?" Candrix asked his father eagerly.

Cadwallon, King of the Ordovices, struggled to find an answer.

He clasped the hilt of his sword, feeling the sticky sweat of his palm on the leather-bound grip. His mouth was dry, filled with the old, never-forgotten taste of fear. Even the presence of his war band, arrayed in a long, ragged line on the gently sloping meadow in front of him, could not banish the terror that gripped his heart.

He was not a warrior. He never had been. He had come to the Kingship by virtue of being the only one of his father's sons to have outlived the old man. Now he was an old man himself and, like his father before him, he had only one son who had survived to adulthood.

Candrix's enthusiasm for the inevitable battle appalled him. The boy's mind had been filled with tales of glory by the songs of bards who praised the deeds of ancient heroes but who had no conception of the reality of war.

Cadwallon swallowed, trying to generate some saliva so that he could speak without his fear being evident. For the sake of his son, he had to show how a King should behave. Yet he had only ever fought once before, many years ago, at the dreadful battle of Caer Caradoc, where the tribes had fled before the might of the Roman Legions. Cadwallon would never admit it openly but he knew in his heart that he had been one of the first to turn tail. The sight of the awful savagery, of the blood, the hacked limbs and piles of fallen warriors had been too much for him. He had turned to run without striking a blow because he had known that to stand before the power of Rome was to die.

The memory of that dreadful day had never left him and he had wished never to see such sights again. Yet here he was, facing another battle. Steeling his nerves, he tried to tell himself that today could not be as bad as that distant morning when the hopes of the free tribes had been smashed.

"Father?" Candrix asked, thinking his father might not have heard his question.

Cadwallon managed to nod his head.

"They will fight," he said softly.

The prospect terrified him but he knew that he had no choice. He had retained his rule by virtue of his wealth, his influence and his ability to maintain a balance between the Romans to the east and the druids to the north-west. He called it a diplomatic balance, but he knew that others called it cowardice. Yet his people had been at peace for the past twenty five years, barring the odd raid or skirmish with their neighbouring tribes, and Cadwallon had been proud of that peace. It was the greatest achievement of his long and difficult reign.

Other tribes had been decimated by Rome, crushed whenever they dared offer any resistance, but the Ordovices had remained untouched by the expanding Empire's ambitions and Cadwallon had congratulated himself on staying aloof from the devastation that had afflicted those who were foolish enough to oppose Rome. He had not even attempted to take advantage of his weakened neighbours when the Legions withdrew because he had known that the Empire would regard any enlargement of his power base as a threat and he had no wish to antagonise an enemy he could never hope to defeat. Peace, he had assured his people, was the prize he sought.

For all his efforts, though, the peace was about to be shattered.

Yet it was not the Romans who posed the threat he had long feared. Instead, the danger had arisen from within his own tribe, where a rebel faction had sprung up, drawing young, disaffected warriors to its charismatic leader and openly challenging Cadwallon's right to rule.

After weeks of defiance, the rebels had seized a village that lay only a day's march from his own mountain homestead and they had called on all the chieftains of the Ordovices to pledge their allegiance to a new King. Some chieftains had done so. Others had refused, remaining loyal to Cadwallon. Most had not yet committed themselves but were waiting to see what Cadwallon would do.

He had no choice. He knew that. If Candrix was to rule after him, the rebels must be crushed and their leader killed. So he had summoned his war band, gathering a force of eight hundred men who now stood in front of him, arrayed in groups under their village chieftains, waiting for Cadwallon's commands.

Doubt assailed him at the thought of issuing those orders. He knew what must be done but he had little idea of how to accomplish his goal.

Candrix seemed oblivious to his father's dilemma. He pointed across the green meadow towards the village.

"Is that him?" the young man asked, his voice rising in pitch with an edge of excitement. "Is that Brennus?"

Cadwallon looked to where his son was pointing. His eyes were not as good as they had once been. In truth, these days he had difficulty making out any detail beyond the length of his outstretched arm. He could see the green of the meadow, the tree-covered hills beyond and the brown smudge of the village at the foot of the hill. Through the fog of his fading vision, he could tell that some of that brown was moving.

"They are coming out to face us!" Candrix declared with savage delight.

"How many of them?" Cadwallon asked anxiously.

After a pause, his son replied, "I think around six hundred. We certainly outnumber them."

Cadwallon nodded but could think of nothing to say. He could barely make out the enemy force but he could see enough to tell that most were on foot, while some were mounted on small, shaggy-coated horses. One of those riders would probably be Brennus, his new rival for the rule of the Ordovices.

He narrowed his eyes, straining to make out details but after few moments of fruitless squinting into the bright morning sunlight, he gave up.

"That could be him," he conceded.

"He's a big man," Candrix observed.

"So they say."

Cadwallon had never met Brennus, had never even heard of him until a few weeks earlier, but he hated the man for the turmoil he had brought to the Ordovices with his talk of waging war on Rome. Such dreams were for fools, Cadwallon insisted to anyone who would listen to him, yet the truth was that fewer and fewer people paid any attention to his words. Instead, the young

3

men flocked to join Brennus and now events had reached the stage where bloodshed was inevitable.

Briefly, Cadwallon wondered whether he should have surrendered the Kingship to Brennus but he knew that would only have resulted in he and his family being put to death or, if they were lucky, exiled. No, he must settle this, must kill Brennus so that Candrix could rule the Ordovices in peace.

It was too late to change his mind now. A ragged cheer echoed across the meadow and the rebel force began to move, crossing the uneven grassland towards Cadwallon's army.

Knowing he must make some effort to encourage his warriors, the King called out, "Let them hear you!"

His men responded with a cheer of their own. A carnyx, a huge, curved war horn, blared out its defiance but Cadwallon thought that his men sounded less than enthusiastic about this fight. They outnumbered the rebels, it was true, but many of the eight hundred warriors he had assembled were old men like himself. Some of them had sons who had joined Brennus' revolt and none of them were keen to spill the blood of their own tribesmen. Fighting the Demetae, or the Deceangli, or even the bloodthirsty Silures, was one thing. Fighting your own kin was quite another matter.

The rebels appeared to have no such qualms. They marched steadily closer, brandishing spears, holding leather-covered wicker shields to protect their bodies.

Their chanting filled the air around them as they crossed the wide meadow.

"Bouda! Bouda!"

Victory!

Cadwallon ran his left hand over his armour. He wore a shirt of mail, hundreds of small, bronze leaf-shaped plates sewn onto a leather tunic. Beneath the tunic he wore a padded coat of wool, thick enough to protect him from spear or sword. Why then, he wondered, was he so afraid? Most of his warriors wore no armour, their only protection being a shield and the blue war paint that covered their bodies with mystic designs.

"We should have druids," Cadwallon muttered to himself.

"Father?"

Candrix shot him a look of concern.

"Nothing."

It was an idle thought but one that made Cadwallon long for the days of his youth, when disputes such as this one would have been settled without the need for men to die. A powerful druid would have sat in judgement and issued a decree as to who should rule and every warrior would have honoured the decision or risk being declared an outcast. As a wealthy King, Cadwallon knew that he would have been able to offer sufficient gold to ensure that the decision was made in his favour.

But the druids had been virtually exterminated years before, when the Romans had stormed the sacred island of Ynis Mon, slaughtering the inhabitants and burning the oak groves to the ground. Cadwallon knew that some druids had returned but few of them were bold enough to venture beyond the confines of their island, which meant that Cadwallon had no option except to fight.

He sensed his men edging backwards, ignoring the grumbling threats of their chieftains. He should have done something, should have called out some words of encouragement, but he could not. He managed to draw his sword, circling his fingers round the unfamiliar, leather-banded hilt and lifting the blade high but no words would come to his lips. His throat was as dry as he could ever remember, so parched that it burned.

"Father? What do we do?" Candrix almost pleaded. "They are coming."

The rebels were barely fifty paces away. At a shouted command, they stopped. Then they began stamping their feet, rattling their spears against their shields, setting up a booming, rolling sound that echoed across the field like thunder as they continued to chant their victory cry.

Cadwallon's men watched them in anxious, nervous silence.

One of the chieftains looked back over his shoulder, calling to the King.

"Do we charge?" he asked, his voice betraying his uncertainty.

Cadwallon blinked, struggling to make a decision.

Should they charge? Should they stand? He had no experience of such things.

Before he could make up his mind, the rebels made the decision for him. A group of horsemen surged into a gallop from the right flank of the enemy force, riding in a wide arc to circle behind the left of Cadwallon's line. All eyes turned towards them.

5

The men on Cadwallon's left turned nervously, lowering their spears to present a wall of sharp blades to the horsemen, then jostling one another as they realised that the riders had no intention of charging at their front but would soon be behind them, leaving the hedge of spears facing in the wrong direction. If the spearmen turned to face the horsemen, their backs would be to the enemy's main force. Bereft of orders, the formation became a tangled mass as some men faced the front while others turned to track the riders.

Cadwallon was transfixed. Unaware of what he was doing, he lowered his heavy sword until the rounded tip of the blade was resting on the grass at his feet. His misty eyes watched as the rebel cavalry dashed beyond the left flank of his army, ignoring the warriors who could only stand and watch them as they galloped past.

A sudden warning cry made Cadwallon whirl his head. From the front, Brennus' warriors were charging his line, yelling at the tops of their voices.

"Father?" Candrix begged. There was a note of panic in his young voice now.

Cadwallon gaped in horror, anticipating the awful clash when the two armies met but the impact did not come because his men broke. Devoid of leadership, they turned and ran, dropping their weapons as they went. By the time the rebel charge reached where the army had stood, only a handful of the bravest men faced them. They were cut down without mercy.

Candrix turned to grab his father's arm. A handful of warriors, the King's personal guard, clustered close around him, presenting their spears to the fleeing mob who surged around them as they ran in panic from the field. Within the space of a few heartbeats, the King and his companions stood alone and isolated as the rest of Cadwallon's army vanished like deer fleeing from a pack of wolves.

Then the horsemen arrived. They rode through the scattered remnants of Cadwallon's army, not even bothering to hack down at the running men. Hoofs thudded on the earth as the riders reined in to leap down from the horses. They held their long, heavy swords in their hands and wore small, round shields on their left arms. Long-haired, bare-chested and with their bodies adorned by tattoos and war paint, they were as savage a bunch of warriors as Cadwallon had ever seen.

6

One of them stalked towards the knot of guards who defiantly stood around Cadwallon in a protective ring of shields and spears. The rebel was surprisingly young, in his early twenties. He was a big man, taller than any of the others, broad-shouldered and with massively muscled arms and legs. His long, dark hair fell straight around his shoulders and his eyes blazed sapphire blue as he approached.

He stopped a few paces from the King, apparently unconcerned by the lethal points of the spears confronting him. His lip curled in a sneer as he addressed the King's guards.

"You may live if you go now," he told them. "My fight is not with the men of our tribe, only with its useless King."

"We are sworn to protect the King," one of the warriors replied.

"I am the King now," the big man told them.

Candrix pushed his way to the front, sword in hand.

Furiously, he yelled, "You are a rebel. A nobody!"

Signalling to the warriors behind him and pointing his sword at the rebel leader, the young man ordered, "Kill him!"

Cadwallon's guards did not move. The whole of Brennus' rebel force was closing in on them, moving to surround them. Six guards against six hundred.

They shifted uneasily, their eyes darting in all directions as they watched the encircling warriors draw nearer.

Anxiously, one of them asked the rebel, "What happens to the King?"

The dark-haired man said, "I am the King. There can be no other claimant. Decide now whether you will oppose me or serve me."

Candrix did not allow the guards time to make a decision. With a scream of outrage, he threw himself at the big warrior, his sword raised high.

Cadwallon found his voice at last, crying out in horror as he watched his son attack Brennus.

"No!"

Brennus reacted with astonishing speed. He dodged aside, allowing Candrix's blade to sweep down, missing him completely. Then his own massive sword was swinging. It smashed into the young man's waist, digging deep into his flesh. Candrix screamed as he fell to the ground. Without hesitation, Brennus slashed down, silencing his cries with a casual swipe of his blade.

7

Two of the guards, jolted out of their inaction, gave a yell as they tried to rush Brennus but the rebel chieftain swept their spears aside with contemptuous ease, his sword lashing to left and right, sending one man down with a vicious slash to his head and felling the other with a cut to his shoulder.

His own warriors closed in, quickly finishing off the fallen men and threatening the four remaining guards who, after some nervous glances to one another, dropped their spears and stood aside.

Ignoring the guards, Brennus strode across the blood-stained grass to stand in front of Cadwallon. He glanced down at the sword the King still held in his hand.

"Are you going to try to use that thing?" he asked, his every word dripping with contempt.

Cadwallon stared at him. Brennus was close enough now that, for the first time, the King's aged eyes could make out his features clearly. He blinked in astonishment.

"It is true!" he gasped. "You are his son."

"Yes, it is true."

"I knew your father."

"I know."

Cadwallon closed his eyes, as if trying to recall old memories. When he opened them again, he said, "He would not have done what you have done."

"I am not him," Brennus replied coldly.

"No, you are not," Cadwallon sighed sadly.

He felt suddenly calm, resigned to his fate. It was over, he knew. The sun was shining, the air was warm and the day promised to be a fine one but his son was dead and he knew that he would join him in the underworld very soon. The fear had left him. Too late now, he thought. If only it had left him years ago.

"Let my family live," he said to Brennus.

"Why should I?" the rebel leader asked, his voice harsh.

"Your father would not kill women and children," Cadwallon told him.

Brennus shook his head.

"I told you, I am not him. I am King now and I will make this tribe great. I will drive out the Romans and become lord of all the tribes. That is my destiny. The only thing my father gave me was life. I will show the world that I am stronger than he ever was."

8

Cadwallon felt his eyes stinging. He looked up to the clear, blue sky where he could hear the cawing of crows already circling far above his head, too indistinct for his eyes to make out.

The sun was warm on his face, its light dazzling him, mixing with his tears to render him almost entirely blind. With a sigh that was almost a sob, he released his grip on his sword, letting the heavy blade fall to the ground at his feet.

Still looking skywards, he said to Brennus, "No, you will never be as strong as your father."

Cadwallon closed his eyes. He heard Brennus move but did not see the sword coming for him. His death was mercifully quick for Brennus aimed his blow at Cadwallon's unprotected head, smashing the blade through the skull, killing the old King instantly.

Brennus let his sword fall to the ground, then stooped to wrench the golden torc from around Cadwallon's neck. He wiped the bloody smear from the shining gold, then stood, placing the torc around his own neck. He turned to face his warriors who cheered him loudly, raising their spears and swords to the sky as they chanted his name.

"Brennus! Brennus! Brennus!"

He acknowledged the cheers with a nod, then walked to face the four surviving guards who had once sworn to protect Cadwallon.

"I am King now," he told them. "You will follow me, or you will die. It is your choice. If you follow me, I will lead you to greatness."

One of the guards stirred.

"You are truly who you claim to be, Lord?" he asked nervously.

Brennus nodded, "Yes. I am Brennus, son of Calgacus."

Chapter II

Under a warm sun, caressed by a gentle breeze, Calgacus stood beside his friend, both of them gazing down at the newly covered grave. Around them, the villagers began to slowly disperse and make their way back to their homes. They had paid their respects but it was time to move on. Death was a part of life, a painful part to be sure, but for those who remained, life must continue and there was much work to be done.

Springtime was a bad time to bury a loved one, Calgacus mused sadly. It was a time of new growth, of rebirth after the long, cold darkness of winter. Death was difficult enough at any time, but to bury someone in springtime was especially hard.

Gazing off to the distant horizon, his eyes caught sight of a kestrel hanging in the air, heralding the imminent arrival of another small death. He watched, fascinated, as the raptor suddenly dropped to the ground, moving so quickly he could barely follow it. It reappeared moments later, wings flapping vigorously as it bore its prey back to its nest. Another act in the constant cycle of life and death, he thought bitterly.

The bird vanished into the distance, forcing Calgacus' attention back to his surroundings. The rites had been observed and he knew it was time to move on. He placed a hand on his friend's shoulder.

"She had a good life," he said softly.

Runt sniffed. His eyes were damp with tears that he fought to hold back.

"Aye, she did."

He seemed about to say more, but no words came. Elaris, his wife for the past twenty years, was in her grave now, buried with the jewels and trinkets she had treasured in life, and with a garland of spring flowers around her neck. She was gone and her spirit was now in the care of Dis, Lord of the Underworld.

Beatha, Calgacus' wife, said gently, "Come, Liscus. You and Adelligus will join us for our mid-day meal."

Runt did not protest. He and his son, Adelligus, the only one of Elaris' children who had survived infancy, walked slowly

10

back up the low hill to Calgacus' homestead which stood on the long summit of a ridge overlooking the village on one side and a broad river estuary on the other. They walked in virtual silence but warm drinks, some ale and some hot food soon had then talking about inconsequential things. Runt, his balding forehead shining in the firelight from the hearth, even managed to laugh as he recalled some of the things Elaris had done over the years. She had reached the age of forty three, a good age for someone who had spent her life working as hard as she had and who had been through childbirth four times. The unspoken pall that hung over the others was that she had been the youngest of their generation. Calgacus himself was now forty eight years old and though he felt as fit and strong as he had ever done, Elaris' death was an unwelcome reminder of the fate that awaited them all. Calgacus shivered as he felt a finger of doom run down his spine.

Time, people said, heals all things but it cannot make people forget. Over the following weeks, Runt threw himself into the never-ending work of ploughing, sowing, tending the crops, and watching the livestock. There was charcoal to be burned, tools to be made, walls and fences to be repaired. Runt tackled all of these like a driven man.

But he did not forget his loss. To those who knew him, it was plain that something inside him was missing. He no longer laughed as much as he had done before and the slightly mocking cheerfulness that had always marked him out was often absent.

"I don't know what to do for him," Calgacus confessed to Beatha.

"There is nothing you can do," she told him, "except be here for him when he needs you. That is all any of us can do."

"I will always do that," he promised.

Beatha laid a gentle hand on Calgacus' arm.

"I know. And so does he. I hope he gets over it soon, for both your sakes."

Calgacus frowned, "What do you mean?"

"I mean that he is just about the only person who can make you smile. Without him poking fun at you, you are like a bear with a sore head."

"You make me smile," he protested.

"Not often enough, Cal. But it is Liscus we should worry about. Try to keep him busy."

That was not difficult, but although Runt never shirked any work, he tackled each task with grim determination rather than his usual good humour. As the summer months passed, Calgacus kept hoping that his friend would recover, but even after the mock combats they used to teach the younger men how to be warriors, the dull, far-away look in Runt's eyes told Calgacus that he had not forgotten his loss.

"Adelligus is shaping up well," Calgacus observed after a particularly strenuous training bout.

Runt nodded. At eighteen years of age, his son was already a head taller than him, with the same brown hair and sharp eyes that his mother had possessed.

He said, "Aye. He's got a knack for it. He damn near caught me today."

"You must be proud of him," Calgacus said. "He's a fine son."

"I am," agreed Runt, before nodding towards a slender young man who was approaching them.

"Speaking of sons, here comes yours."

Calgacus looked up to see Togodumnus hurrying towards him.

Like Adelligus, Calgacus' son was now eighteen years old but he looked younger, his face handsome yet delicate. He was of average height, his hair being neither the raven black of Calgacus' own nor the wheat-gold of Beatha's, but a light brown. Only his bright, blue eyes betrayed his relationship to Calgacus, with his slender build and gentle voice more reminiscent of his mother.

He walked towards them with an unusual spring in his step for he was normally reserved and diffident around his father, but something had clearly energised him enough to seek out the war practice he normally avoided.

"There's a Roman ship approaching," the young man informed them excitedly.

Seeing the spark in his father's eye, he hurriedly added, "It's a merchant ship. No soldiers."

"What do those bastards want?" Calgacus growled.

He jumped to his feet, his hand reaching for his longsword.

Holding out a hand, Togodumnus pleaded, "Father, let me speak to them. They came once before. There is no need to fight them until we know what they want."

12

"Romans only ever want one thing," Calgacus asserted.

Togodumnus gave him a pained look.

"Please, Father. I hardly ever get a chance to practise the Latin that Mother taught me."

"If they are merchants, they might give us news," Runt put in quietly.

Calgacus hesitated for a moment then nodded to Togodumnus.

"All right. But be careful what you say to them. Don't give anything away. And take Garco with you. I'll stay in the background unless there's any trouble. Liscus, you gather the lads just in case."

Togodumnus' face lit up and he blurted his thanks before setting off for the village at a run.

"Come on," Calgacus told Runt. "Let's go and see what the buggers want this time."

The Roman merchant ship, a fat-bellied, single-masted vessel with only one bank of oars on each side, had beached on the sandy shore. A balding, plump man, wearing a white tunic and a blue cloak that was fastened by a large, silver brooch, had clambered down and trudged across the sand to the grassy foreshore where he waited while a gang of sailors unloaded a few sacks and three large amphorae which they set on a brightly coloured rug on the ground in front of him. Once this was done, most of the sailors returned to the ship but four large, burly men stood by the unloaded cargo, each of them armed with a heavy club.

A throng of people came down from the village, descending the steep, wooded slope to the seafront to see these visitors from the Empire. They formed a wide semi-circle in front of the merchant, men, women and children mingling together, chattering excitedly although they made sure to keep a respectful distance from the four sailors who idly waved their cudgels as a warning that the Britons should not crowd too close to the plump little merchant.

While Calgacus and Runt remained with the villagers, Togodumnus strode forwards to greet the Roman. Old Garco, round-shouldered and grey-haired, accompanied him.

Togodumnus held up a hand in greeting.

"Welcome, Roman," he said in Latin.

13

The merchant smiled broadly, spreading his arms in a gesture of openness.

"Ah, you speak our language. Excellent."

He shot a look at Garco as he asked, "This is your chieftain?"

"No. Our head man is not here. I speak for him."

"Indeed?"

The merchant's eyebrows rose in surprise as he studied Togodumnus' young face.

Ignoring the man's obvious scepticism, Togodumnus introduced himself and asked the Roman's name.

"I am Junius Lucullus," the man smiled. "I am a humble merchant, seeking a fair trade for my goods."

Gesturing towards the pile of sacks and amphorae, he went on, "I have brought some fine pottery, some trinkets, some grain and, of course, some excellent wine. I hope that you can offer me goods of equal value in exchange."

Standing in the crowd, Calgacus edged closer, listening while Togodumnus bartered with the Roman.

"He's very good at this sort of thing," Beatha whispered.

"What?"

"Togodumnus. He is very good at this. His Latin is a bit basic but he talks well."

Calgacus grunted.

"I suppose so," he conceded grudgingly.

"He is not cut out to be a warrior," Beatha reminded him gently. "You should know that by now."

"I know. He's clever and he learns quickly. He can read and write Latin, which is more than most of us can do. But what will he do when the Romans come with soldiers?"

"They have not come with soldiers," she pointed out.

"One day they will," he insisted. "Talking will be no use then."

It was an old argument and one that he knew he would lose.

As he had expected, Beatha chided, "You are too hard on him, Cal. You cannot blame him for not being like you. He is more like his uncle, whose name he carries, and you know it."

That was the argument which always defeated Calgacus. His older half-brother, the former King of the once-mighty Catuvellauni, had been the greatest man he had ever known, yet the older Togodumnus had always been more interested in trade and crops than in war. Calgacus' son was so like his namesake that Calgacus was confused by his own reaction to young Togodumnus' nature. All he could mutter was that Togodumnus the King had still gone to war when the Romans had arrived. He had fought and he had died.

"But at least he fought," Calgacus murmured under his breath.

"There is nobody to fight nowadays, thank the Gods," Beatha insisted. "That is why we came so far north. The Roman army will not come here."

He gestured for her to be quiet. The bargaining had been concluded, with Togodumnus having agreed to hand over some animal pelts and a selection of iron tools in exchange for Lucullus' goods.

Runt whispered to Calgacus, "That Roman is no merchant. That's a rotten bargain he's made."

Calgacus nodded, "I expect we'll find out in a moment what it is he really wants."

Togodumnus called for men to carry his newly acquired goods up the hill while he and Lucullus shared some wine to seal the bargain. The crowd, unable to follow the conversation and losing interest in the visitors, began to disperse. Soon, only Calgacus, Beatha, Runt and a handful of the warriors remained.

Calgacus listened intently because this, he knew, would be the most important part of the discussion. Once the bartering of goods was complete, news and information was normally exchanged.

As he had expected, Lucullus began asking questions. He appeared friendly but his enquiries were probing and pointed.

"Which tribe rules here?" he asked.

"The Boresti," Togodumnus informed him.

"And you represent their chieftain?"

"Only the chieftain of this village," Togodumnus replied.

"And what lies upriver?" Lucullus asked smoothly. "How many towns and villages? Who are the chieftains?"

Calgacus, who understood Latin reasonably well, grew increasingly concerned when he heard the Roman. He could tell from the stiffening of Garco's stance that the old soldier was also uneasy but Togodumnus gave suitably vague responses, pretending that he knew little about places beyond the borders of his own village. Calgacus relaxed slightly. He was forced to concede that Togodumnus, despite his youth and inexperience, was handling the situation well. He might not know one end of a sword from the other but he dealt with the discussion with apparent ease, presenting Lucullus with the image of an innocent and rather gullible young man while still managing to divulge nothing of any significance.

Casually, as if he were merely being polite, Togodumnus asked the merchant, "What news from the South?"

Lucullus shrugged, "There is not much to tell. The province is at peace since the Brigantes were subdued and the Silures crushed. But the Emperor has seen fit to appoint a new Governor of Britannia. He has not arrived yet but he will be here before long. His name is Julius Agricola. He is a very famous soldier. Perhaps you have heard of him?"

"No," said Togodumnus.

"No? Well perhaps you will hear more of him in time. I am sure he will wish to befriend the people of the North."

He gave Togodumnus a pointed look as he enquired, "I assume that he can rely on your friendship? Rome rewards her friends."

Togodumnus smiled and nodded, assuring the Roman of his undying admiration for Rome.

Pleased with the response, Lucullus clasped hands with Togodumnus once more, then gathered up his cloak and returned to his ship.

"He was a spy," Calgacus announced once the Roman galley had rowed its way out of sight.

"I didn't tell him anything important," Togodumnus assured him.

"I know, but he told us a few things. The Brigantes are conquered, which means that the Empire is expanding its hold on the tribes. It won't be long before they march north. Especially if they have a new Governor who wants to make a name for himself."

Togodumnus said nothing. He had disagreed with Calgacus too often in the past to want to repeat the same arguments. He had felt confident and sure of himself while speaking to the Roman merchant but he could never retain that same confidence when dealing with his father. Calgacus held an implacable hatred of Rome and nothing Togodumnus could say would ever sway him. Togodumnus lowered his gaze, avoiding the challenge he knew he would see in his father's expression.

"There's nothing we can do about it," Runt observed.

Calgacus pursed his lips. He could feel the palms of his hands pricking, as if they were eager to lash out at the enemy he could only see in his mind's eye.

"What are you thinking?" Beatha asked. "I know that look."

"Nothing," he assured her.

Beatha shook her head, seeing through the lie.

"You want to go and fight them, don't you?" she challenged.

"They are our enemies," Calgacus admitted. "That so-called merchant was spying out the land, offering bribes so that they can march in here without a fight. You heard what he said. The Brigantes have been defeated. Who will be next?"

"We can't fight them on our own," Runt pointed out. "We've got fewer than two dozen men of fighting age in our village. The Boresti will follow you but they can only muster a few thousand warriors at most. It's not nearly enough."

"I know," Calgacus agreed.

He looked at his son, knowing that Togodumnus was holding back his usual question. *Why fight them at all?*

But Calgacus had sworn never to submit to Rome. He knew that Runt was correct but he gave a brief smile as he declared, "We need to bring all the tribes together."

There was a short silence while the others exchanged glances. Then Runt said, "You know that can't be done. Trying to unite the tribes is like trying to build a house on the beach when the tide is coming in. It's impossible."

"It hasn't been done so far," Calgacus argued. "But maybe now is the right time. I need to speak to Cadwgan."

Chapter III

"I thought you disliked druids," Bridei frowned.

"Cadwgan is different," Calgacus told him. "He's an old friend."

Bridei scratched at his chin. Nominally, he was King of the Boresti although that tribe was a scattered one, with many local chieftains who acknowledged him only because of his strength and the number of warriors he commanded. A typical Pict, he went bare-chested most of the time, displaying a host of tattoos on his stocky chest and muscular arms. He was brash and boastful, forceful to the point of being abrasive, and always ready to settle an argument by drawing his sword.

Calgacus liked him immensely. When Calgacus had led his small band of refugees northwards in the aftermath of the failure of the Great Revolt, Bridei had been the only King prepared to offer him a home. In the years that had passed since then, Calgacus had helped the Boresti fend off their larger and more powerful neighbouring tribes. As a result, he and Bridei had become firm friends, their relationship enhanced by the fact that Calgacus, despite his fame, had no designs to become a tribal leader. He was content to govern his small village and to act as War Leader when required but he deferred to Bridei in most matters.

That was why, having conceived the idea of building a tribal alliance, he had come to speak to the bellicose King.

To his surprise, Bridei seemed quite receptive to the idea, even though he shared Runt's scepticism about the feasibility of bringing the tribes together.

"Druids?" Bridei mused. "They don't have much influence these days but I suppose it is worth a try. If you are determined to build an alliance, you'll need all the help you can get. Support from the druids would certainly make a difference."

"We must combine the tribes," Calgacus insisted. "The Romans are pushing further north every year. They will reach here sooner or later."

"So you have been telling me ever since we first met," Bridei grinned. "I hope it is later."

"Me too," Calgacus agreed. "So, I'll go and speak to Cadwgan. You could come with me if you like."

Bridei laughed, "No, my friend. The Boresti are a small tribe. You should go as a famous War Leader, as a Prince of the Catuvellauni, not as a friend of Bridei of the Boresti."

"But I can count on your support? You will join an alliance if I can persuade the druids to help?"

"Does a bear shit in the woods?" Bridei chuckled. "My lads will fight anyone, any time."

He held out his hand as he promised, "You have my word. I am proud to be the first to pledge my people to your alliance. I just hope I am not the last."

Calgacus decided that only a small party would travel to the western island that was the home of the druids. Beatha would go because their elder daughter, Fulvia, had made her home there and Beatha had not seen her for several years. Their younger daughter, fifteen year old Fallar, also wanted to go and Calgacus decided it would be easier to take her. Fallar was a quiet girl who had inherited her mother's striking looks and long, blonde hair. Several men had already asked for her hand in marriage but Calgacus had been reluctant to commit to anything. He still recalled the aborted arrangements he had made for Fulvia to marry a chief of the Taexali. Fulvia had run off with one of the chief's warriors the day before the wedding had been due to take place. War with the offended princeling's tribe had been averted but the risk of vengeance being exacted against Fulvia and her husband had remained a threat. To ensure their safety, they had been forced to leave the lands of the Boresti and now lived in exile among Cadwgan's small community of druids in the far west. Mindful of those events, Calgacus wanted to be sure that the right choice of husband was made for his younger daughter.

Matters were complicated because the Picts reckoned descent from the mother, and Beatha was known to be of royal birth. The fact that her tribe, the Regni, lived far away, on the southern coast of the island and were friends of Rome, did not appear to concern the Picts at all. Neither did it appear to matter that she had thrown off her past to accompany Calgacus. To the Boresti, she was a Princess, and her daughter would be the mother of Kings. Rivalry for the young girl's hand was growing. Whichever tribe Fallar married into would help Calgacus build his alliance but whatever choice she made, several other chieftains would be disappointed. It was another concern that Calgacus could have done without, so the opportunity to take Fallar away for a few weeks was one that he welcomed.

They had horses and pack mules laden with all the things Beatha had deemed essential for the journey. Runt, Adelligus and ten young men from the village would act as escort. That left the settlement dangerously undefended but Bridei had promised to watch over their homes while they were away and it was unthinkable for a famous War Leader to travel without an escort of at least a dozen warriors.

Togodumnus was left in nominal charge of the village, but Garco, a solid, dependable old soldier, would be there to advise and guide him. Calgacus thought it would do his son good to have some responsibility but Garco's presence provided peace of mind that Togodumnus would have somebody he could rely on for help if he required it.

Calgacus spoke to his son before he left but their conversation was one-sided and turned into something of a lecture that Togodumnus listened to obediently, if unenthusiastically. Calgacus came away feeling annoyed with himself for not being able to talk to his son the way he thought a father should, the way his older brothers had talked to him when he was growing up.

Beatha patted his arm gently.

"Togodumnus is a grown man now," she reminded him. "He is eighteen years old. You cannot treat him like a boy any more."

"He never listened to me when he was a boy, either," Calgacus grumbled.

The small party left the village under a warm sun and a bright sky studded with floating, flat-bottomed cumulus clouds. Riding slowly, they followed the course of the broad river westwards. The fertile river plain was heavily wooded but dotted with isolated farmsteads and tiny villages, with a rough, well-trodden trackway winding through the trees from one settlement to the next, always more or less parallel to the river but following a convoluted route to avoid the marshy and boggy ground or the reed-beds which were home to a host of cranes, herons and ducks.

On the first night, they stayed at a settlement crowded on the banks of the river where it narrowed. Calgacus was known here, and welcomed, but the next day's journey saw them leave the territory of the Boresti.

Once beyond the tribal border, Runt constantly reminded the young warriors to remain alert. Although there was no clear demarcation, they were now travelling through the territory of the Caledones, one of the most powerful of the free tribes who held so much land that a man could walk for several days and still be within their borders. The Caledones were generally friendly towards the Boresti but the power of tribal leaders to impose their will was sometimes patchy, and local chieftains often resorted to banditry.

Calgacus made a point of stopping at every village they passed, letting the local leaders know who he was and where he was going. His fame and reputation, often a source of difficulties in the past, now proved its worth as the village chiefs of the Caledones welcomed him and his followers, providing hospitality without asking for payment. In return, Calgacus always presented their hosts with some small gift. He would have to travel home the same way, so it would be wise to ensure that he would receive an equally hospitable welcome on the homeward leg of the journey.

After several days of leisurely travel, they reached the home of Coel, overlord of the Caledones. He lived in a tall broch, a tower built of stone, which stood on a hilltop overlooking a long sea-loch. The broch dominated the landscape all around, standing as a symbol of Coel's authority, telling the world of the power wielded by the man who lived there.

Calgacus had seen the stone tower before but the massively thick walls and imposing height of Coel's home still impressed him. As a warrior, he understood the broch's defensive purpose, although he also recognised that its other purpose was to intimidate any visitors. In a world where most people lived in wooden roundhouses, an enormous, circular tower of stone was something to be wondered at. Calgacus could only imagine the huge effort in time and manpower it must have taken to construct the broch. Coel, he knew, was a man to be respected.

The chieftain of the Caledones was over sixty years old, with long, grey hair and taut, yellowing skin. He wore a torc of gold around his neck but everything else about him appeared outwardly typical of his people. His tunic, leggings and cloak were of fine make, but no better than those of many of his warriors and artisans. He was of average build, not especially tall or short, not especially thin or fat. At first glance, he appeared quite ordinary and unremarkable. Only when Calgacus looked into Coel's dark eyes did he recognise the spark of dangerous intelligence and cunning that everyone said were Coel's trademark.

Coel's greeting was, though, anything but dangerous. He seemed delighted to receive unexpected guests and entertained them royally, giving a feast in their honour. He welcomed Calgacus warmly, greeting him like an old friend, although they had met only once before, when Calgacus had taken Fulvia to stay with the druids on Iova. Coel claimed that the island was under his protection, so Calgacus had visited him on the way there. It had been a brief meeting but at dinner that evening, Coel placed Calgacus on his right side at table and spoke as if they had known each other for years.

Like all men, Coel could not hide his admiration for Beatha, nor did his keen eyes fail to notice Fallar.

"Do you have a husband for her yet?" he asked.

"Not yet," Calgacus admitted. "Though there are several chieftains who have offered themselves or their sons."

"Don't wait too long," Coel advised. "She is fifteen now, you say? Time to find a husband for her."

His eyes sparkled with amusement as he added, "I would be interested myself, but perhaps my grandson would be more appropriate."

He gestured to a good-looking young man of around eighteen years of age who was sitting a few places away and whose eyes were constantly drawn to Fallar. "Hey, Tuathal!" called Coel. "You are not betrothed yet, are you?"

Tuathal was mildly embarrassed at being the sudden focus of his grandfather's attention and knowing that the old man knew precisely where he had been looking. Flushing slightly, he replied, "You know I am not."

"He's a good lad," Coel told Calgacus. "His mother, my daughter, was married to a King of Eire. She had to come back here when her husband was murdered and some bastards stole the Kingship. Tuathal was just a child at the time, but one day soon, he will go back and reclaim his Kingdom."

Calgacus smiled politely but made no comment. Squabbles between Kings were commonplace. He did not know anything about Eire except that it lay across the sea to the west, but he suspected that it was much like everywhere else. The tribes would be busy fighting among themselves and when the Romans came, they would fall one by one. It was a reminder of what he had to achieve, although he was more concerned at Coel's interest in Fallar. The old King had sounded affable enough but Calgacus wondered what thoughts lay behind the old man's words.

Beatha appeared to take the chief at face value. Looking around the smoke-filled hall, she asked Coel, "Where is your daughter now?"

A brief look of sadness crossed Coel's lined face.

"She died a few months ago. Just after Midwinter."

"Oh, I am sorry," Beatha said.

Calgacus shivered slightly. Death seemed to be everywhere this year. Coel, though, merely shrugged, making Calgacus wonder whether the suggestion of sorrow he had seen in the old man's expression had been genuine or simply displayed because the King knew that was what was expected.

Coel said, "It happens." Then he swiftly changed the subject, asking Calgacus, "So you are going to Iova?"

The abrupt switch surprised Calgacus but he was relieved that the talk had moved to more positive matters.

He replied, "Yes. My friend, Cadwgan, is the chief druid there."

Coel nodded, "I know him. He is even older than me. He's a good man, although he doesn't travel much these days. What is it you are going to see him about?"

The question was asked casually but Calgacus knew that a man like Coel did not remain as ruler of a large tribe without being well-informed. Trying to appear relaxed and casual, playing Coel at his own game, if indeed it was a game, Calgacus took a swig of ale before replying.

"Several reasons. Our elder daughter lives there and we have not seen her for a long time. And, as I said, Cadwgan is my friend."

Coel popped a small piece of meat into his mouth and chewed thoughtfully. "Your daughter? Ah yes, I remember now."

Calgacus smiled. They both knew well enough that Fulvia had lived on the island for the past nine years. Coel was too sharp to have forgotten that.

Calgacus went on, "I am also hoping to build an alliance of the free tribes. I think Cadwgan could help with that."

Coel's eyebrows arched upwards.

"An alliance? For what purpose?"

"To stand against Rome when the day comes," Calgacus told him.

Calgacus had half-expected Coel to scorn the idea but the old chief rubbed his chin thoughtfully for a moment before saying, "We would certainly be stronger if we stood together. But trust is hard to build among people who have fought against one another so often."

"That is why I am seeking help from the druids."

Calgacus was aware that most of the people nearby had stopped their own conversations to listen to this exchange, although Coel affected not to notice.

After a short pause, the Caledones' King remarked, "Well, I wish you luck in your quest. An alliance would have many benefits. Provided the question of who leads it can be resolved."

"I would not have thought that was a difficulty," said Calgacus with a smile. "Your tribe is the most powerful, so you should lead."

Coel gave him a gap-toothed grin.

"Really? That had never occurred to me," he said smoothly, almost sounding sincere. "But that would certainly be of interest. You would not mind?"

"Why should I mind?" Calgacus responded. "A wise leader such as you will always listen to the advice of experienced men. I am sure you would remember that when it came to appointing a War Leader."

Coel laughed aloud, scattering scraps of food as he thumped his hand down on the wooden table.

"I think we understand each other," he chuckled as he wiped a tear of laughter from the corner of his eye. Then he wagged a conspiratorial finger at Calgacus, adding, "But a marriage alliance would certainly add weight to my decision."

Calgacus sensed Beatha stiffening but he nodded his head and said to Coel, "Perhaps we can discuss that when I am on my way back from Iova. We can do nothing without the support of the druids."

"Good enough," nodded Coel with a satisfied smile. It was the smile of a wily old fox and it left Calgacus wondering what other bargains he would need to make if he was to build the alliance he was seeking.

"You know nothing about the boy!" Beatha accused later.

"No, but Coel is a strong King, a man we need on our side. Without him, there is no hope of an alliance. Fallar could do worse than marry his grandson."

Beatha scowled, "I need to know she will be happy."

Calgacus understood her concern. Beatha's own brother had married her off to a Roman Centurion who had despised her barbarian roots and had frequently beaten her. Such harsh treatment was not an uncommon fate for women but Beatha was determined that her daughter would not suffer the same hardship she had endured.

Calgacus shrugged, "So speak to Tuathal when we come back. Let Fallar speak to him. Anyway, if she is not happy, she can always divorce him. Women are not possessions among the tribes, you know. They have rights."

"Even if a divorce wrecks this alliance you are planning?" Beatha asked pointedly.

Calgacus sighed, "All right, if it will make you happy, I will speak to the lad and explain how to treat her."

Beatha held up a hand in mock horror.

"No, that would only make things worse. You will terrify him. I will speak to him."

"When we get back," Calgacus insisted.

Despite Beatha's reservations, he was feeling pleased with the way things were turning out. He was experienced enough not to dream too much of what might be, but the future looked suddenly bright. With the help of Cadwgan and the druids, and with Fallar married to Coel's grandson, the chances of building an alliance were beginning to look good. If two or three more tribes could be persuaded to join, then, when the Romans came north, Calgacus would be able to lead an army the likes of which the invaders had never encountered. He would smash them to pieces and send then reeling back to the south.

In his dream, the tribes of the conquered southern province would rise up and perhaps the Romans would, at last, be evicted from the lands of the Pritani.

He shook his head. One step at a time, he cautioned himself. First, he needed to get the druids on his side. After that, it

25

would be time to make plans. But the vague restlessness that had afflicted him was definitely gone, replaced by an impatience to make things happen. To build an army capable of defeating Rome.

Chapter IV

The horses trotted briskly out from the gates of the small Roman fort, their harnesses jingling and the highly polished tack gleaming in the morning sun. The cavalrymen rode in pairs, lances held high, following the Centurion and the Vexillarius who proudly held aloft the standard displaying the squadron's banner.

Quintus Sempronius Casca could not quell his pride as he led the twenty riders out of the fort. His armour had been polished, his cloak had been cleaned, and his helmet gleamed. He was particularly proud of his helmet. Its red horsehair plume was stiff and immaculate, as befitted his rank, but the helmet also had a hinged face mask. When lowered, Casca's face was almost completely concealed, only his eyes visible through the mask's empty eye sockets. The hinged mask not only offered Casca some protection, it meant that his face was hidden from any enemies who would see only an impassively cold, silver visage staring down at them from the back of the tall horse. The helmet had cost him a small fortune although he considered it had been worth the price to have the mask fitted. The silver-coated faceplate had been made in the image of the Emperor Vespasian, copied from one of the busts that everyone knew so well. The end result of the smith's work was imposing and intimidating, just as Casca had intended. Most cavalry officers wore such ornate masks only when on parade but Casca had decided it would serve to intimidate the barbarians he so frequently encountered and he had taken to wearing it at all times.

He was a proud man and his pride extended to his squadron. His men were as smart as any in the army. They were also, he knew, very good at their job. He had made sure of that. The reward for their efficiency had been this posting, one that Casca knew many of the men grumbled about when they thought he could not hear them. For Casca, though, the toughest jobs demanded the best troops and he took it as a sign of his ability that his *turma* had been sent to garrison the wild mountains that were the home of the Ordovices. It was a thankless task, one that nobody else had wanted, because it offered the worst combination a soldier could imagine. The Ordovices rarely caused any trouble, and even when they did, it was only in small, sporadic flurries involving no more than a handful of the younger men, so there was little chance of any trooper growing rich from taking plunder or earning glory from some act of bravery. On the other hand, the *turma* was based far from any other units, so, if any serious trouble did start, they were effectively on their own. Casca's squadron of thirty men was stuck in the middle of nowhere with very little to do except ride around the countryside making sure that the Ordovices stayed quiet. The troopers hated it but Casca took pride in being given such an important, if unglamorous, role.

Casca was a Roman citizen, a native of Veii, although most of his men were Illyrians or Thracians, with a couple of Britons thrown in to make up the numbers. He had taken the post as commander of an allied *turma* because it offered a faster route to becoming a Centurion and Casca had been growing disillusioned as he saw men of lesser ability gain that rank in the legionary cavalry simply because of seniority or, more usually, because they came from well-connected families or, in a few cases, because they were rich and could bribe the Legate into promoting them.

Casca had no connections and little money but he desperately wanted the chance to prove himself so he had jumped at the opportunity when the vacancy had arisen in the auxiliary cavalry. It mattered little to him that his men were not citizens. He was a Centurion and that was what counted.

As for his troopers, they all spoke Latin and most of them had Roman names. They fought for Rome and, as far as Casca was concerned, that was enough.

Whatever the official status of his men, Casca was the representative of Rome in these wild, isolated hills and he made sure that the local chieftains were fully aware of what that meant. He had even visited old Cadwallon, the tribal leader, several times. The man was no warrior, and Casca enjoyed displaying his authority in front of the elderly chief, making sure that the man remained in a permanent state of anxiety.

Thirty men could not hold down a whole tribe, of course, but the fear of retribution could. Casca had let it be known that if any serious trouble began, the legions were only a few days' march away. Cadwallon had understood that message perfectly, a fact that kept his tribe peaceful and made Casca's job relatively simple.

Today would be another routine day. The sun was shining, the air was as warm as it ever got in this part of the world, and the men were in good spirits. Casca worked his squadron hard, constantly training them, making them practise their horsemanship and their weaponry skills. He did it so that the men looked forward to the patrols as being less onerous than the training.

"Look smart now, lads!" he called. "No lagging."

He spoke to keep the men alert although he knew that the warning was unnecessary. Few legionary cavalry units were as smart or as efficient as his. Many Romans who possessed enough wealth to afford the cost, chose to join the cavalry as an easier option than foot-slogging in the Legions, but the legionary cavalry had a poor name in the army, often viewed as being useful for little more than scouting.

The allied cavalry were different. Raised from people who were used to horses and to fighting on horseback, units like Casca's were tough and efficient, equally adept at scouting or fighting.

"Usual route, Sir?" the Vexillarius asked.

Casca nodded.

"Yes. A quick tour of the local villages, then back before nightfall."

He led them into the hills, moving at a steady trot, a pace the horses could maintain for hours, following one of his usual routes that would take him past several farmsteads and through three small villages. Casca would make a point of stopping at each place they passed and he would spend some time talking to the barbarians. Or rather, his interpreter, Tarcus, would talk to them. Casca could not understand more than a handful of words of the barbarians' coarse language, and only a few of his men knew much more than he did.

It was, of course, too much to ask to expect any of the savages to speak decent Latin, although Tarcus had managed it passably well. The interpreter was in his late thirties, and still wore his hair long in the style of the barbarians. He had injured his left leg in some accident long ago and walked with a permanent limp and a grimace of pain on his face. But he was happy on horseback and he was useful to the Romans, so Casca let him stay in the fort and fed him from the squadron's rations. Casca knew that Tarcus was not above pilfering small items from the stores to sell to the barbarians but he turned a blind eye to that because having Tarcus with him showed the locals that it was possible to benefit from the material wealth that Rome offered. A couple of the men in Casca's squadron were Britons and could have acted as interpreters but Casca was convinced that having a man of the Ordovices as his translator made more of an impression on the simple minds of the savage hill tribes.

Tarcus was whistling to himself as he rode behind Casca. The man was invariably amiable. Even when Casca turned round in his saddle to snap at him to cease the noise he was making, Tarcus merely smiled and nodded happily. After a while, he began softly humming the same inane tune that he had been whistling earlier. Casca gave up. Barbarians were so foolish that it was hardly worth the bother of complaining to them.

The sun grew uncomfortably warm for the armoured riders as the day wore on. Casca stopped several times to allow men and horses to rest, to take in water and to wipe the sweat from their brows. He watched idly while Tarcus talked to the farmers at these stops. As he had expected, they learned nothing useful from these conversations but their very presence served to remind the barbarians of who was in charge.

At the first village, though, the interpreter gave Casca a look of some alarm when he spoke to the settlement's chieftain.

"What is it?" Casca asked, wondering what could have upset Tarcus' usual good humour.

Tarcus took a hobbling step towards him, his demeanour unusually agitated.

"The chief says that Cadwallon is dead," the interpreter reported.

Casca raised his eyebrows in surprise.

"Really? Well, he was an old man, I suppose."

"No," the interpreter said with a shake of his head. "He was killed. Cut down in battle."

Tarcus was clearly unnerved by what he had heard. In a low whisper, he informed Casca, "It was Brennus who killed him."

Casca frowned, "Brennus? Isn't that the brigand we've been trying to find?"

"That's him. Apparently he has an army now and he has set himself up as the new King of the Ordovices."

"Has he indeed?"

Casca felt a tingle of excitement at the news. Maintaining an expression of calm determination, he wiped his forehead, then placed his crested helmet back on his head.

In a firm voice, he declared, "Then we had better go and pay our respects to this new King. We can remind him where his loyalties lie."

Tarcus' face betrayed his concern.

"He is said to be a man of violence," the Briton warned.

Casca replied with a short laugh.

"Then we should stamp on him before he gets any ideas."

He turned to his men, waving his arm in signal.

"Mount up!"

One of the troopers cupped his hands to help Casca climb onto his horse. The Centurion swung into the saddle then waited until the whole troop was ready. When he was satisfied that they presented a display of efficiency that would cow any rebel, he waved his arm to urge them into motion. The day, he thought, was getting better by the hour.

The village that had been home to Cadwallon was deep in the high mountains, a journey of several hours even on fast horses. Casca knew that going there would require him to stay overnight, so he sent a rider back to the fort with a message for the Decurion he had left in charge, explaining where they were going. The rest of the patrol pressed on, setting a fast pace as they headed into the hills.

They stopped only once, briefly, for a light meal, then pushed on again. Casca was in a good mood. The prospect of intimidating a barbarian chieftain was one that brightened his spirits.

Tarcus was less sanguine. His weather-beaten face was lined with concern when Casca summoned him to ride alongside.

"What can you tell me about Brennus?" the Centurion asked.

"Not much, Sir. Just that he is very dangerous."

Casca laughed, "The last time I saw Cadwallon, he insisted that Brennus was nothing more than a minor nuisance. It seems he underestimated him."

The Briton turned to look meaningfully back over his shoulder.

"There are only twenty-one of us," he observed glumly.

"More than enough," Casca responded brusquely.

"With respect, Centurion, Brennus evaded all the patrols you sent out to find him."

31

Casca shot an irritated glance at the interpreter. Whenever anyone said, "with respect" it meant that they did not respect him at all.

He said, "It is not easy to find one man in these hills. Now that he has taken over from Cadwallon, we know where to find him."

"He has the whole tribe with him now," Tarcus pointed out.

"And I have the entire Empire with me," Casca replied.

He dismissed the interpreter. Like all Britons, the man was boastful in times of peace but timid whenever danger threatened. Casca was made of sterner stuff. He was not stupid enough to believe that he could defeat an entire tribe with only twenty men but he had no intentions of fighting. All he needed to do was to make sure that Brennus was left under no illusions as to what Rome expected of its subjects. A show of bravado, riding into the man's own village and demanding his allegiance, would settle things. Casca had no interest in avenging Cadwallon. There was no point in trying to stop the perpetual squabbles among the barbarians, and one chieftain was much like another. Brennus would probably bluster and boast but he would see sense eventually.

The sun passed its zenith and slowly drew closer to the hilltops as it sank westwards. The horsemen were climbing now, their route wending its way higher into the steep-sided hills. Soon, the hills crowded in around them, narrowing the valleys, the trees towering high above the troopers as they rode along the mountain passes.

Casca kept a sharp watch but the attack, when it came, caught him completely by surprise. One moment the troop was trotting along briskly, the sound of the hoofs echoing around them, then men suddenly erupted from the wooded slopes, showering javelins and slingstones down on the riders.

The Romans came to a juddering halt as troopers twisted in the saddles. Horses reared, screamed and fell. Men tumbled from their mounts under a hail of missiles.

Some way in front of Casca, a tree toppled, crashing down to block the way ahead. An instant later, scores of screaming tribesmen were pouring down onto the Romans, thrusting viciously with long, wickedly sharp spears, or leaping up to drag the troopers from their horses.

Casca whirled. He had drawn his sword without realising that he had done so but one glance was enough to tell him that his troop would be annihilated if they did not escape quickly. Close fighting like this was not what cavalry should do. They needed to get moving, to use their mobility and speed, but they were trapped on this narrow path, hemmed in by the encroaching trees and horribly outnumbered by the swarms of vengeful Britons who howled around them like madmen.

Casca screamed, "Forwards! At the gallop!"

He pointed with his sword as he slapped his legs against the flanks of his terrified mount, urging it into motion.

The horse obeyed instantly, desperate to escape the slaughter. The Vexillarius echoed Casca's order, calling to the soldiers to follow. Then Casca heard the Standard Bearer's horse scream. From the corner of his eye, he saw it tumble to the ground in a whirl of thrashing limbs, a long spear shaft jutting from its side. The squadron's standard, a tassled square of bright, orange cloth that hung from the cross-piece of the long wooden pole, was trampled into the grass and the Vexillarius, struggling to his feet, was swamped by three wild-eyed, long-haired tribesmen who bore him to the ground where they hacked at him with long knives.

Casca hauled hard on the reins, wheeling his horse, sword held high, but he instantly realised that the fight was almost over. His column of troopers was all but gone, men and horses overwhelmed by the ferocity of the attack. There were no horsemen left alive close to him, and only a handful still struggling against impossible odds further down the trail.

Casca swore in frustration. For a moment he was tempted to gallop into the carnage in a charge that would inevitably lead to his death. Then he heard more shouts of triumph from behind him. Twisting, he saw more barbarians coming for him. He yanked on the reins once more, turning the horse, then yelled as he clapped his heels to its flanks, forcing it into a charge towards the newcomers.

These Britons had been guarding the barricade that had been formed by the fallen tree, but they had deserted their post, rushing forwards in their eagerness to join the slaughter before all chance of glory was gone.

Casca rode straight at them. It was foolish, he knew, because all they had to do was stand firm, spears ready, and his horse would swerve away, leaving him exposed to their weapons.

33

Horses will not charge a solid body of men. Casca knew this, but still he urged his mount on, holding his sword high and screaming defiance at the barbarians as he thundered towards them.

They broke.

Casca yelled in delight as the Britons scattered. He laughed aloud at their stupidity and cowardice. They could have killed him but they had not had the nerve to face a charging horse and so they had given him a chance to escape. Guiding his horse with the pressure of his thighs, he dashed between the barbarians, swinging his sword as he thundered past to take one man down with a vicious cut to the back of the head. Shouting with delight, Casca galloped on.

More men appeared in front of him. He saw that there were only three of them. One was a big man with long, dark hair, wielding a long sword. Casca rode at him. The man jumped aside, placing himself in front of the thick foliage of the fallen pine tree. The other two men leaped to Casca's left. Casca crouched low over the horse's neck, using his legs to ease the beast slightly to the left, aiming for the lower end of the trunk of the fallen tree where no branches blocked his path.

The horse jumped, soaring over the crude barricade. Casca glanced to his right to where the big swordsman was making a futile attempt to hack at him as he passed. Casca caught a glimpse of a stern face framed by long, dark hair and with eyes of piercing blue which glared hatred at him as he flew out of the man's reach. He noticed that the barbarian wore a torc of gold around his neck and his mind registered the name, *Brennus*, as he shot past the warrior. Then the barbarian was gone from view as the horse landed on the far side of the blockade.

Casca urged the frightened mount to run faster. From behind, the sounds of fighting were gone and only yells of triumph followed him as he galloped into the hills.

Chapter V

The daylight seemed to last forever. Even high in the hills, where the towering slopes hid the sun early, the summer nights were short in the northern provinces. Casca rode hard, trying to head roughly eastwards, but he was forced to make a wide detour to evade the barbarians, and the damned hills were so steep and difficult for horses that he was obliged to follow the endlessly twisting valleys that always seemed to take him further north than east. By the time nightfall eventually shrouded the land in grey shadows, his horse was all but exhausted. He guided it into a stand of trees, a thick tangle of oak, ash, alder and birch. Ducking his head as he moved deep into the dark woods, he coaxed his reluctant horse beneath the low branches. When he was sure that he was far enough into the woodland to be out of sight, he gratefully climbed down from the saddle and stretched his aching muscles. His heart continued to beat fast and his legs felt weak, but he was still very much alive.

He calmed his mind by reverting to routine. First, he unsaddled the sweating horse then, groping in his pack, he found his brush and spent some time grooming the animal. Even in the darkness, he could do this easily, because all cavalrymen knew how to tend their horses. The horse, tired and frightened, was reassured by the familiar feel of his hands and the stiff bristles of the brush.

When he was done, he found a tiny rivulet, locating it by the sound of the water trickling through the woodland. The horse drank thirstily while Casca knelt to re-fill his own small waterskin. Then he retrieved the last morsels of a smoked sausage from his pack and chewed on it slowly while his horse tugged at what few patches of grass it could find beneath the densely packed trees.

With nothing else to do, Casca found a soft spot to rest, wrapped himself in his now filthy cloak, and tried to sleep. He lay awake for a long time, his mind racing with recollections of the ambush and the slaughter of his troop but exhaustion eventually overtook him and brought some respite from the tormenting memories.

He woke early, roused by the chatter of birds in the branches above his head. Stiff and sore, he stretched his muscles before replacing the heavy saddle on his horse's back. Then, leading the beast to the edge of the woods, he allowed it to spend some precious time cropping the long grass. His own stomach was rumbling in protest at the lack of food, but all he could find was a handful of dark berries. They tasted deliciously sweet but scarcely served to quell his hunger.

As the sunlight filled the valley, Casca unfastened his red cloak and bundled it into his small pack. It would be difficult enough to travel unseen without advertising his presence, so the brightly coloured cloak would have to be hidden.

Carefully, he examined his surroundings for any signs of life but there was nobody in sight, no tell-tale smudges of smoke that would show the location of a farm or village, nothing except the call of birds and a hawk, slowly circling over a meadow far across the valley, ready to stoop on any small creature that had failed to return to its burrow before dawn.

Climbing wearily into the saddle, Casca set off once more. The disaster of the previous day hung heavy on his mind. He could imagine what would be said when he, the commander, returned alive while all his men were dead. He had led them into an ambush but he had escaped. It was the sort of calamity that caused some soldiers to fall on their swords through shame but Casca was determined that he would not do that. Someone had to return with the news of what had happened. Besides, there was another way to expunge shame, and that was to take revenge.

His mind reeled with ideas and plans for vengeance. He would return to the fort, he would send word to the Legate and the legion would come to crush the rebels. Casca would make sure of that. And he, personally, would kill the rebel leader, the one called Brennus. He would remove the barbarian's head from his body and he would help himself to the torc of gold the man wore around his neck.

Dreaming of revenge, Casca rode eastward, pushing the tired horse as fast as he dared. His greatest fear was that the rebels would reach the fort before him, for they had less distance to cover. Spurred on by that fear, he rode all morning and on into the afternoon. All the time, he scanned the surrounding hills for signs of pursuit but he seemed to be alone in this mountain wilderness.

36

By early evening he arrived at a place he recognised and less than an hour later he reached the plain where the fort sat in splendid isolation on a low ridge that was scarcely more than a bump on the ground. He studied it carefully. Everything appeared calm. There was no barbarian war band in sight. Relieved, Casca trotted his exhausted mount towards the gate.

The sentries were astonished to see him. The gates were opened and the men gathered to greet him.

The Decurion saluted, a puzzled look on his face.

"Sir?" he asked, the word imbued with questions.

Casca dismounted.

"We were ambushed," he told them. "The Ordovices have raised rebellion."

"What about the rest of the patrol?" the Decurion asked.

Casca replied with a question of his own.

"Has nobody else returned yet?"

"No, Sir."

"Then we must assume they are all dead," Casca stated flatly.

He could see the shock on their faces, hear the fear in their whispered voices, but he took command, allowing them no time to panic.

"The barbarians will probably come here," he told them. "They will want to destroy the fort before help arrives."

He could see what they were thinking. There were only twelve of them, including Casca himself.

"We will have a chance to avenge our comrades," he declared confidently.

He thought the men might panic but their inherent discipline asserted itself. He was an officer, giving orders as if he expected to be obeyed. The troopers were shocked and fearful but they offered no argument.

He demanded a writing tablet and iron-tipped stylus, then wrote out a message for the Legate. He handed the tablet to Hortensius, the youngest of his remaining troopers.

"Take this to the legionary fort at Deva," Casca told the young man. "Bring back help as quickly as you can."

Hortensius was a Briton, from the tribe of the Atrebates who had been loyal supporters of Rome ever since the invasion. He had joined the squadron only the year before but had quickly proven to be one of the best riders in Casca's command. If anyone could get a message to Deva quickly, it was Hortensius. Still, the young man's face was pale as he saluted and took the hastily scribbled message from Casca. He was on his way only a few moments later, galloping off to the north-east. Casca did not watch him go. However fast Hortensius travelled, it would be at least five days before any help could reach them. Casca and his ten remaining men were on their own.

To keep them busy, he ordered an inventory of the fort's stores and told them to sharpen their swords on the old grindstone. Two troopers were sent to watch the approaches from the hills. Then Casca went to his small office where one of the troopers brought him some hot food, the first meal he had eaten in two days. Eagerly chewing the first mouthful, Casca told the trooper to send the Decurion to him.

The Decurion's name was Sdapezi. He was a few years older than Casca, over thirty, with twelve years service. In the past, his simmering jealousy at the younger man's promotion had caused some friction between them, although Sdapezi was too much of a soldier to do anything more than grumble. He was, though, experienced enough to know that they were in trouble.

"What do you intend to do?" he asked without preamble as soon as he had closed the office door.

Still chewing, Casca looked up at the standing man.

"Do you have any suggestions?" he asked, choosing to ignore Sdapezi's familiarity.

Casca suspected that the Decurion might be hiding some inner delight that Casca had led the turma into a trap, but then he recalled that many of the men who had died in the ambush were friends of the veteran Decurion. That friendship was Sdapezi's problem, Casca thought to himself. The Decurion still considered himself one of the ordinary rankers, still sought the men's friendship and approval. Casca had no such weakness; an ambitious man could have no close friends.

He stared hard at the Decurion, waiting for a reply.

Sdapezi gave a slight shrug.

"We only have two choices as I see it," he explained pensively. "We can stand here and die when they come, or we can run for it."

Casca scooped another mouthful of gruel into his mouth, taking time to consider Sdapezi's words. He knew the man was right. The fort was not large but with only eleven men, they had no chance of defending its perimeter against a determined attack. Besides which, his men were cavalry, trained to fight from horseback, not to defend walls or face the enemy on foot. They would be lucky to hold the fort for five minutes, never mind five days. Added to which, Casca wanted revenge, not a glorious death battling against hopeless odds.

He swallowed his food, then said, "The honourable thing to do would be to stay and fight. We should not abandon the fort."

Sdapezi did not flinch.

"If that is your decision, Sir, then that is what we will do."

"But you disagree," Casca said softly.

"A lot of good men are dead already," Sdapezi shrugged. "Why add more to that without good reason?"

There was no hint of accusation in his tone but a flash of his eyes told Casca that Sdapezi thought the man responsible for leading his troops into an ambush should fall on his sword. That, rather than holding the fort, would truly be the honourable thing to do.

Casca nodded.

"As it happens, I agree with you. This rebellion needs to be crushed quickly but we do not have enough men to do it. If we stay here, we will all die, which will only add to the barbarians' confidence. However glorious that death may be, I would prefer a chance to avenge our defeat."

Sdapezi nodded. He had not missed the fact that Casca had referred to "our" defeat, but he simply asked, "So, what are your orders, Sir?"

Briefly, Casca outlined what he intended to do.

"Have the men ready as soon as you can," he told the Decurion.

The corners of Sdapezi's mouth twitched slightly as he observed, "It's a bit risky, Sir."

"Yes, but that is what we are going to do. Our men are trained to fight on horseback, not to hold a perimeter wall. This way, we have a chance to strike a blow at the enemy."

Sdapezi saluted.

"Very good, Sir."

He made no protest but it was clear that he thought Casca was making another mistake.

To Casca's surprise, the first of the five days passed without any sign of the tribesmen, but on the second morning, the scouts came galloping back to report that they had seen more than five hundred barbarians heading along the distant valley that opened out onto the plain.

One of the scouts said, "There were at least thirty on horses, Sir. The rest are on foot."

"Only five hundred?" Casca smiled. "You see how little they think of us? I had expected a couple of thousand at least. The rest are probably at home, afraid to march against us."

The men grinned at his bravado and he knew that, even though they were horribly outnumbered, they would follow his orders.

He turned to Sdapezi. "Everyone to their positions," he snapped. "Have the oil poured out now."

Sdapezi shouted orders, sending troopers scurrying to obey. Within moments, the troop had formed up in a column of twos inside the fort, facing the eastern gate, the one furthest from the approaching barbarians. The gates were unbarred and two troopers stood ready to open them when Casca gave the signal. Casca and Sdapezi tethered their own horses at the far side of the fort, near the western ramparts, then climbed to stand beside the wooden palisade. Casca took up position to the left of the gates while Sdapezi went to the right, where he crouched low, out of sight of anyone approaching the fort.

Casca looked around. His men had been busy over the past day. Anything of use to the barbarians had been burned, buried or destroyed. All fires had been extinguished except for two burning torches that were stuck into the earth beside the main barracks rooms and the stables. The fort was an empty shell. Now, there was nothing to do except wait.

Casca looked west, towards the hills. The barbarians were in no hurry. He saw them a long way off, marching steadily towards the fort in a large, disorderly crowd, crossing the open ground with no fear. A group of horsemen galloped ahead, drawing near to check the fort.

Casca hefted a javelin, trying to give the impression that he was a patrolling sentry. He watched the horsemen wheel to a halt some fifty paces distant, look the place over, then turn away, kicking up a flurry of dust as they rode back to the main war band.

Casca felt a grim satisfaction. The barbarians had not ridden round the fort to check the far side. That was good. He glanced to his right to see Sdapezi watching him. He gave the Decurion a sign to remain calm and to stay hidden from view.

The barbarians took an age to cross the wide, flat land between the fort and the hills. They halted around two hundred paces from the gates, then two men left the crowd and began walking towards the fort. As they drew nearer, Casca recognised the awkward, limping gait of Tarcus, his interpreter.

The second man was Brennus. Casca noticed that he wore brown leggings and a homespun shirt, like any barbarian peasant. Only the golden torc around his neck and the long sword in his right hand betrayed that he was a man of rank. A rank that he had seized by the strength of his sword arm. To Casca, though, Brennus was still nothing more than a barbarian. A strong one, to be sure, but a barbarian none the less. Casca knew how to deal with such men.

The two men came to within five paces of the outer ditch that surrounded the fort. There were three ditches, each one steep-sided and as deep as a man is tall. Only at the two gates was there a pathway giving access to the fort. With a full *turma* of thirty men, Casca could have held the place long enough for help to arrive, but with two thirds of his force annihilated, his hope now was to persuade the barbarians that the fort was undefended. The rare prize of destroying a Roman fort was, he hoped, one that would lure them in.

The two Ordovices stopped, standing opposite the point where Casca stood on the rampart.

Casca called down, "They let you live, Tarcus? What price did they pay for betraying us?"

"I have not been paid yet," Tarcus replied, his voice dull and flat.

Casca frowned. Something was not right here but he could not tell what it was.

"What do you want?" he asked.

"I am ordered to give you a message."

Tarcus gestured to the man beside him.

"This is Brennus, the new King of the Ordovices. He says to tell you that you must abandon your fort and leave his lands or you and all your men will be slaughtered. He says you are to tell your masters that Rome is not welcome in the lands of the

41

Ordovices, and any Romans who cross into his territory will be killed."

"He is a fool!" Casca shouted back. "Does he not know that a Legion will be here in three days? When they arrive, it is he and his mongrel band who will die."

Tarcus exchanged a few words with Brennus before calling back, "He says he is not afraid of Rome. He claims that his father defeated a Legion once before, and he can do the same."

"His father?"

"He claims to be the son of Calgacus, who led the Silures when they destroyed the Second Legion."

Casca knew that story. It had happened many years before he came to Britannia, but the soldiers still spoke of it, using the tale as a way to frighten new recruits, to weave stories of the monstrous, blue-painted Britons who fought like crazed demons and took the heads of any Romans they killed. Casca had heard the tale, and he knew the Second Legion had suffered a heavy defeat, but the legion was still here, while the semi-legendary Calgacus was long gone.

Casca said, "I couldn't care less who his father is. You tell this Brennus that he is a dead man already. Rome shows no mercy to rebels."

After another short conversation with Brennus, Tarcus shouted up, "He repeats his order. You must leave the fort. Brennus offers you the chance to depart before he sends his men to destroy it."

Casca laughed, letting them see he did not fear them.

"The fort is already abandoned. I am the only one left. The others ran when they heard what had happened in the mountains. But if he wants to storm it, I will be here waiting for him."

Tarcus and Brennus had another brief conversation, then Tarcus called, "He asks whether you are determined to die."

"No, I am determined to kill him," Casca replied.

Tarcus nodded, "Then there is no more to be said. It is time for me to receive my payment."

Casca watched, puzzled, as the interpreter fell awkwardly to his knees, his crippled leg forcing him to twist as he sank to the ground.

In a move so unexpected that Casca could scarcely believe what he was seeing, Brennus, towering over the kneeling man, gripped his massive sword in both hands and swung the blade in a sweeping arc that sliced into Tarcus' neck.

The interpreter toppled to the ground. He was clearly dead but Brennus hacked at him until he had removed the man's head.

Casca watched as Brennus kicked Tarcus' head into the first ditch. Grinning fiercely, Brennus stood to stare up at him. The barbarian lifted his bloodied blade in a mock salute.

Casca, holding the warrior's gaze, pointed an accusing finger at him, then purposefully dragged his finger across his own throat to signal what he intended to do to Brennus. Dropping his hand below the level of the palisade, he then signalled to Sdapezi who raised his head over the parapet, as if trying to sneak a look at what was going on.

Brennus saw the second man on the ramparts. He hesitated a moment, then laughed before turning away and walking casually back to his war band.

Casca told Sdapezi, "Be ready."

"The bastard killed Tarcus?" Sdapezi asked in a low growl.

"He'll kill the lot of us if we let him," Casca responded. Again, he warned, "Be ready."

They did not have long to wait. When Brennus reached his war band, he gave a signal and the barbarians let out a raucous yell before drawing their weapons and running eagerly towards the fort like a pack of hounds scenting their quarry.

Casca waited only long enough to see that Brennus and his horsemen had stayed at the rear, then he turned to Sdapezi and yelled, "Go!"

The two officers leaped down from the ramparts. Quickly, they climbed onto their horses, then rode to the sides of the fort. Even while they were moving, the rear gates were being hauled open by the troopers charged with clearing the way. Casca leaned down from his saddle to grab one of the blazing torches. He reined in his horse, checked that Sdapezi had gathered the other brand, then tossed his burning torch in through the open doors of the barracks. The oil they had poured onto the floor ignited with a whooshing sound and a crackle of instant heat. Casca saw that Sdapezi had set light to the stables. Quickly, the two men rode to the head of the small column where Casca drew his sword.

"Follow me!" he called.

43

The eleven cavalrymen rode out through the gates, hidden from the barbarians' view by the bulk of the fort and the rise in the ground. Casca led the column towards a stand of trees which they circled, then followed a low dip in the land which curved back towards the plain. He had often worried about that dip, for it afforded a way for an enemy to approach within a hundred paces of the fort without being seen, but now he was grateful for it.

He called a halt as they reached the limit of the low ground, then rode slowly forwards on his own until he could look across the open plain.

The barbarians had reached the fort. Dozens of them were hurling themselves at the gates, vainly trying to smash down the thick wooden doors by slamming their shoulders against them. Casca almost laughed. The fools had not even brought a ram to batter the gates down. Some, he saw, were scaling the ramparts and would soon drop into the fort. He had been right. The Ordovices could not resist the almost unheard of opportunity to sack a Roman fort. Not that there was much left for them, and what was there would soon burn to the ground. He could already see the pillars of dark, oily smoke rising into the sky above the walls.

The smoke did not deter the attackers. Brennus, though, was being cautious. He had told his followers that the place had been abandoned, but when Sdapezi had shown himself, the chieftain had clearly suspected a trap of some sort, so he had taken his own horsemen to the rear, sending in his foot soldiers to spring the trap.

Casca smiled to himself. There was a trap, but it was not inside the fort. He had merely used that as bait.

He raised his arm, calling his tiny troop forwards. When they had joined him, he told them, "A quick in and out the other side. We aim for the leader and we kill him if we can, but don't get caught. Whatever happens, keep moving."

The troopers grinned nervously. Their long lances were ready, their heavy swords hanging at their sides, within easy reach.

Casca lowered the face mask on his helmet, drew his sword, then ordered the advance.

To a man on foot, even one man on horseback can be terrifying. A horse gives the rider immense speed, power and reach. When a horse is at the gallop, the earth seems to shake beneath the pounding of its hoofs. Casca led his ten troopers in a wedge formation, keeping together as they increased the pace from a trot to a canter, angling towards the rear of the barbarian force. This was what cavalry were for, Casca told himself. He wished he could have struck at the men on foot, for they were easy prey, but his target was the rebel leader, the big, dark-haired warrior who called himself Brennus, son of Calgacus. If he was killed, the revolt would crumble as quickly as it had risen.

The barbarian horsemen had seen them now. Brennus was there, his long sword in his right hand, a small shield of hide-covered wicker now held on his left forearm. He was yelling at his men to face the charge, to turn towards the Romans and meet the attack. They responded willingly, but Casca ordered the full gallop and his small formation, outnumbered three to one by the barbarian cavalry, shot across the ground like a living arrowhead, hoofs drumming on the earth.

They crashed into the barbarians, the long lances seeking their targets, just as the men had been trained.

Casca had been aiming for Brennus but the big warrior had turned away to one side. Still charging, Casca hacked at the nearest rider, feeling the edge of his sword bite home. He kept his arm straight, allowing the blade to fall behind him as he passed his stricken opponent, then tugged it clear, a perfect kill, just the way he had practised so many times. Screaming, the barbarian fell from his horse. Casca rode on, twisting to look for Brennus.

The face mask of his helmet restricted his peripheral vision, forcing him to constantly turn his head, seeking out his prey, but the barbarian chief was to his left, too far away to reach. He saw the man block a lance with his small shield, then smash his own sword into a trooper who yanked on his reins as he reeled in pain but somehow kept moving, his armour having protected him.

Casca wanted to turn to pursue Brennus but his charge had taken him through the barbarians and out the other side. The enemy had been shaken by the ferocity and discipline of Casca's charge but they were rallying. To turn for another attack would be suicide. Cursing with disappointment, he yelled at his men to keep moving.

They thundered on, leaving a devastation of fallen men and horses in their wake. Some barbarians tried to follow them but the larger Roman horses soon outpaced the smaller mounts of the Ordovices and the tribesmen soon gave up the chase.

Raising his faceplate, Casca looked around, counting.

Sdapezi, the tip of his lance dark with blood, called over the noise of the galloping horses.

"Africanus went down," he informed Casca. "Two others injured, but I reckon we took down at least twelve of the bastards."

"Brennus? Did we get him?"

Sdapezi shook his head.

"The big one with the gold around his neck? No, I don't think so. He was too quick."

"Damn!" Casca blurted with feeling. "I wanted him dead."

"We'll get him next time," Sdapezi replied cheerfully.

Casca gritted his teeth. Next time. Would there be a next time? He had gained a small victory over the barbarians but he knew that the greater disaster of losing nineteen men would not be easily expunged. Killing Brennus would have made him a hero. Now, he would have to return to the legion with the news that he had lost most of his men and been forced to abandon the fort. He could guess how well that news would be received. He would be lucky to remain in charge of his diminished *turma* at all, let alone be given another chance to catch the rebel leader.

Yet he had no choice. With his fort burning and a horde of rebels swarming across the land, he had a duty to reach Deva and the Legion.

All was not lost. While he lived, he would battle to prove his worth. As he led his men onwards, he vowed that he would find some way to ensure he was given another chance to kill Brennus.

Chapter VI

The island of Iova was nominally part of Coel's Kingdom and under his protection. No rival chieftain had ever bothered to dispute the old King's claim because Iova was a small place with nothing particularly special or important about its location or its resources. It was remote from the mainland and for generations it had been home to only a handful of fishermen and their families who had eked a precarious living from the surrounding sea. Because Iova was one of the smallest of the many islands that lay off the western coast of the lands of the Caledones, Coel had not had much use for the place, so he had allowed a handful of refugee druids to make a home there when they had fled north after the Romans had sacked their former home on the sacred island of Ynis Mon. The leader of this small community was Cadwgan, still as portly as Calgacus remembered, though his hair was all but gone and his long beard was now silvery grey rather than brown.

The old druid greeted his visitors warmly, ushering them into his roundhouse and calling for food and drink to be brought. At Cadwgan's invitation, other people crowded into the house to see the famous Calgacus. Among them was Fulvia, who rushed in and joyfully flung her arms around Beatha and Calgacus before presenting two small children to them, a boy of five and a girl of three.

"Your grandchildren," she beamed, gently ushering the two children forwards as she introduced them. "Calgacus and Reuda."

Beatha was in her element, cuddling the children and speaking to them in a light, happy tone that they instantly warmed to. They were, though, unsure of Calgacus. He knelt down, trying to say something soothing and friendly, but the boy, who had been named after him, hid behind Fulvia's skirts.

The boy's father, Durcar, also stood rather anxiously behind her. He nodded nervously when Calgacus congratulated him on his fine children but neither of the men was at ease. When Fulvia had run off with Durcar, Calgacus had been left to face a potential war with the powerful Taexali tribe. While he had managed to avert that crisis, he found it difficult to be friendly towards Durcar. In his turn, the younger man was clearly intimidated by his famous father-in-law.

Beatha, sensing the awkward discomfort, announced that she would go with Fulvia and the children to Fulvia's home.

"We'll leave you to talk to Cadwgan," she said. "Come and find us when you are done."

She picked up her granddaughter and kissed her before going off with Fulvia and the two children. Fallar followed them and so, too, after a moment's hesitation, did Durcar.

Inwardly, Calgacus sighed. No matter how hard he tried, his family seemed to regard him as some sort of ogre. As he watched them depart, he felt a tinge of regret that he was excluded from their animated happiness and yet he also felt a sense of relief that, with them gone, he could relax and be himself. Perhaps the fault was his, he reflected as he turned to face Cadwgan.

His old friend smiled happily, apparently oblivious to the domestic tension, although Calgacus knew that the druid was too astute not to have noticed.

Cadwgan smiled, "Your daughter is a strong-minded woman. I sometimes think she is in charge around here, not me."

"She gets that from her mother," Calgacus replied.

"You think so?" Cadwgan laughed.

Still grinning, he made the introductions. The roundhouse was almost full, for as well as Calgacus, Runt, Adelligus and their warriors, there were several druids present, mostly younger men who, Cadwgan explained, were nearing the end of their training.

"Soon," he told them, "we will send Brothers to the various Kings to act as advisers. It is time that the druids regained some of the authority they lost when Ynis Mon was sacked."

He gave Calgacus an amused look as he went on, "Although I don't expect that there will be any point in sending anyone to advise you."

Calgacus shook his head.

"I have no need of a druid for myself or my village. But I am not a King and perhaps Bridei of the Boresti will welcome one of your followers."

"You have grown modest over the years if you think you are nothing more than a village chieftain," Cadwgan said with a smile. "But enough of that for the moment. Come, let us sit by the fire and talk."

The central hearth was ringed by stones, the fire fed by small sticks and blocks of peat that filled the house with a smoky, earth-scented atmosphere. The smoke hung in a pall above their heads, slowly escaping through the thatched roof.

Cadwgan sat on a small, three-legged stool, offering a second stool to Calgacus as guest of honour. The other men stood or sat, cross-legged, on cushions stuffed with straw and moss.

Two young druids poured ale into clay beakers. When every man had a cup, Cadwgan formally welcomed his guests then poured a small libation to the earthen floor as an offering to the Gods. The formalities observed, everyone raised their beakers to sip the dark brew.

"To the Gods," they intoned.

The drink was heady and potent, filling Calgacus' nostrils with a mixture of strong smells while the liquid tingled his taste buds.

"What is in this?" he asked.

"It's our own secret blend," Cadwgan replied with a smile. "Something to warm the heart as the fire warms the flesh."

He took another sip from his mug before asking, "So, Calgacus, what news do you bring from the East? We seldom see visitors from so far away."

"There is little to tell. The tribes maintain an uneasy peace. There has been little raiding in the past few years."

"That is not surprising since you removed the heads of the last raiding party who attempted to steal your cattle. As I recall, you stuck them on poles along the beach."

"That deed served its purpose," Calgacus agreed.

He sensed the attitude of the younger druids shifting from one of polite curiosity to slight awe. Cadwgan's words, though spoken in a light tone, had helped to reinforce Calgacus' reputation. The druids of old would never have spoken to a warrior as a friend in the way that Cadwgan was chatting to him, but the old druid had cleverly told the other men that Calgacus was no ordinary warrior.

Only one of the watching druids seemed unimpressed. He was a tall, spindly man, perhaps in his mid fifties. His long hair and beard were already tinged with flecks of grey. He stood, holding a long staff as a mark of his seniority, watching Calgacus through dark, hooded eyes that lurked beneath bushy eyebrows.

Cadwgan had introduced him as Broichan, saying only that he was one of Cadwgan's advisers.

Broichan seemed to bristle with innate hostility towards Calgacus and he was apparently unimpressed by tales of martial prowess. He reminded Calgacus of some of the druids he had met on Ynis Mon years before, men who were almost fanatical in their devotion to the Gods and unswerving in their disdain for anyone who did not share their own views.

Calgacus felt as if Broichan had already judged him and found him wanting. Pointedly ignoring the man's hostility, he turned his attention back to Cadwgan.

The old druid asked, "And what of Emmelia? Your niece has settled well since you rescued her from the Brigantes?"

Calgacus nodded, "She is well. She and Caedmon have a home in the glens. Emmelia prefers a solitary life."

"Ah yes, she would have made an excellent druid."

Calgacus smiled at that. He said, "I think you should be glad she has made her own life away from here. You may think Fulvia is strong-willed, but she is nothing to Emmelia."

"Your family has always produced its fair share of strong men and women," Cadwgan observed. "But tell me, what brings you here other than a desire to see your daughter and her children?"

"Does there have to be another reason?" Calgacus asked.

Cadwgan chuckled, "No, but I know you, my old friend, and I can read it in your face. So unless it is a great secret, why not tell us all?"

"It is no secret," Calgacus admitted. "I need your help with something."

Before Cadwgan could respond, Broichan interrupted. His voice was as harsh and prickly as his demeanour as he rasped, "By what right do you ask for our assistance when you claim not to need the guidance of those who have learned the ancient lore?"

Cadwgan waved a hand at Broichan.

"Calgacus has good reason to distrust the motives of some druids," he explained airily. "But he has done more to resist the Romans than any man I know. Besides, he has helped me many times in the past, and he deserves our friendship."

Broichan did not argue but the fiery expression in his eyes told Calgacus that the druid's acquiescence was given grudgingly. Calgacus, though, had faced hostile druids before, so Broichan's ill temper did not worry him unduly. He decided to ignore the man as much as possible, although he could not entirely ignore the air of tension that Broichan's words had created. The other druids were wavering now, torn between fascination with their famous visitor and Broichan's portrayal of him as an outsider.

Cadwgan tried to smooth things over by asking, "So what is this matter that you need our help with?"

Addressing the whole room, Calgacus outlined his plans for building an alliance of tribes, adding that Coel, King of the Caledones, had been receptive to the idea. He could see that most of the druids were more than interested in what he had to say, although Broichan snorted dismissively.

When Calgacus had finished his explanation, Cadwgan gave him an amused smile.

"What do you think we have been intending to do?" he asked. "An alliance is essential if we are to stand against Rome. I know that better than anyone. That is precisely why we will be sending our newly trained druids out to all the Kings of the free tribes."

"Then we have a common purpose," Calgacus said.

"Indeed we do," agreed Cadwgan. "And we will begin it very soon. Broichan himself will be going to Coel's homestead before the year is out."

Calgacus glanced at Broichan, who gazed back at him darkly. Calgacus wondered whether he was pleased at the prospect of travelling to Coel's fortress home. He suspected that Cadwgan might be trying to get rid of his belligerent advisor because he threatened Cadwgan's own position as leader of the small island community, but he doubted that sending him to Coel was a good idea. Broichan was undoubtedly strong-willed and probably very clever, but whether he would see eye to eye with an old fox like Coel was another matter. Calgacus suspected that the King of the Caledones would not take too kindly to a druid trying to interfere in his rule.

He recalled Runt's warning about trying to build a house on the beach when the tide was coming in. The tribes had seldom worked together even when the druids had been at the height of their power. Old rivalries, ancient feuds and clashing personalities were the normal state of affairs between the various people of the North. Placing two ambitious men like Coel and Broichan together would be like putting two rutting stags in the same field. He

51

wondered whether Cadwgan realised the potential for disaster but this was not the time or the place to discuss that. He would mention it later, when he could talk to Cadwgan alone.

For the moment, he said, "That is good news, my friend. If we can bring all the tribes together, we can defeat the Romans."

Despite his misgivings over Broichan, Calgacus realised that his journey here had proved to be far easier than he had anticipated. In only a few days, and with no arguments, he already had Coel and Cadwgan agreeing with him. The prospect of an alliance was becoming very real indeed. His pulse beat faster at the thought of being able to achieve what no other man except his famous brother, Caratacus, had ever accomplished. It had taken Caratacus years to persuade a handful of tribes to combine their efforts in a fragile alliance, an uneasy pact which had collapsed after the battle of Caer Caradoc when Cadwallon's Ordovices had broken and run.

Since that dreadful defeat, no tribe had been prepared to trust any other, allowing the Romans to defeat them piecemeal. Now, at last, Calgacus had an opportunity to change that.

Cadwgan broke his musings when he said, "It is good that you have come to the same conclusion as us. I must admit that I thought you were here for some other reason."

Calgacus frowned, "What other reason would there be?"

"You have not heard the news from the South?"

"I have heard that the Brigantes have been conquered and that a new Roman Governor is coming," Calgacus replied.

Cadwgan nodded slowly as he said, "Yes, we have heard those things too. But have you heard nothing else?"

Calgacus shook his head.

"No. Why? What has happened?"

Cadwgan cleared his throat. His expression took on an almost reluctant mien as he explained, "It seems that the Ordovices have risen against Rome. We heard from some of our fellow druids who have returned to Ynis Mon. The sailors and fishermen often bring us news from them, you know."

"Yes, I know," Calgacus confirmed, unable to hide his surprise at the news, and feeling his heart beat a little faster at the thought of a revolt.

He remarked, "I am surprised that Cadwallon would dare start a rebellion. Have any other tribes joined them?"

Cadwgan shook his head sadly.

"No. The Deceangli will not help. They are friends of Rome nowadays. And the Silures, who have themselves rebelled several times, were almost destroyed a couple of years ago. The Ordovices act alone."

"Then they, too, will be destroyed," Calgacus sighed.

"Sadly, I fear that is probably true," Cadwgan agreed. "But there is more that you need to know."

He hesitated for a moment before saying, "I think you should consider going to help them."

Runt, who had remained silent throughout the conversation, gave a soft exhalation of wry amusement but Calgacus fixed his blue eyes on Cadwgan and asked, "Why do you think I should do that? Cadwallon is no friend of mine and has proved himself unreliable too many times in the past."

Cadwgan held his gaze as he replied, "Because Cadwallon no longer leads the Ordovices. The new King is a young man called Brennus."

Calgacus noticed Broichan studying him, a slight smile playing round the druid's thin lips as if he was party to some secret joke at Calgacus' expense.

Turning back to Cadwgan, he shrugged, "Well, I wish him luck, but I've never heard of him."

"Really?" Cadwgan appeared genuinely surprised. "That is strange, since he claims to be your son."

"Your son?" Beatha exclaimed when Calgacus relayed the news to her. "How can that be?"

"I don't know," Calgacus admitted.

He had not known how to tell her Cadwgan's news. He had found her with the rest of his family but he had insisted that she walk down to the sea shore with him so that he could tell her in private.

"I don't understand it," he said.

"It usually only happens one way," Beatha shot back.

He could not tell whether she was angry or amused. Somewhere in between the two emotions, perhaps.

"I know you had other women before we met," she sighed. "One of them must have had a child."

"Not as far as I know," he insisted. "I was usually too busy fighting the Romans to have any long term relationships."

"It doesn't need to have been long term," Beatha pointed out sharply.

"I know. But still, I'm not aware of getting any woman pregnant."

"And yet you have a son."

He shrugged, "I have no idea who he is. Maybe he just made it up."

Beatha fixed him with her blue eyes. Fists planted on her hips, she shot him an accusing look.

"You want to go and find him, don't you?" she challenged.

"Yes."

"Even if it means abandoning your plans for this alliance you are trying to build?"

Calgacus could only nod his head.

She stated, "You want to find a son who is like you, don't you?"

"That's not fair!" he protested.

"I'm sorry," she apologised. "But we both know you wish Togodumnus was more of a warrior."

He could hardly deny the accusation but he shook his head vigorously.

"That doesn't mean I don't love him as my son."

"I know, Cal," Beatha sighed. "But I also know you too well to think you will let this news pass without trying to learn the truth. You want to know if there really is a blood tie between you and this Brennus."

She smiled then, a sad, resigned smile.

"Even if he is not your son," she said, "he probably needs your help. Just remember you are a grandfather now, and don't try to outdo the young men."

"I don't feel old," he protested. "I am only forty-eight."

Beatha smiled, "Cal, I know you will go, whatever I say, but you will go with my blessing. Just be careful. I worry about you, you know."

"There is nothing to worry about. We're only going to find him, speak to him and help him with his war strategy. I'll just be an adviser. I probably won't need to do any fighting."

"Really?" she asked, her delicate eyebrows arching. "I hope you don't expect me to believe that."

"All right, but I'll do my best to do as little fighting as possible. And Runt will be with me. You know he always watches my back."

"It should be you watching out for him," she warned. "He has not been the same since Elaris died."

"He'll be fine. And so will I."

Beatha stepped towards him and they wrapped their arms around one another. For a few moments, neither of them spoke. They simply stood together on the lonely, windswept sea shore, sharing the closeness.

After a while, Beatha looked up at him and asked, "How will you get there?"

"Boat," he said with a grimace.

She laughed softly at his expression.

"Boat? You hate the sea."

"I know. But it's the fastest way to get there. Cadwgan says there are always boats travelling down to Ynis Mon and beyond. There is one leaving tomorrow."

"So soon? And when will you be back?"

"I can't say," he admitted. "It depends on what happens when we get there."

Beatha nodded, her expression pensive.

She said, "I will wait here. It will give me a chance to get to know Fulvia's children while you are away."

She gripped his arm as she added, "If you are not back by spring, I will take Fallar home."

He could feel the tension in the touch of her fingers on his arm but he knew they must face the possibility that he might not return.

"I'll leave most of the lads here with you," he told her.

She hugged him again, her voice failing her. She would not cry, because she was the wife of a warrior, but she felt as if she had already lost him.

"Go and find your son," she eventually managed to whisper. "But make sure you come back."

"I'll come back," he promised. "I always do."

Chapter VII

Far from the lands of the free tribes and the troublesome frontier zone, a ship docked alongside a wooden wharf on the southern coast of Britannia. The oarsmen, experienced rowers of the imperial navy, gratefully rested their muscles and looked forward to a night of pleasure in the small coastal town's inns and brothels. It had been an easy crossing from Gesoriacum, for the sea had been mercifully calm and their oars had propelled the ship across the straits in excellent time. No oarsman could ask for any more than that. Above all, their passengers had been delivered safely, so there was every chance that the Captain would be generous with his silver that evening.

Up on deck, the two passengers said a brief farewell to the Captain while their slaves carried their luggage onto the wharf where a string of pack mules was waiting. There were horses for the noblemen, but no carriage, because they were soldiers, used to riding.

An escort of cavalry awaited them, the Centurion in command snapping a smart salute as the two men crossed the gangplank and made their way onto the wharf.

The Centurion stepped forwards to meet them.

"Welcome to Britannia, Governor!" he barked. "Lucinius Avistus, at your command."

The Governor returned the salute with an easy smile.

"Thank you, Avistus. It is good to be back. How are you?"

"I am well, thank you, Governor."

Avistus almost shouted the response as if it was a reply to an order he had been given rather than a friendly question from an old comrade.

The Governor gestured to the Tribune who accompanied him.

"This is my son-in-law, Cornelius Tacitus. He will be on my staff."

"Sir!" Avistus snapped, acknowledging that the young Tribune would be a man he would have to obey.

He exchanged a brief look with Tacitus who inclined his head in a friendly, if rather nervous, greeting.

"Well, let us be off," the Governor said amiably. "We are to dine with King Cogidubnus this evening."

Avistus led them to their waiting horses. The escort of troopers stood ready, armour and weapons gleaming, their horses immaculately groomed. The baggage was hastily piled onto the pack mules and Gnaeus Julius Agricola, the newly appointed Governor of Britannia, set off for his first formal duty, a meeting with Rome's most loyal ally on the island.

Following well-made Roman roads, they arrived at Cogidubnus' residence early in the evening. Here, it was as if a small piece of Italy had been transported to Britannia. The British King, whose father had sent him to Rome as a boy so that he could receive a proper education, had decided that he would live, not in a traditional roundhouse, or even in a Roman villa, but in a palace.

The construction work, which had been going on for several years, was now almost complete, although some traces of masons and carpenters could still be seen. What they had achieved, though, was stunning.

Tacitus, fresh from Rome and on his first visit to the island province, could not help but marvel at the scale of the building.

"It's enormous," he breathed admiringly as they approached the front facade.

"Fit to rival the Golden House," Agricola agreed, referring to the huge palace the former Emperor Nero had built for himself in Rome.

They reached the monumental entranceway, built in the Roman style with several tall columns towering high above the road, supporting a triangular entablature that was decorated with gaudily painted statues.

A score of servants hurried to meet them as they rode through the gateway. With a minimum of fuss, the troopers of the escort and the Governor's slaves were shown to quarters that had already been prepared for them. The horses and mules were taken to the stables, while Agricola, Tacitus and Centurion Avistus were escorted through a paved hallway and on through to the central garden.

Here, they could appreciate the massive scale of the palace. It was two storeys high, built in a square which enclosed the formal garden. Each side of the square was fully one hundred and fifty paces long, so that the garden seemed immense. A colonnaded portico ran around the inner side of the lower storey of the building, providing shelter against sun and rain. The upper storey, covered by a tiled roof, peeked out from above the portico, revealing small, shuttered windows lining the walls.

The garden itself rivalled many that Tacitus had seen in Rome. It had gravel pathways, lined with shrubs and elegant statues. Rows of small trees had been planted, providing shade for visitors and perches for small birds which chattered and chirped as the men crunched along the pathway that led across the garden to the west wing. Here, a freedman dressed in a spotlessly white tunic greeted them formally and led them inside to a large audience chamber where Cogidubnus, King of the Regni, ally of Rome and ruler of a large part of the southern province, was waiting to meet them.

The hall was so large that the handful of men waiting at the far end to greet the Governor was dwarfed by the room's cavernous bulk. The men all wore togas, as upper class Romans did on formal occasions. Tacitus knew that most men disliked wearing the traditional garment because it was cumbersome to put on and difficult to maintain, requiring the constant use of one arm simply to hold the folds of cloth in place. The King, though, stepped forwards smoothly and apparently effortlessly, looking as imperious as any Roman senator, although Tacitus noticed that, King or not, Cogidubnus deferred to the Governor's status by coming to greet Agricola rather than waiting for his guest to approach him.

The King's greying hair was cut short in the Roman fashion. His clean-shaven face and his belly were plump, the legacies of good living, although his eyes were watchful and quick. He spoke perfect, if slightly accented, Latin as he came to meet them.

"Julius Agricola!" he declared, his voice echoing around the large hall. "Such a pleasure to see you again. Your journey has been uneventful, I trust?"

"Greetings, Cogidubnus," Agricola replied. "Yes, thank you. An easy crossing and a safe journey."

The King beamed, apparently genuinely pleased to meet them.

"And this must be your son-in-law, about whom you wrote to me."

Tacitus held up his hand in formal salute.

"Publius Cornelius Tacitus," he announced.

"Delighted to meet you," Cogidubnus smiled.

He clasped Tacitus' forearm warmly, then did the same to Centurion Avistus, who tried to remain grim but was clearly impressed by the scale and opulence of their surroundings.

Cogidubnus said, "Forgive me using this rather formal chamber to meet you, but I rarely get the chance to show it off."

He gestured around the high-ceilinged hall as he asked, "What do you think of my humble home?"

"It is very impressive," Agricola said, apparently with genuine admiration, although Tacitus knew that his father-in-law generally disliked ostentation.

Cogidubnus gave a soft, self-deprecating laugh.

"The whole place is much too large, of course, but I thought it was important to make a statement to my people. I wanted to show them the grandeur of Rome, as it were."

He introduced them to the other men, all of them local magistrates who were rather self-consciously putting on their best manners for the Governor's visit. Then Cogidubnus gestured towards a doorway.

"I am sure you would like a bath after your journey. My home is at your disposal. After that, my cooks have prepared a feast in your honour."

The three Roman officers were led to the King's private bath-house which, like the rest of the enormous palace, was finished in luxurious style. The walls were covered with marble tiles, the floors decorated with mosaics. Slaves were on hand to massage the men's backs, arms and legs, rubbing oil into their skin, kneading the muscles, then using small, curved, metal strigils to scrape away the oil, removing all the ingrained grime of their journey, leaving their flesh tingling and refreshed.

Then there were the bathing pools. The hot pool was filled with deliciously steaming water, the cold pool fresh and invigorating.

"It is just like home," Tacitus observed as he relaxed in the glorious warmth of the hot water.

"Better," Avistus declared.

Agricola said, "One day we will see places like this all across this island. We can make that happen."

They dressed in fresh clothing which their slaves had laid out for them, then went to join Cogidubnus in his opulent dining room. The King's cooks had gone to enormous lengths to provide a meal that any Roman would have been proud to serve in their own home. They ate reclining on comfortable couches, their places at table denoting their rank and importance, although everyone, even those at the lower end of the long table, was served with the same dishes and the same high-quality, imported wine. Tacitus knew that many Romans served food and drink of poorer quality to the less important of their dinner guests but Cogidubnus was either one of those who was higher-minded or who was so rich that it did not matter to him what his guests ate.

The table contained so many dishes that Tacitus was unable to sample everything. There were several platters of beef, pork and lamb, which was something he had been warned to expect, for the Britons liked their meat and it was one of the few things their country was well stocked with, but there were also chopped vegetables, fish, several kinds of roasted bird, eggs, bread, cheese, and a riot of spicy sauces.

In deference to his guests, Cogidubnus had also provided some garnished sheep's brains and sea urchins stuffed with peppers. There was, naturally, plenty of wine to wash the food down.

While they ate, Cogidubnus talked at length about the work of building his palace.

"I have kept an army of skilled artisans in work for nearly five years," he informed them. "We have everything an Italian villa could boast, including a proper hypocaust to keep us warm."

He laughed, "That is essential in the cold winters we have here, of course."

"It is certainly very impressive, Sir," Tacitus said politely. "It must have been quite an undertaking."

"It was, it was," Cogidubnus agreed. "But the worst thing was actually the garden. I tried importing all sorts of plants and trees from Italy but very few of them survived their first winter. Beech trees and apple trees are just about the only ones we have left. They, at least, seem to thrive. We have an excellent harvest this year."

He picked up a piece of sliced apple which he popped into his mouth.

"I do like apples," he smiled cheerfully.

Addressing his son-in-law by his praenomen, Agricola advised Tacitus, "Do not get used to this, Publius. When we begin our campaigns, the food will be soldiers' rations."

Tacitus smiled, acknowledging the warning.

"Then I shall be sure to enjoy and appreciate this while I have the opportunity," he replied.

"Of course you must," beamed Cogidubnus affably before giving the Governor a more serious look.

"So you intend to continue campaigning?" he asked.

"I am a soldier," Agricola replied in a rather grim tone. "I see no reason why the boundaries of the empire should not be extended. According to the reports I have read recently, there are still too many tribes who cause problems by raiding across our frontier."

"Yes, of course," Cogidubnus agreed. "Although subduing them may not be easy. Your predecessors have fought many wars here recently."

Agricola smiled, "I know. When I was a young man, I served with Paulinus during the revolt of Boudica."

Cogidubnus nodded sagely.

"Ah, yes. I remember. That was a desperate time."

Agricola continued, "A few years later, if you recall, the Emperor sent me back to command the Twentieth Legion. I served under Governor Cerialis when he subdued the Brigantes."

Cogidubnus sipped his wine.

"A very successful campaign, as I recall," he commented.

Agricola gave a weak smile.

"At the time, yes, but I understand that Cerialis' successor was unable to finish the job."

Cogidubnus said, "Yes, Frontinus was obliged to spend most of his term as Governor suppressing the Silures."

He sighed, rolling his eyes as he added ruefully, "Suppressing them again, I should say."

"The Silures are a very warlike tribe, I understand," observed Tacitus.

Cogidubnus smiled, his eyes twinkling.

"I think it is more appropriate to say that they *were* a warlike tribe. Frontinus did a most thorough job of subduing them this time. I don't think you need to fear much from them. Mind you, it is not before time."

Agricola nodded, "Indeed. But the Brigantes have had three years to recover themselves. We never did catch their leader, Venutius. That will be out first task. We will complete the conquest of the Brigantes next year, then we shall march north and subdue the Picts."

Cogidubnus raised his goblet.

"I wish you well, Governor. It is an ambitious target you have set yourself but I am sure you will succeed."

"Ambitious? Perhaps," Agricola conceded. "But no war was ever won by being timid. Still, there is more to be done than simply fighting. We must also do our best to show the tribes the benefits of Roman rule. We must give them proper towns and cities, with markets, temples, baths, theatres and amphitheatres. We must persuade the young sons of the tribal chieftains to learn Latin, to wear togas and to throw off their barbarian ways."

He raised his own goblet to Cogidubnus, saying, "You, Sir, are an example I wish others to follow."

Cogidubnus acknowledged the compliment by inclining his head slightly.

"I will do my best to help in any way I can," he assured the Governor. "I think I can safely say that it is an honour to have a Governor who understands this island so well. Many of the people here are, sadly, like children. If you catch them early enough, they are easily trained to conform to civilised ways, but there are also those who stubbornly refuse and who understand only violence."

Agricola said, "I intend to deal with people in whatever way is most appropriate."

"I am sure you will," smiled Cogidubnus. "But you should be wary of the tribes who live in the North. I understand that Calgacus lives among them."

Agricola's face betrayed a slight frown.

Tacitus, who had never heard the name, asked, "Who is Calgacus?"

Cogidubnus gave a slightly embarrassed cough before explaining, "He is a most notorious renegade. A brother of Caratacus, so they say."

He paused for a moment before adding rather hesitantly, "My, ah ... younger sister had the effrontery to run off with him some years ago. She has, I regret, turned her back on civilisation and refused to become a Roman."

Agricola observed, "That was rather a long time ago. Calgacus was famous once but I have not heard his name mentioned for some years. Do you know whether he still lives?"

"I have not heard otherwise," said Cogidubnus. "But I try not to think about him too much. It is a painful memory for me. Even though it was many years ago, that my own sister should elope with such a savage is still hard to bear."

"I understand. But, in truth, Calgacus does not matter," Agricola declared firmly. "He must be an old man now. He has not caused any trouble for years."

"He will not yet be fifty years old," Cogidubnus pointed out. "He was much younger than Caratacus, you know. But I dare say you are correct. He has not been heard of for some years. Still, if you should happen to find him, I would be grateful if you could dispose of him and bring my sister back to me. She may have thrown her lot in with the barbarians but she is still family."

He hesitated, sipped at his wine, then added, "I would pay a handsome reward to the man who brings her back to me."

"I will let my officers know," Agricola promised. "Now, I fear I must bid you good night. We must be off early tomorrow. I need to go to Londinium, then I wish to visit each of the Legions and make preparations for next year's campaign. I need to be sure that no trouble will break out while I am fighting the northern tribes. I have seen that happen before, as you know."

"Oh, I don't think you need worry about that," Cogidubnus assured him airily. "None of the tribes would dare rebel. They have seen what happens when they do. Surely you don't think anyone would be foolish enough to repeat the mistakes of the Iceni and the Silures?"

"Let us hope not," agreed Agricola as he drained his goblet. "I intend to have this whole island under control by the time I finish my term as Governor. I will encourage obedience when I can, but I learned years ago that any opposition must be quickly and utterly crushed."

He placed his empty goblet on the table as he went on, "Unfortunately, I have been in Britannia often enough to know that some of the tribes here do not seem to have learned that lesson very well."

"You expect trouble, then?" Cogidubnus enquired, his chubby features betraying some concern at the thought.

"I expect victory," Agricola replied firmly. "But I will not take anything for granted. I will anticipate trouble, and I will prepare for it. Any tribe that rebels will be exterminated. That is a promise."

Chapter VIII

Summer in Britannia was not too bad, Tacitus thought to himself as he woke to another fine morning. The climate was wetter and cooler than Italy, of course, but the soil was rich and fertile, producing abundant crops and providing excellent grazing for livestock. Many of the natives were rather backward and rustic, but that was only to be expected from a province that had been part of the empire for less than forty years.

The growing town of Londinium was an exception, being, like so many Roman towns, a cosmopolitan mix of people from all over the empire. Traders flocked there, sailing across the straits in search of exotic goods from this mysterious island at the edge of the world. Artisans came to find a place they could make their fortune, and some people came simply in search of somewhere new.

Londinium was certainly new. It was now the effective capital of the province, having supplanted the original capital of Camulodunum which had never really recovered from being sacked by Boudica eighteen years previously. The original settlement at Londinium had also been destroyed but the broad river allowed ships crossing the sea from Gaul to sail deep into the heart of the province, making the town's location ideal for a river-port.

Londinium, like the mythical phoenix, had grown again from the ashes of its destruction. The bustling town was filled with shops, warehouses, inns and workshops. It was also the nominal residence of the Governor, although Tacitus had enjoyed few opportunities to relax in the comfort of his father-in-law's official home.

In the few days since their arrival in Britannia, Agricola had been a whirlwind of activity, dashing down to the south-west of the island to inspect the Second Legion and to briefly tour the territory of the Silures, a tribe which, the Governor noted with satisfaction, was very firmly under control. That visit had been followed by a lightning trip to the other side of the island, to see the wide, flat lands of the Iceni. That famous tribe had been utterly crushed after the Boudican revolt and Tacitus could see that, even after eighteen years, many farmsteads still lay abandoned, while some villages appeared to be almost entirely deserted. It was plain that the retribution meted out to the tribe after the failure of the rebellion had been brutal, even by Roman standards.

With grim humour, Agricola had mentioned that peace with the Iceni was now guaranteed since they scarcely existed as a cohesive tribe. Tacitus had shelved that comment away as one that might prove useful to him in the future, though he reckoned it could do with some polish if it was to be recorded for posterity.

Leaving the sorry remnants of the Iceni to their misery, Tacitus had accompanied his father-in-law back to Londinium where they intended to spend a few days before heading north to prepare for the following summer's campaign. Tacitus was exhausted by the days of hard riding and had been looking forward to a short rest which would allow him some time to record his impressions. He knew that anyone who had any ambitions in Roman society was obliged to serve some time with the army, but his real passion was for writing. His aspiration was to be a historian, a writer who could tell the people of Rome about the far-flung places of the empire and the men who had built that empire. Men like Agricola.

Tacitus felt enormously privileged that his father-in-law had permitted him to join his staff during Agricola's term as Governor of Britannia. The least Tacitus could do was to pen a work that would tell the world what a great man Agricola was.

Tacitus sat at his table, considering where he should begin that day's notes, but a knock at the door interrupted him before he could begin writing.

"Come!" he called.

A freedman stuck his head round the door, giving Tacitus an apologetic look.

"Sir? The Governor has asked that you join him in his office immediately."

Tacitus sighed as he laid down his writing stylus.

"Did he say why?"

"No, Sir. But it seems to be urgent. All of the senior officers have been summoned."

Reluctantly putting aside his thoughts about writing, Tacitus made his way to Agricola's office. He discovered that he was the last to arrive, for the other Tribunes, the Quaestors and the senior Centurions were already assembled, crowding into the small room to hear what the Governor had to say. An air of nervous apprehension hung over them, for they all knew the Governor would not call them together unless his news was important.

Agricola nodded when he saw Tacitus arrive.

"Gentlemen," he announced briskly, "we must go north without delay. I want everyone ready to leave by noon."

The men stirred. Avistus, the senior Centurion, asked, "What has happened, Sir?"

Agricola's face was stern as he explained, "I have received news that the Ordovices have risen in revolt. They have almost wiped out a squadron of cavalry that was stationed on their territory."

He looked around the room, holding each man's gaze for a moment. Then he continued, "This is our first test, Gentlemen. We must get to Deva quickly. Then I will lead the Twentieth Legion against this tribe and we will wipe them out. Completely."

He flattened his palm on his desk, crushing an imaginary foe.

The officers were bursting with questions but Agricola had few answers to give them. His one concern was to stamp out the revolt quickly. Years before, as a young Tribune, he had been on the staff of Governor Paulinus when the Iceni had risen in revolt under their infamous Queen, Boudica. That rebellion had almost ended in disaster for Rome but Paulinus had acted decisively and, above all, swiftly. Agricola had learned the lesson well. He issued orders for the march and sent his officers scurrying away to carry out those orders.

Tacitus hurried to his room to gather some essential items, including his writing materials. He had a slave pack them into some small leather bags along with some spare clothing.

"Have them fastened to my horse," he told the slave. "The rest of my kit can follow later."

"Yes, Master."

Taking a last look around the small room, Tacitus sighed. He had been warned that Britannia was an unruly province but he had not expected trouble to erupt within three weeks of his arrival. His writing, it seemed, would have to wait.

He went to the stables but found that everything there was under control. Freedmen, slaves and scribes scurried to and fro under the watchful eyes and bellowed curses of the Centurions. A newly appointed and inexperienced Tribune could do nothing to help so Tacitus returned to Agricola's office where he found the Governor rattling out commands to half a dozen secretaries, dictating letters that were to be sent to various officials and military posts throughout the island.

One of those letters was a brief note to the Emperor, advising him of the news of the revolt and what Agricola intended to do about it. Agricola signed the letters, then passed his seal to one of the secretaries who pressed it into the hot sealing wax before handing it back to the Governor.

"Will that be all, Sir?" the secretary asked.

"Yes. See that messengers are sent without delay."

The secretaries hurried out with their precious letters, leaving Tacitus and Agricola alone. The Governor raised an eyebrow as he looked at his son-in-law.

"Well, Publius? How are you enjoying Britannia so far?"

"I feel rather superfluous at the moment, Sir."

"Don't worry about it. You are here to watch and to learn. There is no better place in the entire Empire to learn how to deal with barbarians."

"Yes, Sir," Tacitus replied uncertainly.

Agricola laughed, "Don't look so worried, man. Put on the face of a stern patrician. We must let everyone see that this rebellion is an inconvenience, not a disaster. If the Britons scent weakness, they can turn on us in an instant. So we must not panic but we must act quickly and decisively."

"Yes, Sir. I see that. But if I may ask a question?"

"Of course."

"We do not yet know how serious the problem is. I was wondering whether it was necessary to advise the Emperor before we know the full facts."

Agricola's thin lips twitched in wry amusement.

He said, "It is always wise to keep the Emperor informed. If it turns out to be nothing serious, then I will be able to tell him how easily we suppressed the trouble. Besides, we cannot afford to wait. You know, of course, that the Emperor's secretaries always provide a new Governor with a list of detailed instructions as to how he is to carry out his duties."

"Yes, Sir."

Again, the faint smile played on Agricola's lips as he explained, "You will learn, Publius, that initiative is not a trait that

Emperors like to see in their officials. That is why these instructions are issued, so that there can be no doubt as to what I am permitted to do and what I must not do. My letter of instruction covers a great many situations but there are times when guidance must be sought. However, it will take several weeks for a letter to reach Rome and for the reply to arrive. If we are to deal with this rebellion, we do not have the luxury of time."

His smile broadened as he added, "In any case, there is one over-riding command implicit in my instructions. I must keep the peace. Anyone who threatens that peace must be dealt with."

"I understand, Sir," Tacitus acknowledged.

"Good. Then let us go and see how soon we can be on the road."

They left Londinium before noon. To Tacitus' surprise and admiration, the Governor was on the way north within two hours of ordering the departure, riding alongside Tacitus with Avistus and the cavalry escort streaming behind them. The Quaestors, scribes and freedmen would follow in wagons, bringing the officers' personal belongings and the mountains of official paperwork that were so essential for governing a province.

The journey was two hundred miles to the north-west but Agricola set a fast pace, leaving the wagons far behind in his wake as he pushed up the military roads. They travelled through a green land that was slowly turning to russet, gold and brown as the trees of the great forests began to shed their leaves. Overhead, flying in ragged vee-formations, geese were migrating from the North, seeking their winter habitats. Mists and rain dogged the Governor's progress but Agricola pushed on, resting only briefly during the day and spending the nights at staging posts before rising at dawn to set off again. Travel-worn and dusty, they reached the legionary fortress at Deva on the morning of the fourth day after leaving Londinium.

Tired as he was, Agricola did not rest. He immediately summoned the Legion's senior officers to an emergency meeting. Wearily, Tacitus accompanied his father-in-law, wondering at the man's seemingly boundless energy.

The officers gathered in the main hall of the Principia, the headquarters building. Agricola sat at the tribunal bench alongside the Legate of the Twentieth Legion and the senior Tribunes.

Silencing the buzz of conversation with a call to order, the Governor explained what he wanted done.

"I want our retribution to begin immediately," he announced. "Legionary and Auxiliary cavalry are to raid inside the Ordovices' territory and destroy homes and farms. Anyone who resists is to be killed. The rest of the barbarians are to be driven into the hills so that they can spread the news of our intentions."

He paused, noting with satisfaction the looks of approval on the faces of his officers.

He continued, "While that is happening, I want messages sent to all the nearby legionary detachments and Auxiliary units. They are to gather here as soon as possible. And I want ships out patrolling the coast as far as Mona."

He shot a glance at the Legate, a fresh-faced man named Hordonius Piso.

"How many fit men can the Legion put in the field?" he demanded.

Piso reacted rather nervously to the question. This was his first command and he was only too well aware that the Governor had commanded the Twentieth Legion some years before him. Most of the legionaries remembered and revered Agricola, and Piso often felt that his men regarded him less favourably.

Under the Governor's intense gaze, he ran a hand through his thinning hair and swallowed nervously before replying, "We have just under three thousand legionaries in the fort, plus around fifteen hundred out on various detachments."

Piso pursed his lips, as if wondering whether to continue, but the Governor's orders to call in the detachments could only mean one thing. Taking a deep breath, he asked, "Do you intend to march against them this year, Sir?"

"Of course!" Agricola responded curtly. "Why not?"

Piso flushed slightly as he mumbled, "Well, Sir, it is just that the summer is almost over. There are very few weeks of reliable weather remaining."

Agricola's response was firm.

"I will not wait until next year. We will march whatever the weather. Is that understood?"

"Absolutely, Sir," Piso replied instantly, silently angry that he had been so publicly reprimanded.

As if recognising the Legate's discomfort, Agricola's stance softened slightly and he said, "My apologies, Piso. I understand your concerns. The mountains are treacherous, I know. But we cannot allow the Ordovices time to cause more trouble or to persuade other tribes to join them. They must be stopped as soon as possible."

He paused, then added with a smile, "Anyway, this damned island's weather is so unpredictable, we could have snow in July and warm sunshine in October."

Mollified by the Governor's placatory words, Piso smiled back while the other officers laughed dutifully at the old joke.

Agricola went on, "Now, what of the other tribes?"

"No problems reported so far, Sir," Piso informed him. "The locals round here never cause trouble. To the west, the Deceangli have promised us they will maintain the peace."

With some pride, he continued, "I sent a message to their King reminding him of the consequences of not remaining loyal."

"Well done," Agricola nodded approvingly. "So we have only one tribe to worry about for the moment. Let us hope that remains the case. Now, which of your men knows the Ordovices best?"

Frowning slightly, Piso replied, "That would probably be Sempronius Casca, Sir."

He signalled towards a young cavalry officer who was standing to one side of the hall, his plumed helmet tucked neatly under his arm.

"Casca is a Centurion of Auxiliary cavalry," Piso explained. "It was his unit that was ambushed at the start of the revolt."

The Legate tried not to sound disapproving but did not quite succeed in keeping a trace of disappointment from his voice.

Agricola smiled as he saw the Centurion stiffen to attention.

"Casca? I don't believe we have met. How are you?"

Casca's face was hard, his eyes dark pools of simmering resentment, but he spoke confidently.

"Well enough, Sir. Thank you."

Agricola nodded. He noticed that the other officers were maintaining a discreet distance from Casca. Not only were the men under his command Auxiliaries, and so of lesser status than legionaries, but his unit had been ambushed, most of his men killed, his fort destroyed, and yet he had escaped. The taint of his disgrace was enough to make other men unwilling to be seen close to him.

Agricola did not appear to be concerned as he said, "Good. Now, you and Piso must stay and talk to me in private. We have much to discuss while your colleagues are preparing for the campaign."

He looked around the room as he told the officers, "Carry on, Gentlemen. I intend to set off as soon as the detached units have joined us. That will take several days but I want to be on the march as soon as possible. Make sure your men are ready because we have some barbarians to kill."

The officers laughed, saluting before filing out of the room. Agricola smiled as he heard the murmur of their voices receding. They were professionals, he knew, and they would not let him down.

He gestured to Tacitus, Piso and Casca to join him at a large table that stood to one side of the hall.

Fixing Casca with a frosty stare, he said, "You lost nineteen men in an ambush, I hear."

"Yes, Sir."

Casca's face was a hard, stony mask as he made the admission.

Agricola nodded thoughtfully, appreciating the younger man's honesty and the fact that he made no attempt to offer excuses.

"Well," Agricola smiled softly, "it happens to the best of us. One of my predecessors as Governor, Petilius Cerialis, was ambushed when he was Legate of the Ninth Legion. He was marching to put down the rebel Boudica and he walked straight into a trap. He lost a couple of thousand men, but his career recovered and he went on to become Governor here."

Casca inclined his head slightly as he said, "Thank you, Sir. I appreciate that."

He did not voice the opinion that Cerialis had been from a wealthy family with connections to important people in Rome. Casca did not enjoy those privileges and he knew that his own career was unlikely to recover as well as Cerialis' had done.

Agricola seemed to understand Casca's concerns.

"Just don't do it again," he warned with a quick smile. "I will reward men of talent and ability, but I will remove any who are dishonest, corrupt or incompetent. Promotions will be on merit from now on."

He glanced at Piso, making sure that the Legate also understood his message.

Then he turned back to Casca and asked, "So you want revenge, I expect?"

Casca's mask of indifference slipped as he eagerly replied, "Yes, Sir!"

"Good. Now, let us review the maps, and you can tell me how we go about tracking these rebels down."

Piso gave a slight cough as he asked, "Will they not simply melt away into the hills when we advance?"

Agricola smiled, "That is their usual tactic. But I do not intend to chase their army through the mountains. We will target their villages and farms. The harvest is in. There will be places where they store their grain. If they see that we intend to destroy those places, they will have only two options; they will either have to fight us or starve. Either way, they will die."

He spoke with such conviction that the other men could not help but believe him.

Tapping a map which Tacitus had spread out on the table, Agricola said, "Now, Casca, tell me what you know."

The four men spent almost an hour going over what Casca knew and what information Piso's scouts had brought back before Agricola eventually seemed satisfied.

"This man Brennus," he asked Casca. "He is an experienced chieftain?"

"No, Sir. We only heard about him a few months ago. I would guess that he is in his mid-twenties. He is a bandit chief. Nothing more."

Agricola nodded, "So, he keeps power by showing his followers that he is the strongest. I suspect that a man like that will fight us, even if we don't destroy his granaries. He will lose his authority if he does not face us. All we need to do is provoke him enough so that he gathers his forces for a battle. Then we will crush them."

Piso nodded in quiet agreement with the Governor's plan.

Casca asked, "Sir? May I make a request?"

"Of course," Agricola nodded.

Casca explained, "My unit is severely under strength. We have been assigned to escorting the supply wagons."

He did not look at Piso as he went on, "I would like the opportunity to redeem myself."

Piso frowned in annoyance but Agricola asked Casca, "What is it that you want? I will not interfere in the dispositions of the Legion."

"I understand, Sir," said Casca. "But I cannot take my revenge on Brennus if I am acting as nursemaid to the muleteers. I and my men would be grateful if you could give us a special commission."

Piso struggled to contain himself at Casca's impertinence but Agricola seemed amused.

"What commission might that be?" he asked.

"To hunt down Brennus," Casca replied with a cold, merciless glint in his eyes. "I know what he looks like. You know these Britons, Sir. If Brennus dies, the revolt will die with him. I wish to seek him on the battlefield and kill him personally."

Agricola studied the young officer for a few moments. He could sense Piso's annoyance but he recognised the need in the young cavalryman. Desire for revenge emanated from Casca's every movement, every small gesture.

After some thought, Agricola remarked, "A battlefield is not the place for personal revenge. We are Romans. We will fight the way we have always fought."

Casca's face stiffened. Barely masking his disappointment, he said, "I understand, Sir."

Agricola held up a hand as he went on, "However, I think that a man with such determination could be better employed than merely guarding our stores."

He turned to Piso and asked, "Could you detach Centurion Casca and his men to serve on my staff? Temporarily, of course. I could do with having someone close to me who knows the land and the people."

Piso's expression was dark but, faced with such a request, he could hardly refuse.

"Of course, Sir," he nodded grudgingly.

"Excellent," smiled Agricola breezily. "Well, Casca, I cannot promise you personal revenge on this Brennus, but I can promise you that you will be at the heart of our war against him. Will that do you?"

Casca smiled for the first time as he said, "Thank you, Sir."

"I will work you hard, mind," warned Agricola. Then he gave a soft laugh as he added, "And if I know anything about barbarians, Brennus will flee when we destroy his army. If that happens, I will indeed need somebody to hunt him down."

Casca was smiling broadly now, but it was the smile of a predator about to strike.

He vowed, "If he runs, I will find him for you, Sir. I will bring you his head."

Chapter IX

Brennus knew he must be utterly ruthless if he were to establish a proper hold on the kingship. After killing the old King, he had ordered his men to hunt down Cadwallon's remaining relatives and kill them so that there would be nobody to dispute his right to rule. It was an order the warriors obeyed reluctantly but they were afraid of Brennus, so Cadwallon's young grandsons were executed.

Brennus had been forced to kill the old King's wife and daughters himself because few warriors took pride in killing innocents. Rape and murder after a battle were one thing but cold-blooded killing of women was a different matter. Brennus, though, needed to be certain that there could be no rival claims to his Kingship, so all of Cadwallon's family had to die.

It was an unpleasant task, certainly not one he enjoyed, but it was a necessary one and Brennus was determined that he would do whatever was required. So, hardening his resolve, he ignored the pleas and fear of Cadwallon's women and took his knife to their throats.

He knew that his followers were not happy with what he had done. Contests over leadership were not uncommon but few victors went so far as to kill anyone except their main rival. Yet in recent generations, Kingship of the tribes had tended to pass from father to son, rather than falling to the strongest chieftain as had been the case in the old days. Cadwallon had been King for a long time. He had been unpopular with many of his people because of his neutrality towards Rome and because he had been a weak and often ineffectual leader. But because he was descended from tribal leaders, he had remained in power despite his faults. This modern attitude to inheritance had removed much of the internecine strife that had bedevilled the tribe in past generations but Brennus realised that it meant he could not afford to leave any of Cadwallon's descendants alive. To do so would be to invite a challenge. For Brennus, it had been a simple decision to kill the entire family.

Yet he understood that the rest of the tribe would be horrified at his brutal take-over, so he distributed Cadwallon's silver, gold and cattle to his followers, he coerced other warriors into joining his band, and he led them in the ambush of the Roman cavalry patrol. That victory, and the subsequent destruction of the Roman fort had brought acceptance from the warriors. Brennus was a strong leader, a powerfully built man of awesome strength and with a ruthless determination to drive the Romans out of his tribe's territory. After years of grumbling about Cadwallon's policy of appeasement and servitude, the warriors had found a leader who could defeat the Romans.

That victory acted as a talisman. While most of the older people of the tribe were still sullen and shocked by Cadwallon's death, Brennus' victory brought the young men of the Ordovices flocking to join his war band.

Gold, silver, cattle and victory. These were the things that Brennus used to build his powerbase.

Then there were the slaves. Brennus freed those who had been owned by Cadwallon. Most of them had known nothing except a life of slavery and were bewildered by the sudden change in their status. To the freed men, he gave small plots of land, telling them to repay him by farming the land and providing food for the warriors. The women were given to his warriors as wives. He was pleased with that idea, for it was another way to reward those who had been loyal to him.

Then he had seen the girl. Although she was nominally free, his men were arguing over her while she stood, arms hanging loosely at her sides, head bowed, her long, dark hair falling around her face. She was slightly built, slim and delicate, but clearly desirable if the reaction of the men was anything to go by.

One of the warriors reached out to raise her chin so that they could study her face. The dull, frightened expression she wore sent an arrow of long-forgotten anger and grief through Brennus' heart. The emotion was so strong that he knew he could not ignore it. Scarcely aware of what he was doing, he pushed through the crowd of warriors and walked over to face her.

The arguing men fell silent as they took a step back, making way for him. Brennus looked down at the girl.

"What is your name?" he asked her.

She looked back at him with wide, frightened eyes. When she spoke, her voice was a whisper on the summer breeze.

"Tegan," she said. Then she lowered her gaze again.

"Look at me, Tegan," Brennus commanded.

He gestured with one arm, indicating the warriors who stood around her.

"Which of these men do you desire as a husband?"

She gave a slight shake of her head.

"I don't know," she whispered. "I don't care."

He had guessed that from the way she stood there, but his heart beat faster when he heard her say it. Slowly, he reached for her hand.

Clasping it gently, he told her, "Then I will have you."

Nobody argued. Tegan certainly made no protest. She meekly went with him while the other men turned their attention to the remaining women who had not yet been selected as suitable wives.

Brennus told some of the other women to help her wash and to give her new clothes. Among the plunder he had kept for himself he found some gold rings to put on her fingers and a necklace of jet beads which he placed around her neck. Tegan accepted his gifts in silence, her eyes always lowered.

As evening drew on, the other couples were assembled in the open air and a mass hand-fasting ceremony was held. Brennus, as tribal leader, officiated, witnessing the vows and placing the cords over the wrists of the betrothed, symbolically binding them together.

He decided that there was nobody senior enough to witness his own marriage to Tegan, so he sent a messenger to Ynis Mon, the sacred island, asking for a druid to come to the village to perform the ceremony. That was a gamble, for there were few druids left alive and those who had survived the Roman slaughter were not easily persuaded to answer a summons from anyone. But Brennus was always lucky in such things. Three weeks after the message had been sent, a druid came to perform the ceremony in the presence of the entire tribe.

During those three weeks of waiting, Brennus had showered Tegan with gifts of sparkling jewellery, replacing her necklace with a golden torc, a symbol of rank and authority. She did not live with him but was cared for by a wealthy old chieftain and his wife because Brennus wanted his marriage to be seen and acknowledged by the tribe. He was King and he would sire an heir. He wanted no accusations that he had not done everything properly.

When the day eventually arrived, the druid hung the cords over the couple's wrists, a great feast was held by firelight, Brennus distributed yet more gifts and, as night fell, he took Tegan to his bed.

She was soft and delicate, tiny in his massively muscled arms. She barely spoke to him, but she dutifully undressed him, then submitted to him as he took possession of her body by the light of the hearth fire. Only when he had spent himself and they were lying together under the furs of the bed did she speak.

"Why did you choose me?" she asked softly.

"What?"

He raised himself on one elbow to look down at her perfect face, realising that it was the first time she had ever asked him anything.

"What do you mean?"

"Why did you choose me?" she repeated. "You are a King. I am just a slave."

"You are not a slave any longer," he told her. "You are Tegan, wife of Brennus, the chieftain of the Ordovices."

She fell silent, closing her eyes as if deciding that there was no point in pursuing the question.

Brennus moved the furs aside so that he could gaze down at her body. Gently, he ran one hand over her skin, caressing her.

Absently, he said, "I chose you because you are very beautiful. Is that not enough?"

Tegan said nothing. Her eyes remained closed as he touched her.

Impelled by her silence, he told her, "You reminded me of someone. Someone who had no choice when she was told to give herself to any man who visited her master."

Tegan's eyes opened, her interest aroused.

"A slave girl?" she asked.

"Yes."

His hand moved to gently stroke her cheek as he went on, "You don't look like her, but your situation was the same. I could not do anything to help her, but I can make things different for you. Are you not happy?"

"Yes," she agreed, closing her eyes again, though the truth was that she did not feel happy. She did not feel anything. Nor did she believe that she had really had much of a choice.

Harvest time arrived. This year, the feast of Lughnasa was held with more abandon than was usual among the Ordovices. They had rebelled against Rome and killed Roman soldiers, and everyone knew that retribution would come sooner or later. The Romans had an immensely strong military presence on the island but they could not be everywhere. Their strategy was based on ensuring that everyone knew what the response would be to any tribe who rose in rebellion.

Brennus was no fool. He knew he would not be left in peace, so he sent emissaries to the Deceangli, asking for their aid. Ceawlin, their King, replied with a blunt refusal.

Undeterred, Brennus asked for help from the Silures who lived to the south. They were famous for their resistance to Rome but that resistance had brought the vengeance of the Empire down on them. Their response to Brennus' envoys was bitter recrimination.

"The Ordovices did not help us when we fought Rome," they accused. "We have lost too many men in the past, and our land is now garrisoned by Roman forts. Why should we help those who did not help us?"

Brennus had hoped that the name of his famous father would be enough to rouse the Silures. They still sang songs about him. In fact, everyone sang songs about Calgacus. But the Silures were under the Roman heel, and they would not fight.

Brennus was disappointed but his resolve was unshaken. He was young, strong and confident in his own ability. He had made his plans knowing that aid from neighbouring tribes would be a bonus and he had always known that, ultimately, the Ordovices might stand alone. He had heard the old men talk about the power of Rome but he doubted whether the Governor would be able to bring more than four or five thousand men against him. Already, six thousand men of the Ordovices had sworn to fight and more were gathering every day.

"Let the Romans come," Brennus told his people. "With our superior numbers and the mountains to aid us, we will defeat them. My father did it once before and I shall do no less."

The people listened, taking heart from the memory of Calgacus' famous victory a generation ago, but despite their open show of bravado they knew that the step they had taken was a bold one, so they celebrated Lughnasa as if it might be their last feast, drinking and eating as much as they could.

And when the feast was done, they prepared for war.

Roman cavalry patrols returned, skirting the lowlands at the foot of the hills, though they never ventured as far as the mountains. Instead, the men and women who farmed the lowlands found their harvest confiscated, their grain and livestock seized to feed the approaching army, and their homes burned to the ground. A few Britons were killed, some taken away into slavery, but most were allowed to go free. Agricola knew that homeless, starving people would have no choice but to flee to the hills, seeking Brennus, asking for his protection. These refugees helped spread fear and panic, as well as adding to the mouths that the Ordovices needed to feed.

With dozens of homeless refugees spreading the dire news of an imminent Roman attack, Brennus knew that he must be seen to do something. He led his men out, drove away the cavalry as best they could, set watches on the hilltops and prepared to defend their land.

Day after day they waited, watching and patrolling, occasionally skirmishing with the Roman horsemen but mostly simply sitting idle. Boring hours turned into monotonous days and, as the summer waned, Brennus began to think that the Romans would not come after all and that winter might prevent an invasion.

His hopes were dashed when, as the leaves were carpeting the ground brown and gold, his scouts brought news of the Roman army.

"They are heading straight for us," one of the scouts told him.

Brennus gripped the hilt of his sword as he declared, "Then we shall go to meet them."

Messengers galloped through the hills, summoning the men of the Ordovices. One of the advantages of not having fought Rome was that the tribe's numbers had not been thinned by years of warfare, so the warriors came in their thousands from all across the tribal territory until the whole tribe came together, a force more than eight thousand strong. They brought their women and children, swelling the throng to nearly twenty thousand, and they brought their cattle, sheep, goats, pigs and dogs.

Brennus rode at their head, leading them north-east to meet the invaders. He knew where he wanted to face them, for he had scouted the land many weeks earlier and knew precisely the best place to stand against the enemy.

He called a halt on a steep hill with a broad summit that afforded excellent views over the approaches from the north and east. They arrived not a moment too soon, for when Brennus looked to the wide lands stretching out to the north-east, his sharp eyes could make out the dark patch of brown that was a massive Roman marching camp. The enemy were near.

"We will stand here," he announced.

The Ordovices made camp on the hilltop. The warriors sharpened their spears, tightened the leather coverings of their wicker shields and drank their dark beer. Some of them painted their faces and chests with blue war paint, drawing swirling patterns designed to ward off the enemy's weapons. Others painted themselves with images of horses or bears, wolves or eagles, hoping that the spirits of these fierce and powerful creatures would aid them. Men plastered their hair with lime, spiking it high to make themselves appear tall and terrifying. This was how their fathers and grandfathers had prepared for war and the Ordovices were determined to honour the old ways.

Fires were lit, small shelters constructed. The men who had their wives with them made love, paying no heed to the thousands who surrounded them because the following day could bring battle and there might never be another chance for them.

Brennus lay with Tegan under a makeshift shelter of strong branches and leather hides. As usual, she was passive, barely responding to his touch.

"Will you win tomorrow?" she asked him.

Her voice was calm and soft, no trace of concern evident in her tone. She asked it in the same way she would enquire whether he had enjoyed his dinner.

"Of course we will win," he assured her. "I am Brennus. Nobody is as strong as me."

"Cadwallon used to say that nobody could defeat the Romans. He told tales of the great battle at Caer Caradoc, where even Caratacus was beaten."

"That was long ago," Brennus said dismissively. "Cadwallon was a witless fool and now he is dead. As for Caratacus, he was not of the Ordovices. We will win. I always win."

He pulled her close and kissed her lips.

"Now, come here," he told her.

Unresisting, Tegan closed her eyes as he rolled on top of her, kissing her and almost crushing her beneath his muscular body.

He was unexpectedly interrupted when they heard a voice calling from outside the shelter.

"Lord Brennus!"

Brennus froze.

"What is it?" he snapped, irritated at the interruption.

"There are some people asking to see you."

"Tell them to wait. I am busy."

He leaned down to kiss Tegan's lips. She waited but he paused again, a frown of annoyance on his face.

"Who is it that wants to see me?" he called out.

The voice from outside sounded worried and uncertain as it replied, "Their leader says his name is Calgacus."

Chapter X

Although Calgacus was keen to discover the true identity of the man who claimed to be his son, he had still viewed the journey south with some trepidation. When he saw the means of transport, he was less enthusiastic than ever.

Standing on the edge of the wooden landing jetty, he eyed the boat warily. He had never been comfortable on the sea, distrusting the constant, stomach-churning rocking motion of the vessels that always seemed to accompany any voyage. Despite its impressive size, this particular boat looked no better than most he had seen before. It was not one of the sea-going curraghs but a proper, oak-built sailing vessel although that did nothing to allay Calgacus' fears as he studied it.

The boat's wooden hull was nearly forty feet in length from the high, pointed prow to the large, wooden steerboard that was fixed to the centre of the blunt stern. It had a tall, single mast, with a cross-spar near the top, from which hung a furled, leather sail. Wide rowing benches spanned the fore and aft sections but two large, rectangular, wooden structures filled the spaces immediately in front and behind the mast. These were where the ship's cargo of goods were stored because this was a trading vessel rather than a warship.

A group of sailors were just finishing their task of stowing bales of wool into the holds while he watched.

On the jetty, the Captain stood patiently, chewing on a ragged fingernail while he watched Calgacus' inspection of the sailing vessel.

Frowning, Calgacus gave the shipmaster an enquiring look.

"That will get us all the way to Ynis Mon?" he asked.

The Captain, a small, wiry man with thinning hair, replied with a throaty chuckle, "Who knows? If the gods allow it, yes."

"You don't sound very confident," accused Runt.

The Captain's tanned face broke into a gap-toothed grin.

"Well, I've been a sailor long enough to know you should never take anything for granted, especially in these waters. But if it is any comfort, I've been doing this trip for more than fifteen years now and we've made it every time."

He paused, then hawked and spat on the ground for luck.

"So far," he added with a broad, mocking smile.

Seeing Calgacus' worried expression, the Captain continued, "I can promise you this is the finest, fastest ship you'll find anywhere in these islands. If you want to reach Ynis Mon, you'll not find a better means of getting there."

Calgacus' anxious expression did not alter but he sighed, "Right then. Let's get going."

The shipmaster was a small man but he stood his ground in front of Calgacus' towering bulk, holding up a hand to prevent them from boarding.

"You'd better take off that armour first," he advised.

Calgacus looked down at his battered breastplate. It had been a gift from his half-brother, the great Caratacus. He had brought it because, despite its age and the battle scars that marked its surface, it was more impressive than the coat of chainmail he usually wore in combat. The chainmail was for fighting, the breastplate's main use for him now was for display. Made of gleaming bronze, it marked him out as a wealthy and successful warrior. Although Calgacus was seldom concerned with the use of symbols, he understood them well enough. He had set out on this trip to gain friends and allies, so he had left his chainmail at home and brought his polished breastplate, a symbol of his status, little expecting that he might have to go to war after all.

"What's wrong with it?" he asked the Captain.

"Nothing. But it's heavy. If you fall into the sea with that on, you'll sink like a stone. Best take it off. And that bloody great sword you've got on your back."

Reluctantly, Calgacus undid the straps that held the breastplate in place. Unlooping his sword, he nodded to the Captain.

"Can we board now?"

"Be my guest," the Captain grinned, sweeping his arm ostentatiously to invite them onto his sea-worn vessel.

Calgacus clambered aboard awkwardly, staggering slightly when the vessel tipped and rocked as he stepped into the wooden hull. The sailors laughed but showed him to a place near the stern where he could stow his breastplate and sword into a long, wooden chest. Runt and Adelligus followed him aboard, as did two of his warriors. Both were young men, untried in battle, but keen and skilled in using their weapons.

The taller of the two was named Dunnocatus, a wiry youth who was the son of one of the exiled Catuvellauni warriors who had followed Calgacus to the North.

The other man, dark-haired and stocky, was called Cawrdaf, named after his mother's father who had been a warrior of the Deceangli.

Looking around at his companions as they piled their heavy weapons into the chest, Calgacus could not help thinking that they were a mixed bunch. Descendants of Catuvellauni and Deceangli, they had grown up among the Boresti as exiles from their paternal tribes. The Romans, he reflected, had done more to meld the tribes together than anyone.

As the Captain stepped aboard and began shouting orders, Calgacus and his companions took their seats on a bench at the stern and waved to the small crowd of onlookers who had come to say farewell.

Beatha and Fallar were there, as well as Fulvia, with her husband, Durcar, and her two children who waved dutifully to their grandfather. Calgacus waved back, trying to appear cheerful, although the sight of the children depressed him slightly. He did not feel old enough to be a grandfather and did not know how to behave like one. He had tried to be friendly towards the children but he knew that he had not succeeded in winning them over. That, he knew, was his fault because he could not help seeing them as a reminder of the undeniable fact that he was growing older.

"Good luck!" called Cadwgan.

"Let's hope we don't need to rely on luck," Calgacus whispered to Runt through his teeth as he kept smiling.

"You've always been lucky," Runt replied.

The druid Broichan, looking stern and officious, cast a silver brooch into the sea, then poured a libation of dark ale into the water as he beseeched the gods to provide safe passage for the travellers.

Satisfied that the proper offerings had been made, the Captain took his place on the rearmost bench and gripped the long arm of the steerboard. He called out more orders, the mooring ropes were untied and the agile sailors leaped to their stations.

Four of the men manned long oars. The two on the port side used the heavy, wooden poles to push away from the jetty.

The other crew members went to the mast where they unfurled the large, square sail. Made of wide strips of leather that had been carefully stitched together, it cracked and flapped as the light breeze caught it, then the vessel slowly edged away from the shore and turned out into the narrow channel that separated Iova from the neighbouring island.

Calgacus kept his eyes on his family and friends as the boat carried him further away from them. It had been a long time since he had left Beatha to go on a journey like this and he felt the loss of separation because he knew that, whatever she might have said, she did not want him to leave.

But he was a warrior, there was a war to be fought, and, if the stories were true, he had a son to find.

He sat on the bare plank that served as a bench, twisting round to look back over his shoulder, occasionally giving a wave in response to the farewells from the shore. He did not feel as if the boat was moving very quickly but in a surprisingly short time it had carried them out of sight of their friends and family on the shore.

"Ship oars!" the Captain called.

The rowers pulled the oars in, stowing them along the side of the low gunwales. The Captain sat at the stern, holding the steerboard lightly as he guided the ship south, moving through the scattering of islands, both large and small, that dotted the western coast.

He grinned at Calgacus.

"The name's Risciporus," he said. "But while you are on board, you can call me Captain. You do as I say. Is that understood?"

"Understood," Calgacus nodded.

Risciporus was friendly, chatting amiably to his passengers while they sat on the low benches in front of him.

"She's a good ship," he declared lovingly. "Old, but seaworthy and, with a good wind in the sail, she can still outrun most other ships. She'll get us there."

Runt, always keen to learn new things, looked up at the wide sail and asked, "How does that keep us moving if the wind dies?"

"It doesn't," Risciporus replied. "But the wind rarely dies away in these waters. If it does, we try to use the currents and the tides. If that fails, we use the oars."

Runt nodded. They had all noticed how much stronger the wind was out on the sea.

"What if the wind is coming from the wrong direction?" he asked.

Risciporus laughed. He wetted a finger and held it up.

"Which way is the wind blowing now?" he asked in return.

Runt wetted his own finger, tested the air, then pointed.

"From the west?" he suggested.

"Near enough. A bit west-north-west I'd say. But we are heading south."

Risciporus grinned happily as he informed them, "We can adjust the sail a bit, using the lines, but when the wind is against us, the trick is to tack the ship."

Seeing the puzzled looks on the faces of his passengers, he explained, "We move in a zig-zag course."

He motioned with his hands to demonstrate the ship's movements as he went on, "That way, we catch the best of the wind. Believe it or not, we actually sail faster with the wind coming off the quarter, that is from an angle, than we do when it is directly behind us."

"That can't be right," frowned young Adelligus, who was intrigued but suspected that the shipmaster was having fun at their expense.

Risciporus laughed, "Just you watch. You'll see."

He eased the tiller slightly to one side and the boat seemed to take a leap forwards as the wind filled the sail. Risciporus shot Adelligus a satisfied smile.

"It sounds difficult," said Adelligus, impressed although not really understanding.

Calgacus quickly put in, "Not if you practise, I expect."

Risciporus nodded, "Exactly. The more often I sail, the better I get at it."

"It's the same for everything," Calgacus agreed.

Runt had another question.

"I thought the steerboard was usually on the right side of the ship," he remarked, gesturing to where Risciporus sat at the centre of the flat stern.

"On Roman ships, maybe," the Captain confirmed. "Not on ours. It's more complicated to fashion a central steerboard and rudder but it gives us far greater control."

Demonstrating again, he pushed the rudder slightly and they felt the vessel turn before he steered it back on course once more.

"We're a lot lower in the water than a Roman galley," he informed them. "That means we can use a stern rudder and tiller instead of one of their huge steerboards. It also means we can turn a lot faster than any Roman ship."

Calgacus shot the Captain another questioning look.

"So how long will this voyage take?"

Risciporus shrugged, "Hard to say. I've done it in two days with the wind coming from the north but that doesn't often happen. If the sea remains calm and the wind comes from the west, it will probably take three or four days because we'll be heading into the wind for the last part of the voyage."

He regarded them with another amused smile as he added, "And if the wind and tides are against us, it could take longer."

The sea, though, did not remain calm, or at least, that was how it appeared to Calgacus and his companions, who felt the swell grow rougher. The sailors appeared not to notice the waves that battered against the hull as the boat pitched and rolled its way southwards, but young Cawrdaf was sick, hanging over the side to empty the contents of his stomach into the sea.

Calgacus felt like joining him but gritted his teeth, swallowed hard, and refused to let the motion of the ship beat him. He often gazed down at the wooden planks beneath his feet in an attempt to quell the queasiness but that only made him imagine the depths that loomed beneath the boat's hull. The thought that less than a finger's length of wood separated him from countless fathoms of ocean frightened him more than the prospect of facing the Roman legions.

His fear of the depths, allied to the queasy lurching of his stomach, made the ship's crew laugh. The rolling motion of their vessel did not appear to affect them in the slightest and they made a point of telling jokes at their passengers' expense. It was, though, all done in good humour, an attitude which extended to the sailors' work. They clambered around the ship and even scaled the mast with unfailing good humour but Calgacus noticed that they were always quick to obey any shouted command from Risciporus.

There were eight sailors in Risciporus' crew. In appearance, they were as diverse as any group of men could be, ranging from tall and thin, to short and wiry, to huge and powerfully built. What they had in common was an air of easy familiarity with one another and with the sea, and each of them was tanned from their constant exposure to the sun. They were rough men, some bearing scars or with noses that had obviously been knocked out of shape in some brawl. They spoke to one another in a peculiar, nautical language that was largely incomprehensible to Calgacus and his companions. Calgacus suspected that they rather looked down on men who did not understand the ways of the sea. For his part, he left them to get on with their jobs, most of which seemed mysterious and arcane.

Yet for much of the time there seemed little for the crew to do because the Captain and the wind carried the ship across the waves with little need for any assistance. When this happened, They would throw lines and nets over the sides, laughing and joking with one another as they worked. Once or twice they managed to hook a fish, hauling it, flapping wetly, into the boat. A great cheer always greeted these successes, for it meant they could trade their catch for a meal and shelter when they went ashore in the evening.

Adelligus, who had quickly gained his sea legs, gazed over the side, looking down into the dark depths.

"There must be big fish down there," he commented. "Have you ever seen a sea monster?"

Calgacus winced slightly. His loathing of the sea was partly fuelled by his terror of the monsters that he knew must lurk in the deep water. He was tempted to tell Adelligus to be quiet but Risciporus smiled gleefully as he answered, "Oh, yes. It's a bit late in the season for basking sharks but early in summer you see a lot of them. Huge, they are, as long as this ship some of them, with mouths that are wide enough to swallow a man whole."

Seeing Adelligus stiffen slightly, the Captain joyfully continued, "And there are whales, of course. Massive, they are. They generally leave us alone but if they get close enough, they could pitch us right over and sink us as easy as anything."

Adelligus looked incredulous. Risciporus, warming to his tales, went on, "But they are nothing compared to some of the creatures that live in the deeps. There are huge monsters down there, with great tentacles and some with jaws that could swallow the ship whole. or with tails that could smash us with one blow. I've heard many a tale, I can tell you."

Calgacus had heard enough.

"Save your tales for another day, Captain," he said sharply. "Just get us to Ynis Mon as quickly as you can."

"As you say," grinned Risciporus mischievously.

He gave Calgacus a broad wink as soon as Adelligus had turned away from him.

"But the lad did ask. I was just trying to be helpful. I wouldn't want you being surprised if we come across some creature you've never seen before."

Unwilling to admit that he had been frightened by the sailor's tales of sea monsters, Calgacus simply muttered, "We'll take that chance. There is no point in scaring the youngsters unnecessarily."

Risciporus grinned and gave him another wink, showing that Calgacus had not fooled him at all.

Despite the Captain's dire stories, they saw no monsters although the sea brought other unexpected surprises. When they were moving, the wind and spray clutched and clawed at them, however calm Risciporus and his crew considered the seas to be. Yet often the sunlight dazzled their eyes as it reflected off the wide surface of the water. Risciporus informed them that he usually sought a landing place before evening because the glare was so intense when the sun sank to the west that it was sometimes almost impossible to see. To Calgacus and his comrades it seemed that there was never a time when the voyage did not present some difficulty.

"I could never be a sailor," Runt admitted ruefully.

While the passengers suffered, the sailors constantly adjusted the sail, furling or unfurling the leather or pulling on the lines that adjusted the angle of the great sail in response to Risciporus' commands. Despite his queasy stomach, Calgacus could appreciate the skill and hard work that kept the ship moving, always seeking the best wind, following the coastline southwards in response to Risciporus' gentle use of the rudder and the crew's constant adjustments to the sail.

As evening approached, Risciporus turned the prow towards the shore and headed for a narrow, shelving beach in a tiny inlet that was home to a small fishing community. He ordered the sail to be furled and the oars to be used to propel the ship slowly to the shore until the boat gently grounded itself on the sand. Then he had two enormous anchors thrown over the sides. Each of these was a great block of stone with a large hole drilled through it at one end. A thick, horsehair rope was passed through the hole and tied firmly in place.

"They'll stop her drifting out to sea when the tide turns," Risciporus explained to his passengers.

Once ashore, Risciporus traded some of his cargo and their small catch of fish for the promise of a night's shelter. The head man welcomed them, inviting them into his home which soon became crowded as other villagers arrived to listen to whatever news their visitors might bring. Most people rarely ventured far beyond the immediate vicinity of their homes, so news brought by sailors, merchants and other travellers was always welcome although Calgacus knew from experience that much of what these people heard was little more than rumour.

As food and drink were passed around and Risciporus relayed some gossip to the attentive villagers, Calgacus was surprised to discover that the small coastal settlement they had arrived at was in the land of the Brigantes. He had not realised that they had travelled so far south so quickly and the discovery made him feel a little uncomfortable because his relationship with the Brigantes had been far from smooth over the years. He had even fought against them while he had briefly served in a Roman auxiliary unit, a fact that still caused him some uneasiness.

The villagers, though, barely reacted when they heard his name, although one old man asked if he was the same Calgacus who had won his sword from a giant, the way the bards' songs recounted.

Calgacus shook his head.

"No, that wasn't me," he assured the old man, taking care not to catch Runt's eye as he made the denial.

While he would normally gruffly acknowledged that the songs were about him, he would always claim that they were exaggerated. Now, in the territory of a tribe who had so often been his enemies, he decided it would be safer to keep his identity secret.

The villagers appeared to accept his word and he turned the conversation to other matters because he was interested in what they could tell him about events in Brigantia. The last time he had been there had been nine years previously, when he had helped Cartimandua, the tribe's Queen, to escape from the army of Venutius, her former husband. Venutius, a long-time enemy of

Calgacus', had seized the Kingdom, forcing Cartimandua to flee into exile among the Romans.

Calgacus often felt guilty about his relationship with the beautiful Cartimandua. She had been his lover once, when they had both been young, but she had also been a friend to Rome. Helping her and opposing Venutius had placed Calgacus in a difficult position for him to justify to himself, let alone to anyone else. His only argument was that he hated Venutius, whose one concern was to gain power for himself, and who had tried several times to have Calgacus killed. One of those attempts had left Calgacus badly wounded and another had resulted in the death of his woman, Senuala. Calgacus had plenty of reasons for his hatred of Venutius, who he knew had no real interest in fighting against Rome, wanting only to be King of the Brigantes. But even though he could almost persuade himself that his stance was justified, a part of Calgacus still felt guilty that he had never fought alongside the Brigantes against Rome. Fate, and Venutius' enmity, had made that impossible.

And now, if the tale told by the Roman merchant, Junius Lucullus, was to be believed, the Brigantes were under Roman control.

"What happened after Cartimandua left?" he asked the village chieftain.

The old man's face contorted in a grimace of distaste.

"The Romans used that as an excuse to make war on us," he explained bitterly.

"I had heard that Venutius wanted peace with Rome," Calgacus prompted.

"Maybe he did," the Brigante replied. "But Rome did not want peace with him."

He shrugged as he went on, "And our tribe had a lot of men who were eager for war. Venutius was forced to fight."

"We tried to keep out of it," one old man put in. "We are fishermen, not warriors."

"Some of the younger men went off to join Venutius," another explained. "Only one of them came back."

He nodded his head, indicating a slim young man who bore a scar on his forehead, a white slash against the sun-burned tan of his face.

Calgacus asked the young man, "What happened?"

The villager shrugged.

93

"The Romans came," he recounted reluctantly. "Venutius tried to ambush them but some of the men attacked too soon. We killed a few, but they were too strong for us. The warriors broke and ran."

Calgacus nodded. It was a familiar story.

"What happened to Venutius?" he asked.

The fisherman replied, "I don't know. I'm sure they didn't catch him. After the battle, there was a lot more fighting, but it was all just small raids, or when war bands were trapped and had no option except to fight. The Romans hunted us wherever we went."

He shrugged again, a gesture signifying the helplessness he must have felt during the disastrous conflict.

He sighed, "Eventually, our army just broke up as men went back to their homes and hid their spears."

One of the older men piped up, "We still hear reports of raids and some fighting. Some say that Venutius still leads a small war band, but the tribe will not gather again. Too many men were lost."

There was much nodding of heads and murmurs of agreement from the villagers.

Another man said, "Most of the chieftains have made peace with Rome now. We heard that old Cynwrig has taken Dun Brigantia and claims to be our King now."

The man spat into the fire as he rasped, "He is King only because the Romans suffer him to rule. They know he will not fight them."

"It is not worth fighting the Romans," agreed the head man. "If anyone does, they just send more soldiers to destroy our villages."

"Some people still oppose them," Calgacus remarked. "We have heard that the Ordovices have risen in rebellion."

The villagers had heard that too, but most of them had little interest in the tale for the Ordovices lived several days' march to the south and west, too far off to be of much concern.

When Calgacus asked whether they had heard any recent news about the rebellion, the head man said, "A trader brought some word last week. He said the Romans are sending a legion against the Ordovices. Claimed he had seen thousands of them preparing to march. The rebellion will be over soon, if it isn't already."

94

Calgacus felt a chill of dread seep into his bones. He knew enough of war to know that what the villager had told him was probably true. If the Romans reached the Ordovices before he did, he might never find the man who claimed to be his son; might never know the truth.

He exchanged an anxious look with Runt, who replied with a barely perceptible nod of his head. They both understood what was at stake.

Time was now against them.

Chapter XI

It took another two days of relatively calm sailing before the island of Ynis Mon hove into view as a dark smudge on the horizon.

After they had left the Brigante fishing village, the Captain had asked Calgacus whether he wanted to make landfall along the northern coast of the territory of the Deceangli but Calgacus had shaken his head.

"We have no friends there any more," he frowned.

Nodding in understanding, Risciporus had veered his boat westwards, further away from the coast and out into deep waters.

"We want to keep away from any Roman ships that might be patrolling around the mouth of the Deva," he had explained. "Also, if we follow the coast south, we would have to turn west toward Ynis Mon. That would be into the teeth of the prevailing wind. I'll cut the corner off the journey but we'll be well out to sea for a while and we'll still be heading more or less into the wind, so it will be a slow passage."

The deep swell did nothing to comfort Calgacus' queasy stomach but the boat sailed on, laboriously tacking to and fro in response to Risciporus' guidance.

When the low, green hills of Ynis Mon eventually came into view, the shipmaster gave his passengers a warm smile.

"I told you we'd get you there," he beamed.

Calgacus risked standing upright, stepping forward carefully and ducking beneath the sail to get a better view. He stared ahead at the fabled island. After a few moments, he turned, stepping cautiously over the benches until he reached Risciporus' station at the stern. The Captain raised an eyebrow in silent question as he approached.

"Can you land us on the mainland opposite the island?" Calgacus asked.

"If you like. You don't want to go to the island?"

"No. I need to head inland, so there would be no point. Is there somewhere we can get horses?"

Risciporus nodded, "There's a small settlement on the coast. You might be able to buy horses there."

"Let us off there, then," Calgacus decided.

Taking a small pouch from inside his tunic, he counted out some silver coins which he handed to the Captain.

"Will these pay for our passage?" he asked. "I have some of the old-fashioned bronze or iron rings but most people prefer Roman silver these days."

Risciporus, one hand still easily clasping the steerboard, looked at the money, each coin bearing the head of a Roman Emperor and the strange markings that made sense only to the Romans.

"That is too much," he said.

"Keep it," Calgacus told him.

Risciporus grinned happily as he took the coins.

"We will drink some ale in your honour," he promised.

He beached the vessel in a sandy cove near the narrow waters that separated Ynis Mon from the mainland. Calgacus and his four companions leaped ashore, then helped push the boat out again. Risciporus waved as he turned the prow towards Ynis Mon and the crew used the long oars to propel the boat away from the shore.

"I'm glad that is over," sighed Runt as he strapped his twin swords at his waist.

"Me too," Calgacus agreed.

He held his bronze breastplate to his chest while Dunnocatus fastened the leather straps at his back.

When the armour was in place, Calgacus adjusted his cloak, looped his sword over his back and declared, "Let's go and buy some horses. Then we can start looking for Brennus."

The village was a sorry place. Calgacus knew that there had always been a small settlement on the mainland, a place where travellers could purchase passage across to the sacred island but, like so many settlements, the village had been destroyed by the Romans when they had stormed across the strait to ravage Ynis Mon. The rebuilt village was a small and rather forlorn place. Cadwgan had told them that some druids had re-occupied Ynis Mon but they were few in number and, if the few hovels clustered near the shore were anything to go by, it seemed they had even fewer visitors.

Runt gestured towards a row of fishing vessels drawn up on the shore.

"It looks like the folk here make their living from the sea rather than from pilgrims these days," he remarked.

His comment seemed accurate. Where there had once been a thriving inn with large stables, there was now a small hut next to a paddock with a three-bar wooden fence behind which a dozen sorry looking ponies cropped the windswept grass.

Calgacus bartered some gold trinkets to acquire five thin, underfed mounts from a surly trader who, like everyone else in the settlement, stank of fish.

The man bit the gold suspiciously, checking that it was real. Calgacus was tempted to hit him but restrained his temper and asked instead for news of the Ordovices and their new chieftain.

"Are you going to join Brennus?" the trader asked, eyeing their swords.

In response, Calgacus gave him a hard stare.

"Just tell me where I can find him."

The trader scowled, waved an arm vaguely towards the hills and said, "They say he's gathered an army somewhere away over there."

"Very helpful," Calgacus muttered with heavy sarcasm which the trader ignored.

Shaking his head, Calgacus turned to his companions.

"Come on, let's get moving."

They rode south-west, following the trails that led into the mountainous territory of the Ordovices. It was a land of majestic, dramatic hills, lush green valleys, and huge tracts of untamed, empty land that was home to deer, wolves, boar and bears. The Ordovices lived in small, scattered settlements, many of them sited on hilltops with walls of stone to protect them. Calgacus knew roughly where Cadwallon's mountain village was. He had visited the old King a few times, although the last time had been many years before and his memory was hazy as to the correct route to take. He asked the way whenever they came to a farmstead or village but they quickly learned that there were few people left to ask. Most of the tribe, it seemed, had gone to join Brennus' war band.

As they passed another deserted village, Runt commented, "This is a proper uprising. The whole tribe has gone to war."

With a grim smile, he added, "It reminds me of Bonduca's rebellion."

"Let's hope it ends up differently," Calgacus replied, remembering the disastrous final battle in which his sister's rebel army had been destroyed.

It took them six days to track Brennus down. Six days during which Calgacus and Runt taught the three younger warriors everything they could about fighting the Romans and about travelling unseen. They showed them how to build fires that would not create smoke, how to cross the country so that they were never silhouetted against the skyline, and they told them as much as they could of their past battles. The young men listened, although Calgacus suspected that they did not believe half of what they heard. To Adelligus and the others, he and Runt were probably just old men who talked about past glories.

In the evenings, he insisted they all spend some time practising their swordplay. That was one thing they all enjoyed. They wrapped the blades in their cloaks to prevent injury, then faced each other in mock combat. Calgacus was annoyed to find that he struggled to match the speed of the younger men, and needed longer to recover from the exertions. Adelligus beat him twice, and Cawrdaf caught him with a whack to his leg that stung for a while.

"We're not as young as we used to be," Runt sympathised with a wry smile.

"You still managed to beat them all," grumbled Calgacus as he rubbed his leg where Cawrdaf's blade had caught him.

With a flash of his old humour, Runt grinned, "What can I say? When you have talent, you have to use it."

Calgacus gave a weak smile. Runt wore two short, Roman swords and could fight as well with his left hand as with his right. He had watched Calgacus' back for years, ever since they had been boys. Calgacus began to worry that he would need Runt's skill more and more if his own fighting ability had been diminished by age.

"I don't feel old," he sighed softly. "I just can't seem to do things as easily as I used to."

Runt tossed a handful of small twigs on the camp fire.

"Mock fights don't really count," he shrugged. "You'll be fine if you have to do any real fighting. Then we can all just stand back and watch you slaughter the Romans."

"I promised Beatha I wouldn't do any fighting."

"Did she believe you?"

"No, not really."

Runt laughed, "She's a smart woman. Don't worry. We can still show the youngsters a thing or two, I'm sure."

"I bloody hope so," grunted Calgacus.

"I suppose we'll find out soon enough," said Runt.

He paused, as if he were about to say something more, but fell suddenly silent.

Calgacus knew what his friend was thinking. The one thing they had not talked about was what they would do when they found Brennus. Even Runt, who was as close to Calgacus as anyone, had not broached the subject. All the reports they heard agreed that Brennus claimed to be the son of Calgacus. As unlikely as Calgacus thought that might be, the only thing he was sure about was that he wanted to know the truth behind the claim. What he would do after that, even he did not know.

They eventually found the Ordovices on the eastern fringes of their territory, camped on a wide hilltop overlooking a broad plain, although the encampment was so vast that it spread all the way down into the valley on the western slope.

In the dim twilight of dusk, Calgacus rode slowly up the slope, picking a way between small fires and tiny, crudely-fashioned shelters that had been formed by draping cloaks over short branches stuck into the ground.

Here on the lower slope of the hill, the camp was occupied mostly by women, children and the elderly. Most of the warriors, Calgacus knew, would be on the hilltop, and that was where Brennus would be. He did not ask directions but picked his careful way up the steep slope, ignoring the curious looks of the people as he passed between them.

Beside him, Runt clucked his tongue in disappointment.

"They are doing this the old-fashioned way," he said in a low voice. "Gathering together and inviting the Romans to attack."

Calgacus nodded but said nothing as they passed through the forest of tiny shelters, crackling fires, small carts, heavy wagons, and hordes of people who were cooking food, eating or preparing for sleep. Children and dogs roamed the camp, sheep and goats were mixed among the tribespeople, and he could hear the distant sound of lowing cattle. As Runt had observed, this was an old-fashioned tribal uprising, where everyone followed the warriors, taking all their belongings with them.

Calgacus found the thought depressing and felt his irritation growing as they neared the wide summit of the hill. He knew the sense of frustration he was feeling was partly borne of uncertainty over how he would react when he met Brennus but seeing the Ordovices gathered together in an apparent attempt to fight in a manner that had failed so many times before, only added to his anger.

As they reached the crest of the hill, he stopped his mount alongside one fire where several young men were sitting, drinking ale from clay beakers.

"Where do I find Brennus?" he asked them.

The men looked at one another. One of them waved his beaker to the eastern side of the broad, flat hilltop.

"Over there, I think."

"Perhaps you could take me to him," Calgacus said in a tone that implied his words were more than a suggestion.

The young warrior sat still. He looked Calgacus up and down, taking in the armour of the breastplate and the hilt of the large sword that peeked over the big man's shoulder.

"Who are you?" he shot back, grinning at his friends who chuckled at his bravado.

"My name is Calgacus."

There was a brief silence around the fire, accentuated by the general murmur of background noise from the vast camp all around them.

The man sitting nearest to Calgacus rose slowly to his feet. He studied Calgacus' face for a moment, then asked, "*The* Calgacus?"

"That's right," Calgacus growled.

"I thought you were dead," the warrior said, looking round at his companions with a broad smile as they laughed at his boldness.

Calgacus did not laugh. He leaned forwards slightly, putting his face closer to the young warrior. He sniffed the stink of stale beer on the man's breath.

As the warrior turned back to face him, Calgacus rasped, "Just take me to Brennus."

The man blinked, then nodded as he acknowledged the threat of violence in Calgacus' eyes.

"Follow me, then," he shrugged.

Walking with the deliberate care of someone who had drunk several pots of beer, the warrior led them on through the camp. The other men who had been sitting round the fire with him gathered up their spears and followed. Soon, more people were tagging along, intrigued by the mention of Calgacus' name.

The rumour of his arrival spread quickly. By the time they reached the eastern edge of the hilltop and found a small shelter of skins and furs that was ringed at a distance by spearmen, Calgacus reckoned there must be over four hundred tribespeople close by, with more gathering all the time. With a gesture to Runt and the others to stay on their horses, he climbed down from his saddle and walked towards the shelter.

Two of the spearmen stepped in front of him, their expressions hard and suspicious.

One asked sceptically, "You are Calgacus?"

"That's right. Now go and fetch Brennus. I want to talk to him."

He thought the man was about to argue but the warrior took a step closer, peering at his face in the dim light. As he did so, the man's eyes widened in surprise.

"Wait here," the guard instructed before turning and hurrying towards the shelter.

Calgacus waited patiently, ignoring the stares and whispers of the gathering crowd. After a short time, he saw a figure emerge from the shelter, a tall, strongly-built man with long hair. In the gloom, he could not make out the man's features but, when he drew near, both men stiffened in astonishment.

Calgacus' breath caught in his throat. When he saw the man's face, it was almost like looking at a reflection of himself.

A hushed silence fell over the watching crowd as everyone looked on in awed expectation. Standing only a few paces apart in the firelit darkness, the two men stared at one another, unspeaking, for what seemed an age.

It was Calgacus who recovered first.

"We need to talk," he said, instantly regretting his words because they had come out sounding like a command, a gruff insistence, the way a father would speak to an unruly child who had misbehaved. The way, he thought ruefully, he usually spoke to his son, Togodumnus.

Brennus, although he was clearly surprised at seeing someone who looked so much like him, was not prepared to be cowed, especially when the people of his tribe were looking on.

He took a deep breath, shot Calgacus a challenging look, then asked, "Why?"

"You know why," Calgacus replied. "You claim to be my son. I am Calgacus, son of Cunobelinos, son of Tasciovanus, son of Cassivellaunos. I am the rightful King of the Catuvellauni and was once the War Leader of the Silures and the Deceangli."

Brennus was not impressed by the recitation of Calgacus' lineage and status.

He bared his teeth in a humourless smile as he retorted, "We have nothing to talk about. Where were you for the past twenty five years? I have managed well enough without you so far. I can manage without you now."

Having recovered from the initial shock, his voice seethed with an undercurrent of suppressed anger that surprised Calgacus.

Calgacus' own temper began to rise in response.

"I want to know the truth of your claim," he stated, eyes blazing. "And if you have any sense, you will listen to what I can tell you about fighting the Romans."

He glanced around before suggesting, "Perhaps there is somewhere more private?"

For a moment, Calgacus thought that Brennus was going to refuse to speak to him. The hostility in the younger man's demeanour was plain to see. Then a young woman, scarcely more than a girl, came out of the shelter behind Brennus. She was slim, quite pretty, with long, dark hair, and wearing a long, traditional dress with a woollen shawl wrapped around her shoulders. She had obviously heard their exchange for she wasted no time asking what was happening.

Brushing back a strand of loose hair, she walked up to stand beside Brennus, gently placing a hand on the warrior's arm.

"If this is truly your father," she said softly, "you should speak to him."

Brennus pursed his lips, then gave a curt, fierce nod.

"Join me at my fire," he snapped.

It was an ungracious invitation, grudgingly given, but Brennus had ensured that he was the one who was seen to be in charge of events. Turning brusquely, he barked an order to his spearmen to create a cordon to give them some privacy, then

103

stalked back towards the small fire that glowed in a ring of stones a short distance from his sleeping shelter.

Calgacus looked at the girl.

"Thank you," he said.

Her face remained calm and unsmiling as she informed him, "I am Tegan."

"I am Calgacus."

A hint of a smile flickered around her lips and he thought it made her look much prettier.

She said, "Welcome, Calgacus. Please accept the hospitality of our camp."

They walked to the fire while Brennus' warriors ushered the tribespeople back, forming a loose perimeter some twenty paces from the flickering flames. Runt and Adelligus dismounted, leaving the horses in the care of Cawrdaf and Dunnocatus, and came to join Calgacus. This made the Ordovices spearmen nervous but Brennus sat by the fire, quite unconcerned at having three armed strangers near him. His one concession to the potential threat was to lay his sword on the ground at his side, his hand resting lightly on the hilt. He watched carefully while the others took their places, sitting cross-legged on the grass beside the small fire.

They sat in silence, looking at one another awkwardly. Seeing that Brennus did not intend to speak first, Calgacus made the introductions while Tegan poured strong-smelling beer that Brennus had called for. Eyes lowered so as not to meet their gaze, she handed round the pewter mugs.

Calgacus took the drink then ceremoniously tipped a small amount of the dark, foaming liquid onto the ground in front of him.

"To Camulos," he intoned as he made the libation.

Brennus poured some of his own beer onto the earth.

"To Nodens," he retorted, naming the war god of the western tribes rather than the god of the Catuvellauni whom Calgacus had invoked.

Giving Calgacus a dark look that showed he had made the correction deliberately, Brennus added, "May he bring us victory."

Calgacus raised his beaker in salute.

"To Nodens," he agreed.

His face hard and unyielding, Brennus turned his attention to Runt.

"I have heard of you," he told the little man, his voice still challenging and unfriendly. "One of the songs tells how you killed a Roman General in single combat. They say you fight with a sword in each hand."

"That's true enough," Runt agreed, trying to sound amiable despite the tension in the air. "But it was a Centurion I killed, not a General."

Calgacus put in, "You shouldn't believe everything you hear in songs."

"I don't," Brennus replied sharply. "All my life I have heard songs about you. The bards sing of your exploits as if you are some sort of hero from legend."

"Like I say, you shouldn't believe them. I once had a friend who was a bard. He used to make up all sorts of nonsense about me."

"I can see that," Brennus snorted disparagingly. "You are big but you don't look like a hero."

Runt leaped to Calgacus' defence, saying, "The songs aren't all wrong. Calgacus is more of a hero than any other man you'll ever meet."

"Not to me," Brennus replied harshly, hostile eyes fixed on Calgacus' face.

Slowly and deliberately, Calgacus placed his beaker on the ground at his side.

"Enough of this," he sighed. Pointing a finger across the fire at Brennus, he stated, "You claim to be my son. I want to know whether that is true or not. Can you prove it?"

"Is it not evident?" Brennus asked, gesturing towards his own face.

"He has a point there," Runt told Calgacus with a rueful smile. "He has the same build, the same dark hair and the same eyes. His nose is a bit different, and his face a bit rounder, but he looks a lot like you."

"That means nothing," Calgacus said dismissively. He asked Brennus, "Who was your mother?"

Brennus gave a snort of derision.

"What do you care? You wouldn't remember her."

"Try me."

Brennus drained his beaker before staring back at Calgacus.

105

"No," he said with an air of finality. "I told you, I owe you nothing. You owe me nothing."

"So your claim is a lie, then," Calgacus persisted, trying to goad a response from the young chieftain. "You have just used our physical similarity to make a baseless claim."

Brennus shook his head.

"Don't be stupid," he said bitterly. "I have never seen you before. I had no idea whether I looked like you or not. My mother told me the truth of my birth."

He glared angrily at Calgacus, the glow of the orange firelight on his face seeming to reflect the suppressed rage burning inside him.

"I am your son but I ask nothing from you. I have used your name because it helps gather men to my cause. Some men do believe the songs, you see."

Calgacus took a deep breath, struggling to keep his temper under control. He wanted to shout at Brennus in frustration, to force the young man to tell him the story of his birth but he knew that giving in to his anger would only make things worse.

He looked at Tegan, hoping she would intercede, but the girl said nothing, merely lowering her gaze when he looked at her.

Feeling aggrieved, he turned back to Brennus and sighed, "Very well. If you won't talk about that, at least let us talk about how to defeat the Romans."

"I don't need your help with that either," Brennus asserted with a wave of his hand. "I have beaten them once already and have chased them out of our lands."

"How many of them were there when you beat them?" Calgacus challenged.

"Enough."

"I heard it was one squadron of cavalry. Thirty men?"

Brennus shrugged, "The number is unimportant. What is important is that we killed most of them and the ones who lived ran from us in fear."

"That is true," Calgacus conceded. "Even a small victory gives your warriors heart. But what is really important is how the Romans react. You are faced by thousands of them now. You cannot stand and face them in battle."

"What would you know about it?" Brennus sneered. "You have hidden away from them for the past twenty years. I have no interest in old stories about old battles, told by old men. Such things will not help us."

Calgacus bunched his fists in anger as he shot back, "You can learn from old battles. I was at Caer Caradoc."

"That was long ago," Brennus frowned, unsure what Calgacus meant. "I was not even born then. And you lost that battle."

"Precisely. That day we did what you are planning to do tomorrow. We stood on a hill and we dared them to attack us. We had forty thousand warriors and we had made our position as strong as we could. We were led by the great Caratacus who gave us such confidence that we truly believed we would win. But the Romans came across the river and although we fought them as hard as any men could, they kept coming, and kept coming, and we could not hold them."

He paused, then added, "There were men of the Ordovices there that day. Speak to them and learn the truth of it."

Brennus' lip curled as he sneered, "They are old men now. They ran from that battle because they were led by the coward, Cadwallon. I don't think I need lessons from them."

"Then listen to me!" Calgacus snapped, his voice rising to a shout. "I was the War Leader of the Silures when they destroyed the Second Legion. I led the Deceangli when they held back the very legion that faces you now. I led the Iceni when they annihilated half of the Ninth Legion. I know how to beat the Romans!"

He stared hard at Brennus, his face flushed with emotion, daring the young man to disagree with him.

Speaking softly but insistently, Runt told Brennus, "He is right. You should listen to him. Nobody knows more about fighting Rome than Calgacus."

Brennus looked at them. The anger in his expression had not faded. If anything, it grew to match Calgacus' rising temper.

He said, "The Silures are conquered. The Deceangli are friends of Rome. The Iceni were slaughtered. All these victories you claim mean nothing. Whatever the songs say, your victories were ultimately useless. You have failed every time. You are welcome to remain in the camp because your name will encourage the warriors. They will fight better because you are here. But you may not join us in the battle and I will not listen to your words."

He stood up, picking up his sword in one hand and gesturing with the other for Tegan to join him.

"I am going to sleep now," he told them. "I need to be ready for tomorrow." Staring down at the seated Calgacus, he added, "You may be my father, but you are not my friend. I need no help from you."

With that, he turned his back on them and walked away, leaving Calgacus angry, mystified and helpless.

Chapter XII

Cornelius Tacitus shivered in the cold morning air. He had been roused before dawn, emerging from the tent he shared with his father-in-law to find a soft, wispy mist blanketing the ground, rising to around knee height. It lent a strange, ethereal air to the clear stillness of the early morning. Tacitus permitted himself a small smile when he saw that men who were some distance from him appeared to move with the lower part of their legs bitten off by the ground-hugging mist. He blew air out of his mouth, watching it steam and curl in front of him.

"A fine day!" Agricola announced as he came out of the tent, rubbing his hands together to warm them.

"Yes, Sir," Tacitus replied.

He looked upwards. The sky was a clear, frosty blue, with not a cloud to be seen except some thin wisps of mares' tails far off over the western hills.

"A bit chilly, though," he observed.

"Marching to battle will soon warm the men up," Agricola declared cheerfully.

Tacitus nodded. The sounds of a bustling army camp were all around, ringing clear in the eerily still air. Not a breath of wind disturbed the pennants of the legion's standards that stood proudly near the Governor's tent.

A soldier brought them some breakfast, a thin porridge of mashed grain with some chopped, dried fruit mixed in. Holding the wooden bowl in one hand, Tacitus spooned it into his mouth, recalling the warning his father-in-law had given him about soldiers' rations when they had enjoyed the feast at Cogidubnus' palace. That luxurious meal seemed so long ago now.

He forced the mush down despite the unease in the pit of his stomach. Today he would witness his first battle. It was a worrying prospect but he was a Roman, so he knew he must do his duty and, above all, must not show any outward signs of fear. He stretched his leg and back muscles, painfully aware of how sore they were from so many days of hard riding.

Beside him, Agricola gave no indication that the strenuous efforts of the past few days had affected him in any way. The Governor was eating hungrily, smacking his lips as if the bland gruel had been the tastiest food he had ever eaten. He stood, looking around the camp, apparently taking immense pleasure in simply watching the legionaries eat their own breakfast. It was the start of a typical day in an army encampment, although the men were a little quieter than usual.

"The prospect of a battle always has that effect," Agricola observed. "But they'll soon be eager to get to grips with the enemy."

He washed his breakfast down with a small beaker of watered wine, then arched his eyebrows as the senior officers came to greet him.

Piso, the legion's commander, approached, accompanied by a gaggle of Tribunes and the Twentieth Legion's senior Centurion whose chest was decorated with badges of honour. Avistus, commander of the Governor's bodyguard, joined them. They all greeted the Governor with smart salutes.

Agricola asked, "Anything to report?"

The senior Centurion, known as the *primus pilus*, the first spear, replied, "No, Sir. All quiet during the night. The barbarians are just sitting on the hill, waiting for us."

Tacitus felt suddenly foolish. He had almost forgotten the enemy. He covered the lapse by feigning indifference to their presence. Looking towards the distant hill, he saw a swarm of small, dark figures moving on its summit.

Agricola said, "Well, it is a straightforward approach. There is nowhere for them to set any sort of trap for us, so we may as well attack. They obviously aren't going to come to us."

He glanced at Piso, asking, "How many are there?"

"Our scouts were unable to get too close," the Legate reported uneasily. But they estimate there are several thousand on the hilltop and more behind. There could be as many as fifteen or twenty thousand, Sir. That means we are outnumbered at least three to one."

Agricola smiled, like a teacher correcting a student who had made a fundamental error.

"Their number includes the women and children, does it not?" he enquired.

110

Embarrassed by the question, Piso flushed slightly as he admitted, "Probably, Sir. The scouts did say they thought there were some women there, though they could not tell how many."

"This is a tribal gathering," Agricola explained, waving a hand towards the hill. "At least half of them will be women and children, probably more. I expect there are fewer than ten thousand warriors. They will make a lot of noise and act with great bravado but if the legion closes with them, they will run. They always do. Tell your men that."

"Yes, Sir," said Piso. He was clearly unhappy at the prospect of marching his men up a steep slope to attack so many barbarians but he was unwilling to argue with the Governor.

Agricola went on, "Send your cavalry to the flanks. This will be an infantry attack but the cavalry should be ready to pursue the enemy when they break. They should circle round the hill when I give the signal."

He gestured with his hands, showing how he wanted the cavalry to ride around either side of the hill to cut off the enemy's inevitable retreat.

"Yes, Sir," Piso repeated dutifully.

Agricola glanced around the group but when he asked whether there were any questions, his gaze was firmly on the senior Centurion.

The *primus pilus* knew why the Governor had directed the question at him. Whatever the Legate and the Tribunes might believe, when it came to fighting, the men followed their Centurions, the officers who had risen through the ranks, earning their positions by virtue of being meaner and tougher than their fellow soldiers. They were the experienced men, the men of iron will and unyielding resolve who had fought and survived and who knew what needed to be done. The aristocratic officers might be the brains, but the Centurions were the backbone of the Army.

Agricola understood this, so he asked the *primus pilus* whether there were any questions and the Centurion promptly replied, "No, Sir."

"Very well, Gentlemen. Break camp and let us advance. And tell the legionaries that I will march with them."

"Yes, Sir."

Piso looked puzzled by the Governor's decision to march in the ranks but Tacitus saw the broad grin on the face of the senior Centurion as he saluted.

When the legionary officers had gone to prepare for the advance, Avistus asked, "Do you really intend to march with the soldiers, Sir?"

Agricola gave a firm nod of his head.

"Absolutely. If I left it to Piso, the advance would be half-hearted. We cannot afford that. We must go straight for the enemy. The men will be more eager if I am in their midst."

"It will be dangerous," Tacitus warned, echoing Avistus' concern.

Agricola laughed, "Have no fear. I will stay out of trouble. But you will be my eyes, Publius. Stay with Avistus. Mind you take his advice, too. I want the two of you to watch for any danger. I don't expect the savages to do anything clever but you never know."

"Very well, Sir," Tacitus acknowledged, wondering how his father-in-law could treat the danger so casually.

Avistus was clearly unhappy at not being able to stay close to the Governor. As commander of the bodyguard, it was his duty to see that no harm came to Agricola. But Avistus knew the Governor well enough to know it would be futile to argue.

He promised, "Don't worry, Sir. We will keep a good eye open. If there is any trouble, we'll come straight in and get you."

Agricola acknowledged the Centurion's devotion with a nod.

"I'm sure that won't be necessary," he smiled. "But I need you to keep an eye on young Tacitus, too. This will be his first real taste of battle."

Tacitus stiffened, aware of his youth and inexperience compared to these two veterans.

"I am sure I will acquit myself well, Sir," he protested.

"Of course you will," Agricola replied. "You are a Roman."

Tacitus relaxed slightly but the Governor had already moved on to other concerns.

Looking around, he said, "Ah, there is Sempronius Casca."

He waved a hand, beckoning the Centurion of Auxiliaries to join him.

"Good morning, Casca."

"Good morning, Sir."

Casca saluted smartly. His manner was stiff and formal but his dark eyes radiated eagerness and hunger.

"My men are ready for your command," he announced.

"Excellent," smiled Agricola. "I want you to stay near to Tacitus and Avistus. Keep your unit in reserve. When the enemy break, you may pursue them. If Brennus survives the fighting, you must hunt him down. Should someone else have the good fortune to kill him, I want you to identify the body so that we can be certain he is dead."

Casca's earnest expression broke into a craggy smile as he replied, "It will be a pleasure, Sir. An absolute pleasure."

In well-practised response to the blasts of the horns, the tents were packed away, the overnight stockade dismantled, and the legion set off, ready for war.

The soldiers marched unencumbered, their heavy packs left behind with a rearguard whose duty was to watch over the baggage. Most legionaries now carried only their large shields, their short swords and two long javelins, the dreaded *pila* that would be hurled at close range to break up the enemy formation before the Legion closed for the final killing.

Some Centuries were equipped with longer, heavier spears, the *hasta* which were used to ward off enemy cavalry. These units marched on the flanks, ready to ward off any barbarian horsemen who might try to assault the Legion as it advanced.

The Twentieth *Valeria Victrix* Legion was an experienced unit, the men well trained and reliable. The Governor, who had once been their Legate, marched in their midst, in the second rank, sword in hand. He spoke to the soldiers as they marched, encouraging them, telling them that he trusted them to do their duty. His presence in the ranks would make them fight all the harder because the Legion would suffer endless shame if the Governor were to die while under their protection.

Each Century's standard bearer wore an animal skin headdress and held aloft the banner that proclaimed the Century's identity while, in the midst of the formation, the A*quilifer,* the Legion's standard bearer, went bare-headed, carrying the Eagle standard, the emblem without which the Legion would not exist.

The Eagle, sitting proudly with outstretched wings and surrounded by a silver laurel wreath, was the essence of the Legion. In many ways, the A*quilifer* was the most important man in the entire Legion, for if he were to fall or simply drop the standard, the soldiers would regard that as an omen of bad luck and would refuse to march. But this fine, crisp morning, there were no mishaps. The polished Eagle glinted in the bright sunlight as the legion crossed the plain towards the enemy.

They marched in open formation, divided into staggered blocks. Each block comprised two Centuries and was known as a Maniple. Each Maniple was either slightly ahead or behind its neighbours, leaving gaps between them but providing mutual support.

Spread out on the flanks were auxiliary units, dressed in chainmail, carrying long spears and short swords. They were there to support the Legion but the men of the Twentieth knew that it would be the heavily armoured legionaries who would win this battle.

Some men who joined the Imperial Army never saw a battle, serving their twenty-five years in relative peace, with nothing more dangerous than drunken brawls to police or the occasional unarmed mob to put down. In Britannia, things were different, for many of the tribes remained hostile. Full-scale battles were still rare but danger was ever-present for the Roman troops in this wild province. The Britons often carried out small raids, pouncing on some band of soldiers then vanishing into the hills, forests and marshes before they could be cut down.

Today was different. Today, the war-hardened men of the Twentieth would have the opportunity to come to grips with their enemy. The soldiers marched steadily and cheerfully, because the Governor had given them only one command.

Kill every barbarian you can find. Man, woman or child, it made no difference. The fate of the Ordovices was sealed; every one of them must die.

The ground mist cleared as the sun rose higher in the cold, blue sky, the long grass swished under the tramping feet of the legionaries, and death closed in on the Ordovices.

The same chill dawn that had greeted Tacitus found Calgacus in a sour mood. He had not slept well, tossing and turning with his mind full of whirling emotions. All through the long voyage south he had tried to put the question of Brennus' parentage to the back of his mind, yet when he had seen the young chieftain, he had been convinced as to the truth of the rumours. The man was so similar to him it was almost frightening. Brennus looked more like Calgacus than young Togodumnus did. There was, though, no doubt about Togodumnus' parentage. It was the question of who Brennus' mother was that kept Calgacus awake for most of the night.

There had been women, of course. In the years before he had met Senuala, and during the time between her death and when he had found Beatha, there had been many young women who had been only too keen to be with the famous exiled Catuvellauni prince. But Calgacus had never made any secret that he was not particularly interested in them, apart from the one obvious thing that they offered. Even then, he was fairly certain that none of them had become pregnant. Not while they were with him, anyway.

Yet there was no denying Brennus' resemblance to him. Against all expectation, Calgacus was convinced that he now had another son, a son he had not known about, not even dreamed about. A son, moreover, who was a warrior, a leader, an enemy of Rome.

Brennus was all the things that Calgacus had wished Togodumnus would become. That thought wrung Calgacus' heart. He knew that Togodumnus had grown into a fine young man but he was not a warrior. Calgacus' relationship with him was so strained at times that they were almost like strangers. Calgacus knew that the fault was as much his as his son's, yet he also knew that it was a fault he would never be able to change. When he looked at Togodumnus, it was hard to ignore the disappointment he felt.

Yet with a man like Brennus as a son, things could be so different. The two of them had more than a physical resemblance in common; they shared a desire to defeat the Romans. Together, what could they not achieve?

But what had happened? Calgacus almost groaned aloud when he recalled his first words to Brennus, a peremptory order lacking any friendliness. Worse than that, Brennus had rejected him. The young man had scorned his desire to know the truth of his birth and, moreover, had derided all of the achievements that Calgacus was famed for.

What hurt most was that Brennus was right. For all his victories, Calgacus often felt that he had achieved nothing.

Nursing his injured pride, Calgacus sat apart from the others, using his old razor to shave. He had run out of oil, so used some cold water to wet his face before carefully scraping the sharp

115

blade across his chin and neck. The chill morning air made his skin tingle as he removed the overnight stubble. When he was done, Runt ambled over, bearing two mugs of steaming hot tisane. He handed one to Calgacus before sitting cross-legged on the damp grass beside him.

"It's got some honey in it," he said.

Calgacus grunted his thanks, then sipped at the liquid, swearing when he almost scalded his mouth on the piping hot drink. He lowered the beaker as he licked at his lips. Glancing up, he saw that Runt was watching him intently.

"What?" he asked.

"Nothing."

"Don't give me that, Liscus. I know when something is bothering you."

Runt's lips twitched in a sad smile. Keeping his voice low, he explained, "I got the youngsters to ask around a bit."

Calgacus raised an eyebrow.

"And?"

"You won't like it."

"Just bloody well tell me," snapped Calgacus.

Runt sniffed but he was used to Calgacus' moods so the reprimand did not upset him.

Calmly, he said, "Apparently, Brennus didn't just kill Cadwallon. He cut him down while the old man was alone and unarmed."

Calgacus pursed his lips, his expression pensive. All through his life, he had lived by a personal code that would not allow him to kill unarmed or helpless men. It was a vow he had made to himself after seeing a captive sacrificed to the gods by the druids. The man's terror had awakened a deep dread inside the young Calgacus who had witnessed that and he had sworn to leave such killings to the druids.

He exhaled deeply, then forced a nonchalant shrug.

"So he is ruthless. Maybe that makes him stronger and better than me. Cartimandua always used to say I wasn't ruthless enough."

Runt had often cursed Calgacus' inability to finish off wounded enemies but he knew it was one of the things that made Calgacus who he was.

He responded, "It makes him more ruthless than you. Not better. But there is more."

116

"What?"

"You really won't like it."

"So you keep saying."

Runt hesitated slightly before continuing, "The word is that he also killed all of Cadwallon's family. Wife and daughters. Even the grandchildren."

Calgacus felt his blood run cold.

"Are you sure?" he asked.

"It's no secret. Ask anyone."

"I will. I'll bloody well ask him."

"Don't start a fight, Cal," Runt warned. "Maybe you should leave it until after the battle."

Calgacus gave a derisory snort.

"You think there will be anyone left alive to ask after the battle? They are just going to stand here and wait for the Romans to slaughter them."

"Then it won't matter what he did," Runt observed drily. "But if you ask him now, you'll just cause trouble. You'll get angry and so will he. If you fight him, one of you will die. Either way, that won't help the rest of us."

"So what do you expect me to do?" Calgacus demanded.

"We should leave," Runt stated earnestly. "You are right about one thing. The Ordovices won't win this battle. If you were in command they might have a chance, but that isn't going to happen. They are desperate for a fight and they trust Brennus. Even if the five of us joined in the fighting, we couldn't make much difference."

Calgacus picked up his beaker and took a sip. The tisane was still hot but at least it was drinkable now.

Over the rim of the clay mug, he remarked, "You are not usually this pessimistic."

"I'm just being realistic," Runt replied with a shrug. "I see no point in throwing away our lives to help people who don't want us."

"Maybe they'll win," Calgacus countered, though without much conviction.

Runt said nothing, merely raising a questioning eyebrow to show what he thought of the suggestion.

Calgacus drained his drink.

"I can't leave now," he told his friend. "Not until I have tried to speak to him again. Maybe I can persuade him to fight the Romans properly."

Runt clucked his tongue.

"Just don't fall out with him."

Leaning forwards, he added, "I mean it, Cal. We should leave. We are getting too old for this sort of thing. You have a wife and family to go back to. You've got grandchildren, by Toutatis."

"I'm a warrior," Calgacus argued. "They all know that."

Runt sighed, "I thought you'd say that. Well, you know we'll stand by you, whatever you decide to do."

"I know," Calgacus nodded.

He felt a pang of guilt, knowing that Runt's unspoken thoughts were that the little man no longer had anyone at home. Calgacus suspected that if it were not for young Adelligus, Runt would quite happily die on the battlefield. He could still see the loss in his friend's eyes. He wished there was something he could say to help but there were no words that could heal the empty hurt that Elaris' death had left behind.

Runt jerked his head, pointing with his chin.

"If you want to speak to Brennus, now is your chance."

Calgacus saw Brennus striding along the edge of the broad summit of the hill, a score of warriors following in his wake. As he passed, men rose to their feet, cheering loudly.

Putting down his beaker, Calgacus stood, gathered up his sword and crossed the hilltop to intercept his new-found son.

Brennus stopped when he saw him, his expression hard, almost annoyed.

Calgacus forced a smile to his face as he stood in front of the man who looked so much like his younger self.

"Good morning," he said, doing his best to sound friendly. "It looks like being a nice day."

"A good day for a fight," Brennus responded cautiously.

"That depends on who you intend to fight," Calgacus told him.

Brennus looked puzzled.

"The Romans, of course. Who else?"

Calgacus gave a weak smile as he said, "I thought for a moment you were going to fight me."

"I don't make war on old men," Brennus retorted, his face still hard.

118

Calgacus' own expression grew serious.

"That's not what I heard," he challenged. "Cadwallon was older than me. I heard that he didn't even try to defend himself when you killed him."

Some of Brennus' warriors shifted angrily and hands clutched at the hilts of their swords as their expressions hardened. What their reaction told Calgacus was that what Runt had told him was correct.

Brennus, though, merely shrugged dismissively.

"It was necessary," he stated flatly.

"Even his womenfolk and grandchildren?"

"It was necessary," Brennus repeated icily. "Now, I have a battle to fight, so you had best keep out of my way."

Brennus made to push past but Calgacus held up his arm, blocking the path the young man intended to take.

"All right. Forget Cadwallon for the moment. We need to talk about the Romans. You can't beat them by just standing here and waiting for them to attack you."

Brennus glared angrily at him, his nostrils flaring.

"Let me pass or I will have you killed right here," he hissed through clenched teeth. "I am the King of the Ordovices. I decide when and where my people fight, not you. We have the high ground. When the Romans attack, the climb will tire them and we will sweep them away with our charge."

Calgacus felt his temper rising. He pushed his head forwards, staring into Brennus' blazing eyes.

"Yes, you must be of the Ordovices. You obviously got your brains from your mother because no son of mine could be so stupid."

Brennus roared, his face turning red with fury. Without warning, his right fist flashed out, jabbing for Calgacus' face. Calgacus instantly swayed back, raising his left arm to deflect the blow. Furious at being thwarted, Brennus jumped at him, twisting so that his left shoulder barged into Calgacus' chest, striking against the hard bronze of Calgacus' breastplate. The force of the blow made Calgacus stagger backwards, arms flailing. Struggling for balance, he slipped on the damp grass and fell backwards.

He landed heavily, grunting as he hit the ground. Dazed, he looked up to see Brennus standing over him, his sword drawn and raised as if to strike.

"Enough!"

119

It was Runt's voice, cutting through the fight, demanding attention.

Staring up at the dark bulk of Brennus' outlined against the blue sky, Calgacus could not see Runt but he knew his friend was close by.

He heard him shout, "You should be fighting the Romans, not each other."

Brennus stood almost motionless, sword still held high. He was breathing heavily, nostrils flaring, eyes wide and filled with rage. Slowly, he lowered the sword.

"We will finish this later," he snarled down at Calgacus before glancing up to address Runt.

"Keep him out of my way," he commanded. "Stay with the women, children and other old men."

Then he spun on his heel and stalked off. His warriors followed, many of them laughing or casting disdainful looks at Calgacus as they passed him.

Runt hurried to help Calgacus to his feet.

"I'm glad you followed my advice about not starting a fight," he muttered. "Are you all right?"

"I'm fine," Calgacus replied.

He looked around to see Adelligus, Cawrdaf and Dunnocatus watching him. All three of them wore anxious expressions, but all three had their hands near the hilts of their swords. He understood that they would have tried to protect him and that realisation made him feel foolish. He waved a hand towards them.

"It's all right. No harm done. Come on, you may as well learn something by watching how not to fight the Romans."

"We are staying?" Runt asked, his brow furrowed in a disapproving frown.

Calgacus gave a self-mocking laugh as he nodded, "Yes, let's go and stand with the other old men and watch the fight."

The Ordovices would fight on foot. They had some horses but the slope in front of their position was steep and rough, unsuitable for cavalry, so the warriors who normally rode into battle dismounted, picked up their spears and shields, and joined the mass of tribesmen who gathered on the crest of the hill to await the enemy.

Calgacus and his four companions saddled their own horses and mounted them, standing in a small group behind the

120

warriors. Calgacus chose a position near the left flank, from where he could see the Romans approach. This vantage point had the added advantage that it was a little distance from the remainder of the women and children whose mocking looks made it plain that none of the Ordovices wished to stand too near to them.

Unexpectedly, there was one exception. Tegan arrived, strolling casually along the crowded plateau towards them.

She had combed her dark hair, tying a thin band of leather cord, twined with strands of silver, around her head. At her throat she wore a golden torc, similar to the one that Brennus wore. Her face was serious, her eyes sad, and Calgacus found himself wishing that he could see her smile again.

She looked up at him, her expression apologetic.

"I am sorry for what he did to you," she said.

"It was nothing," Calgacus assured her.

"He does not like to take advice," she told him.

Runt laughed, "That doesn't surprise me, considering who his father is."

A flicker of a smile crossed Tegan's face at that but she quickly shifted the conversation away from any further discussion of Brennus' faults.

"Why are you on horseback?" she asked.

"To get a better view," explained Calgacus.

"And so that we can get away quickly when everything starts to go wrong," added Runt.

Tegan frowned, regarding him intently.

"You really think the Romans can beat us?" she asked.

"It will be a miracle if they don't," Runt told her with a sigh of regret.

She glanced at Calgacus who gave a nod of agreement.

He said, "I have seen it too often to believe it can be any different this time."

Then, remembering that this young girl was Brennus' wife, he softened his expression as he added, "I am sorry. Perhaps it will be different this time. Who knows?"

Tegan's face showed no emotion as she regarded him.

"I will fetch a horse for myself," she decided. "To get a better view."

"That would be wise," Calgacus agreed. "You should stay near us."

"In case things go wrong?" she asked searchingly.

"It is always better to be prepared," he told her.

Her mouth twitched in the beginnings of a smile that did not quite succeed in lighting up her face before dying away. Without another word, she turned away, heading towards the rear slope where the Ordovices had gathered their livestock.

Calgacus watched her go, admiring the sway of her hips but noting, too, the stiffness in her manner as if she expected someone to challenge her at any moment. It was the walk, he reflected, of someone who had not quite come to terms with their new status.

"Strange girl," he muttered.

"She's pretty, though," said Runt as he, too, watched Tegan walking away from them.

"She should smile more often," Calgacus observed.

"Maybe she doesn't have much to smile about," suggested Adelligus.

Runt agreed, "She certainly doesn't seem too bothered at the prospect of becoming a widow."

Tegan returned a few moments later, riding on a small, shaggy-coated pony. Her long dress had been cut at the sides, allowing her to sit on the saddle and revealing her legs. Calgacus saw the young men eyeing her admiringly. Runt too, was smiling. Few women were permitted to ride horses but Tegan was the wife of a King, so nobody would dispute her right.

Calgacus, who had ridden horses since he was a boy, noticed that, despite her efforts to appear relaxed, she sat stiffly and awkwardly, clinging to the animal as if she did not trust it.

Trying not to look at her legs as she approached, he smiled, "I'd guess you don't have much experience of riding horses."

"I had never been on a horse until a few days ago," she admitted.

Runt told her, "Don't worry. We'll look after you."

"Hopefully we won't need to," said Calgacus, determined now to try to give the girl some encouragement despite his private misgivings about their chances of victory.

Wanting to change the subject, he said to her, "I'd like to know more about Brennus. What can you tell me about him?"

She frowned slightly before saying, "I don't think there is much I can tell you. What do you want to know?"

"For one thing, I'd like to know who his mother was."

Tegan shrugged, "I don't know. He talks about her a lot, but not in any great detail. He just says things like, 'my mother told me this' or 'my mother said that'. He never mentions her name, or says what happened to her."

"She is dead, then?" Calgacus asked.

"Yes," Tegan confirmed. "He told me that much."

She narrowed her eyes as she asked, "Do you really not know who she was?"

"No," Calgacus admitted.

Tegan's brown eyes gave him a look that might have been an accusation but she quickly lowered her gaze.

Not looking at him, she informed him, "He doesn't know what to make of you. Before you arrived, he was proud to call himself the son of Calgacus. Now, he is confused and angry."

"Yes, I noticed that."

Runt chuckled, "I think everyone noticed that."

Tegan turned her head to look into Calgacus' eyes as she explained, "He is not really angry with you, though."

"You could have fooled me," he grunted.

Tegan shrugged, "All right, perhaps he is. But I think he is more angry that he never knew you until now. He has spent his whole life blaming you for not being there for him. For not being there for his mother. I think she had a sad life. That is why he is angry."

Calgacus pondered that for a moment before pointing out, "That is hardly my fault. I had no idea he even existed."

"That, I suspect, is the whole problem," observed Runt.

Staring out over the plain beneath them, Calgacus sighed, "Well, let's hope he directs his anger at the Romans. They'll be here soon."

They all looked to the north-east. Approaching the hill was a neatly-arranged mass of men and horses, of brightly coloured standards, of red and yellow, iron-bossed shields, of iron-tipped javelins and sharp, deadly swords.

The Legion was closing on them.

Chapter XIII

The legionaries maintained their steady pace as they reached the foot of the slope. As always, they advanced in silence. While the barbarians would shout and scream at their foes, the Romans would make no sound. Only the steady, uniform tramp of their feet heralded their approach. From the hilltop, they could hear the barbarians yelling fiercely but the men of the Twentieth remained determinedly silent. They knew that their steady, inexorable and soundless advance would unnerve their opponents.

Watching from the right flank, Casca held his small band of riders back, letting the infantry move ahead of them.

Raising the faceplate of his ornate helmet so that he could obtain a better view, he eyed the slope warily. It was steep; difficult although not impossible for horses, but certainly unsuitable for a rapid charge.

"We'll go at a slow walk," he told his troop. "Stay behind the legionaries. And remember, we are not here to fight. Our task is to find Brennus."

As he rode up the lower part of the hill, his eyes scanned the horde of barbarians that waited some three or four hundred paces above him. He was looking for the large figure of Brennus, wanting to pick him out so that he could follow him wherever he went. Casca's main fear was that the barbarian chieftain would fall victim to someone else when the opposing lines closed together. He wanted that glory for himself so that he could redeem himself from the shame of having lost most of his men to ambush. He more than wanted it; he needed it.

"I can't see him," Sdapezi commented.

"He's there somewhere," Casca grunted in response.

Sdapezi said nothing. The barbarian could stay there as far as he was concerned. The Decurion was unhappy at this latest task the remnants of the squadron had been given. After months of garrison duty in the middle of hostile territory, he thought the men could have done with some time carrying out the relatively easy duties of guarding the baggage and supply columns. Instead, Casca had persuaded the Governor to give them this special mission. The only redeeming thing that Sdapezi could think of was that, whatever Casca did, Brennus would soon be dead and the revolt would be over. Then they could go back to some dull, routine and, above all, safe sentry work.

First, though, they must find Brennus.

Casca gave a sudden bark of satisfaction and pointed up the hill.

"There he is!" he grinned. "In the front rank. Right in the middle."

Sdapezi followed Casca's pointing finger. To say that the barbarians were in ranks was an exaggeration, for the host on the hilltop was nothing more than a mass of chanting, shouting men. In the centre of the horde, though, there was one figure that was larger than the others.

"I see him," he confirmed, although the truth was that he had no idea whether it was Brennus or not.

"Keep your eyes on that big bastard, lads!" Casca called out to the men. "He's the one we want."

The Legion was nearing the summit and, at last, the marching was over and the fighting could begin.

The barbarians opened the contest, giving a loud yell as they showered missiles on the advancing Romans. Javelins and rocks rained down on the legionaries who raised their shields for protection. The rattle of metal and stone striking home could be heard all across the field of battle. It echoed across the hillside like an irregular tattoo of wild drums, a sound that mirrored the barbarians' savage ferocity. The impact was so violent that the legionaries faltered for an instant but then, with shields held high, they resumed their attack, urged on by their Centurions and by Agricola who stood in their midst with his sword drawn and ready.

"They should throw," Sdapezi muttered, referring to the heavy pila the Roman troops carried.

Casca told him, "They are moving uphill. They'll need to get closer or they'll just waste the javelins."

Casca could still see the barbarians over the heads of the advancing Roman infantry. That showed just how steep the slope was. On that sort of terrain, the legionaries would struggle to hurl their *pila* any distance at all.

"Get in close and kill them," Casca urged.

Brennus was bare-chested despite the chill. He had daubed blue paint across his torso, a mass of circles and wavy lines, mystic symbols befitting a chieftain. Sword in hand, he watched as the Romans drew closer to his position in the centre of the war host. The noise all around him was incredible as the Ordovices chanted their war songs, encouraging each other to feats of valour. Screaming defiance, they hurled their spears and stones down on the legionaries, cheering whenever a soldier fell to the ground under the onslaught.

The sound as the missiles struck home drowned out even the raucous yells of the tribesmen but the advance continued, making Brennus frown when he saw that barely a handful of Romans had been struck down.

The moment was near. The Romans had climbed a long way, wearing heavy armour, carrying their weapons. They must be tired. Brennus decided to let them come another ten paces, then he would order the charge and his warriors would sweep them away.

His men were ready, eagerly waiting for his signal. From somewhere behind the war host, he could dimly make out the screams of encouragement from the watching women. In a few moments, he and his warriors would give them something to celebrate.

The Romans came on. Five paces. Six. Seven. Brennus took a deep breath, ready to shout the order to charge.

Then the Romans halted. Brennus heard a shouted command from within the ranks, saw the leading soldiers draw back their arms, then gaped in horror as the dark javelins came arcing up towards him. He threw up his shield, ducking his head instinctively as screams assailed his ears. There was a tremendous thump on his left arm and he shouted in alarm as a wicked iron point powered through the leather and wicker of his shield, its sharp tip scraping across his forearm, drawing bright blood.

His shield suddenly felt incredibly heavy. He lifted his head to see that the long metal spike of the javelin had bent on impact, leaving the javelin hanging from his shield. Its weight rendered the shield useless.

Cursing, he slipped his arm free, letting the ruined shield drop to the ground.

The man standing on Brennus' right suddenly screamed as he fell, a javelin having caught him in the belly. Brennus ducked

126

again as the Romans' second volley crashed home. He had to jump to one side as a pilum came skimming towards his legs.

Confused by the tumult around him, Brennus collided with the warrior on his left. The man gave a strangled gasp as he was punched backwards by a javelin that thudded into his chest, shattering bones and spraying blood. As he fell, he twisted, swinging the long, wooden haft of the pilum towards Brennus. With its tip still buried in the dying man's torso, the flailing haft of the pilum caught Brennus on the forehead just above his left eye. The blow stunned him and he felt himself falling, dimly aware of the screams and yells of fright all around him.

He tried to order the charge. He knew his warriors must attack now or the moment would be gone. He opened his mouth, desperately trying to shout the command, but no words would come. His head was spinning and he felt suddenly weak. Without warning, his knees collapsed under him and he hit the ground with a thump.

He lay there, unable to move, his head throbbing. The grass was mercifully cool against his face and chest, and for a moment he wanted nothing more than to lie there until his head cleared, but the cold chill of the earth revived him slightly. Then he felt hands grasping at him, hauling him upright. Men were shouting his name in anxious, almost terrified voices, urging him to stand.

Brennus took a deep breath as he slowly came to his feet. He blinked, frantically trying to clear his blurred vision. He could make out shapes but everything was chaos and confusion. Miraculously, he discovered that his sword was still in his hand and he readied himself to fight.

"I'm all right!" he yelled to his warriors. "Attack them!"

He wished he could see properly but he knew they must attack now, so he shouted the command in an effort to make himself heard over the riot of noise that surrounded him.

Few men heard his order. None of them obeyed. The Roman javelins had cut down dozens of men, creating carnage among their ranks, and the rumour of Brennus' death had spread through the tribe faster than the wind. Unnerved by the chaos, even the bravest men were edging back from the edge of the plateau, while others simply turned away and ran from the impending onslaught of the Legion.

That onslaught followed hard on the heels of the *pila*. The Romans charged up the last few paces of the slope, shields held determinedly in front of them, the tips of their swords jutting forwards between the curved shields. They battered into the leading men of the Ordovices, easily blocking the clumsy swings of the long swords or the jabbing points of spears. The shining blades of the Roman swords stabbed forwards, taking men in the legs or lower body because of the angle of the slope. It did not matter where they struck, for the Ordovices wore no armour and every thrust of a sword bit home, taking men down.

In moments, the summit of the hill became a hell of blood, pain and terror.

Brennus, now with several men between him and the Romans, roared at his warriors to attack but the Romans pushed on, gained the summit and kept moving forwards, cutting down everyone in their path.

The remaining Ordovices, unable to withstand the deadly assault, fled, and the retreat of a few suddenly became a widespread, panic-stricken rout.

Only a handful of men, those who had been Brennus' most loyal followers, held their ground, but the press of bodies streaming away from the battle drove them all backwards. In moments, Brennus found himself facing the entire legion with only half a dozen warriors beside him.

He blinked, wiping his eyes with his free hand, wishing his blurred vision would clear, but all he could make out was the bright red and yellow of the wall of large shields coming towards him, drawing closer with every heartbeat.

He wanted to attack but the part of his mind that still functioned through the throbbing pain in his head told him that the chance had been lost. The battle was over already, his tribe shattered in only a few, dreadful moments.

The battle may have been lost but Brennus was a warrior. With the bitter taste of defeat in his mouth he knew that there was nothing left for him except death. If that was inevitable, he decided to make it a glorious death. He gripped his sword and prepared to charge, determined to take a few of the enemy to the underworld with him.

Before he could move, the men of his bodyguard grabbed him, several of them hauling him away. He swore at them, trying to shake them off, but the blow to his head must have weakened him for he could not resist them. He found himself running, sword still unbloodied, a small group of warriors surrounding him, still prepared to protect him.

Brennus had never run from a fight in his life. Only cowards ran, he told himself, and he was not a coward. But everyone was running now. Many of the warriors discarded their weapons, intent only on getting away. Women and children, who had expected to witness a great victory, were now screaming in terror as they fled the hilltop.

The animals, frightened by the panic, also ran, turning the flight into utter chaos as cattle, sheep, goats, pigs and dogs mingled with the people, blundering across their path.

The Romans were still coming for them, moving more quickly now. The lighter-armed auxiliary troops who had been on the flanks were closing in from either side, cutting down anyone who was unfortunate enough to cross their path. While these troops ran to encircle the Ordovices, the legionaries swept across the hilltop, their swords red with blood.

Somewhere in the fleeing mob somebody fell, bringing down those around them in a horrible tangle of limbs and bodies. Others tumbled over the fallen, screaming in terror as the mob trampled them.

As he saw the crush, Brennus' befuddled mind began to clear at last. He called to his men to angle right, to where the slope was steepest on the far side of the hill. Most of the tribe were running to the left, where the gradient was easier, but that way was now partially blocked by the herds of livestock and the people who had fallen. The press of the crowd was so great that there was no quick escape in that direction. Already, the Romans were charging into the mass of tribespeople and slaughtering them.

Brennus and his small band of warriors dashed down the far slope, angling right. There were several hundred others ahead of them, running at reckless speed as they tried to escape.

"Keep going!" Brennus yelled. He pointed as he ran. "Head for the trees!"

His warriors ran. If they could reach the foot of the hill and run another five hundred paces beyond that, they could reach the heavily wooded slopes of another low hill. However slim, it was their only chance of escape.

Arms pumping, their breath coming in heaving, ragged gasps, they ran.

They were half way down the slope when Brennus heard the thunder of hoofs and saw more than a hundred Roman cavalry gallop along the foot of the slope, lances held high. Still running, he watched in horror as the horsemen rode into the fleeing tribesmen ahead of him, cutting them down mercilessly. The riders rode and stabbed, rode and stabbed, losing their formation as they spread out to hunt for more victims, but seemingly invulnerable because the Ordovices were so terrified that none of them made any attempt to defend themselves. They fell in their hundreds.

"Cut right!" Brennus yelled, angling to pass behind the horsemen who were still streaming away to his left as they pursued the fleeing tribespeople.

His own tiny group, growing more scattered now as the weaker men lagged behind, made for the narrow valley floor. With lungs burning and muscles aching, they reached the foot of the hill, dodged past the bodies of the fallen, then ran for the trees.

For a while, Brennus thought they would make it. He knew that the carnage, both on the hilltop and away to his left, was not done yet because he could still hear the sounds of killing, but he and his small group, only five of them now, were still alive. They had a chance.

The trees were barely a hundred paces away when the cavalry returned.

There were three of them, all with lances or swords dark with blood. They had obviously decided to give up the chase and had returned with the intention of looting the bodies of the fallen, but now they had seen Brennus and his four companions, so they slapped their bare legs against the heaving flanks of their horses and charged.

"Stand!" Brennus yelled.

He shoved his men into a small huddle.

"Swords ready!" he barked at them.

The men were exhausted and frightened, all of them streaked with sweat and breathing heavily, but they obeyed. They had no choice. There was no chance of outrunning the horsemen, so there was nothing they could do except stand and fight.

The three Roman horsemen were overconfident. Their squadrons had rampaged along the foot of the hill, cutting down barbarians indiscriminately. Not a single Roman horseman had been killed as they had massacred the fleeing rebels. Now they rushed at this small group of barbarians, confident that they would ride them down just as easily. Eager for plunder, they saw the golden torc gleaming at Brennus' throat and galloped straight for him.

Brennus yelled again, attempting to bolster his men's flagging resolve.

"Stand firm! They won't break us!"

The warriors held out their long swords, presenting a small wall of blades to the horsemen. The horses swerved at the last moment, as Brennus had known they would, but one of the riders jabbed with his long lance as his mount skittered past. The tip of the lance caught a warrior on his shoulder, driving deep into his flesh. Screaming in pain, the man staggered, moving away from his companions. In an instant he was dead as the lance plunged again, piercing his back.

The horsemen swirled round the tiny group of warriors who whirled to face them, but they could not face in all directions at once and the mounted Romans had greater height and reach over men on foot. Another warrior went down, screaming, his face smashed to pulp by a heavy sword blade.

A rider hacked at Brennus with his sword. Brennus blocked the blow, the clash of metal ringing in the air, then he leaped upwards.

He grabbed for the rider's leg, fingers clutching desperately for a hold. The Roman hacked down again but Brennus raised his sword to block once more. Then he brought his blade down in a vicious cut that gouged deep into the rider's leg.

The Roman let out an agonised yell as blood sprayed from the awful wound. He should have ridden away, leaving Brennus standing alone, but the horse was turning and Brennus hacked again, smashing his sword into the rider's arm. With a mighty heave, Brennus hauled the Roman from the high saddle.

The Roman fell and the terrified horse reared. Ignoring his wounded victim, Brennus grabbed for the reins, steadied the beast and vaulted up onto its back. Now he could fight his enemy on equal terms.

Sword in hand, he turned back to the fight, just in time to see the last of his warriors being cut down. With a roar of fury, he jabbed his heels into the horse's sides and rushed at the nearest cavalryman.

The Roman did not see him until it was too late. Brennus' sword smashed into the back of his shoulders, sliding on the rider's armour but gouging into his neck below the rim of his helmet. The cavalryman gasped, stiffened, then slumped away. Brennus almost lost his sword as he charged past but he yanked it free and rode on.

Still full of rage, he wheeled again, ready to face the third horseman but the Roman quickly decided that he did not want to risk his life. He turned away, galloping to safety.

Brennus sat on the horse, his chest heaving, his long sword dangling from his hand. Beneath him, he could feel the horse quivering slightly, uncertain about its new rider.

He rubbed his forehead, wincing slightly as he felt a large lump above his left eye. Grimacing, he looked around, seeking a way to escape, but a movement on the hillside caught his eye.

He swore bitterly as he realised he was not yet free from danger. More cavalry were coming for him.

Chapter XIV

There had been so much confusion on the hilltop that Casca had lost sight of Brennus. When the Ordovices broke and the legion had surged forwards, he had urged his horse upwards, calling to his men to watch out for the big barbarian with the golden torc around his neck, but by the time the squadron reached the broad summit of the hill they were greeted by a scene of utter devastation.

The battle line was marked by piles of mangled, twisted bodies, some of them still feebly moving. All across the grass of the flat summit, bodies lay scattered and weapons littered the ground. Some soldiers were busy finishing off the wounded and looting the corpses, while other pursued the fleeing tribespeople in a thirst for more bloodshed.

Casca surveyed the scene, looking for Brennus, but the bodies were piled so deep that it was almost impossible to make out any details.

"Spread out," he ordered his men. "Find him!"

While they were searching, The Governor appeared, now on horseback, with Tacitus and his bodyguard riding close behind.

"Any sign of him?" Agricola asked.

"Not yet, Sir."

Agricola did not appear concerned and gave a broad grin, clearly in an expansive mood after having gained such a rapid victory.

"Not to worry," he told Casca. "If he's not dead already, I'm sure he will be soon. The enemy are completely routed and we are hunting them down."

The Governor turned to his son-in-law and added, "You see, Tacitus? These barbarians will not stand when faced by a determined Legion."

"It was an impressive victory, Sir," agreed Tacitus.

"Yes, it was," Agricola beamed cheerfully. "But it is not over yet. We must destroy this tribe as an example. The task now is to hunt them down and kill every last one of them."

Turning back to Casca, he said, "Carry on, Casca. Find Brennus for me."

"Yes, Sir," Casca nodded, although he wondered how he was supposed to locate one corpse among so many.

Agricola led his staff away, heading for the far side of the hill, leaving Casca and his nine cavalrymen to search the wide plateau. Casca ordered them to dismount so that they could search through the piles of dead and wounded, but they had barely had time to climb down when young Hortensius let out a cry of excitement.

"Sir! Sir! Over here!"

Casca quickly guided his horse through the debris towards the northern part of the hill where Hortensius, his face flushed with elation, was waiting for him.

The young trooper pointed down the hillside.

"I think that's him!" he blurted excitedly.

Casca stared down at the lower ground where a small group of barbarians had been trapped by three Roman horsemen. He watched as the cavalrymen rode the rebels down, then his eyes blazed as he saw one of the barbarians, a big man, his upper body bare, haul one of the riders out of the saddle, then cut down a second horseman. Despite the distance, Casca had no doubt who it was.

"To me!" he bellowed, summoning his troop.

He drew his long sword, testing its comforting weight in his hand and waiting impatiently for his men to gather around him.

"There is our target, lads," he announced as soon as they had joined him. "Ten denarii to the man who kills him."

With a determined gleam in his eye, Casca lowered the face mask of his helmet then led the remnants of his squadron down the slope, intent on gaining his revenge.

Brennus took only an instant to make up his mind. The Roman horsemen were coming down the steep slope that faced him, although they were unable to goad their mounts into moving too quickly in case they fell on the uneven terrain. Still, there was no escape for him that way. Behind him, the trees beckoned, but his newly acquired horse would be of little use among the woods. The ten riders who were coming for him would be forced to dismount but they could still hunt him down, or they could remain on horseback and encircle the woods with a loose cordon so that he would be seen as soon as he tried to escape.

He looked to his right, where the main force of Roman cavalry was pursuing what remained of his scattered and defeated tribe. There was no escape that way.

Which left him with only one direction.

Brennus slammed his still bloody sword into the scabbard on his back, hauled on the reins and yelled the horse into a gallop, heading to his left, back towards the plain the Romans had crossed only a short time earlier. He would have a head start on the ten riders and he hoped that they would ignore a solitary fugitive. There were plenty of dead bodies for them to loot and, with any luck, the temptation would prove too much for them.

He decided to circle the low, wooded hill. Once he had reached the far side, he could head west, into the rugged mountains where he would be safe. He was sure they would not follow him that far. Leaning low over the horse's neck, he whispered into its ear, urging it to hurry.

The horse was already tired, for it had been in two charges that morning and Brennus was a big, heavy man. He could feel the beast's gallop wavering beneath him. "Not long now," he told the horse.

He glanced back over his shoulder to check on the ten Romans and cursed when he saw that, instead of stopping to gather loot from the bodies of the fallen, they were pursuing him, riding hard and, what was worse, gaining on him.

He slapped his legs against his mount's sweating flanks, dug his heels into its sides and shouted at it to run faster. Obediently, the horse picked up the pace. The wind blew his long, dark hair out behind him. It stung his eyes and chilled his bare chest as the horse raced along as fast as it could carry him.

He eased it left, following the contour of the low hill. Soon he was heading west, towards a line of yet more hills. He looked back once more, grinning when he saw no signs of pursuit, then groaned aloud when the Roman horsemen appeared around the curve of the woodland, still hunting him down and, he thought, closer than ever. They were perhaps six hundred paces behind him. If he faltered now, they would soon catch him.

He galloped towards the hills. There was a gap, a narrow gully that was lined on either side by dense woods. He aimed for it. His horse was tiring rapidly now, slowing with every step but it carried him to the tree-shadowed entrance to the pass. The ground began to rise slightly as the gap narrowed and the sounds of the horse's hoofbeats echoed back around him. He wondered how far behind him the Romans were, but he dared not look.

As the horse gamely struggled up the shallow slope, he knew he would need to stop soon. The animal could carry him no further. He would have to risk going on foot.

The woods were thick here, with broad-leafed trees towering above him. Their branches were almost bare but the undergrowth was still dense enough to conceal him despite the lateness of the season. His problem would be moving quietly through the thick layer of fallen leaves that covered the ground. But he had no choice. The pursuit would catch him if he did not hide.

He saw the ground ahead of him reach a small summit, a mere saddle of land between the sides of the narrow pass. Once he crossed that, he would be out of sight of his pursuers for a few moments. He decided that he would abandon the horse and run for the trees as soon as he reached the far side.

Without warning, a figure appeared ahead of him. Barely ten paces away, a big man stood up from behind some concealing rocks and held up an arm, signalling for him to stop.

Brennus hauled on the reins, bringing the startled horse to a juddering, twisting halt. It stood, mouth and nostrils frothing, while Brennus stared at the man in front of him, unbelieving.

"Come on," said Calgacus urgently. "Get across this ridge."

"What are you doing here?" Brennus demanded.

"Saving your skin," snapped Calgacus. "Now get over here. Quickly."

Brennus forced his horse on, cresting the low ridge, then gratefully dipping down the far side. There he saw Tegan waiting for him, sitting on horseback. Beyond her were five other horses with empty saddles, tethered loosely to the bare limbs of the trees.

Tegan's face barely registered any emotion as she said, "Hello, husband."

Brennus could not understand how she had got here. He whirled, turning to Calgacus.

"There are ten riders after me," he warned.

Calgacus gave him a grim nod, speaking rapidly.

"I know. We saw them chasing you. Stay here. Take one of the other horses. That one is near dead. If this goes wrong, get the girl away. Go to Ynis Mon. Find a boat and sail north to Iova. Find Beatha. She will welcome you."

Before Brennus had time to properly take in his instructions, Calgacus turned, jumped lightly over the crest of the small ridge and drew his sword.

Casca called a halt as the squadron reached the entrance to the narrow pass. He had watched Brennus disappear over the low saddle of land at the far end, and he had known that they would catch him soon. At worst, the barbarian would abandon his horse and take to the trees, but Casca was confident they would still find him.

Then another figure had appeared at the far end of the rocky pass. Casca's senses screamed a warning at him. He held up his right arm, signalling for the squadron to halt.

Sdapezi pulled alongside.

"There is only one man," the Decurion said.

"We can only *see* one man," Casca replied.

He raised the faceplate of his helmet to get a better view.

"Wait here," he ordered.

"Brennus is getting away," Sdapezi pointed out.

"Just wait here," Casca repeated.

He nudged his horse into a slow walk, moving between the tall trees that crowded on either side of the pass. Snorting and tossing its head, the horse carried him along the shadowy path.

His eyes scanned the woodland as he ventured further into the gully. The autumn sun was still low in the sky and the trees were shrouded in gloom. Small, tangled bushes and a thick carpet of fallen leaves provided cover for an ambush. Still, he could see only the one man ahead of him. The figure stood waiting patiently, sword drawn, the tip resting in the ground in front of him, both hands clasped lightly around the hilt. He was a big man, Casca could tell, wearing a breastplate of bronze. He was clean-shaven, with long, dark hair, like an older version of Brennus. The breastplate and huge sword marked him as a man of some importance but why, Casca wondered, was he standing there alone?

There could only be one reason.

Casca heard a movement in the trees to his left, a swishing rustle from the leaf-strewn ground. He saw the big man wave a hand in a signal, as if telling someone to sit down. Another rustle from the undergrowth was the only acknowledgement. Then Casca thought he caught a glimpse of a dark shadow among the trees to his right, as if someone was trying to move along the hillside to get behind him.

He stopped his horse, waiting. Slowly, he laid his sword across the twin pommels in front of him.

Silence.

No, not complete silence. Casca could hear the sounds of the woodland, faint but audible. There was a bird warbling somewhere nearby and he could hear his horse's tail swishing. There was an occasional sound as his mount moved its feet on the stony path. But nothing else moved. He sat on his horse, watching the warrior who blocked the far end of the pass. The man eyed him carefully but made no other move.

Still Casca waited. He considered lowering the faceplate of his helmet. That would hide his features as well as providing some protection if he was attacked. But it would hamper his peripheral vision and perhaps give the wrong signal. He had no wish to start a fight here in this narrow, tree-lined cleft where he could be surrounded in moments. Memories of the ambush sprang into his mind. He pushed them away, deciding to show that he was prepared but unafraid. Let the barbarians see that he was not frightened of them.

After what seemed an age, the barbarian casually lifted his sword and began walking slowly towards Casca. He approached to within ten paces, then stopped, resuming his former stance. He looked up at Casca, his eyes a brilliant blue.

"I will let you live, Roman," he said in a not unfriendly tone. "I was hoping to catch all ten of you, but one is hardly worth the bother."

Casca's eyes flickered to either side, looking for more movement among the trees.

"How many men do you have?" he challenged.

The barbarian chuckled, "Enough."

Casca decided a little bluster would not be out of place.

"Then I think I will send a man back to fetch more soldiers. When they come, you will die."

"Go ahead," the barbarian replied calmly. "The rest of you will be dead by the time they get here."

"We have horses," Casca pointed out.

"So do we."

Casca hesitated. He had seen some movement in the trees but, so far, he had detected signs of no more than three barbarians. Yet the man facing him appeared unconcerned at the prospect of fighting ten mounted soldiers. His manner was that of a man who was supremely confident that he held a position of strength. Which meant that he was either very sure of himself or too stupid to appreciate his danger. Or bluffing.

Casca studied his opponent, trying to guess which.

The man was not old but the first tinges of grey were visible in his hair. His face, so reminiscent of Brennus, showed his years, but he was strong and powerfully built. Casca also noticed that the man moved lightly, apparently unaffected by the weight of his breastplate and the huge sword he held. But it was his sparking eyes that drew Casca's attention. They shone with a keen intelligence and an apparent willingness to engage in violence if Casca made the wrong move. Whatever else he might be, Casca decided that this man was not stupid.

He recalled the Governor's warning about not repeating the mistake of riding into an ambush. But if this was an ambush, it was the strangest one Casca had ever heard of. Why had this barbarian shown himself? It had given away his plan. Casca was almost convinced that the man was bluffing. Yet the big warrior appeared quite calm and relaxed. Casca was not sure that being almost convinced was enough. If he led what was left of his squadron into another ambush, his career would be finished.

If he survived.

"Who are you?" he asked while he tried to decide what to do.

The barbarian grinned, "My name is Calgacus. You may have heard of me."

Casca frowned as he searched his memory.

"Brennus claimed to be the son of Calgacus. Is that you?"

"That's right," Calgacus acknowledged.

"I thought you were dead," Casca told him.

Calgacus snorted, "No. I have been away for a few years. Now I am back. Unfortunately, my war band and I were not able to reach the battle in time to influence it. If I had, you would not have won."

"That is a proud boast," Casca said.

Calgacus shrugged, "It is the truth. You should go back to your new Governor and tell him that I will oppose him the way I have opposed others. Tell him that he will meet the same fate as Scapula and Nepos."

He gave Casca a wolfish grin as he explained, "I killed both of them, you know."

Casca hesitated. Like all Romans in Britannia, he had heard tales about Calgacus' exploits but he had not believed most of them. Now he was not so sure. Scapula and Nepos, former Governors of Britannia, had both died violent deaths and this man looked perfectly capable of having killed them.

"Maybe I should just kill you now," Casca said lightly, indicating the sword in his hand.

"You could try," Calgacus invited. "You won't succeed. I have been fighting Romans for twenty-five years. I am good at it. Anyway, my men will cut you down before you reach me."

A flicker of Calgacus' eyes made Casca look to his left. A warrior appeared, a young man with a long sword, standing poised as if preparing to jump down from the embankment onto Casca. A sound to the right heralded the appearance of another barbarian from among the trees.

"Three of you?" Casca asked, forcing himself not to show any concern.

Calgacus laughed, "Oh, no. I have more than that. I am a chieftain and a War Leader. But three is more than enough to dispose of you if I want. But, as I said, I am feeling generous today. I am happy to let you live because I want you to take my message to your Governor. Be sensible. Go back and tell him what I said."

Casca's hand tightened on the hilt of his sword. He looked at each of the three barbarians in turn, then back at Calgacus.

"Tell Brennus I will hunt him down and kill him," he rasped. "He ambushed my men and I want his head."

"I will tell him," Calgacus promised. "But he is my son. If you want him, you will have to kill me first."

"Naturally."

Calgacus laughed again.

"Let us leave that for another day," he suggested.

He waved a hand as he added, "Go now, before I change my mind."

With an ostentatious flourish, Casca sheathed his sword. He nodded to Calgacus, turned his horse, and rode slowly back to his men. As he went, he cursed himself for a coward. He was fairly sure that there were no more than three barbarians. On the other hand, he was absolutely certain that he could not risk being caught in another ambush.

Sdapezi greeted him anxiously.

"There are barbarians in the trees just over there," the Decurion informed him nervously, waving to the trees at the near end of the pass.

Casca pursed his lips. His spirits lifted slightly. Perhaps it had been an ambush after all. At least Sdapezi would be able to back him up when he explained to the Governor why Brennus had escaped.

He told his men, "They wanted to ambush us but at least we have managed to avoid that."

"Why did they let you live?" Sdapezi asked.

"That man claims to be the famous Calgacus. He wants me to take a message to the Governor."

Sdapezi looked to where Calgacus still stood, calmly watching them.

"I thought he was dead," he remarked.

"Apparently not."

"What about Brennus?"

Casca's decision was made.

"Brennus will have to wait for a while. Come. We must tell the Governor there is another barbarian war band in the hills."

He signalled to the troopers to turn, then moved the horses into a canter as they rode back the way they had come.

Chapter XV

"How did you do that?" asked Brennus in a voice that contained a mixture of wonder, admiration and suspicious hostility.

"Let the enemy see what you want them to see," Calgacus replied in a matter-of-fact tone. "That Roman wasn't sure whether there was an ambush or not, but we let him see enough to convince him that there might be."

He gave Brennus a questioning look as he added, "He says he will hunt you down. He wants revenge for some ambush. Does that mean anything to you?"

With a sour nod, Brennus spat, "It must have been Casca. No wonder he chased me."

"Well, we have gained a little time," Calgacus said, "but now we must go."

He signalled to Runt and the three young warriors who had hurried back from their hiding places in the woods as soon as they were sure that the Romans had gone. They quickly ran to their horses, making ready to depart.

Brennus did not move. He remained standing while the others mounted. Folding his arms across his bare chest, he demanded, "Go where?"

"First to Ynis Mon. Then north. I have family and friends there."

"I don't," Brennus retorted. "I must stay here. My people need me."

"Your people are being hunted," Calgacus reminded him. "We saw it. The Romans are showing no mercy. Even if you stay, nobody will join you. You will be hunted down by Casca or by some other Roman. You should come with us."

Brennus stared pugnaciously at his father.

"Why should I do as you say?" he challenged. "I am King of the Ordovices."

"The Ordovices are dying," Calgacus replied. "Just like my tribe, the Catuvellauni, died years ago. Staying here won't change that. If you stay, you will surely be killed. Better to live and to fight again."

Brennus' head was throbbing with pain and anger. He looked at Calgacus again, seeing not the old, tired warrior who had sat by the fire the night before but a big man, well-muscled and strong with a look of determination on his face that suggested he might be capable of anything.

Brennus looked around at the others. He could see that they were all ready to follow Calgacus without question. Even Tegan, who sat watching him expectantly. Her acceptance of Calgacus' leadership hurt him almost as much as anything that had happened all morning.

He took a deep breath and faced Calgacus with as much determination as he could muster.

"I'm no coward," he insisted. "I will not run away."

Calgacus sighed, "You cannot fight the whole Roman army on your own. Your rebellion is over. The Ordovices will not fight again. The Deceangli are friends of Rome these days. Apart from a few druids and renegade bandits on Ynis Mon, there is nobody left here who will fight."

"So you want to run away?" Brennus demanded scornfully.

Calgacus did not rise to the taunt. Remembering how he had lost his temper the last time they had spoken, he did his best to remain calm.

He explained, "In the North, I am building an alliance of tribes. Sooner or later, this new Governor is going to march north. When he does, we will face him with an army the likes of which he has never encountered."

Calgacus took a step towards Brennus, holding his gaze. Lowering his voice, he implored, "Come with me. Help me fight them. Together we can defeat them."

Brennus swallowed hard but his gaze did not soften as he stared back at Calgacus. Like two great bulls, they faced one another, gauging each other's strength.

Then Tegan put in, "Husband, we should go with them. If we stay, we face a life of hardship as fugitives. If we go, we have a chance at a better life. A life of freedom and perhaps a chance to fight another day. At least let us go as far as Ynis Mon."

Brennus slowly turned his head to look at her. She dropped her gaze immediately. He studied her thoughtfully for a few moments before turning back to Calgacus.

Taking a deep breath, he sighed, "Very well, we will go with you. To Ynis Mon, anyway."

Calgacus smiled, "You are welcome, my son."

Agricola's face was grim as he listened to Casca's report. The Governor had assembled his small staff on the plain while his soldiers continued the task of hunting down the rebels. He had been in a good humour because the battle had been won easily and quickly, with few casualties on the Roman side, but the news of Brennus' escape and the arrival of another notorious rebel had rather spoiled his mood.

"He told you he was called Calgacus?" he asked.

"Yes, Sir. That is what he said."

Agricola rubbed his chin thoughtfully.

"But you don't know how many men he has?"

Casca felt embarrassed about this part of his story but he made the best of it.

"No, Sir. I saw only him and two others, but my men saw signs of several more hiding in the trees. He seemed very sure of himself. I decided it was better to bring you the news rather than take a risk."

Agricola nodded, "You did the right thing, Casca. Although I suspect that he does not have many men at all."

Casca flushed slightly, feeling he was being criticised, but he decided it would be best not to argue the point. Fortunately for him, Piso asked the question he had been thinking of.

"Can we be sure of that, Sir?" the Legate enquired.

Agricola smiled patiently as he explained, "I have never come across this fellow Calgacus but I know him by reputation and I know men who have met him. He is an experienced warrior. He is also, as I recall, very skilled. If he had wanted to ambush Casca and his men, he would not have let them see anyone. He would simply have sprung the trap."

In an effort to justify his actions, Casca offered, "That thought occurred to me, Sir. But I could not be certain."

"I understand, Casca. As I say, you did the right thing. But if Calgacus came with an army of his own, they would have been seen. They cannot march through our province undetected, and our fleet would have seen a large number of boats coming south. No, I suspect he probably has no more than ten or twenty men. Maybe less."

Piso nodded in deferential agreement.

"So what do we do now, Sir?" he asked.

Agricola, as always, made up his mind quickly.

"Leave one cohort and the allied cavalry to continue hunting down the Ordovices. I want every village destroyed. They are to kill or enslave any member of that tribe they find. The main thing, though, is to seize their grain and destroy their homes. Leave them with no food and nowhere to shelter for the winter."

"Yes, Sir."

Turning to Tacitus, Agricola ordered, "Send word to Deva. I want some naval galleys to patrol the coast and make for the island of Mona. That is our next objective. If the druids have re-occupied the island, we must stamp them out this time."

Tacitus gave a nod of acknowledgement.

"Yes, Sir."

"What about this fellow, Calgacus?" Piso asked.

"He will go to Mona," Agricola told him. "There is nowhere else for him to hide."

The Governor looked at Casca as he went on, "Your men should scout to the west. Brennus still lives. But now, I want you to find both him and Calgacus. Do whatever it takes."

Casca saluted, giving the Governor a fierce smile.

"Yes, Sir."

Tacitus asked, "Will we not need transport boats to cross to the island of Mona?"

"It will take too long to gather enough boats," Agricola replied. "No, I want to press home the advantage we have gained. We will head to Mona as quickly as we can. The strait is not wide and we have auxiliary troops who are used to swimming. The British and Batavian units will be able to swim across to the island before the rebels are ready for them."

Tacitus wondered how the Governor could be so confident. He sensed that some of the other officers, and certainly Piso, were less certain that matters would turn out as the Governor intended. Yet none of them voiced any objections. Agricola's brisk decisiveness and conviction was sufficient to silence any dissent.

Agricola rubbed his hands together. Now that he had made his plans, his mood had brightened once more.

"Very well, Gentlemen. Carry on. The season's campaign is not quite over. Let us finish it quickly."

The ride west should have been everything that Calgacus could have wished for. He was beside his son, and behind them rode Runt and Adelligus. Two fathers, two sons, as it should be. But instead of the joy he should have been experiencing, there was a tension that he could not ignore. Brennus appeared determined to maintain his brooding hostility however much Calgacus tried to encourage him to speak. The conversation between them became more of a monologue as Calgacus explained how they had taken Tegan away from the hilltop as soon as the Ordovices' battle line had crumbled.

"We got away quickly enough," he explained. "When we saw the Roman cavalry coming round to block the escape, we headed north, into the trees. We crossed the hill and were going to make straight for Ynis Mon when we spotted you being chased."

Brennus nodded but said nothing. He merely rubbed at the darkening bruise above his eye while staring straight ahead, not meeting Calgacus' gaze.

Trying to suppress a growing feeling of exasperation, Calgacus went on, "It is not your fault that you lost, you know. Nobody I know has beaten the Romans in a fight like that. Not even my brother, Caratacus, could do that."

"Whose fault is it, then?" grunted Brennus angrily.

Calgacus could not answer that. Having been on the losing side before, he knew the despair that Brennus must be feeling.

He said, "It is in the past now, anyway. What is important is that we get back to the free tribes so that we can build a strong alliance. You have seen that one tribe alone cannot defeat Rome. We need to persuade all the people of the North to combine."

"Can you do that?" Brennus asked sceptically.

"I can bloody well try," Calgacus insisted. "We have made a good start. The Caledones and the Boresti are already committed. With your help, we will turn a wider alliance into a reality."

"You don't need my help," rasped Brennus in a surly tone.

"Yes I do. You are my son. One day I will give you this sword. It is the sword that Caratacus carried into battle. Before him, my uncle, Epaticcus, wielded it. Before him, my grandfather, Tasciovanus and before him, the great Cassivellaunos."

"I get the message," Brennus said sourly. "But these names mean nothing to me. I don't want your sword. I want nothing from you."

Calgacus stared at him but the young man was looking directly ahead, determined not to return his gaze.

The burning intensity of Brennus' anger sent a shiver of distress through Calgacus' whole body. *I want nothing from you.* The words struck him like a dagger to the heart. He had come in search of a son, a man he had hoped would be like himself but any resemblance that Brennus bore was merely physical. Brennus had been shaped by the circumstances of his birth, circumstances that Calgacus desperately wanted to understand.

I want nothing from you.

As gently as he could, Calgacus prompted, "Tell me why."

For the first time, Brennus turned to face him but the younger man's expression was dark, his eyes harsh. The visible mark of the ugly bruise on his forehead reflected the throbbing anger inside him.

He seemed to struggle with some internal conflict for a while but, at last, he reached a decision. With a heavy sigh, he confessed, "My mother was a slave. She was of the Ordovices but when she was young, her village was raided by the Silures and she was captured. Later she was sold and eventually she returned to the Ordovices, where she ended up in Cadwallon's home."

Calgacus frowned, "Did he not free her? She was of his tribe."

Brennus gave a snort of disgust.

"She was a slave. Why should he believe what she said? She had no proof of who she was."

In a voice filled with emotion, he went on, "Then one day, not long after the battle of Caer Caradoc, you arrived to speak to Cadwallon."

Calgacus felt a chill as recollection came to him. He had lost many good friends in that battle. They had been so close to victory but it had been snatched away from them when the legionaries had forced their way across the river and broken the Ordovices. In the aftermath of the defeat, Caratacus had fled to Cartimandua, Queen of the Brigantes. That had been a mistake, for she had promptly imprisoned him and handed him over to the Romans.

With Caratacus gone, Calgacus, the last remaining son of the great King, Cunobelinos, had been appointed War Leader of the western tribes. His first task had been to visit Cadwallon to recruit his aid for the continuing fight.

147

He recalled how frightened Cadwallon had been at that meeting. His tribe had been the first to run from the battlefield and everyone knew it. But Calgacus had decided to fight war a different way and had asked Cadwallon only for supplies of food and weapons. The King of the Ordovices had been so relieved that he would not be asked to do any fighting himself that he had thrown a small feast in Calgacus' honour.

And after the feast, Calgacus remembered now, Cadwallon had given him a slave girl for the night.

Calgacus half closed his eyes. It had been a long time ago. He had been barely twenty years old but he could never forget the events of that momentous year. They had been burned into his memories like the writing that the Romans carved into stone.

"I remember," he said softly, feeling guilty because he could not recall the girl's face.

"You never even asked her name," Brennus accused.

"I was young and foolish," Calgacus shrugged, knowing it was a poor excuse.

Brennus continued, "I was born the year after. The same year you destroyed the Legion that marched against the Silures. She was very proud of that when she heard the news. When I was growing up, she talked about you all the time, told me what a great hero you were."

Brennus spoke with enough venom to make the word, hero, sound like a taint.

Calgacus now understood Brennus' bitterness.

He sighed, "But I wasn't there to help her, or you."

"No, you weren't."

"What was her name?" Calgacus asked.

Bitterly, Brennus spat back, "Does it matter? She is dead now."

Calgacus briefly closed his eyes as he fought to control his emotions. It seemed that whatever he said only served to enrage Brennus further but there were questions that needed to be answered.

Taking a deep breath to calm himself, he asked, "What happened to her?"

After a short pause, Brennus recounted, "We were both sold when I was quite young. To a chieftain of the Demetae, the tribe who live by the western coast. We stayed there for years, but when I was twelve years old she caught a fever and she died."

148

"I am sorry," Calgacus said.

Brennus' expression was scathing as he shot back, "Being sorry now is too late. She had a hard life. Nobody ever helped her. She was passed from one master to the next, like some sort of animal. The only thing that she ever spoke of with any joy was that she had borne your son."

He shook his head as he added, "I never understood why that made her happy. She never saw you again after that night and you never did anything to help either of us."

There was nothing Calgacus could say to defend himself from Brennus' accusations but he tried anyway.

"I am truly sorry. But what about you? You were still a slave. How did you escape?"

Brennus at last gave a slight hint of a smile, as if some memory had reminded him of at least one good thing that had happened to him.

"When I was sixteen," he explained with grim satisfaction, "I killed my master. The bastard wanted to whip me for something I hadn't done, so I hit him. It was a good punch. He fell and broke his filthy neck. Then I ran. His warriors chased me but I made it to the hills. Eventually I found my way back to the land of the Ordovices and I gathered a few men. I wanted revenge on Cadwallon, so I used your name to attract a war band to me."

Darkly, he added, "That was the only good thing you ever did for me."

"Do you think I would not have done something if I had known?" Calgacus asked, his own anger rising once more. "You can't expect people to help when they don't even know about you."

Brennus said nothing but his expression remained clouded. The two men lapsed into an angry silence which Brennus ended when he turned his horse and went back to ride alongside Tegan, leaving Calgacus to fume in a welter of regret and anger.

He discussed the conversation with Runt as they sat at a small fire that evening. Brennus and Tegan sat some distance away, near a camp fire of their own, refusing to have much to do with any of the others and pointedly ignoring Calgacus.

Adelligus and the other two young warriors discreetly announced that they would stand watch for the first part of the night, leaving Calgacus and Runt alone by the fire.

"I must be a failure as a father," Calgacus grumbled softly. "You get on well with Adelligus, don't you?"

"I always have," Runt agreed. "He's a lot like his mother in many ways. Maybe that is why. He never really got on with her, though. Too much alike, I suppose. They were always arguing."

"You're lucky," Calgacus told him. "I just can't seem to get on with Togodumnus at all. And now that I've found another son, I discover that he hates me."

"You're not listening to what I'm saying," Runt chided. "Children don't always get on with their parents. I told you, Adelligus and Elaris were always clashing over something or other. There is often one parent a child is closer to. Beatha gets on well with Togodumnus, doesn't she?"

"Beatha gets on well with everyone," Calgacus retorted.

"Fair enough. But as for Brennus, he doesn't really hate you. He just hates the fact that he never had a father. He grew up as a slave, by Toutatis. What sort of a life is that for the son of a King? He's just taking out his anger on you."

"Maybe you should talk to him," Calgacus suggested.

He knew that Runt's circumstances had been very similar to the life Brennus had led. Runt had never known his father and his mother had died when he was still a child. He had escaped from slavery when his master, a Roman merchant, had visited the Catuvellauni. Runt had seen an opportunity to slip away from the guards and had literally run into Calgacus who had hidden him from the enraged merchant. They had been friends ever since.

Because of their lifelong friendship, Runt usually went along with whatever Calgacus suggested. This time, though, he held up his hands in a gesture of refusal.

"No thanks. I'm keeping out of it. Don't worry, though. Once Beatha meets him, he'll come round. Like you say, she gets on with everyone. She'll convince him to stop being so angry with you."

"Maybe," Calgacus said grudgingly. "But I just can't understand him. Were we that stubborn when we were young?"

"You were," grinned Runt with a rare flash of his old humour. "In fact, you still are. I was always the sensible one."

That brought a smile to Calgacus' face.

"You weren't all that sensible," he countered. "Remember the time you got caught with that farmer's wife?"

"I *nearly* got caught," Runt corrected. "He was too slow to get hold of me. Anyway, at least I didn't go around arguing with druids."

They both smiled at the memories as Runt went on, "I remember Caratacus complaining about us when we were young. I think it will always be the same. Young men see the world differently."

Calgacus idly tossed some twigs onto the fire.

"I suppose you're right," he admitted.

He glanced over to the other fire where Brennus and Tegan were sitting. They did not appear to be talking to one another, but were simply staring into the small, wispy flames. Calgacus took a deep breath. Recalling his own youth had stirred more memories within him.

Trying to lighten the mood, he said, "This is just like old times, isn't it? Travelling across country, avoiding the Romans. The young lads are doing well."

Runt nodded, "A bit of real war makes them learn fast."

Then his mouth twitched in the habitual way that Calgacus knew heralded some acerbic comment. Runt did not disappoint him.

"It is just like old times," the little man agreed. "You moaning because nobody ever listens to you and the Romans winning another victory so that we have to run and hide. Story of my life."

Calgacus gave a soft laugh.

"Never mind, Liscus. It will be over soon. We'll get back home and we will forge an alliance of tribes. When Agricola comes north, we will beat him. With Coel and Cadwgan backing me, I'll be the War Leader. Then we will fight them properly. And this time, we'll win."

Runt smiled at the determination in Calgacus' voice but his own personal grief kept the smile from reaching his eyes.

"I hope you are right," he said softly. "But we will only get one chance. We will need to make it count."

"We will."

"Then let's make sure we reach home safely. It's a long way."

"We'll get there," Calgacus assured him. "But right now I am going to get some sleep."

He lay down, pulling his cloak tightly around his body. Silently, he told himself that everything would work out when they got home but the memory of Brennus' words, *I want nothing from you,* chimed through his restless mind, keeping sleep at bay. He

151

rolled over on the hard ground, trying to make himself comfortable. Then he worried because when he had told Runt it would be over soon, his friend had smiled. It had been a smile of hope, but hope for what? The two of them had faced death often enough but for the first time, Calgacus began to fear that the ending Runt was seeking would be a final one.

He sighed. Life, he reflected, was becoming complicated.

They sold the horses at the village on the shore opposite Ynis Mon, to the same trader they had purchased the mounts from. The man offered them barely half the price they had paid to buy the animals.

"You're kidding!" Calgacus exclaimed. "You sold us five horses but you're buying seven for less than we paid."

The trader gave a careless shrug.

"That one's a Roman horse," he replied, pointing to the mount that Brennus had stolen. "A man can get into trouble having one of those."

His eyes lingered on Brennus and Calgacus knew that the man had guessed the young warrior's identity.

"You're a bloody thief," Calgacus growled menacingly, stepping close and thrusting his head towards the merchant's face.

The trader realised he had made a mistake. He swallowed nervously and promptly increased his offer, producing a small collection of bronze and silver rings. Calgacus bullied him into also providing a tunic and cloak for Brennus who had lost his clothes at the battle and had travelled the length of the country wearing only his trousers. He had not complained but he took the clothes with a nod of thanks, fastening the cloak with a bronze brooch that Tegan produced from her small backpack.

As they were leaving the sullen merchant, Calgacus said to Brennus, "You'd better take off that torc from around your neck."

"Why?" bridled Brennus as he touched a hand to the thick circlet of gold.

"We may have some bargaining to do to get passage home. If people see that, they will think we are rich. Or they'll guess who you are and ask a ridiculous price. They might even decide to turn us in to the Romans. Better to keep it out of sight."

For a moment, he thought Brennus was going to argue but the young man tugged the torc loose, handing it to Tegan who shoved it into her backpack. She had already removed her own, more slender, torc which suggested to Calgacus that she, at least, was thinking ahead.

Satisfied that they looked like nothing more than a band of rebel warriors, he led them directly to the shore where they purchased passage across to the island. The boat was small and rocked alarmingly when they stepped into it but they made the short crossing without mishap. On the far side, they were greeted by a small band of ragged warriors and nervous druids who grew even more anxious when they heard the news of the battle.

Brennus hung back, still maintaining a barrier between himself and the others. For the first time, Calgacus was grateful for his son's dark brooding. He knew how druids thought, so he announced his own name but did not divulge who any of his companions were because he suspected that if the old longbeards discovered Brennus' identity, they would insist on sacrificing him to the gods in an attempt to gain divine aid to drive away the Romans. He wondered whether Brennus had realised that this was the real reason he had told him to remove the torc. Probably not, he decided. Brennus was too wrapped up in his own anger to think straight.

It did not take long to learn that there were only a few druids on the island. These remnants of a once proud tradition were far removed from the more gentle and subtle ways that Cadwgan had adopted on Iova. These were men of the old school, the men who believed that only blood sacrifice could persuade the gods to aid the free tribes. In the past, Calgacus would have argued with them, for he had seen sacrifice after sacrifice performed and still the Romans had been victorious. He had no time for druids, especially not for these dregs of the ancient calling. Masking his distaste, he simply told them that the Ordovices had been defeated, then asked where he could find a boat to take him and his companions north.

One of the druids directed him to a small cove on the eastern side of the island, not too far from the strait that separated Ynis Mon from the mainland. It was a place that sailors used to beach their boats for the winter and there they found Risciporus.

The shipmaster was overseeing the loading of cargo onto his boat which lay in the small bay. He greeted them warmly, though his face fell when he learned what had happened to the Ordovices.

He gave Brennus an appraising look before saying to Calgacus, "I see you found your son."

"Yes."

Calgacus introduced Brennus and Tegan, though neither of them gave Risciporus more than a curt nod.

The Captain gave a shrug, ignoring their poor manners, then asked Calgacus, "I suppose you want to sail back north?"

"That's right. When can you leave?"

"It's not that easy," Risciporus replied evasively. "The season is coming to an end. There will be gales and storms. It is a dangerous time to make such a long journey. I was planning one short trip to the south, then I was going to haul the boat ashore for the winter. The hull needs to be checked over. Caulking and other repairs are always needed, you know."

"That would not be wise," Calgacus told him.

"Oh? Why not?"

"Because the Romans are probably coming this way."

"They'll wait till next year," Risciporus asserted.

"Maybe, but I don't want to wait that long. I need to get home now."

Risciporus looked uncertain.

"It is too dangerous," he insisted.

"I will make it worth your while," Calgacus told him. "How much do you want for our passage?"

The Captain's expression softened slightly. The dangers of the journey suddenly appeared to be less serious when faced by the prospect of making a profit. He gave a small smile as he scratched his chin.

"How much have you got?"

Casca led his small troop into the village at a gallop. There was little resistance. The villagers had seen the Roman infantry approaching, just as the Governor had intended. Some had fled to their small boats, frantically making for the doubtful sanctuary of the island across the strait. Others had run south, hoping to escape from the advancing soldiers and head into the distant hills. Anticipating this, Agricola had sent his cavalry to block off that route, catching the barbarians in a classic pincer attack.

Eager to find Brennus and Calgacus, Casca's troop led the way, outstripping the other cavalry units.

The villagers panicked when they saw the horsemen charging towards them. Some turned, heading back into the village. Others tried to run past the Romans, while many simply stood still, resigned to their fate. That fate was death, and Casca's men were happy to deliver it. Their lances stabbed as they rode into the helpless Britons.

Yelling at his men to show no mercy, Casca swung his own heavy sword. He cut down one woman, his sword smashing her skull to bloody pulp, then he rode down a teenage boy who had run at him waving a short knife. Guiding his horse with the pressure of his knees, Casca sent the boy reeling and charged on.

As he entered the huddle of roundhouses, he hacked down an old, grey-haired man whose twisted and gnarled legs slowed him so much that he could not escape.

Casca called to his men to stay together. Killing these helpless savages was all very well but he was in search of bigger prey. Leaving the other cavalry squadrons to hunt down and finish off the scattered villagers, Casca led his troop deeper into the cluster of roundhouses. There were Roman foot soldiers approaching from the opposite direction, darting into the houses, dragging out any Briton who had attempted to hide, and killing them on the spot. The houses were being burned, the livestock seized. The Governor had decreed that there should be no rape, because rape was a barbaric crime and his men were civilised, but the barbarians had rebelled and so must be destroyed. As with every other task they undertook, the Roman soldiers carried out that destruction quickly, efficiently and ruthlessly.

Casca reined in, whirling his horse to look all around. He had hoped to see a band of barbarian warriors defying the attack. He wanted to see the two big men, Brennus and Calgacus, offering resistance so that he could ride them down, trample them under the hoofs of his horse, then hack off their heads as trophies to be presented to the Governor.

He looked in vain. There was no sign of the men he wanted. Cursing, he told his men to rest their mounts, then he sent four of them to plunder the nearest homes before the legionaries took everything of value. Not that there would be much worth looting here, he thought ruefully, but perhaps they would find some freshly baked bread or bannocks.

155

The Governor and his escort arrived in a flurry of hoofbeats, Agricola's red cloak flapping in the air behind him. As he slowed, his helmeted head turned towards Casca.

"Any sign of them?" he asked tersely.

Casca raised his faceplate.

"No, Sir. They must be on the island."

"Then we have them," declared Agricola. "I am sending men across as soon as I can muster them."

He paused as he saw Casca's expression.

"What is troubling you?" he asked.

"They have some boats, Sir. What if they sail away?"

"There is a galley from the Imperial Fleet heading this way," the Governor told him. "It will be here soon."

"Permission to join that galley, Sir? I'd like to be sure of cutting off their escape."

The Governor nodded, "You may do as you see fit."

Then he was off again, riding fast to gather the troops who would make the assault on the island. Tacitus and the other members of the Governor's staff and bodyguard hurried after him, raising a cloud of dust that hung in the air behind them.

Sdapezi looked at Casca enquiringly.

"What next?" the Decurion asked.

Casca noticed that Sdapezi's lance was unbloodied. He considered making some comment about the man's squeamishness over killing barbarians but decided against it. It was possible that Sdapezi had cleaned the blade while he had been busy speaking to the Governor. Casca doubted that but he had larger issues to consider than his Decurion's dislike of slaughtering unarmed savages.

Giving himself time to think, Casca unfastened his water flask from the rear of his saddle. He took a long drink while he considered his next move.

Wiping his lips with one sweat-stained hand, he announced, "If we cross with the soldiers, the rebels might escape by sea. But if we board the galley, they might stand and fight on land. Someone else will find them before us."

Sdapezi gave a sour grin.

"So either way we could be buggered."

Casca stared across at the island. He could see the dark shapes of people gathering on the shore as the small flotilla of boats that had fled the mainland scrambled onto the beach. There had been a great battle on that same beach years before, when Governor Paulinus had stormed the island. The druids had been all but exterminated but the rebel Queen, Boudica, had raised a revolt, forcing the Governor to call off the final work of hunting down the few survivors. There would be no such mistake this time. Already, Agricola was gathering his lightly armed auxiliary troops, men from Britannia and Batavia, men who knew how to swim carrying weapons. Many of them used inflated pigs' bladders to help them stay afloat. Others simply swam. All of them streamed into the water, heading directly for the island.

Casca watched, still pondering what to do. The druid's sanctuary had as good as fallen already, he knew. There were scarcely two hundred men waiting to meet the attack and they would be swept aside easily enough. He scanned the far shoreline, looking for any men who were taller than average, but he could see no sign that his quarry was there.

"Calgacus is a runner," he said, half to himself. "When that lot run, he won't stand."

Snapping out of his musing, he spoke to Sdapezi in a voice full of official authority.

"If some other men kill them, they will still be dead. That is the main object. Let's find that galley in case they try to flee."

"Very good, Sir," Sdapezi acknowledged with a formal air, as if he believed the order to be a waste of time.

Nevertheless, he called the men back, assembling the troop, barking at them to hurry.

Turning his back on the island, Casca led them east, along the coast. This was a gamble, he knew. The sailors of the Imperial Fleet had no great love for the Army. No galley commander would allow horses on board his ship, that was certain, but Casca reasoned that he would either find Brennus and Calgacus on the sea, where a horse would be no use, or on the island, where he would not need horses to hunt them down. This time, he would catch them.

Chapter XVI

Cawrdaf came running towards the ship, his arms waving frantically.

"The Romans are coming!" he yelled.

His face was flushed with exertion, his breath heaving in his chest as he reached them.

"They are swimming across the strait," he gasped, as if he could scarcely believe what he had seen. "Hundreds of them. There are thousands more on the far shore."

Calgacus immediately turned to Risciporus.

"We must leave. Now!"

The shipmaster waved a helpless hand towards the stores his crew were loading into a coracle before transferring them to the ship that lay a little way offshore.

"We're not ready," he said.

Calgacus gripped the man's shoulder.

"We leave now, or we are all dead. Move!"

Risciporus was too stunned by the ferocity in Calgacus' tone to offer any resistance. He turned, shouting at his crewmen to drop what they carried and to get to the ship. While the bewildered sailors scurried off, Calgacus and his men hurried towards the boat.

Risciporus had floated the ship off the beach and dropped the heavy, stone anchor. His crew had been loading supplies by ferrying them across on the tiny coracle. It was a time consuming exercise but it meant that the ship did not have to be pushed off the beach while fully laden. The precaution proved its worth now. Calgacus plunged into the sea, ignoring the sudden chill as he ploughed into the water. As he went, he waved at his men to get aboard quickly.

Brennus lifted Tegan as if she weighed nothing and carried her in his arms as he waded into the water. The sailors paddled the coracle towards him but Brennus sent them away.

"Get the ship ready," he told them. "I can manage."

The water was up to Calgacus' waist by the time he reached the boat. Runt, following behind, was submerged to his chest, with the gentle swell of the waves sending water lapping up to his face.

The sailors who were on the boat reached down to help them aboard. The ship heeled alarmingly as the men grabbed the sailors' outstretched arms and began to clamber up. Dripping with salty water, they hauled themselves up into the boat.

As soon as he was aboard, Calgacus turned to reach down for Tegan. Brennus hoisted her high and Calgacus caught her, lifting her easily over the ship's side. She staggered against him as he landed her on her feet. When she clutched at him for balance, he could not help noticing the soft feel of her body beneath her dress.

He cursed silently. This was no time to be thinking of such things.

"Sit over there," he told her, pointing to the benches at the far side of the boat, furthest from the shore.

Tegan scrambled away, obedient as always. Calgacus' eyes lingered on her retreating back for a fraction longer than they should have. Then Brennus was clambering aboard, water cascading from him, pooling on the planks beneath his feet.

The sight reminded Calgacus that he, too, was dripping sea water everywhere. The slight breeze chilled his legs as the wet cloth of his trousers clung to his skin. It was a sodden, uncomfortable sensation but he knew that if he was able to feel the discomfort, it meant that he was still alive. Now he had to make sure that they all stayed that way.

He lined his three young warriors near the ship's port side, where they stood awkwardly with their legs braced on either side of the ends of the rowing benches.

"Shields ready!" he commanded.

He asked Cawrdaf, "How long before they get here?"

The young warrior shrugged uncertainly.

"Not long."

Runt had drawn his swords and was trying to dry them off while he scanned the shore. He pointed.

"There are already people running away from the far beach," he observed.

Calgacus turned to Risciporus who was sitting by the steerboard, barking orders. One sailor, a huge, bald-headed, bull-necked man, hauled the heavy, stone anchor aboard while the rest

159

of the crew untied the lines that held the furled sail in place. The huge sheet flapped loose, fluttered noisily in the breeze, then was caught by the sailors who tied yet more lines into position under Risciporus' directions.

The wind filled the sail almost immediately. Slowly at first, the ship edged away from the shore, then it picked up speed as it edged away from the shelter of the cove and the westerly wind pushed it on.

Calgacus shivered. The sea breeze was cutting through his sodden clothing, the smell of salt lingered all over him and his feet squelched in his boots whenever he moved. Despite the danger, his mind seemed to focus on these small, irrelevant details. He knew that he often reacted that way, that his brain wanted to take in everything around him. It was a habit that still annoyed him although he understood that it was a way of handling the situation, a mechanism to allow his instincts for battle to take charge. He was at his best when he did not have too much time to think about what he needed to do, so he allowed his mind to occupy itself with small matters while his subconscious worked out what he should do.

He looked back to the shore where he could now see people running in panic. Then the soldiers came into view over the low rise that overlooked the cove the ship had just left. The Romans were running after the fleeing Britons, their swords bright and hungry for blood.

Brennus clambered over the benches to stand beside Calgacus. In a low voice, he growled, "We should have stayed. We should fight them."

"We would die," Calgacus told him.

Brennus pointed angrily to the distant people, now mere small, dark shapes against the green of Ynis Mon.

"They are our people!" he snapped. "We should protect them."

"There are not enough of us," Calgacus replied calmly. "I don't like it any more than you do but we cannot protect them."

"You are only saying that because you do not know them," accused Brennus. "If it was your home, your family, you would fight."

"Possibly," Calgacus conceded. "But I like to think I would not be foolish enough to set up home where the Romans could catch us so easily."

160

He shook his head sadly as he went on, "I am sorry. There is nothing we can do. There is an entire Legion coming this way. Six of us could not defeat them."

Brennus glared at him.

"So you only fight when you think you can win, is that it?"

Once again when faced with Brennus' accusations, Calgacus struggled to keep his own temper under control. Why, he wondered, did all his conversations with his son turn into arguments?

He retorted, "No. I only fight when I *know* I can win."

Brennus spat in disgust, "That is not the way of a warrior."

Calgacus' voice rose angrily as he insisted, "It is the only way we will beat the Romans. People have been trying for years and failing because they think they can win by making loud boasts, by parading in their war paint and strutting up and down on an open field, daring the enemy to attack. But that is exactly what the Romans want us to do. That is what they train for, what their Army is designed to do. Believe me, I know what I am talking about. We cannot defeat them if we fight the old way. We must fight to win, by whatever means we can. If that means refusing to stand and face them, then that is what we must do. They are not invincible. I know, because I have beaten them before, but if we are to have any hope of defeating them, we must use our brains to outwit them. Stay with me and I will show you how we can do it."

It was a long outburst, and one that attracted the attention of everyone around them, but Brennus' nostrils flared as he lowered his voice to a menacing whisper.

"You may have won a few victories when you were young, but you are an old man now. I think you have lost whatever courage you ever had. There is nothing you can teach me."

Before Calgacus could react, Runt stepped between them.

"Now is not the time for this," he warned.

He jerked his head to indicate the sailors and the young warriors who were watching them with appalled expressions.

The two big men stared at each other, neither willing to back down. The air between them almost crackled with the tension and anger, but Risciporus' shout of alarm broke the spell.

"A war galley!" he cried.

All eyes turned to see where he was pointing. Along the coast, its square sail furled, but with its oars splashing the surface of the water as they moved in perfect unison, a long, low, deadly and sleek warship was heading straight towards them.

Calgacus squelched his way to the stern and sat down beside the Captain.

"Can you outrun them?" he asked.

Risciporus looked around, as if seeking some inspiration from the sky and the waves. He gave Calgacus a smile that radiated confidence.

"It won't be easy," he replied, "but if anyone can, I can. The hard part will be getting past them and out into open water before they ram us."

"How hard?" Calgacus asked.

Risciporus shrugged, "It depends on how good a seaman the Captain is. But we have the wind behind us and I know a trick or two."

"And if you can't get past them?"

"We surrender or we fight," Risciporus answered.

"I won't surrender," Calgacus growled.

"I didn't think so," the Captain grinned.

Calgacus hurried back to his men.

"Clean your weapons," he ordered. "If Risciporus can't get us away, we will need to fight."

"So you think you can win, then?" Brennus asked sarcastically.

"We can bloody well try!" Calgacus snapped. "I suggest you prepare yourself."

Brennus turned away but he drew his sword and grabbed a rag from the sailors to clean the blade.

With a frustrated shake of his head, Calgacus turned his attention to his own sword, carefully wiping the shining blade to remove the salt water. The last thing he wanted was a rusted sword. He almost laughed aloud when he realised that the sword would probably not have time to rust before the Romans caught them. The chances of an old sailing ship outrunning an oar-powered war galley were slim, to say the least.

The ship's sail was bulging now, the vessel rocking and dipping as it moved out into the deep water, driven on by a strong westerly breeze. Calgacus looked at Risciporus who jerked a thumb back over his shoulder.

"I'd say there is a storm coming," the Captain informed him with a cheerful grin. "That will either save us or kill us."

"If the Romans don't kill us first," muttered Runt.

Calgacus looked forwards, beyond the taut cloth of the sail, towards the galley. It was closing fast, heading as if to cut them off, but Risciporus appeared to be doing nothing to avoid it.

Calgacus looked back at the Captain once again. Risciporus was sitting in his habitual place at the stern, his hands clutching the steerboard while he shouted to his men to make minor adjustments to the rigging.

Frowning with concern, Calgacus called out, "You are heading towards them!"

Risciporus replied with a manic grin.

"I know. Just watch. And sit down. This could get rough."

Calgacus ducked under the sail and perched himself on top of the forward hold, a deep, rectangular chest of solid oak which he knew would provide a better platform for fighting than the awkward rowing benches.

He turned his attention back to the galley. It was close now, perhaps only four hundred paces away. It was long, its sleek hull low in the water. A single bank of oars drove it towards them, the blades of the heavy, wooden oars digging into the water to power the boat through the deep swell in a regular, practised rhythm.

He had heard stories that some Roman galleys were monstrously large, with as many as three banks of oars. This one was no giant but it was still nearly twice the length of Risciporus' ship.

Like all war galleys, it was designed for speed, the rowers able to make steady headway even when heading into the wind. Calgacus was convinced that, despite Risciporus' apparent confidence, the clumsy cargo ship could not hope to outrun the galley.

He gripped his sword tightly. Idly, his left hand ran down the length of the bronze armour that covered his chest. It's hard coldness reminded him of Risciporus' warning about what would happen if he fell into the sea wearing a breastplate. He briefly considered taking it off, then dismissed the idea. If it came to a fight, he would need it. The thought of drowning sent a shiver of fear through his bones but he vowed that he would not jump into the sea whatever happened. Better to die fighting, he decided.

163

He studied the approaching galley once more. He had told Brennus that he only fought when he knew he would win, but this time there was no option except to fight. He recalled a conversation he had once had with his older brother, Caratacus, when the great King was teaching him the art of warfare. Caratacus had been a War Leader before he became King, and had fought many battles. When the Romans had invaded, the tribes had tried to fight them in the traditional way and had been defeated.

Caratacus had learned the lesson quickly. Calgacus had a brief mental image of his brother, sitting on a tree stump, carefully oiling and polishing the blade of his mighty sword, the same sword that Calgacus himself now carried. While he worked, Caratacus had spoken to his younger brother about the ways of war.

"There is a trick to it," Caratacus had told him. "An easy one to remember but a difficult one to put into practice."

"What is it?" the young Calgacus had asked.

He had been fifteen years old, little more than a boy, but he had been desperate to learn the ways of a warrior.

Caratacus had smiled as he worked his oily rag up and down the shining blade.

"Planning," he had said. "Deceive your enemy. Fight on your terms, not his. Forget honour and glory. Fight to win."

"That doesn't sound so difficult," Calgacus had frowned.

"It's not. Not if you have the talent. But most men don't have it. They blunder in and hope for the best. That is the difference."

He had smiled again, that familiar, confident smile that Calgacus missed so much.

Then Caratacus had added, "Victorious warriors win first and then go to war; but defeated warriors go to war first, and then try to win."

It was a lesson Calgacus had never forgotten. Now, faced by the approaching galley, he desperately sought a way to win the inevitable fight.

The sea was not his home. He felt uncomfortable on the constantly moving boat and knew it was a poor choice of battleground. The rowing benches impeded movement and the wooden planks were wet and slippery underfoot. If the Romans boarded them, the fight would be messy and brutal. This, he knew, was not a good place to make a stand.

He studied the Roman galley again. Unlike Risciporus' ship, the rowing benches were inside the hull, covered by a wide, flat deck around which ran a low, wooden rail. He could see men standing on that deck now, men in armour, men with swords ready. They, too, were taking a chance by wearing heavy armour, but they, too, were ready for a fight.

Runt remarked, "I heard once that their ships have a ram at the front, beneath the waves. They will try to ram us and sink us."

"That's what Risciporus said," Calgacus agreed.

"Then why is he heading straight for them?" Runt wondered.

"He says he knows some tricks."

"They'd better be bloody good ones," Runt muttered. "I don't fancy fighting here."

"We won't," Calgacus replied. "We'll take the attack to them. When they hit us, we should climb onto the galley. There's more room and a flat surface."

Runt sucked in his cheeks as he considered the idea.

"Risky," he commented. "They won't stand back and let us do that. Their deck is a lot higher than us and we'll be easy targets as we try to climb up."

"I know, but it's better than standing here on a sinking boat."

"You have a point there," Runt agreed. "All right. I'll tell the lads."

He moved off and Calgacus saw him put a hand on Adelligus' shoulder. Father and son, facing death together.

Calgacus looked to the far side of the boat where Brennus was busy wiping his sword blade while Tegan sat behind the rear storage hold, her eyes fixed on the approaching galley. Calgacus knew that he should speak to Brennus, that this could be their last chance for reconciliation, but their argument still hung over him like a dark storm cloud. Every time he had tried to speak to Brennus he had been rebuffed. His pride would not let him try again. Let Brennus do whatever he wanted. Calgacus would show him that, old or not, he still knew how to fight.

Runt and the others scurried under the flapping sail and gathered round the forward storage hold. Calgacus gave them an encouraging smile as they clustered around him. Adelligus, Cawrdaf and Dunnocatus had determination etched on their young faces as they watched the distance between the two ships close to a hundred paces.

"How many of them?" Calgacus asked, knowing that Runt's keen eyes would have counted the enemy soldiers.

"Thirty on deck. That bastard Casca is one of them," said Runt.

"He's a determined sod," Calgacus observed. "I suppose I'd better kill him first."

He turned, making a point of addressing the three young warriors.

"All we have to do is kill five each and we've won," he told them as cheerfully as he could.

"What about the rowers?" Adelligus asked. "There are lots of them."

Calgacus laughed, "One problem at a time."

He pointed to the galley as he went on, "Look, some of those men are obviously marines. They're used to fighting on ships. The others look like that fellow Casca and his cavalry. They won't be used to it at all. Kill them first, and the others will lose heart."

Dunnocatus gave a nervous laugh.

"I'm not used to it, either," he pointed out.

"Then you'd better learn quickly," Calgacus told him. "Remember, go for their faces. Don't waste time hitting their armour unless it is just to gain an opening."

Runt asked, "What about Risciporus and his men?"

Calgacus looked around. Some of the crew were big, tough men who looked as though they would be handy in a fight. Several of them had found heavy cudgels and wicked iron spikes and had gathered near the prow in readiness to repel the Romans, while a few of them concentrated on constantly adjusting the sail in response to Risciporus' shouted commands. They had tugged some of the sail up so that only around two-thirds of it was catching the wind. Calgacus wondered why Risciporus was not using full sail. Then he heard the splash of oars and he knew it did not matter because the galley was coming for them.

"Hold on to something!" Risciporus yelled.

His face wore a wide grin as the ship suddenly leaned to the right. Calgacus and his warriors felt the hull tip beneath them as the Captain made a sharp turn that took his ship on a direct collision course with the galley.

166

Risciporus laughed aloud when he saw the look of alarm on Calgacus' face.

The Captain shouted, "They want to ram our side, not the prow. Now watch!"

Calgacus saw some of the Romans on the galley's deck waving their arms and shouting orders. Risciporus' unexpected change of direction had surprised them but they were still heading directly towards the merchant ship. They were so close now that he could make out the frothing surge of water where the bronze-covered ram jutted from the galley's prow just beneath the surface of the waves.

Calgacus swore.

"We need to get to the front," he said.

"The prow," Runt corrected.

"Just bloody well get there!" Calgacus shouted.

Before they could move, Risciporus yelled, "Wait!"

Then he waved a hand to his crewmen.

"Full sail! Now!"

As the sailors released the sail, Risciporus hauled hard on the steerboard, putting all his weight into guiding his ship into another frantic, lurching turn. The sail cracked open, bulging as the blustering wind filled it and the ship heeled to the left.

Calgacus, who had half risen with the intention of reaching the boat's prow, stumbled backwards with the force of the movement. He felt himself slipping as his sodden boots failed to gain a purchase on the wet planking and he toppled over, almost losing his grip on his sword as he flailed for balance and fell backwards, sliding under the sail.

Then his son's hand caught his arm as Brennus braced himself against the rear storage hold and steadied him.

Calgacus gave a sigh of relief. If he had fallen, he might have tumbled over the side of the ship and plummeted into the dark depths that still seemed to lurk beneath him at an awkward angle as the boat leaned precipitously on its desperate turn.

Then, thankfully, the ship righted itself, the sea fell away and the world resumed its proper place.

Calgacus exhaled with relief.

"Thank you," he said to Brennus. "That was close."

Brennus did not reply but a flicker of a smile crossed Tegan's face as she said, "You should be more careful."

167

Calgacus turned as he felt the ship begin to roll again, this time in the opposite direction.

"Sit down!" yelled Risciporus.

Brennus yanked Calgacus down to the bench behind them and they sat side by side, Brennus' fingers clamped around Calgacus' upper arm as the Roman galley loomed above them.

Calgacus swore when he saw how close they were and he realised that a collision was inevitable.

"Hold on!" screamed Risciporus.

Calgacus felt helpless but the wily sea Captain had judged things to perfection. He steered his boat so that it dodged the galley's ram and shot past the Roman ship under full sail, too far away for the marines to leap down but close enough so that its surging prow smashed into the ends of the galley's oars.

His unexpected manoeuvre had caught the galley's Captain completely by surprise.

Calgacus felt the impact juddering through the hull as the ship smashed into the leading oars. He heard the splintering of wood, saw great lengths of broken oars fly up into the air, heard the screams of the rowers as the ends of their oars were flung violently, ripped from their hands by the force of the impact to smash into the heads and backs of the rowers sitting in front of them.

Risciporus turned again. The impact had slowed his ship but he moved it away, seeking open water, leaving the galley floundering with half a dozen of its oars on the starboard side having been smashed. In moments, Risciporus had left the galley behind.

Calgacus looked back to the warship. On the deck, the figure of Casca was running to the stern of the galley as he watched in helpless frustration while his quarry moved further away from him.

Calgacus quickly checked that Runt and the others were safe, then he hurried back to Risciporus. The Captain gave him a nod of welcome.

"I told you to hang on," he scolded, as if he had done nothing of any great importance.

"I wasn't expecting that," Calgacus admitted.

"Neither were they," Risciporus grinned, jerking his head back to indicate the galley. "I told you we could outturn any Roman ship. But it is only a brief respite. Once they sort themselves out and get turned round, they'll have the wind off their beam and they'll be able to use sail as well as oars."

"So they'll catch us?" Calgacus asked.

"Not for a while," Risciporus replied calmly. "I know these waters better than most. There are currents and tides I can use to help keep us ahead of them. For a while at least."

"What happens after that?" Calgacus asked.

"I'll head for shore and let you off. I can always claim you forced me to take you on board."

Calgacus shot the Captain a look, trying to gauge whether the man was serious. He suspected that he was.

"To be honest, I'd rather fight them on dry land, but try to get us as far north as you can before it comes to that."

"I shall do my best," Risciporus promised.

Calgacus stared back towards the galley, amazed at how much distance Risciporus had already put between them and their pursuers. The Roman warship was dead in the water, the oars still. It fell further behind with every passing moment but eventually he saw the oars splash and the warship began to move, turning in a wide arc. As it turned, he saw the large, square sail being lowered from the cross-beam of the mast.

"I hope you have some more tricks ready," he said to Risciporus.

The Captain replied, "No, but look at the sky behind them."

The western horizon was dark, a band of storm clouds stretching as far as Calgacus could see.

He smiled, "I sometimes think that Taranis is watching over me."

Risciporus frowned at the mention of the god of storms and thunder.

"Well, he'll drive them to seek shelter," he said. "If they have any sense. We should do the same."

"Not until after they have," Calgacus told him. "Use the storm to hide us from them."

"I had a feeling you were going to say that. There is a good chance we will all die if the storm catches us."

"Maybe, but we will definitely die if the Romans catch us."

Risciporus grinned, "A most persuasive argument. Very well. Let Taranis do his worst."

Standing near the prow on the deck of the galley, Casca could hardly contain himself. He knew that he should not criticise a fellow officer in the presence of the men but he could not help himself. With his own troopers and two dozen marines watching, he rounded on the galley's Captain.

"We must catch them!" he insisted.

The Captain was a grey-haired, burly man with a weather-beaten face that had seen twice as many years as Casca. He knew that he had made a mistake in underestimating the barbarian vessel but who could have expected a tiny cargo ship to act like a trireme? Yet he was reluctant to admit his mistake and Casca's anger only served to make him more intransigent. Instead of rising to the Centurion's baiting, he simply waved a hand towards the sky beyond the stern.

"Even you can surely see that?" he blustered. "We must make landfall or we will be swamped. This is just a small, coastal galley. It can't survive a storm."

"The barbarians are not heading for land," Casca retorted, pointing to the distant sail that was carrying Brennus and Calgacus to safety.

"Perhaps they are blind," the Captain shrugged dismissively. "But they are not in a war galley. We cannot survive a high sea. I have injured men aboard and even if I didn't, a storm will just wash over a low ship like this. I will not risk my entire crew. We are heading for shelter."

He turned away, clearly indicating that the conversation was at an end.

Casca clenched his jaw. He saw his men watching him, waiting to see how he would react.

"Stand down," he snapped at them. "We will resume the search once the storm has passed."

The troopers gathered into a huddle on the exposed deck, eyeing the approaching storm nervously, while Casca turned to stare northwards at the receding sail, his fists clenched in tight balls of fury.

The gathering wind drove the boat onwards through an increasingly rough sea. Risciporus maintained full sail as long as he dared but, after a couple of hours and with the Roman galley lost beyond the horizon, he eventually ordered the crew to lower the sail to prevent the wind ripping the huge leather sheet from the mast.

As the crew worked feverishly to furl the sail, he gave Calgacus a worried look.

"We have left them a long way behind us but we must find shelter soon. This storm is going to be a bad one."

Calgacus pointed to his right, where he could still see the dark shadow of land on the horizon.

"The coast is not that far away, surely?"

"Open water and no safe beaches," Risciporus responded. "We'll still be exposed and the ship will be smashed on the shore. A Roman shore, I might add."

He jerked his head, pointing with his chin as he went on, "There's a bay I know a little way ahead."

Calgacus staggered as a heavy swell made the boat lurch. He regained his balance, suddenly aware that the nausea he had previously experienced when at sea had returned. The prospect of combat had banished it for a while but now it was back. He swallowed, tasting the bile.

"Can we get there before the storm catches us?" he asked the Captain.

For the first time, Risciporus' face betrayed real concern as he admitted, "I don't think so, my friend. We have run out of time. You had better start praying to Taranis to preserve us from his fury."

"How bad will it be?" Calgacus asked anxiously, all too aware of the looming storm clouds that now seemed to be racing across the sky in pursuit of their escape.

Risciporus gave him a wry grin as he asked, "Have you ever ridden a wild horse down a mountainside in the middle of the night?"

"No."

"I thought not. Try to imagine it."

"It sounds bad," Calgacus frowned.

Gravely, Risciporus informed him, "You misunderstand. This will be much worse than that. I suggest you sit down and hang on as best you can."

Calgacus and his comrades huddled near the stern, clutching onto the benches as the boat began to rise and fall alarmingly. Calgacus soon discovered that what he had thought were rough seas on their first voyage had, in fact, been plain sailing.

As the skies were darkened by towering, black clouds, the waves grew in size and ferocity, their tops decorated by surging, white spray. The boat soon began to resemble a child's toy tossed around on the surface by the power of the ocean.

Rain began to fall, a few spots at first and then a torrent that hammered down on them and pooled on the planks beneath their feet. The rain was, though, the least of their problems as the west wind buffeted and battered at them and drove the sea to a manic frenzy of violence.

Risciporus steered the ship as best he could, somehow managing to evade the most malevolent surges of the sea, but several waves almost swamped the vessel, crashing salt water down on them and forcing the sailors to risk their lives by grabbing buckets and frantically baling the water out of the hull while Risciporus attempted to prevent the next monstrous wall of water drowning them all.

At one point, Calgacus closed his eyes when a vast wave rose up behind them, its height so immense that he needed to raise his head to see its foaming crest. With a skill that Calgacus would have believed impossible, Risciporus coaxed his ship into riding the wave but the boat rose and fell with a stomach-churning motion that ended with a jarring splash which almost drove the prow under the seething water.

Calgacus and his companions were helpless, huddled together under their cloaks, peering out at the rain and heaving sea with nothing better to do than offer prayers to the Gods to preserve them while the ship lurched, rolled and pitched and the heavens poured down.

All the time, Risciporus sat at his post, both arms wrapped around the long pole of the steerboard. His hair was plastered to his head and his clothes were drenched. His eyes were constantly moving, peering in every direction, trying to see through the gloom that had descended as the heavy clouds blanketed the sky above them. He shouted defiance at the skies, gripped the tiller and fought to guide his ship through the teeth of the storm to safety.

Calgacus' senses soon became numb. The rain drummed on his hooded cloak, the ship heaved and rolled beneath him and he was pushed and pulled from side to side by the motion of the vessel in a seemingly neverending torment of wind and water. The ship, which had never seemed substantial to his eyes, now felt as fragile as a flower.

After what seemed an eternity of wild motion, the Captain let out a yell of delight that was loud enough to be heard over the cacophony of the storm. Calgacus lifted his head, wiping the rain from his face as he peered towards the front of the ship.

"The land is close," he told the others. "We are nearly there."

Then the steerboard snapped.

The ship had been struggling, but still surviving despite the battering it was taking from the rain, wind and waves. Risciporus had guided it up the seething side of yet another mountainous wave and managed to retain control as the ship plummeted down the far side of the crest into a deep trough, splashing so fiercely that the bow momentarily vanished from sight. It had surged upwards again but a sudden cross-tide had pitched the vessel to starboard.

Risciporus had felt the movement and had tried to react. He knew these waters and understood that he was approaching the shallows. In normal circumstances, he would have been ready for the sudden change in the direction of the waves but it was so dark and his senses had been so dulled by the pummelling of the rain that he did not sense it coming until it was upon them.

As he tried to compensate, another monstrous wave materialised out of the darkness. It smashed into the side of the wallowing ship with awesome force, swamping the hull with spray and salt water. The ferocity of the surge snatched the steerboard from Risciporus' grip. The long, wooden arm caught the Captain on the chest, sending him reeling. Even as he fell, he heard the sharp crack of snapping wood as the rudder was broken in two.

Calgacus scrambled across the rain-soaked rear benches to catch Risciporus.

"Are you hurt?" he asked, his voice almost lost in the drumming of the torrent and the howling of the wind.

"Of course I'm hurt!" Risciporus snapped back. "But nothing broken, thank the gods."

He pushed himself up to a sitting position, then looked into Calgacus' face with fearful eyes as he moaned, "But the ship is lost. We are at the mercy of the waves."

Risciporus' crew, who had been helpless for some time, were now scrambling to find anything that would float, ripping

173

open the holds and hauling out every object they thought might save them. Then, with the boat floundering beneath their feet, they splashed their way to the stern where the Captain had pulled himself to join Calgacus' group. The sailors passed over wooden battens, a small barrel and some broken bits of planking which Risciporus distributed among the passengers.

"When you get in the water," he instructed, "hang on to these and kick for shore. Be ready when I give the word. We don't want to get caught when she starts to go down. And you'd best dump your armour and weapons."

"Not yet," Calgacus said. "We must be close to land."

"You'll drown when she goes down," Risciporus told him.

"I'll wait a bit longer," said Calgacus.

The fear of being plunged into deep water gnawed at him but he remained stubbornly determined not to lose his armour and weapons unless there was no other choice.

The sailors returned, bringing more large pieces of wood for themselves. Their faces were masks of fear as they clung to whatever they could and waited for the end.

Somehow, the ship survived. With the hull half submerged in sea water, it had gained some stability but it was still being lashed by the storm. Driven by the relentless waves, it lurched towards the coast.

Rain and sea water continued to swamp the hull, pouring into the holds and swirling around beneath the rowing benches, slowly forcing the vessel lower and lower in the water.

Risciporus' face was set hard as he contemplated the destruction of his beloved ship but the vessel did him proud, somehow holding together as it limped ever closer to the shore.

"We're going to make it!" Calgacus shouted, trying to encourage the others.

The coast was close now, barely fifty paces away. The shoreline was deserted. Calgacus could see a low ridge, topped by long grass, edged by a narrow strip of shingle where the waves crashed onto the land. Beyond the grassy hummocks, trees were leaning, their branches swaying and waving violently in the wind that howled all around them.

Risciporus scrambled to his feet, hanging onto the side of the ship for balance.

"We're going to run aground!" he yelled. "We must get off before she breaks up."

174

He gestured to the others to follow him but a great swell lifted the ship and drove it onto the shingle where it was slammed down with a jolt that flung everyone across the benches in a tangle of arms and legs.

The ship rolled, pitching them down towards the surf. The receding waves tried to pull the vessel off the shingle but the wind held it to the shore and the succeeding waves pushed against the hull, driving the boat onto the land.

Calgacus grabbed for the side, hanging on grimly to avoid falling into the seething water. All around him, limbs and bodies were tumbling in a tangled heap.

One of the sailors leaped down, splashing into the surf. The waves drove his legs from under him but he staggered upright and waded for the shore. Where he had first fallen, the water was no more than waist deep.

Calgacus yelled at everyone to jump down. He shoved at the nearest man, Dunnocatus, urging him over the side. Dunnocatus twisted, hung onto the edge for an instant, then dropped into the water. In moments, he was scrambling clear and the others were following him as they swarmed to escape the ship, Brennus clinging to Tegan's arm as he led her into the pounding surf.

A great crack of snapping wood filled the air, cutting through the deafening tumult of the storm.

Risciporus grabbed Calgacus' arm and yelled, "Go! The mast has broken."

The long pole of the mast swept down like a tall tree felled by a woodsman's axe. The end of the cross-beam thudded into the shingle, narrowly missing one of the sailors who leaped away in alarm.

The ship heeled again, forcing Calgacus to hang on desperately. He made a quick check. He and Risciporus were the only ones still aboard. With a heave, he swung himself over the side and dropped into the cold water.

He gasped with the shock but immediately made for the shore. The waves battered against the backs of his legs, impeding his progress but every stumbling step took him closer to safety. As he neared the shore, his left foot slipped on the pebbles under the seething surface, sending a stabbing pain shooting up the back of his leg. He grimaced with pain but hauled himself ashore, limping badly.

Runt met him with a manic smile.

"We made it," he grinned. "We're alive."

"Did everyone get off safely?" Calgacus asked.

"Yes," confirmed Runt. Then he asked, "What's wrong?"

"My leg. I think I've torn my calf muscle."

Runt gave him a look of sympathy but the little man's relief was evident as he said, "That will mend. The main thing is that we are safe. I can't believe we got here."

"Wherever here is," Calgacus muttered.

He turned to Risciporus who was standing on the shingle beach, drenched to the skin but seemingly oblivious to the raging storm as he watched the wreck of his ship with sad eyes.

"Where are we?" Calgacus asked the Captain.

Risciporus, looking bereft and somehow smaller now that he was on land, tore his gaze away from his wrecked ship. He gave a weak shrug.

"Somewhere in Brigantia," he replied.

Runt's mouth twisted in a bitter grimace.

"Oh, shit," he groaned with feeling.

Part II – Brigantes

Chapter XVII

At some point during the dark, rain-drenched hours of the night, the storm died away, leaving the survivors wet, cold and exhausted but very much alive. The sky was now overcast, with a sullen drizzle ensuring that everything and everyone remained sodden.

As soon as it was light, Risciporus and his crew returned to the hulk of their ship to see whether they could salvage anything of value. They returned with a few tools, an axe, two spears that had washed up on the shore and some coils of rope.

"The food supplies are ruined," Risciporus reported glumly.

He gave off the air of someone who had lost a loved one and Calgacus supposed that, in a sense, he had. His beloved ship was now a shattered wreck, smashed beyond repair.

Brennus ignored the Captain's plight.

"There must be villages near here," he declared. "We can find food there."

"Yes, there's one a short distance up the coast," Risciporus agreed without enthusiasm.

Calgacus immediately put in, "No. It is too dangerous. The Romans will come looking for us. When they see the ship, the first place they will look will be the nearest village. We should head inland."

"Who put you in charge?" Brennus demanded angrily. "Anyway, you can hardly walk."

That was true. Calgacus' calf was agony whenever he tried to take a step but he was too proud to admit the full extent of the pain. While most of the others were on their feet, he was sitting on a tussock of wet grass, his leg stretched out in front of him.

"I will manage," he insisted. "As for being in charge, my men and I are used to war on land. Runt and I have experience of avoiding the Romans."

Brennus blew a snort of air down his nose.

"How long ago was that?" he sneered. "Not for many years, I'll bet."

Before Calgacus could respond, Runt stepped between the two men. Turning to face Brennus, he said, "Show some sense, boy. We need to work together if we are to get out of this. Brigantia is not a place we want to be found, not by the Romans or by the locals."

He rolled his eyes as he added, "And I am getting fed up of keeping you two apart. We cannot afford to argue."

His words had no effect. For days, Brennus had been struggling to suppress his anger but now it boiled over. He loomed over Runt, glaring down at the little man. With a snarl, he drew his dagger and held the blade up, turning it menacingly in front of Runt's face.

"I don't have to do what you say," he hissed. "I am King of the Ordovices and I should be in charge. Anyone who wants to argue will have to fight me."

Tegan breathed a soft cry of dismay while Risciporus and his men edged away, watching carefully. Adelligus, Cawrdaf and Dunnocatus all reached for their swords.

Runt stopped them with a wave of his hand, signalling to them to stay out of the argument. All the time, his eyes remained fixed on Brennus.

Calmly, Runt said, "Put that away and don't be so bloody stupid. If you want to be in charge, you'll have to fight all of us because we follow Calgacus. You can't kill us all. Even if you do, all you'll be in charge of is yourself."

Brennus stared hard but this time Runt's words seeped through his anger. After a few tense moments he slowly lowered the knife, placing it back in its sheath at his waist. He tossed his hands in the air as he turned away in disgust.

"Do as you please," he sighed. "But we need food, water and dry clothes. Where will we get them from if we don't find a village?"

He stalked away to join Tegan who was standing watching, her eyes wide and her face deathly pale. With an angry thump, Brennus sat down on the grass beside her and lowered his head, refusing to look at anyone.

Risciporus gave a nervous cough.

"If I might make a suggestion?" he asked.

For a moment, nobody spoke. Then Calgacus tore his eyes away from Brennus and nodded, "Go ahead."

"My men and I could go to the village. We could purchase some supplies, then rejoin you further inland. We are obviously seamen, not warriors."

"That's a good idea," said Calgacus.

Casting an eye over Risciporus' crew, he thought that some of them looked every bit as tough and unsavoury as any warrior, but they did have the air of the sea about them and their story of shipwreck would be believed without question. They were as wretched and wet as any men he had ever seen.

He suggested, "When you have bought some supplies, tell them you are heading back south."

"Of course," Risciporus agreed.

The decision made, the party split into three small groups. Risciporus and his eight men went north along the coast. Calgacus, Runt and their three warriors headed inland, moving slowly because Calgacus' sore leg forced him to hobble rather than walk.

The third small group comprised only Brennus and Tegan, who followed at a distance.

Adelligus found a fallen tree branch which he skilfully stripped with his knife then presented to Calgacus to use as a walking stick. Calgacus took it gratefully. Using the stick, he was able to walk a little faster but every step was agony, sharp shards of pain running the length of his calf. After three hours of stumbling across the wild countryside, he was forced to call a halt.

"I need to rest for a bit," he explained apologetically as he lowered himself to a convenient boulder.

Runt sent Adelligus and Cawrdaf to search for somewhere they could hide in shelter while he crouched beside Calgacus.

"Can you keep going?" he asked in a concerned voice.

"Not much further," Calgacus winced. "I should have stopped a while ago."

Runt pursed his lips thoughtfully.

"If we keep heading inland, we'll reach the hills. There are caves and all sorts of places we can hide up there."

"That will take two or three days, even if I could walk properly," Calgacus pointed out.

"We could try carrying you."

"With Brennus watching and laughing at me? No thank you. I'll keep going somehow."

179

He looked up at his friend and lowered his voice as he went on, "By the way, thank you for what you did back there."

Runt shrugged, "It was nothing. He wasn't going to use the knife. He's just feeling lost and angry."

"He's not the only one," Calgacus muttered glumly. Resignedly, he added, "Come on, then, we'd better get going."

Runt looked doubtful as he reached out to help Calgacus to his feet.

He said, "That injury will take at least a moon to heal, you know."

"I know."

"So we need somewhere safe to hide. We'll need food and water. And right now, we need a fire to dry ourselves out."

"I know that too, but the wood is damp and will produce too much smoke. We can't risk it."

"Well, there is one good thing," Runt said.

"What is that?"

Runt gave a wry laugh as he explained, "Things can't get much worse."

As they resumed their slow trek, Adelligus returned with the news that he and Cawrdaf had found a wood nearby.

"There's a river, and some small caves. Well, overhanging rocks, really, but they will give us some shelter."

"Good lad," Calgacus said with feeling. "Let's get there. Then you young lads had better go back and look for Risciporus."

It took almost an hour for Calgacus to haul himself to the woodland. It was deep and long, following the twisting contours of a narrow stream. The trees were almost bare, their leaves having fluttered down to carpet the ground in a soggy layer of gold and muddy brown. Calgacus swished his way through them until they reached the river, where they found a small hill, little more than a rocky outcrop, by the water's edge. There, they huddled under the overhanging rock, eager to escape the persistent drizzle that had dogged them all morning.

With a sigh of relief, Calgacus sank gratefully to sit on a large stone, massaging his calf as he rested.

Runt looked around.

"We could risk a small fire here," he decided. "The trees will break up the smoke."

Calgacus was too tired and sore to argue, so Runt set about gathering some of the drier twigs and soon had a small fire going.

It was a puny thing but it gave the illusion of warmth, which was welcome. The three young warriors, though, were soon off again, searching for Risciporus and his men so that they could guide them to this small sanctuary.

Tegan knelt on the ground beside the fire, holding out her hands in an effort to warm them. After watching her for a moment, Brennus stalked away, muttering something about checking their surroundings.

"I see he's still in a good mood," Runt observed.

"You shouldn't have threatened to kill him," Calgacus said.

In response, Runt gave a low chuckle.

Tegan gave him a curious look before turning to look at Calgacus.

"What do you mean?" she frowned. "Brennus had the knife. It was him who was threatening to kill your friend."

Calgacus gave her a smile despite the pain from his leg.

"Runt wasn't in any danger," he assured her. "I'm just glad it didn't come to a fight, otherwise Brennus would have been hurt."

Tegan frowned as she regarded Runt curiously.

"I don't understand," she said. "Brennus is a mighty warrior. Everyone is afraid of him."

She paused, then looked directly at Runt, an expression of dawning realisation on her features.

She asked him, "You weren't afraid, though, were you? Why not?"

Runt gave her a smile as he explained, "He wasn't serious about it. He wouldn't have tried anything."

Tegan looked uncertain.

"You can't be sure of that," she frowned.

Runt merely shrugged.

Calgacus put in, "One thing you can be sure of is that if he had tried anything, Runt would have beaten him. He's almost as good as me."

"Except that I'm more modest about it," Runt added.

Tegan looked from one to the other. The two men smiled, then began laughing. Soon she had joined in. It was the first time Calgacus had seen her laugh and he thought it made her look much prettier.

The three of them were still chuckling when Brennus returned. He scowled darkly as he sat a little way from them, under the edge of the sheltering rocks.

"What's so funny?" he asked sourly.

Tegan lowered her eyes, spluttering slightly as she tried to stifle a laugh. Calgacus told him, "We were just saying how nice it is to rest our old bones."

That set Tegan off again and Runt soon joined her laughter, leaving Brennus scowling suspiciously.

Risciporus returned with some smoked fish, half a lamb, some cheese, stale bannocks and a small leather bag filled with pulses. But he returned without six of his crewmen.

"A couple of them have families who might still be alive," he explained ruefully. "The others said they didn't fancy being hunted through the wilds and would take their chances with the Romans."

Brennus growled, "You should not have let them go."

"I am a Captain without a ship," Risciporus shrugged defensively. "I cannot offer them employment, so I cannot tell them what to do."

"But they could tell the Romans where we are," Brennus persisted.

Calgacus intervened, saying, "They don't know where we are."

Brennus was not to be mollified. He rasped, "They could still put the Romans on our trail."

Jabbing a finger at Risciporus, he snarled, "You should have insisted they come back here first."

"Why?" the Captain frowned.

"Because then we could have dealt with them."

Risciporus blanched as Brennus' meaning became clear but Calgacus told his son, "That is enough! They are not here and that is an end to it."

"You would not have killed them anyway, would you?" Brennus challenged.

With an edge of steel in his voice, Calgacus stated, "No, I would not."

"You are too soft," Brennus sneered scornfully. "You will get us all killed."

The others held their breath, anticipating another argument but, as if resigned to Calgacus' lack of resolve, Brennus turned away to resume his place at the far end of the shelter.

Calgacus said to the Captain, "Ignore him. The rest of us are very grateful that you and your two companions came back. I take it that means you don't have any families to return to?"

Relaxing slightly after the shock of Brennus' aggressive response, Risciporus shook his head.

"Not so as you'd know," he admitted.

The two men who had remained with him were almost complete opposites. The first was a rather timid, softly-spoken man with slim build and a shock of dark hair that he tied back in a long pony-tail. His name was Ulcattus. Calgacus judged him to be in his early twenties.

The second sailor was the big, bald man Calgacus had noticed before. He was not very tall but he was barrel-chested and heavily muscled. His massive bull-like neck was wrinkled at the back and his arms were liberally decorated with tattoos depicting all sorts of sea monsters. Calgacus had watched him on the ship and been impressed by the brute power the man possessed in his arms and legs. His name was Ger. Risciporus had more than once indicated that he was not the most intelligent of men, although he was fiercely loyal to his Captain.

"Thank you for coming back," Calgacus said to all three of them.

"We have nowhere else to go," Risciporus admitted glumly. "We don't want to live under the Romans, so we thought we'd head north. There are quite a few chieftains who are always keen to hire good sailors. You're going north, so we'll stick with you."

He sat down beside the fire once more and asked, "So what do we do now?"

"Nothing," Calgacus replied. "I need a few days for my leg to heal. We will need to hide out here for a while. We have food and we have shelter. We'll be safe enough for a little while."

While Calgacus and his small band of refugees huddled in their camp, the Romans were also making their plans. With the Ordovices crushed and Mona conquered, Agricola had returned to the legionary fortress at Deva where he had commandeered an office in the Principia.

Tacitus could tell that his father-in-law liked Deva. The fortress that dominated the slightly raised ground overlooking the river had been Agricola's nominal home during his tenure as Legate of the Twentieth Legion, although he had spent much of that time waging war against the fierce Brigantes whose territory lay to the north. The fortress was strategically placed to separate the Brigantes from the tribes of the west, although Tacitus supposed that function was less essential now that the western tribes had been brought to heel.

Agricola had been effusive in his praise of the legionaries. Thanks to their speedy destruction of the rebels, the province was at peace. For now, at least. The Governor would keep his troops in winter quarters until spring returned. Then he would march north. His first task would be to ensure that the Brigantes remained subservient. After that, he would tackle the northern tribes.

"There is no reason why we cannot conquer the entire island within three years," he announced to his son-in-law.

Tacitus could not argue with him. If the stunning victory over the Ordovices was anything to go by, the barbarians would fall before the Legions like wheat beneath a scythe. Privately, Tacitus wondered whether the island might not be conquered in less than the three years the Governor had set himself.

The Governor looked up from his desk as he signed the last of the heaped parchments and writing tablets that his secretaries had brought him.

"Well, Publius," he said, "I think we deserve a rest this evening. In the morning, I want to visit the town and speak to the leading citizens. I want them to see that Rome cares about them and wishes them to become like us."

"Yes, Sir," Tacitus replied.

His father-in-law's energy remained a constant surprise to the young Tribune. Agricola rarely seemed to become tired, so the prospect of a relaxing evening was welcome. Visiting the town next day would no doubt be a tedious procession of meetings and pep talks as the Governor made a point of being seen by the local inhabitants and being interested in their affairs, however mundane they might be.

There was already a burgeoning Roman-style town growing up around the fortress but Agricola never seemed to be satisfied with the rate of progress in converting the Britons to Roman ways. Time and again he stated that he wanted bath-

184

houses, theatres, temples, schools. He wanted to see Roman tunics and togas being worn. He wanted to hear the local people speaking Latin. Surprisingly, despite Agricola's apparent impatience with the pace of change, these things were happening. It seemed to Tacitus that most of the Britons he met were only too glad to become part of the empire. It was another of the bizarre contrasts that this island province produced so readily. The people of Deva were happy to embrace Roman culture but only a few days' march to the south-west, the Ordovices had been the very model of barbarian savages.

The secretary picked up the papers that Agricola had signed. Then he gave a slight cough to attract the Governor's attention.

"There is an officer to see you, Sir," he said. "He has been waiting for some time."

Agricola replied with a wave of his hand.

"Of course. Show him in."

The secretary crossed to the door. He went through, then re-appeared in the doorway as he ushered in the Centurion, Casca, who strode to the Governor's desk, his ornate helmet tucked under his left arm.

The secretary closed the door as Casca stopped before the desk, saluted and said, "Greetings, Governor."

"Relax, Casca," Agricola replied soothingly. "There is no need for formality here."

Casca's stance barely softened. As if he had not heard the Governor's words, he announced, "I regret that I have failed you again, Governor. Brennus and Calgacus have eluded me."

Agricola sat back on his chair. A faint smile hovered around his lips as if he found something amusing in the Centurion's message.

He said, "I had a report from the Captain of the galley you were on. What was his name, again? Ah, yes. Corvus. He wrote a very lengthy description of events."

"Sir?" Casca asked, unblinking.

"A very lengthy report indeed," Agricola informed him. "I read it most carefully. The man seems incompetent."

For the first time, Casca's shoulders appeared to relax slightly although his face remained impassive.

"That is not for me to say, Sir," he replied cautiously. "I am no sailor."

"Neither, it seems, is Corvus. To have his oars broken by a merchant ship is the height of incompetence. If it had been a warship you were chasing, I might have understood. But a small merchant ship? No, that particular galley will require a new commander, I think. Captain Corvus would be better suited to other duties than patrolling hostile waters."

A flicker of satisfaction crossed Casca's eyes but he said nothing. He remained standing at attention in front of the desk.

Agricola went on, "So, tell me what you found."

Casca cleared his throat before beginning his report.

"When the storm abated, I persuaded the Captain to put back to sea. I instructed him to head north in the hope of catching the rebels."

Agricola smiled, "Yes, he mentioned that in his report. He claims you threatened to cut his balls off if he did not go in search of the barbarian ship."

"He must have misheard me, Sir," Casca stated. "I merely reminded him of his duty and the urgency of the mission."

"Indeed. Go on."

Casca continued, "We found the barbarians' ship wrecked on the shore, sir. There was no-one on board, and no bodies. It was hard to tell because the storm had left so much damage, but we think they headed inland. As we had no horses, I told the Captain to go on to the next coastal village. The people there said that some sailors had come, asking for food. They claimed they had been shipwrecked."

"Sailors? What about Brennus and Calgacus?"

"No, Sir. They were not among the group."

Tacitus ventured, "The villagers could have been lying."

A hint of irritation crossed Casca's face at the implication that he had not considered that.

He replied, "I don't think so, Sir. We questioned them very closely but they would not change their story. Nobody matching the descriptions of the rebels was there. I am certain of that."

Tacitus studied the Centurion's face, wondering whether the officer's definition of close questioning was the same as his own. He suspected it was not.

Agricola said, "So, Casca, it seems your mission is not yet at an end."

Casca visibly brightened at that.

"Sir?" he asked expectantly.

"Give my apologies to your men," the Governor told him, "but I need you to continue the hunt. The Army will be staying in winter quarters for at least the next five months, but I want you to go north, into Brigantia, to see if you can find these rebels."

"Yes, Sir!" Casca almost shouted.

The Centurion's whole body was suddenly like the taut ropes of a ballista, ready to explode into action.

Agricola motioned to him for caution as he warned, "It will not be easy, for I expect they will travel north as quickly as they can. Do your best."

Casca nodded briskly, "Of course, sir."

Agricola regarded him thoughtfully, then said, "If you can, bring one of them back here alive. Either Brennus or Calgacus, It does not matter which."

"Alive, Sir?"

"If possible. A captured barbarian King would be useful. He could be sent to Rome as a gift for the Emperor."

Casca nodded, "I understand, Sir. But it may not be possible. We may be forced to kill them if they resist."

"Do your best, Casca," said Agricola. "Alive if possible, but dead will do."

"Yes, Sir."

Casca understood the order well enough. Roman Generals were no longer permitted triumphal marches through the imperial city, for these spectacular processions were reserved for members of the Emperor's family in case any commander should gain too much popularity. But sending a famous captive back to the Emperor would gain the Governor much honour, triumphal regalia and significant political influence.

Personally, Casca wanted to remove Brennus' head from his shoulders but he recognised that personal satisfaction was a short-term victory. If he wanted to please the Governor, he would need to produce a living rebel. He consoled himself with the thought that he could kill Brennus and hand Calgacus over. That way, everyone would be happy.

Agricola went on, "While you are in Brigantia, scout out the land for me. Locate any hostile villages or hillforts. Speak to the chieftains. Remind them that they have agreed not to oppose us when we march north. They are supposed to be our allies now but some of them may have forgotten that."

"Yes, Sir."

187

Casca seemed to have grown taller as he listened to the orders. He was struggling to contain his excitement, impatient to set off in pursuit of the rebels.

Agricola gave a curt nod.

"Very good, Casca. You may go."

Casca saluted. "Thank you, Sir."

He nodded to Tacitus, then spun on his heel and marched out, closing the door behind him.

When they were alone, Tacitus asked his father-in-law, "You don't really expect him to scout out the whole of Brigantia, do you? He only has ten men in his troop."

"Of course not," Agricola replied with a thin smile. "But I want him out of the way for a while, and this gives him something to do. His unit was ambushed, his reputation tarnished. If he stays with the army, there will inevitably be trouble. There will be taunts and snide remarks from other officers and Casca is not the sort to accept that treatment without reacting. It will lead to fights. I don't want that. On the other hand, he would be wasted on garrison duty, so this little project will keep him busy and also keep him where he won't cause any unnecessary difficulties for us. You never know, he may even find the rebels."

"He certainly seems very driven," Tacitus observed.

"Yes, he is a ruthless, heartless bastard," Agricola remarked agreeably. "I wish I had a few more like him. Pity the barbarians if he does catch them."

"You will need to reward him if he succeeds," Tacitus pointed out.

"Of course. Promotion and glory for young Casca if he brings me Brennus or Calgacus. Obscurity and scorn from the rest of the army if he fails."

"No wonder he is so determined," Tacitus said softly.

For a brief instant he wondered whether it would be a good thing if Casca were to succeed. In Tacitus' opinion, promoting such a dangerous soldier might create more problems than it solved.

Calgacus' leg was slow to heal. The fugitives remained hidden in the wood for four days, by which time the food was running low. Fortunately, the rain and drizzle had died away, allowing them to dry out their sodden clothing, but autumn was definitely turning to winter, bringing overnight frosts, chill winds and damp mornings.

Runt approached Calgacus saying, "We can't stay here. There is not enough proper shelter for all of us."

Calgacus stood up, gingerly flexing his leg. He grimaced but gave a determined nod.

"Let's move on then. I should be able to keep going long enough for us to get into the hills."

Gathering up their few possessions, they left the woodlands, heading north and east, away from the coast and towards the chain of rugged hills that formed the spine of the territory of the Brigantes. Calgacus, though, soon found that his leg was far from healed. The sharp, stabbing pain continued to shoot up the back of his leg every time he took a step. Flexing the muscles to walk uphill was especially painful but he had no alternative. Gritting his teeth, he hobbled on with the aid of his stick.

It was not a happy travelling party. Brennus continued to sulk, rarely offering to help anyone and often muttering snide remarks about the decisions Calgacus made. Tegan, always quiet, stayed close to Brennus. As the only woman in the group, she knew that she was the object of many hungry looks from some of the men. To avoid trouble, she never strayed far from Brennus, who growled threateningly at anyone he thought was taking too much interest in her.

Calgacus was in too much pain to concentrate on very much else, which worried Runt who walked protectively alongside his friend, anxious to ensure that no more harm came to him. That anxiety spread to the three young warriors who were only too happy to escape the tension by walking ahead, scouting the land, leaving Risciporus and his two sailors to trudge along at the rear. These three walked warily, unused to overland treks and clearly uncertain about where they were supposed to fit in to the disparate group they found themselves with.

On the third day of their trek, they climbed the first of the hills. By the fourth day, they were deep into the wilds. Just after mid-day, they found an abandoned hut high on an upland plateau, a place where some local tribespeople obviously came in summertime to watch over their sheep and cattle while the livestock grazed the high pastures.

The hut was crude but serviceable, with walls of wooden stakes and turf, topped by a poorly thatched roof. Runt pushed aside the tattered leather flap that covered the solitary doorway.

Inside, the hut was littered with debris. Broken pots, old rags and torn waterskins had been dropped indiscriminately all over the smooth, earthen floor. There was a small hearth near the centre, a circle of stones surrounding blackened, long-cold ashes. The place was hardly welcoming but it was spacious enough to provide shelter for all of them. A small stream trickled down the hillside not far away and there were trees further down the slope where they could gather firewood.

Calgacus, his face bathed in sweat, dropped to the ground outside the doorway.

"It will have to do for a while," he said, grimacing in pain as he massaged his leg. "I'm going to need a few more days before I can get up and about properly."

They quickly set about making the place habitable, piling the rubbish outside, filling their waterskins and chopping wood. Before long, they had a fire crackling in the hearth, filling the cold hut with smoky warmth. Then they gathered bracken and heather for bedding, piling it up around the edges of the hut.

"Just like home," remarked Runt as he deposited another armful of bracken against a side wall.

Food was their main problem. They all knew that snow often fell on the high ground. The longer it took for Calgacus' leg to heal, the more chance there was of winter snow leaving them trapped high in the hills. Without a regular supply of food, they faced starvation. Even with careful rationing, the supplies Risciporus had obtained were almost gone.

"There must be a village nearby," Calgacus said. "Lots of the Brigantes spend their summers up in the hills at places like this, but they go back down to their villages for the winter. The people who built this place must live near here."

"Then we'd best look for them and see what we can get," said Runt.

Risciporus asked, "Won't that be dangerous?"

"It's either that or starve," Runt pointed out.

Calgacus delved inside his small leather belt pouch. He distributed pieces of silver, some of them coins, some rings, some simply broken pieces of the precious metal. He also had a few old-fashioned bronze and iron circlets of the type that had been used as currency before the Romans brought their minted coins to the island.

"Pay for whatever you need," he told them. "Let them think that you are rebels, still holding out against the Romans. From what those villagers told us earlier, there are probably quite a few war bands roaming these hills."

Brennus snorted, "They are more likely to think we are bandits."

"Then make sure they are frightened of you so that they feed us," Calgacus told him. "But don't do anything more than threaten. And don't even threaten unless you have no choice."

For once, Brennus made no comment. He merely shrugged as if to imply that he would do whatever he thought best.

The men divided themselves into pairs, each couple setting off in a different direction, leaving Calgacus alone with Tegan. She busied herself arranging the piles of bracken into neater bundles, then went to gather more firewood. When she returned, she fed the flames, then piled the wood she had gathered inside the door where it would remain dry. Satisfied, she sat by the fire, holding her hands to the flames to warm them.

Wanting to break the awkward silence, Calgacus said to her, "I am sorry about this. If my leg was better, we would be a lot further north by now. Even on foot, we would reach my home before Midwinter."

Tegan looked up briefly but quickly lowered her eyes.

"It is not your fault," she said softly. "Nobody else blames you. They all follow you willingly."

"Not all," he reminded her.

She almost smiled as she replied, "Brennus? He is still angry, but he has nowhere else to go."

Calgacus asked, "Why is he still angry? I am doing my best to make him welcome. I want him to come home with me, to be a part of my family."

"Do you not know?" Tegan responded, as if she thought the reason for Brennus' hostility should be obvious.

"No. I wish I did. Then I could do something about it."

Tegan shook her head.

"You cannot do anything about it," she assured him. "He is angry because you were right."

Calgacus frowned, "About what?"

Tegan sat back, lifting her knees and clasping her arms around them. For once, she regarded him carefully, her eyes meeting his.

She said, "You told him he could not defeat the Romans. He was a King, and you told him he was wrong, so he wanted to prove to you that he was right. Then he lost the battle and you saved him when the Romans were chasing him. That made it worse for him."

"I can't help it if I am right," Calgacus protested.

"No, but he sees you every day and you are a reminder to him that he failed. That is why he is angry."

"He should try to learn from his mistake," Calgacus insisted. "I lost battles when I was younger. He should listen to my experience rather than sulk about being beaten."

"He has always had to rely on himself," Tegan explained. "It is not easy for him to take advice."

"Yes, I noticed that," Calgacus grunted.

Tegan gave a tentative smile as she ventured, "Your friend, Liscus, says he gets it from you."

Calgacus had not been aware that Runt had spoken more than a few words to the girl but he dismissed the comment with a shake of his head. Running his hands through his long, matted hair, he sighed, "See if you can persuade him that I want him to join with me, to be my son."

"I will try," Tegan promised, although she did not sound confident that she would succeed.

Brennus had been paired with the sailor, Ulcattus, the person who was least likely to argue with him. The two of them had climbed the hill above the hut, with Brennus setting a fast pace. Ulcattus did not protest, but simply followed, apparently unconcerned at the exertion. He did not say much, which suited Brennus perfectly.

They crested the hill to see a vista of more steep slopes, scattered woodlands, rounded hilltops and deep valleys, but far below them they could make out a huddle of roundhouses, smoke lazily drifting from the thatched roofs. There was no stockade, no defensive ditch, but a patchwork of fields and pastures, lined by walls built of stones piled on top of one another. From their high vantage point, they could make out a few cattle, goats and sheep. There was even a large paddock where a dozen horses were penned. It was a sizeable village, and Brennus thought that it looked a prosperous place by the standards of Brigantia.

Some way to the east of the settlement, he could see the unmistakeable heaps of slag which betrayed that the village was a place where men worked iron. That alone would denote it as an important place.

Brennus set off down the steep hillside with Ulcattus silently following on his heels.

As they approached the outer limits of the village, Brennus ordered, "You wait here. I'll go and speak to them. If there is any trouble, go back and fetch help."

Ulcattus nodded. He was used to taking orders and he was more than a little afraid of the big, surly warrior, so he was happy to let Brennus do the talking while he waited at the edge of the small settlement. Quite what help he would be able to bring quickly, he was not sure, for it would take the rest of the afternoon to climb back up the hill and fetch the others. Ulcattus, though, was not going to argue with Brennus, so he hefted the long staff he was holding, made sure his knife was in easy reach, and waited.

Brennus wasted no time. He marched into the village, accosted the first man he saw and demanded to see the head man.

The villager shot him an alarmed look before scurrying off, presumably to fetch the local chieftain.

Brennus waited, knowing that his arrival had created a stir. Children gaped at the huge sword strapped to his back, while their mothers tried to usher them away. Men gave the strange visitor nervous looks. Some surreptitiously fetched axes or other implements they could use as weapons, although none of them looked keen to do any fighting. They hung back, muttering amongst themselves but making no overt move to challenge him. Brennus gave them little more than a cursory look as he waited for the head man to appear.

The village chieftain was an old man, his hair greying and his once burly frame showing signs of flabbiness. He looked at Brennus with unfriendly eyes, then glanced to the waiting Ulcattus, clearly trying to work out whether there were any more men he could not see. In a surly voice, he bade his visitor a formal welcome and announced that his name was Tumnorix.

Towering over the chieftain, Brennus got straight to the point.

He said, "My men and I need food. We are staying in the area for a short while, so will need supplies for a few days."

Tumnorix scowled. With a helpless wave of his hand, he indicated his village.

"We are poor enough as it is," he complained. "We have barely enough to feed ourselves over the winter."

Brennus took a step closer to the old man. Leaning down slightly, he hissed, "Let me make this simple for you. I can pay silver for some food. Meat, grain, whatever you have. But if I have to, I will simply return with more men and take what I need. Do I make myself clear?"

Tumnorix visibly paled.

"But we have already given food to Venutius," he protested. "We cannot give more."

Brennus hesitated for a moment. Even far way in the west, he had heard of Venutius, one time King of the Brigantes, now a renegade, hunted by the Romans.

Fixing his hard eyes on Tumnorix, he asked, "Venutius is nearby?"

Tumnorix shrugged his shoulders as he replied, "He was here four days ago, but he moves around. I do not know where he is now."

"Which way did he go?" Brennus demanded. Then, seeing Tumnorix's reluctance to betray his nominal King, he added, "My men and I have been seeking him. We want to join him."

Tumnorix chose to believe the statement. He waved a hand, vaguely pointing to the east.

"He went that way."

Brennus nodded thoughtfully. After a moment, he said, "Then he is gone and I am here. I want food. Now."

Brennus could see that Tumnorix was considering having him killed but the threat of more brigands was enough to make the old chieftain give in. His people reluctantly produced a small sack of grain, a few half-rotten vegetables and a slab of salted beef. Brennus gave the chieftain a silver ring, hefted the sack onto his shoulder, signalled to Ulcattus to come and fetch the rest, then strode away, leading Ulcattus back up the hill. This time, there was a spring in his step. For the first time since his disastrous battle against the Romans, he felt a sense of purpose. He had found food, which would enhance his standing among the group, but, more importantly, he had learned that Venutius was nearby.

Brennus had heard stories about Venutius' resistance to Rome. Unlike Calgacus, who seemed determined to run from the Romans at every opportunity, Venutius had been fighting them for the past four years. Venutius may have been defeated by the

Romans, may have lost his Kingdom, but he was still leading the resistance in Brigantia, still opposing Rome. He was, Brennus decided, the very opposite of Calgacus.

The fact that Calgacus was his father meant little to Brennus, especially now that he had met the man. For all his swagger and confident words, Calgacus was old and fearful, quite unlike the stories that people told and the songs they sang about him. Brennus felt no loyalty to him. Venutius, though, was a fighter, a War Leader. Brennus vaguely recalled that Venutius had sent the Romans scurrying from his Kingdom when he had first seized the throne from the pro-Roman Queen Cartimandua. Any man who could do that was worthy of respect in Brennus' eyes.

As he trudged up the hill, he decided that he knew what he must do. Let Calgacus skulk back to his home in the wild north with his fanciful dreams of an alliance. Brennus would not go with him. Instead, he would join a real warrior.

He would find Venutius.

Chapter XVIII

Brennus departed early the following morning, taking an obviously reluctant Tegan with him. He stood by the door of the hut, facing the others with an expression of determination mixed with scorn as he announced his intention.

"I am not coming with you," he declared, directing his words to Calgacus. "I have decided to seek some other home here among the Brigantes so that I can continue the fight against Rome."

There was a moment of surprised silence. Then Calgacus forced himself to his feet, ignoring the protests of pain from his injured leg.

"Why?" he asked. "You know nobody here. The Brigantes are already a defeated tribe."

"Some of them still fight," Brennus snapped back. "Anyway, I know nobody in the far north, either."

"You know us," Calgacus countered.

Brennus looked around the hut, his eyes showing nothing but disdain.

When he looked back at Calgacus, he said, "All the more reason for me to leave, I think."

Gesturing to Tegan, he commanded, "Come."

Tegan slowly rose to her feet, reluctantly gathering up her pack.

Calgacus reached out a hand, trying to catch Brennus' arm, but the young chieftain shook off his attempt to make contact.

"Leave me alone!" he snapped roughly. "I have made up my mind."

Calgacus stood in the middle of the hut, not knowing what to do.

"Brennus, please," he whispered, his voice almost choked with desperation. "Son, you must stay."

Brennus pushed aside the leather door-flap, ushering Tegan outside. He turned his head to look back over his shoulder as he followed her.

"I wish you well enough," he said. "But I want to lead my own life. I told you before that I want nothing from you."

Then he was gone.

Calgacus made for the door but Runt intercepted him.

"Leave it, Cal," he insisted as he grabbed his friend's arm. "You'll only make it worse if you go after him."

"But he's my son!" Calgacus protested.

"He's a man. His own man. You cannot control him."

Calgacus shrugged off Runt's grip, pushed through the door and went outside. From the doorway, he watched as Brennus and Tegan, already growing smaller as they headed down the slope, walked away from him. He saw Tegan turn to look back but Brennus obviously snapped at her to keep moving, for she turned to hurry after him. Standing silently, Calgacus watched them for a long time, until they became mere specks of movement against the dull greens and browns of the rolling hills. Then they crested a rise and vanished from his sight.

"Where are we going?" Tegan asked as she hurried along, forced to walk quickly in order to keep up with the pace Brennus was setting.

"To find a new home. To find a real warrior," Brennus replied.

She wanted to ask him more questions but she could tell from his tone that he was in no mood to answer her, so she remained silent.

Under leaden grey skies, he led her north and east, through the hills and woods, sometimes climbing steep slopes but more often staying to the lower ground where they could make better progress.

She grew tired and hungry but she was determined not to protest. She understood why Brennus felt the way he did about his father, but Tegan thought that he was wrong to leave. Calgacus had offered a chance for all the things that neither Brennus nor Tegan herself had ever had. She envied the easy friendship she had witnessed between Calgacus and Runt, marvelled at the unquestioning loyalty, tempered by respect, that the younger warriors showed to Calgacus. Only Brennus could not see his father's worth, she thought to herself.

She had tried to tell him but he had refused to listen, determined to maintain his obstinate hostility. Now they had left

197

the chance of a new life behind them. A safe home among friends was all that Tegan had ever wanted but she doubted that Brennus would find that among the Brigantes.

Yet she followed him. Deep inside, she knew that she did not have to go with him. She was no longer a slave but a free woman. Among the tribes of the Pritani, a woman was not the property of her husband, but Tegan was young, with little experience of anything except the life of a slave. However much she told herself she was free, she did not know how to stand up to Brennus, could not match the strength of his will.

Another voice inside her told her that she must go with him because she owed him more than she owed Calgacus. It was Brennus who had freed her, Brennus who had elevated her to be his Queen, and so it must be Brennus who commanded her loyalty, whatever misgivings she may have about his choices.

Always heading north and east, their trek occasionally took them past isolated farmsteads or small settlements. Whenever they came across other people, Brennus would tell Tegan to wait at a safe distance while he went to speak to them. He did not tell her what he discussed with the locals, but once or twice he changed his course after one of these brief conversations. She often saw arms pointing as if the farmers were giving him directions. Fortunately, these brief halts also allowed Brennus to barter for some scraps of food, although it was rarely enough to satisfy Tegan's hunger.

After three days of walking, during which they were buffeted by winds and showers of freezing rain, Brennus found a village where he spoke to the local chieftain for a long time. When he returned to the spot where Tegan waited, his face was flushed with excitement.

"Come on," he urged. "We are close."

"Close to what?"

"To Venutius," he replied, giving her the first smile she had seen in days.

With Brennus setting an eager pace, they climbed a nearby hill, a long, low, gentle slope of damp grass, liberally dotted with small clumps of woodland. The far side of the hill revealed more of the same countryside, but Brennus set off towards the north, angling for a dip in the ground. Tegan scurried after him, forcing herself on despite feeling as if her legs were about to give way from exhaustion.

She jumped in alarm when, without warning, two men rose from hiding places in a fold in the ground. They each held a long spear and a small, rectangular shield of leather-covered wicker.

"Stop there!" one of them called. "Where are you going?"

Brennus spread his arms wide.

"I am looking for Venutius," he replied. "I wish to join him."

"And who are you?" the spearman demanded, his demeanour full of suspicion.

He could not fail to notice the large sword Brennus carried and the sight was enough to make him cautious.

Brennus did his best to appear friendly.

"My name is Rennix," he said, choosing a name that sounded similar to his own. "I am of the Ordovices."

"You are a long way from home," the sentry commented drily.

"I no longer have a home," Brennus explained. "We fought the Romans and we lost. My wife and I are seeking a new home. We heard that Venutius is looking for warriors."

The two spearmen held a brief conversation in low tones, then the first one signalled with his spear.

"Come on, then. I'll take you to him."

They went down the slope until they reached the edge of a deep fold in the land, a narrow cut that was too small to deserve being called a valley but was deeper and longer than a mere dip on the hillside. All along the foot of the defile were small shelters, temporary homes built of wood with leather hides stretched across the long stakes. One or two tattered, Roman-style army tents were in evidence and in places there were lean-to shelters of wood and hastily cut turf. Small cooking fires sent tendrils of wispy smoke into the chill air and wafted the smell of hot food which clawed at Tegan's empty stomach as she passed.

Men, women and even a few children dotted the scene. Tegan guessed there were at least a hundred people there, many of them spear-wielding warriors. All of them wore ragged, patched clothes that spoke of a life of wandering and hardship.

Their guard led them down to the floor of the defile, then towards one of the tents where a handful of men were standing talking to one another. At the tent's open entrance, sitting on a rock beside a small fire, was a man with long, greying hair and hazel eyes. He wore a torc of twisted gold around his neck, similar to the ones that Tegan now carried concealed in her pouch. The man's fingers were decked with golden rings and his cloak, once of finely woven wool but now rather worn and faded, was fastened by a large, golden brooch. Beside him, a scabbarded sword was propped against another stone.

The standing men moved aside as Brennus and his escort reached the tent.

The guard announced, "Lord, this man says he is of the Ordovices and is fleeing from the Romans after his tribe was defeated. He says he wants to join with you."

The seated man looked up, his eyebrows arching. Tegan thought that he had a handsome face, although time and the hard life he led had given him a rather weary appearance. She supposed he must have been very good-looking when he was younger, although something in his manner disturbed her, as if he felt that speaking to them was beneath his dignity.

His mood changed when he saw Brennus. His eyes widened in surprise as he looked the big man up and down. He seemed about to say something, but thought better of it, then turned his gaze over Tegan who had hung back slightly, hoping to escape his notice. A faint smile crossed the man's lips when he saw her, then he looked back at Brennus, giving him an expansive smile, all trace of haughtiness gone from his expression.

"You want to join me?" he asked, tilting his head slightly to one side.

"You are Venutius?" Brennus asked in turn.

The man gave a slow nod.

"I am. And you are?"

"Rennix. Of the Ordovices."

"Ah, you obviously have a story to tell us," smiled Venutius.

He gave a gentle wave of his hand as he indicated the other men.

"These are my most trusted followers," he explained.

The assembled warriors gave Brennus a range of welcomes, from curt nods to hard, suspicious stares.

Venutius, still the only one who was seated, went on, "So tell us your tale, Rennix of the Ordovices. Your tribe has been defeated, you say?"

Brennus nodded. He could sense an undercurrent of danger here, a suspicion on the part of his hosts. He supposed that their suspicion was inevitable since these men were themselves outcasts, fugitives from the Romans. That was bound to make them distrustful of strangers. Venutius himself was displaying a front of friendliness but the man's eyes were cold and calculating. Brennus understood instinctively that, whatever the others thought of him, Venutius was the man he must convince.

Speaking slowly, Brennus related how the newly-arrived Roman Governor had led his legion against the Ordovices and how the tribe had been slaughtered.

Venutius listened patiently. When Brennus finished, the one-time King of the Brigantes sighed, "Sadly, that is a familiar story. We have fought the Romans many times but our victories are rare."

He waited for Brennus to say something but the big warrior remained silent, so Venutius observed, "I had heard that a man named Brennus had declared himself King of the Ordovices."

Brennus managed to keep his expression impassive as he nodded, "Yes."

"What happened to him?"

Brennus shrugged, feigning indifference as he replied, "He is probably dead. The Romans over-ran the battle-line and he was in the front rank."

Brennus had hoped that explanation would satisfy Venutius but the Brigante chieftain seemed to have an unhealthy interest in the fate of the Ordovices' King.

He asked, "This Brennus. He claimed to be the son of Calgacus, did he not?"

Brennus had hoped that news of his rebellion might not have reached this far but Venutius seemed well informed. Too well informed for Brennus' liking but he was committed now.

Giving a cautious nod, he agreed, "So he said."

"Was it true?"

"How would I know?" Brennus responded gruffly.

Venutius gave an amused half-smile as he shrugged, "Of course. Well, if it was true, he clearly did not inherit his father's skills. Calgacus was no friend of mine but even I have to admit that he knew how to fight. The Romans would not have defeated him so easily."

Brennus felt the hairs on his neck bristle. His anger was rising once again, anger that this stranger had compared him to Calgacus and found him wanting. It took all of his willpower to

201

force himself to remain outwardly calm. Yet he also had to stifle an impulse to ask questions of his own. He could see that Venutius was old enough to be a contemporary of Calgacus, though the Brigante War Leader looked somehow older and more worn down by time than Calgacus, but Brennus had never considered that the two men might have known one another.

Trying to shift the subject away from his estranged father, he asked, "May I join your war band, Lord? I know how to fight."

"I am sure you do," Venutius smiled. "Very well, Rennix. Welcome to the tribe of the Brigantes."

Brennus inclined his head.

"Thank you. You will not regret this."

"Oh, I am sure I won't," Venutius agreed smoothly. "Einon here will find you somewhere to sleep."

He gestured towards a young, fresh-faced warrior who had been eyeing Brennus warily ever since he had arrived.

Einon looked none too pleased at being commanded to this duty, as if he thought it was beneath him to act as a guide to newcomers, but although his eyes sparkled angrily, he did not voice any protest.

As if he had not noticed the young man's reaction, Venutius continued, "In a few days you will be able to show me just how useful you can be."

Brennus raised an eyebrow in question.

"Lord?"

"All in good time, Rennix," Venutius cautioned with a grin. "All in good time."

With a nod of his head, Venutius indicated that the audience was at an end. Einon led Brennus and Tegan away as the small gathering around the tent broke up. The young Brigante showed them to a small clump of stunted trees at one end of the defile.

"You can gather wood from here," he told them. "I'll send some others to help you build a shelter. I'll get someone to bring you some food as well."

"Thank you," Brennus replied.

Einon left them, giving Tegan an appraising look as he passed her. She could sense his hostility towards them but despite his unfriendly manner, he was as good as his word, sending half a dozen women and two young warriors to help construct a

202

makeshift shelter. All of them seemed wary of their new companions but they worked willingly enough.

One of the women brought a slab of bread and some goat's cheese which Tegan devoured ravenously. She was so hungry that it tasted better than any food she could ever remember.

The Brigantes worked quickly and efficiently but Brennus made no effort to appear too friendly towards any of them. He knew that being welcome in this group would depend on how valuable Venutius found him, not on how much the others liked him, and he did not want to get too close to anyone until he learned how the inevitably complex social structures of the group were organised. He was also more rattled than he would care to admit by Venutius' interest in Calgacus. There was, he decided, only one way to ensure he was accepted. He resolved to forget all about his past. Brennus was dead, killed by the Romans, just as he had told Venutius. He was Rennix, son of a minor chieftain of the Ordovices. And he had never met Calgacus. He told himself that if he stuck to this story, nobody would ever learn the truth.

Einon scowled as he approached Venutius. The King was still sitting on his stone seat, sipping a steaming mug of honey-flavoured tisane that one of the women had brought him. He glanced up as Einon squatted down to face him.

"Well?" the Brigante chieftain asked.

Bluntly, Einon replied, "I don't trust him."

"Of course you don't," Venutius smiled. "I have taught you not to trust anyone."

Einon blew a snort of air down his nose. What Venutius said was true enough. The old King had chosen Einon as one of his closest companions and advisers some years previously, admitting him to his inner circle when Einon was scarcely more than a boy. Despite his youth, Einon was intelligent and had proved to be a quick learner. He was not sure why Venutius had selected him, though the King's war band was small enough and mere chance could have been the explanation. Einon, though, had heard the whispers that said he was Venutius' bastard son. Nobody had ever said it to his face and the whispers had not even begun until the man whom Einon had always thought of as his father had been killed in a skirmish with the Romans.

Einon's mother had died some years before, taking the truth of his birth to the grave with her, so the only person he could ask with any certainty of discovering his true parentage was Venutius himself, but Einon had no wish to jeopardise his favoured status by being so blunt. The King had never given any hint that he regarded Einon as anything other than a young man of intelligence and promise. For the moment, Einon was happy to leave it at that.

A position as an adviser to Venutius was dangerous enough in any event. The King had lost a procession of Captains over the years, many of them to violent deaths. Einon was in no hurry to join that list.

Now, as he considered the latest member of their small war band, he said to Venutius, "I think there is something he is not telling us."

Venutius waved his beaker vaguely towards the spot where a shelter was being constructed for the man who called himself Rennix.

"I am sure there is a great deal he is not telling us," he conceded.

"You know something," Einon accused.

Venutius took a sip of his drink, slurping the hot liquid noisily while he considered his response.

"I certainly suspect something," he admitted at last.

Einon waited, knowing that the King liked to play these games.

"What do you suspect?" he enquired after a suitable lapse of time.

"You are a young man," Venutius reflected. "So is he. He is a few years older than you, I think, but still young compared to me. It is the way of young men to think that their elders are lacking in some way. We are no longer as quick or agile or as strong as we once were, and young men despise us for these things."

"Nobody despises you, Lord," Einon insisted.

"Hah!" Venutius exhaled. "You know that is not true. But age brings one vital thing, Einon. Experience. I know things that you could not possibly know because you simply do not have that experience."

Einon nodded his acceptance of the King's statement.

"What is it that you know?" he asked.

"I know what Calgacus looks like."

Einon frowned, "You mentioned him before. The name is vaguely familiar. Who is he?"

Venutius smiled conspiratorially. Nobody had ever sung songs about Calgacus when the King of the Brigantes was near, so it was not surprising that Einon had difficulty recalling the name.

Venutius explained, "He was a prince of the Catuvellauni, a brother of the Great King, Caratacus. He became a War Leader, first of the Silures, then of the Deceangli. He is the only man who has ever defeated a Roman Legion in battle."

"You say he *was*. Is he dead?"

Venutius smiled, pleased that Einon had asked the question.

"Who knows? I lost track of him a few years ago, when the Romans came against us. He went to the far north, to the lands of the Picts."

Venutius pulled a sour face as he went on, "I certainly hope he is dead but he has a very irritating knack of staying alive."

"I don't understand," Einon confessed. "If he is an enemy of Rome, is he not our friend?"

"You still have much to learn, Einon," said Venutius patiently. "I fight Rome because of fate, not because I want to. In the long run, nobody can defeat the Romans. They attacked me because I overthrew their puppet Queen, the whore Cartimandua. I would have been content to be a friend of Rome but I made a mistake. Rome does not have friends, only conquered subjects. They used Cartimandua's eviction as an excuse to invade our lands. I fight them because I must if I want to stay alive. Whereas Calgacus fights them because ..." he paused, then went on, "... because he is Calgacus."

"You do not like him," stated Einon.

Venutius gave a smile that was utterly lacking in warmth.

"I would gladly see him dead," he admitted. "I have tried to kill him, or have him killed, several times, but as I said, he had a habit of surviving."

"I am sorry, Lord," Einon frowned. "I still do not understand why he is your enemy."

"It is a long story, Einon. As usual in such tales, it involved a woman. But above all, as I say, Calgacus was an enemy of Rome through choice, while I am their enemy through circumstance. I would rather be their friend than their foe. That is what sets him against me."

Einon considered the King's words for a few moments. Choosing his own words carefully, he suggested, "Could you not go to the Romans and surrender to them?"

Venutius shook his head.

"Do you know what the Romans do to defeated enemies? No, I would not live more than a day if I did that."

He took another sip from his beaker, then went on, "No, if I want to stay alive, I must treat with the Romans from a position of strength. I will not repeat my mistake. I know I must agree to be their subject but I can only do that if they believe that accepting my surrender is more convenient than fighting me."

He gestured around the small encampment as he added, "I hardly think they would consider me a strong King at the moment. That is something I intend to remedy. I have been planning it for a while, and I think the moment is approaching when I should reclaim my birthright."

Einon's interest was piqued.

"You wish to re-take Dun Brigantia?" he breathed expectantly.

Venutius nodded, "It is my home. I was evicted by the Romans but now it is time to return."

Einon understood that there was still something the King had not revealed, something that he wanted Einon to learn. As usual, though, Venutius expected him to probe for the answers.

"If you do that," the young man ventured, "the Romans will know where to find you."

"Indeed they will. Regaining the Kingship properly is only the first step. I have held that position before and been defeated, which is why I need something else. Something I can give to the Romans. Something to make them value me as an ally."

"What can you give them?"

Smiling, Venutius explained, "Years ago, Cartimandua proved her loyalty to Rome by handing them Caratacus as a prisoner. If my guess is correct, I will be able to use the same ploy."

Following the King's gaze, Einon twisted, looking to where the big man who called himself Rennix was hammering stakes into the ground with a large, flat stone as he made a small fence which would form a wall of his overnight shelter.

Turning back to the King, Einon asked, "Who is he?"

"I think he is Brennus, King of the Ordovices. And, more importantly, the son of Rome's greatest enemy among the tribes of the Pritani. I told you, I knew Calgacus. That man is so like him it is uncanny. I am certain that he is the son of Calgacus the Swordsman. And he will be the means by which we will make peace with Rome."

Chapter XIX

The Brigantes broke camp under a dull, mist-shrouded sky with the damp air leaving a sheen of moisture on every surface. Tegan had not slept well and felt dreadfully tired. She was nervous among these strangers, even though there were now other women to talk to. She felt that, in some indefinable way, she had been more at home with Calgacus and his rough crew. But she was here now and would have to make the best of it.

Brennus had reminded her to watch what she said so as not to betray his true identity. She did not really understand why he wanted to keep that secret but he made her promise not to say anything that would give him away so, as she always did, she had agreed without argument.

The shelters were abandoned, a breakfast of warm bannocks, goats' milk and thin gruel distributed, then they made ready to depart. Several of the warriors had horses; small, shaggy beasts ideal for trekking through the barren hills. These men rode off to scout ahead while the others gathered around Venutius. The women packed their belongings on mules, or simply hefted large bundles onto their backs. Even the children were given things to carry.

"Where are we going?" Tegan wondered aloud.

Brennus shrugged, "We will soon find out, I suppose."

She thought he seemed on edge, filled with nervous expectation as if he was eager to tackle some important task.

The young warrior, Einon, sauntered up to them, beckoning Brennus with a curt wave of his hand.

"Venutius wishes you to accompany him," he said before turning away again without waiting to see whether Brennus obeyed the summons.

Brennus gave Tegan a reassuring smile as he told her, "Stay with the other women. I'll see you later."

Then he was gone, walking determinedly to where Venutius had mounted a small, dark-coated horse. He did not look back and the sight of his departing back left Tegan feeling desperately alone.

The men set off, climbing out of the defile in a long, straggling line. The women followed, walking in twos and threes, the children scampering around their feet as they chased one another in some riotous game. Tegan watched them, wondering where she should join the procession. She could not help thinking that they were an ill-favoured group. Dirty, tired and in ragged clothes, they resembled a collection of wandering refugees rather than a war band. But then, she supposed that was precisely what they were. Refugees, hiding from the Romans, seeking shelter wherever they could, always on the move, begging food from people who sympathised with them.

Tegan gave an involuntary shudder. She did not want to be like them but what choice did she have?

Most of the women trudged past, ignoring her, but one of them gave her a smile and waved to her, motioning that she should join them. Feeling awkward and self-conscious, Tegan walked over to her.

"My name is Ambarra," the woman said as Tegan moved alongside her.

"I'm Tegan."

"I know."

Tegan guessed that Ambarra was in her late twenties, although her figure was already blurred and rounded by childbirth.

The woman turned away briefly to shout at one of the children, a boy of around four who was trying to pull the tail of an undernourished mule.

"Get away from there!" Ambarra scolded. "You'll get a kick if you're not careful."

She turned back to Tegan and rolled her eyes as she shrugged, "Kids! You have to watch them all the time."

"He is your son?" Tegan asked.

"That he is." Ambarra turned her head, scanning the procession as she continued, "I've a girl around here somewhere. She's a bit older and more sensible, so I don't need to worry about her so much."

"Is their father with the warriors?" Tegan asked, more out of politeness than curiosity.

Ambarra said, "No, lass. Their father's dead. He was injured in a fight and the wound was infected by evil spirits. He died two summers past."

"I'm sorry."

209

"No need to be sorry, lass," said Ambarra. "I hardly miss him."

Brushing a strand of her dark hair back from her face, she went on, "Maybe I'll get a new man soon." She gave Tegan a sly smile as she added, "Maybe I'll see if I can take yours away from you."

Tegan gave the woman a sharp look but Ambarra laughed, a throaty chuckle of genuine amusement.

"Just kidding, lass. Mind you, he's quite a specimen, isn't he? I bet he tires you out at nights."

Tegan blushed, shook her head, then smiled. She was not sure how to take Ambarra, but the woman appeared to be making some effort at friendliness, so she decided she had better reciprocate.

"He can be quite demanding," she ventured after a while, then immediately wished she had said something less bold.

Ambarra laughed, "He's a man. Of course he's demanding. Still, if he ever gets too much for you, just send him my way. It's been a while since any man demanded much from me, although I haven't forgotten how to keep them happy."

She waved a hand down her front, indicating her body as she pouted, "Still, I don't have the looks I used to. Not like you. You are of the Ordovices, I heard. Is that right?"

"Yes," Tegan replied cautiously.

"You have come a long way. How did you get here?"

Tegan hesitated slightly. Ambarra's face seemed open and honest, her question no more than natural inquisitiveness, but Brennus' warnings about saying too much were fresh in her mind. Still, there were some things he had agreed that she could divulge and it was always better to tell the truth rather than become caught in a web of complicated lies.

Not daring to look Ambarra in the eye, she explained, "After the battle, we fled to Ynis Mon but the Romans came there, too. We managed to get onto a small boat and got away but there was a storm and we were shipwrecked."

She waved a hand vaguely to the west as she recounted, "Somewhere on the far coast. We didn't know where to go, but Rennix had heard that the Brigantes are still resisting the Romans, so he decided to come and join up with a war band here."

"He's a resourceful man, then," remarked Ambarra. "I'll bet he's a good fighter, too."

210

"The best," Tegan agreed.

"He has the look of a chieftain about him," Ambarra observed.

Hoping the lie would not catch in her throat, Tegan said, "He's the son of a minor chief of the Ordovices."

"Is he indeed?" Ambarra's eyebrows arched at this news. "He sounds more and more interesting. You'd best hang on to him, lass. There's more than a few women here who are looking for husbands. Maybe I should get to know him better myself."

Tegan felt her cheeks burning again. Desperate to steer the conversation away from Ambarra's salacious musings, she asked, "Do you know where we are going?"

Ambarra gave a slight shrug as she sighed, "They don't tell us, dearie. But if I had to guess, I'd say we were heading for Dun Brigantia."

"Where's that?"

"A bit to the north and east. A good few days' walk from here, I reckon."

"Why are we going there?"

Ambarra replied, "I don't know that we *are* going there, love. But if we are, it can only be for one reason. Venutius wants his throne back."

Chapter XX

Preparations for the festival were well in hand. All the tribes of the Pritani had long recognised the major turning points of the seasons, marking them with feasts and religious ceremonies.

Of the four great occasions that were celebrated each year, Samhain was the one that brought the greatest mixture of emotions. For most people, if the harvest had been good, food was plentiful at Samhain. There were fat cattle, pigs and sheep to be slaughtered, the granaries were full and the beer had been brewed. Beans, pulses, berries, vegetables and meadow plants provided variety to an otherwise bland diet, while deer, wild boar, fish and wildfowl added to the bounty.

Yet Samhain also marked the coming of winter. Much of the freshly-butchered meat would be salted and preserved to see the people through the cold days and colder nights. Samhain marked the beginning of the hardest time of year, when fresh food was scarce and the weather was harsh.

But Samhain held other fears, for it also marked the night when the veil between the world of the living and the world of the dead was weak. At Samhain, evil spirits stalked the earth, seeking victims from among the unwary.

People would blacken their faces, using ashes from the great festival bonfires so that the creatures of the shadows would not recognise them and would pass them by. The people would sing, dance and tell stories of witches, ghosts and all the other malevolent creatures that haunted the land during the hours of darkness.

Cynwrig's head told him that the stories which would be told around the fires that evening were just that. They were stories, told to frighten the children and the gullible. Yet, deep inside him, he also knew that the stories were very real. However much he told himself that, in all his long years, he had never seen a ghost or an evil spirit, he knew, at a fundamental level, that such things existed and only a foolish man would not take precautions this night. Samhain was a dark night for dark deeds, so Cynwrig would daub his face and hands with ash and he would keep the torches and candles burning throughout the night, just as he had done every Samhain for as long as he could remember.

He wandered around the Dun, his small escort of warriors maintaining a respectful distance while their chieftain spent his time being seen by the Dun's inhabitants. Cynwrig would stop to chat to people from time to time, to enquire as to their health or ask how they were looking forward to the feast. As a chieftain, he would be expected to distribute gifts to his people after the feast. Other local chiefs would come to pay tribute, to acknowledge him as their overlord. He would not only supply the food and drink for the evening, but would hand out gifts of horses, cloaks, spears or swords, rings and brooches of gold and silver, or perhaps some fine Roman glass or jewellery. That was what it meant to be a chieftain. Men owed him loyalty because he was a gift-giver.

Cynwrig did not call himself King of the Brigantes. For one thing, the Romans who had supported his elevated position disliked the term 'King'. Cynwrig knew that they had been happy for him to seize control of Dun Brigantia because he was old and, although he was proud, he was tired of fighting when peace could be obtained by paying tribute to Rome.

Cynwrig had been quick to fall on his knees before the previous Governor. It had cost him his pride but his submission had brought several years of bitter and bloody warfare to an end. That, he believed, justified any personal hurt he might feel.

It was, though, an uneasy peace. The Brigantes were a loose confederation of people, with local chieftains exercising power over their surrounding villages. In Cynwrig's youth, the tribe had acknowledged a King or Queen when it suited them, but things had changed in recent years. When Cartimandua had been Queen, she had gained authority over many of the people because she was a friend of Rome and could keep the empire at a distance, protecting her people from the fate that had overtaken so many other tribes. Cynwrig recalled ruefully how he had been persuaded by the promises of riches and glory to support Venutius when the Queen's former husband had decided to seize the throne for himself. That had been a mistake, Cynwrig knew now. Cartimandua had fled, it was true, but Cynwrig had come to see Venutius in a new and less favourable light.

First, Venutius had refused to fight Calgacus in single combat when challenged. Instead, his Captain, a ferocious warrior named Corlus, had taken his place. Cynwrig could still remember the awesome speed with which Calgacus had defeated Corlus and reclaimed his stolen sword. But that was the moment he saw Venutius for what he was.

The self-proclaimed King of the Brigantes had shown himself to be less than honourable. He had ordered his warriors to cut Calgacus down, despite having given his word that the winner of the combat could go free. Only the resolve of the chieftains, led by Cynwrig, had forced Venutius to keep to the bargain that had been struck.

That, Cynwrig mused, had been the moment when Venutius had lost the Kingship. He had ruled the tribe from the two great centres of Isuria and Dun Brigantia for three more years, but his rule had been a facade because many chieftains despised him and few paid all the tribute they had promised. What use, they had murmured among themselves, was a King who could not be trusted?

When the Romans returned, using Cartimandua's eviction as an excuse to conquer the Brigantes, Venutius had found little support. Some among the tribe had fought, Cynwrig amongst them, but the Romans had been clever and had used bribery as well as force of arms, paying silver coins to many of the minor chieftains to persuade them to abandon Venutius. Cynwrig himself, too proud to accept money from people who were invading his lands, had fought on for a while but he had seen too many of his tribesmen die to no purpose. After two years of struggle, another Roman emissary had come to him and this time he had accepted the coins. Then he had gone home, taking his remaining warriors with him.

That had been three years ago. The last Roman Governor, Frontinus, had broken off the hunt for Venutius because the ever-restless Silures had risen in revolt yet again. Frontinus had personally visited Cynwrig and paid him handsomely to occupy Dun Brigantia from where he would act as a friend and ally of Rome while Frontinus led his legions south to deal with the Silures.

Cynwrig had taken the Roman coins but he had hated himself for it. He had been a warrior all his life but now he was an old man, tired and afraid, and the prospect of peace had been too much for him to resist. He knew that most of his people felt the same way. Too many had died in the fighting of the previous years for the allure of peace and stability not to call to them. And yet ...

And yet Cynwrig despised himself. The Brigantes were a conquered people even if the Roman troops were not actually on their land. The people had wanted peace but now they grumbled at the knowledge of their subservience. Every so often, young men would go off into the wilds to join the rebels who still refused to bow the knee to Rome. That, thought Cynwrig wryly, was a problem to which he had no answer.

He stood atop the mighty wall of the Dun and looked south. Out there somewhere, Venutius was still at large. He may have been defeated, he may have lost the regard of the older chieftains, but he came from a noble line and had been their King for many years, from the time in his youth when he had married Cartimandua, until he had taken the throne for himself. His name still held the power to attract young, disaffected warriors to his cause.

Cynwrig knew that he should send men out to find and kill the old King but he also knew that he would not do that. He had persuaded himself that he ruled because the people wanted him to rule and if they ever wanted him to step down, he would do so without argument. When he was younger, he had dreamed of power, but now that he had it, he did not like the lingering taste of bile it brought. He knew in his heart that he ruled only because the Romans permitted it.

So he went through the motions, played his part and wondered whether it would be Venutius or the Romans who would come for him. One day, one or other of them would depose him. He was certain of that.

The wind drove a fine misty rain into his face as he gazed out across the damp greenness of the fields and forests. He pulled his thick, hooded cloak closer around his body, shivering despite its warmth. Below him, the mighty walls of Dun Brigantia gave the impression of being impenetrable but Cynwrig knew that was an illusion. Dun Brigantia was not a traditional hillfort, built for defence. The walls were tall and strong but were for show rather than anything else. They had been built by Venutius' father and grandfather to display the power and wealth of the family. The place had begun, generations before, as a mere fortified farmstead but had gradually grown and been extended until now, countless years since the first enclosure had been built, the walls encompassed such a huge area that no army could hope to hold the entire perimeter. It would take half a morning to walk the circumference of the walls.

Inside, much of the land was given over to grazing for the chief's cattle and sheep, or for growing cereal and other crops. Dun Brigantia was a settlement whose wide boundaries were merely marked by the walls, rather than protected by them. The Romans had proved that when they had come here. They had launched one attack at the main gate where Venutius' warriors had stood to oppose them, but had then sprung a second assault further round on the eastern side where there were few defenders to prevent them crossing the ditches and scaling the high walls.

It had all been over so very quickly. Venutius had fled and his homestead, including the villa he had built in the Roman style, had been destroyed.

Cynwrig sighed gently as he turned away from the wall to make his way back to his home. This damp weather made his old bones ache but he knew that he must make an effort, for tonight was Samhain and he was expected to play his part one more time. There was one consolation, he told himself. He would be safe from Venutius for another day because nobody would venture far outdoors at Samhain.

"We attack tonight," Venutius announced to his warriors.

Many of the men lowered their eyes, others shuffled nervously or swore in low whispers. Venutius stood, watching them, waiting for someone to speak.

Eventually, it was young Einon who said, "Tonight is Samhain, Lord."

Venutius bared his teeth in a grin as he replied, "Which is why they will not expect us to attack. It is the perfect time. Their warriors will be drunk and, moreover, all gathered together in one place."

The men remained unconvinced. A few nervous coughs betrayed their concerns. With a shake of his head, Brennus took a step forwards then turned to face the other men.

In a loud, confident voice, he told them, "I am of the Ordovices. I do not know what tales your people tell of Samhain but if they are like the stories of my own people, I understand why you are afraid."

He paused, looking at their faces, holding their gaze to show his determination.

"I am not afraid," he continued. "Death holds no fear for a true warrior."

Drawing his sword, he held the long, gleaming blade up for them to see as he went on, "I will carry this against our foes and if any ghost or evil spirit comes for me, I will deal with it as I will deal with any man who opposes me. I say that we can do this. We can blacken our faces, we can stalk our foes like avenging spirits ourselves. We can become the beasts of the night that they fear. You are all warriors. I ask you to accompany me but if you would rather stay safely beside your fires, then I will go alone."

He sheathed his sword, turned and gave a smart bow of his head to Venutius.

"Give the word," he told the Brigante King, "and I will strike down your enemies."

Venutius returned the bow with a nod of his head.

"Well said, Rennix. You see, lads? There is one man who does not fear the darkness. Is there no man of the Brigantes who will dare the same? Who will go with him? For victory!"

The response was muted. Some men echoed the call of, "Victory!" with little conviction or enthusiasm, but most remained silent.

Brennus called out, "What was that?"

He punched his fist into the air.

"Victory! Let me hear it!"

This time there was a better response.

"Victory!"

"Victory!" Brennus shouted again.

"Victory!"

Brennus led the traditional chant of the tribes, the calls echoing around the small valley they had chosen for their camp.

"Bouda! Bouda!"

It was the word that preceded battle, the word that fired a warrior's blood and banished fear.

Bouda.

Victory.

As the echoes of the war cry died away, Brennus gave a satisfied nod. He had altered the mood among the warriors. Where they had been afraid, now they were determined to overcome that fear and prove that no Brigante would be overshadowed by a man of the Ordovices.

Venutius clapped him on the back.

"Well done, Rennix. You have a talent for leading men, I think. Now I want you to lead them to a genuine victory. It is time we overthrew Cynwrig and took back our ancestral home."

Brennus nodded as he asked, "And you want him dead?"

"Cynwrig is a traitor to the Brigantes," Venutius assured him smoothly. "He has taken Roman silver and turned against me, the rightful King. He must die."

"I understand," Brennus confirmed. "But what happens afterwards?"

"Afterwards? I will resume my rightful place and summon all the chieftains to join me. This time, we will not make the same mistakes as before. We will challenge the might of Rome and, with you to lead our War Host, we will defeat their Legions."

Brennus gave the King a grim smile of determination.

"That is all I ask," he stated. "The Romans must be driven out of our lands."

"Then let us go to Dun Brigantia," Venutius told him. "That is where we will begin."

The Brigante rebels set off, scouts moving ahead to check that the way was clear, and Brennus strode alongside Venutius, his mind consumed by one burning desire.

Bouda.

Victory.

He had suffered the humiliation of defeat and he vowed that he would have his revenge. The Romans must be destroyed and the only way to achieve that was to fight them, not to run away and hide as Calgacus had done. Brennus knew he had made the right decision when he had left his father behind because, far from hiding, Venutius was giving him the opportunity to be the instrument of Rome's defeat. With the power of the largest tribe among the Pritani at his command, he was convinced he would be able to slaughter the Legions.

Visions of glory filled his mind with heady euphoria but he tried to dismiss them because the Romans would need to wait. First, he had another task to complete. He must take Dun Brigantia and overthrow a traitor.

Chapter XXI

There were sentries guarding the North Gate but they were hardly alert. One of them had managed to get hold of a skin of ale which was being passed around from one man to the next. They grumbled among themselves because the gates were closed and barred and would not be opened until daybreak. They all knew that gate duty on this night was a waste of time, so they sat around a small fire, drinking their ale, listening to the sounds of music and dancing that carried from the centre of the Dun on the night breeze.

Outside in the darkness, Brennus lay on the damp grass some distance from the gate. There was nothing to see except the faint orange-red glow of the large bonfires that had been lit deep within the stronghold.

Satisfied, Brennus crept away into the shadows. He found the small stream that ran along the northern edge of the Dun, an invaluable landmark on a moonless, cloudy night. Moving carefully, he followed the water eastwards, counting his paces as he went. With his eyes accustomed to the dark, he could just make out the silhouette of the high wall against the cloud-shrouded sky. The walls seemed to go on forever, he thought.

After eight hundred paces, he stopped, crouched low and moved stealthily towards the Dun.

He reached the edge of the ditch where he lay down, nothing more than a dark shadow against the ground. Again he waited. He lay still, straining his ears, for they were of more use than his eyes in this blackness. For a long time he lay there but there was no sound from beyond the wall. This, he decided, was where they should make their entrance.

He returned to the stream where he unfastened his cloak. He spread it on the ground, then scrabbled to find a small rock which he placed on top of the cloak. There was scarcely any wind but he did not want to take any chances of the cloak blowing away. It would act as his marker when he returned.

Moving more quickly now, he retraced his steps, following the sound of the trickling stream until he reached the gate. From there he cut northwards, into the night.

Venutius and his small war band were waiting on the far side of a low hill. The warriors looked at him expectantly as he scrambled down the slope to their hiding place. Every man had blackened his face so that they looked like spectres in the night, white eyes against dark skin.

Venutius' voice asked, "Well?"

"I found a place," Brennus informed him. "There are no sentries nearby."

"Then go and take the fortress for me," Venutius ordered.

Brennus nodded. He could feel the expectancy and tension in the air. Somewhere in the crowd of shadows was Tegan, but he could not see her. He was not concerned, for he knew she would be safe. Venutius and four other men would remain with the women and children. If anything went wrong with the assault, they would be able to slip away unseen. It was Brennus' task to make sure that nothing did go wrong.

He could feel his muscles tensing as the prospect of seizing the Dun grew closer to reality. Once they crossed the ditch and wall, they would be entering the unknown. He summoned the warriors to him.

"Keep silent," he warned them before setting off again, the others following him closely in single file.

By the time they reached the stream, Brennus was feeling frustrated and annoyed. It had taken him a long time to scout out the approaches when he was on his own and half the night had passed by the time he had returned to Venutius. This second march through the night was, though, far more difficult. There were no landmarks, no path to follow except a faint tinge of orange where the firelight reflected from the low clouds, but the night was passing, the fires were burning lower and Brennus could not be certain where he was heading. Worse, the men behind him seemed unable to follow. He had thought it would be easy for them to walk in single file however dark it might be. Somehow, it was not that simple. Plaintive whispers for guidance reached his ears as men lost their way or stumbled in the darkness. To compound the problems, a fine mist was beginning to rise, muffling the world in a haze of grey.

At last Brennus found the stream where he called a halt. Quietly, he counted the men, made sure they all understood what they were to do, then splashed across the water before heading east.

With the faint sound of the water to guide them, they made quicker time. Brennus counted his steps once more, but had reached more than eight hundred without finding any trace of his cloak. He was beginning to think that he had missed it somehow, or that it had been dragged away by some malevolent ghost. That thought filled him with dread, making his heart race, for if some underworld spirit had one of his possessions, they might use it to lure him into their clutches. He tried to push that thought away, then almost tripped as his foot snagged and he realised that he had found the cloak after all.

"What is it?" asked Einon in a concerned whisper.

He had been shadowing Brennus during the entire march and was so close that he almost bumped into him when Brennus stopped.

"This is the place," Brennus whispered back.

He retrieved his cloak, now heavy with dampness, slung it around his shoulders and fastened it with his brooch. Then he pointed into the mist.

"This way."

The war band followed. When they reached the ditch, they stopped, peering at the high walls that towered above them.

Brennus hissed at them to move quickly.

"It's not so high here," he told them. "And the stonework is not as fine as the stuff on the south side. You can climb it."

He hoped he was correct. Venutius and Einon had both assured him that the wall was less imposing on this stretch of the circuit. Looking up at the high, stone wall, he was less confident than he tried to sound.

"Go!" hissed Einon to two of the smaller men who had been given this task.

Each had a rope looped over his shoulder. They clambered down into the deep ditch, cursing softly as they waded through the muck and stagnant water that lay at its foot, then began to scale the stone walls. Soon, two ropes were dangling down, allowing the rest of the men to climb.

Brennus ran down, hurdled the filth at the bottom of the ditch, grabbed at a rope and hauled himself up. He scrambled over the top, dropped lightly to the other side and looked around. The mist hid everything from view but Venutius had told him that this place should be nothing except open grassland, the meadows where the livestock grazed.

As more men crossed the wall, he sent some of them to form a loose perimeter in case there were sentries who might be patrolling. He knew it was unlikely, but he also knew that their chances of success depended on the alarm not being raised too soon.

"We should have brought more ropes," Einon grumbled as he climbed down to join Brennus.

"We didn't have any more," Brennus replied.

Again he fretted while the warriors seemed to take an age to climb the wall. He kept glancing to the sky, trying to judge the time, but the mist and low clouds made it impossible to tell.

At last they were gathered, thirty-two of them including Brennus himself. He had no idea how many warriors Cynwrig had, but it was certain to be many more than that. In addition, Venutius was convinced that other chieftains would be in the settlement, with warriors of their own. Not good odds, Brennus thought. But then, that was why they were attacking using stealth rather than force of arms. Surprise would compensate for their lack of numbers.

He was pleased to see that the men's mood had lightened. They were buoyed by their achievements so far and seemed to be growing in confidence.

Brennus nudged Einon.

"You lead the way," he said. "I've never been here before."

Einon nodded.

"Stay close, lads," he announced in a loud whisper. Then he set off, cutting away from the wall towards the heart of the Dun.

The grass was heavy with dew and moisture from the all-enveloping mist. They swished their way across the uneven fields, staying in a group, spears ready, shields now gripped tightly on their left arms. Brennus had no shield but he drew his sword, holding it ready. All around, he could hear the tramping of feet, the breathing of the men. The mist seemed to bounce the sound around him, confusing his ears as well as concealing the world from his eyes.

Einon halted suddenly. He looked around, then pointed his sword to the left.

"This way," he decided. "And keep quiet. We are too close to the gates."

He moved on, eyes darting around as he sought familiar landmarks. The war band followed.

222

After walking another two hundred paces, Einon stopped again. Ahead, dark shapes loomed in the murk. Brennus took a moment to recognise the vague, mist-distorted outline of a roundhouse.

"We are here," Einon whispered.

"Let's find Cynwrig," Brennus replied.

Gesturing to two other men to follow, he led Einon towards the roundhouse leaving the rest of the war band to guard their retreat should anyone raise the alarm.

This part of the plan had been Brennus' idea. Nobody could say for certain which house would be Cynwrig's home. Venutius had always lived in the large villa at the centre of his homestead, but the Romans had destroyed that building, so Cynwrig could be anywhere. Brennus had suggested discovering his whereabouts by the simple expedient of taking prisoners from the first house they came across and killing the occupants one by one until somebody agreed to lead them to the chieftain. It was the sort of action Brennus knew was necessary. If he had been with Calgacus, he was sure that his father would have forbidden it. Calgacus would have made some weak-minded excuse not to do what needed to be done. But Venutius was made of stronger stuff. When he heard Brennus' plan, he had smiled and nodded his assent without hesitation. Now Brennus gave a grim smile of his own. It was time to make it happen.

He moved silently into the house. The hearth fire was still burning. Like all fires on this night, it had been built high to keep the house lit all through the darkness of Samhain so that ghosts and evil spirits would not enter the home. It was burning low now, suggesting that dawn was close. By the dim firelight, Brennus saw a man and a woman lying under a covering of blankets. Their faces were smeared black but had streaks of white or grey where they had rubbed their skin. Both were sleeping soundly, the man's arm lying across the woman's bare shoulder. To another side of the house lay three young children, their faces also ash-dark. The family had followed the traditional way of keeping themselves safe from danger but this night the precautions had been in vain, for danger was here.

The stink of sweat and stale beer reached Brennus' nostrils as he approached the low bed. Venutius had been right, he thought. Everyone would have drunk too much at the feast. He sheathed his sword and drew his dagger, then crept to the bedside, kneeling to place a hand over the sleeping man's mouth.

The man spluttered, then his eyes opened. Brennus applied pressure, clamping his hand down over the man's mouth while he held the dagger to his throat.

"Make no sound or you and your family will die," Brennus whispered.

The man was tense but he lay back, blinking in terrified confusion. After a few moments, he nodded, indicating that he would not resist.

Brennus said, "I am going to ask you a question. Think carefully before you answer, because your family's fate depends on you telling the truth. Do you understand?"

The Brigante swallowed frantically, his breathing rasping through his nose in rapid gulps. When Brennus showed him the sharp point of the dagger, he gave another frightened nod.

"Do you know which house Cynwrig is in?" Brennus asked.

The man nodded again.

"Good. Now I am going to let you stand up. If you resist, or make any sound, your family will die. Do you understand?"

Another nod.

Brennus moved back, gesturing to the man to stand. The Brigante slipped from under the covers, revealing that he was naked. Hastily, he reached for a pair of leggings which he pulled on.

On the bed, the woman stirred. She rolled over, her arms reaching for her husband. Still sleepy, she opened her eyes when she could not find him.

Brennus stifled her scream by planting a hand over her mouth while Einon held a sword to her husband's throat.

"Be quiet!" hissed Brennus. "If you remain quiet, you will live. Make a sound and you will die, along with your children."

The woman's eyes were wide with terror, their whiteness accentuated by her ash-blackened face. Brennus hauled aside the blankets, revealing that she, too, was naked.

"Get dressed," he told her. "Sit by your children and make sure they remain quiet."

Sobbing, she scurried to obey, covering her flabby body with a rough-sewn dress, then scuttling to sit cross-legged on the earth floor beside her sleeping children. Tears were running down her cheeks, smearing the dried ash.

Brennus gestured to the two men who had accompanied him and Einon.

"Stay here," he commanded. "If there is any trouble, kill them all."

The warriors gripped their spears purposefully, moving into the house to stand over the woman and children.

Brennus turned to the man they had captured.

"Now," he said, "you will take us to Cynwrig."

Led by their half-naked and terrified prisoner, the war band moved through the small settlement. The homes were widely scattered, each one with its own plot of land surrounding it. The men moved as silently as they could, drifting deeper into the heart of Dun Brigantia.

A dog barked as they passed one house. They froze, then hurried on, trusting to the misty darkness to conceal them. The dog's furious yapping slowly faded away and still they had not been discovered. Brennus hurried them on, knowing their luck could not hold for much longer.

Their terrified guide led them to a roundhouse that appeared no different to the rest. He waved a hand.

"He should be in there," he said in a low, rasping voice.

Brennus, Einon and four other men pushed open the door and ducked through the doorway. As before, the hearth fire in this home was still bright but this house, well furnished with rugs, wooden furniture and silver platters, had only two occupants. One was a young woman. The other was an old, grey-haired man. Both were sleeping under a thick pile of patterned, woollen blankets.

Brennus raised an eyebrow as he asked Einon a silent question.

Einon nodded, "That's him."

Cynwrig woke with a start as Brennus' hand covered his mouth and the dagger pricked his neck. He was sleepy, his mind dulled by the ale he had drunk, but he understood Brennus' whispered orders well enough. Obeying without any attempt to resist, he climbed out of the bed and pulled on his leggings.

The woman, little more than a girl, squealed in fright when Brennus woke her, but he slapped her hard, hissing at her to remain silent, then flung her dress at her.

225

The two new captives were marched outside and Einon led them all a little way to the north. Here were the remains of what had once been Venutius' Roman-style home, now a pile of blackened rubble and shattered tiles of red clay. Brennus shoved the prisoners against the low, crumbling wall that was all that remained of the once magnificent building, but hauled Cynwrig a few paces away, forcing the man to stand, bare-chested and shivering in the cold, mist-shrouded night. Two spearmen watched the grey-haired chieftain carefully.

The old man gave Brennus a weary look and asked, "Where is Venutius? Too afraid to do his own fighting, as usual?"

"He will be here soon," Brennus replied.

"Once the danger is past," Cynwrig muttered. "That sounds like Venutius."

He shot a sad look at Einon as he observed, "You are a better man than the leader you follow, boy."

"Be silent," Brennus warned.

Cynwrig looked at him, a puzzled frown on his lined face

"Do I know you?" he asked. "You look familiar."

"We have never met," Brennus told him roughly. "Now be quiet."

Cynwrig gave a sad smile as he asked, "Why? What will you do to me that you do not already intend to do?"

The old man's calm acceptance of his fate annoyed Brennus.

"Enough!" he spat. "It will be dawn soon. We must hurry."

Cynwrig bowed his head resignedly.

"Time to clear the gates," Einon said as he pointed with his chin towards the lightening horizon.

Brennus and Einon led ten men to the main gate on the south wall. Only one guard was awake and he was busy relieving himself against a wall when the raiders arrived. Unarmed and taken by surprise, he surrendered without a fight. The others were disarmed, woken up with rough kicks, then herded back to where the other prisoners were sitting.

"Now for the North Gate," Brennus said.

He gave orders to the warriors.

"Grab anyone who comes out of a house. Kill them if they resist."

Leaving the bulk of the warriors to secure the settlement, he and Einon led their small group to the North Gate.

The mist was thinning as morning arrived. The men at the gate, four of them, were awake, hoping to be relieved soon. As Brennus and the other warriors emerged from the mist, the guards relaxed, thinking they would, at last, be allowed to return to their homes, but then realised that they could not recognise any of the men approaching them.

One shouted a perplexed challenge.

"Who are you?"

In response, Brennus stopped, held his sword up and pointed it at the four sentries.

"Lay down your weapons and you will be spared," he told them. "This place has been taken for Venutius, King of the Brigantes."

"King of the turds, more like," one man growled, spitting on the ground to show what he thought of Venutius.

"Lay down your weapons," Brennus repeated. "I will not tell you again."

"If you want them, come and get them," the surly guard retorted, hefting his long spear.

Brennus charged. He moved so suddenly that he caught his companions by surprise, leaving them standing. He ran at the spearman who immediately raised his shield and jabbed his spear forwards, seeking to drive Brennus away.

Brennus kept moving. A man with a spear has a much longer reach than a man with a sword, but the spearman must keep his weapon constantly in motion, to hold his opponent at a distance. When Brennus closed in, the spearman should have backed away, but the other guards were too close and the barred gates were behind him, so he had nowhere to retreat to.

Fast as lightning, Brennus' sword swept up, knocking the spear high. Brennus barged into the man, forcing him backwards. The guard slammed into the solid wood of the gate, the breath exploding from his body as his back struck the beams.

Brennus was already moving, swinging his sword in an arc to hack at the man on his right. This sentry had grabbed a large, wooden club but was too slow to react. He fell away, crying aloud, blood gushing from a huge gash in his side. Then Brennus was spinning, facing the remaining men just as Einon and the other warriors charged at them.

One man went down, fighting frantically, the other dropped his spear and held up his hands in surrender. Seeing Einon

227

hesitate, Brennus took a step towards the sentry, swinging his sword to take the man on the back of the neck, almost severing his head. Without pausing, Brennus turned back to the first man he had attacked who was now struggling to haul himself to his feet, his back still against the gate. Brennus slit the man's throat with a vicious cut of his blade. A final hack at the last, already wounded man, ended the resistance.

"Open the gates," Brennus ordered tersely.

Obediently, the warriors hauled the bodies aside so that they could swing the huge gates open.

Einon, his sword unbloodied, gave Brennus a quizzical look.

"You are a dangerous man, I think," he remarked in a low voice.

"Only to my enemies," Brennus replied.

Einon returned his sword to its scabbard and reached down to gather up the wooden club that one of the dead men had dropped. He weighed it in his hand, slapping it against his other palm. Then, gesturing towards the bodies of the guards, he looked up at Brennus.

"There was no need to kill them all," he said, although without reproach.

Brennus shrugged, "It will serve as a lesson."

"Indeed. But to whom?"

"To anyone who seeks to oppose us."

The gates were swung open. Brennus strode to stand in the centre of the gateway. He held his sword aloft. Einon, still holding the club, stood a little behind him, conceding the place of honour to Brennus.

Soon there was movement from the distant hillside. Dark shapes moved in the growing light as the sun banished the mist, clearing the way for the returning King of Brigantia.

Venutius, accompanied by his entire band of followers, marched proudly up to the open gates of his former home. He stopped a few paces from Brennus.

Smiling, he asked, "You were successful?"

"Yes, Lord."

"Cynwrig?"

"We have him prisoner."

"Everything went as planned, then?" Venutius persisted.

Brennus thought that the King was rather over-anxious. How many times did he need to be told?

"Yes," he confirmed. "Dun Brigantia is yours again."

"You have done well, Rennix," Venutius said at last. "Very well indeed. It is almost a shame to do this."

Brennus frowned.

"What do you mean?" he asked uncertainly.

Venutius flicked his hand, signalling to someone behind him. Brennus saw Tegan, her wrists bound behind her, her ankles hobbled by a length of rope, being shoved forwards through the crowd by the woman, Ambarra. Tegan's face was a mask of worry and fear, her cheeks stained by the silver tracks of many tears.

Shocked, Brennus looked at Venutius who grinned back at him. Brennus did not understand what was happening but he sensed danger and gripped the hilt of his sword tightly.

Before he could move, the world exploded in pain as Einon's heavy club struck him on the side of the head. Lights flashed in Brennus' eyes, his knees crumpled and he fell to the ground, his head ringing with the sound of Venutius' mocking laughter.

Chapter XXII

Brennus woke with a shock as someone poured cold water over his face. Spluttering, he tried to shake the water off, then immediately wished that he had not moved as a sharp stab of pain lanced through his head. He groaned softly, closed his eyes and tried to work out where he was. Bright lights danced behind his eyelids, his head ached and his stomach was churning. The old, still-throbbing bruise he had received during the battle against the Romans was now competing with a larger, thumping pain that spread across the other side of his head. All he wanted to do was sleep.

Rough hands hauled him up to a kneeling position. He tried to resist but his arms and legs were bound, keeping him trussed like some animal being carried back from the hunt.

With a huge effort of will, he forced his eyelids open. For a few moments, he could see nothing except red light and bright sparks as his eyes tried to adjust. Blinking frantically, he eventually found his vision clearing. The first person he saw was Tegan.

She was sitting on the hard-packed earth floor a few paces from him. She, too, was bound by cords of thin rope wrapped around her ankles and wrists. She was looking at him with concern and fear engraved on her tired and tear-stained face.

Brennus stretched his neck muscles, wincing at the pain in his head. He looked around. He was inside a roundhouse, that much was plain. Three men stood between him and the doorway. One was a warrior, a burly man who had been in the raiding party with him. Brennus ignored him, recognising that he was there simply to act as muscle. Brennus turned his attention to the other two men.

Einon and Venutius.

Venutius stood smiling, his hands toying with a golden torc. Brennus recognised it instantly. It was the one he had claimed from Cadwallon.

Venutius chuckled, "Well, Brennus, I suppose I really should thank you for regaining my home for me. Things went very well indeed last night."

Somehow, Brennus' befuddled brain recognised what was wrong with Venutius' words. His throat was dry but he managed to croak, "My name is Rennix, not Brennus."

Venutius held up the torc.

"This," he said expansively, "is yours."

Brennus looked up at the shining metal of the torc. His eyes flicked to Tegan, whose face wore a miserable expression, then he looked back at Venutius.

"What of it?" he asked. "I stole it from a body on the battlefield."

"Really?"

Venutius appeared to be immensely pleased with himself. But then, thought Brennus, he had good reason to.

The King went on, "Well, if you insist that your name is Rennix, then I suppose we may as well just kill you."

He signalled to the guard, indicating that his suggestion should be treated as an order.

Tegan yelled, "No! You promised."

With a wave to the guard to stand back, Venutius frowned, "Did I? Oh, yes, I think I may have done that. But my promise only extended to Brennus, son of Calgacus. Not to anyone else."

He took a step closer to Brennus, gazing down with suddenly hard eyes. His voice took on an iron edge as he hissed, "Now, I suggest that you stop playing games and admit who you are. The girl has already told me but I'd like to hear it from your own lips."

"Go to hell," rasped Brennus.

Venutius leaned forwards, swinging a hand to punch Brennus on the side of his face. Brennus flinched, his already battered head twisting with the force of the blow. He swayed, almost fell, but managed to retain his balance.

He looked back up at Venutius with dull eyes.

"What if I am Brennus?" he asked. "What difference does that make?"

Venutius took a pace back, the false smile returning to his face.

"Oh, that makes all the difference in the world," he said. "If you are Rennix, then you must die, for I have no use for you. If you are Brennus, then I will let you live. So why don't you tell me the truth?"

Brennus nodded weakly. He knew that Venutius was playing some sort of game but he also knew that there was only one way to stay alive.

"I am Brennus," he admitted softly.

Venutius nodded, "There. That wasn't so hard, was it?"

The King turned to Einon and ordered, "I want the two of them fed, watered, and kept alive in good condition. They are not to be harmed, so long as they do not try anything silly."

Einon nodded, "As you command, my King."

Turning back to Brennus, Venutius added, "I will even have your bonds unfastened so that you are free to move around."

He laughed when he saw the brief flicker of hope flare in Brennus' eyes.

"But if you try to leave this house, the girl will be killed. I brought her here so that you can see that she is alive and unharmed. She will remain safe as long as you do as you are told, but I will remove her to some other place so that you cannot find her. She will be a guarantee of your good behaviour."

Einon stirred, shooting Venutius a warning look.

"He is a dangerous man," he advised. "It would be unwise to free him from the bonds."

"Yes, you are right," Venutius agreed. "Have some iron shackles brought. Drive a stake into the ground and chain him to it. That should keep him quiet."

"Why are you doing this?" Brennus demanded.

"Because I once had your father captive and I made the mistake of not having him securely guarded. I will not make the same mistake again."

Despite his thumping headache, Brennus was intrigued when he heard that, but he had enough problems of his own to worry about Venutius' past encounters with Calgacus.

"I didn't mean that," he insisted. "I meant why are you keeping me alive?"

"I thought you would have guessed by now," Venutius said with a hint of disappointment in his voice. "Still, perhaps that knock on the head has dulled your wits, so perhaps I should explain. I have regained Dun Brigantia and Cynwrig's head now adorns the main gate. The local chieftains have acknowledged me as King once more, and others will soon do so as my messengers spread the word. All of these things are thanks to you, Brennus. But there is one more thing you must do for me in order to make my position secure."

Brennus supposed that his headache was dulling his thoughts because he could not understand what Venutius meant.

"What is it you want me to do?" he asked.

Venutius grinned evilly as he explained, "You are a valuable man, you know. The Romans will reward anyone who delivers you to them. You, Brennus, will be the means of keeping me in power as a friend of Rome."

Brennus' brow wrinkled in confusion.

"The Romans? You said you were going to fight them."

Einon laughed, while Venutius bared his teeth in a smile of triumph.

"I lied," the King admitted happily. "Now I will leave you to consider your gullibility and the fate that awaits you."

"I trusted you!" Brennus shouted angrily, struggling uselessly against his bonds.

"That was your mistake," Venutius replied casually. "But please do not be tempted to make any more errors of judgement. If you do anything to displease me, I will allow my men to rape your woman in front of your eyes. If that fails to teach you to behave, we will mutilate her so that no man will ever wish to look at her again. Do you understand me?"

Brennus could feel Tegan's dread. Miserably, he nodded his head.

"I understand."

"Good. Then let me leave you with a more pleasant thought. If you behave yourself, I will allow her to go free once you have been handed over to the Romans."

Brennus stared at the floor. He felt sick to the very core of his being, a cold sweat breaking out all over his skin. He knew he had no choice but to do as Venutius wanted but he also knew he could not trust the Brigante King to keep any promises. Whatever he did, Tegan's fate would remain doubtful while his own was certain.

He would be delivered to Rome and executed.

The Romans were closer than even Venutius had guessed. Casca had driven his small troop hard, covering great distances every day, visiting farmsteads and villages in his quest to track down

Brennus and Calgacus. As the Governor had instructed, he tried to persuade the various Brigante chieftains that they should not resist when the Roman army came north the following year.

"Rome will reward her friends," he told them, "but anyone who opposes us will be destroyed."

Some of the chiefs had nodded gravely, giving promises of good faith. Others had watched him with calculating looks, clearly trying to decide whether to kill him and his men. None of them was brave enough to make the attempt but Casca marked which men were likely to prove hostile, noted their names and the locations of their villages in his journal, and then moved on.

He did not really care whether the Brigantes intended to resist or not. He had seen enough of them to know that they could not defeat the Legions. If they were foolish enough to try, they would die. Casca would not lose any sleep over that. What he wanted was to find the rebel leaders, Brennus and Calgacus. Yet it seemed that nobody knew anything about them. Nobody had seen them. A few admitted to knowing the old songs about Calgacus but most of the Brigantes thought the famous War Leader was long dead because none of them had heard anything about him for several years.

"This is a waste of time, Sir," Sdapezi complained one evening as they sat beside a small camp fire. "The country is too damn big to find them. They'll be long gone by now. And the weather is turning colder."

Casca cupped his hands around his beaker of warmed wine. Sdapezi was probably correct, he knew, but he could not afford to give up. His career depended on finding the rebels.

"We'll keep looking," he insisted. "It may be cold but it is still early for snow. As long as the weather remains reasonable, we'll keep on hunting for them."

"Very good, Sir," said Sdapezi without enthusiasm. "I suppose we might get lucky."

Casca knew that it would take a great deal of luck but he was not so foolish as to rely solely on fortune. Before leaving Deva, he had made offerings to Jupiter, Greatest and Best, pledging to build an altar to the chief God of the Roman pantheon if his quest proved successful. Then he had decided to make the same vow to Mars, God of War, and to Fortuna, Goddess of Luck. After some hesitation, he had also promised an altar to a local British God, Antenociticus, who was said to be a War God of the local tribes. Casca fervently hoped that having so much divine help would bring success but he knew that the Gods were fickle and that his prayers might go unheeded. Even if he was successful, the cost of having so many altars carved would force him into debt but he felt that was a price worth paying. If he could have offered prayers to Mithras, the soldiers' God, he would have done so, but Casca had never been invited to become a member of a Mithraeum. That was another thing that would surely change if he brought Brennus back as a captive. He would be seen as a lucky man, a man favoured by the Gods, a man worthy of initiation into the secret rites of Mithras.

These were fine dreams, he told himself, but first he had to find the rebels.

They continued the search. day after day they patrolled far and wide, braving the cold and the driving rain that Britannia was so famous for. They had come equipped with long, woollen trousers, oiled to keep the worst of the rain out. The troopers hated wearing them, even if they were essential in this bitterly cold northern province, for it meant that they could not feel the sides of their horses with their bare legs when they rode. The bond created between man and beast by that touch was part of what made a good cavalryman and the heavy leggings removed the intimacy. It was yet another thing for the troopers to grumble about, although they made sure not to do so when Casca might hear them.

Braving the elements, Casca led the troop ever deeper into the high hills that dominated the central part of Brigantia, where the clouds hovered just above the mountaintops and the wind brought a chill to their bones.

"Reminds me of home," Sdapezi observed one day as they rode slowly down yet another long slope. Smiling, he added, "Not as warm, of course."

"Where is home?" Casca enquired.

"My family are from Sardica, in Thrace," Sdapezi informed him.

"You intend to go back there one day?"

Sdapezi gave a low chuckle as he shook his head.

"No, I think I'd rather settle in Italy. I passed through Umbria once. It looked a nice place. You know, plenty of good farmland. When I retire, I think I'll ask for a plot of land there. Grow vines, make wine. That sort of thing."

Casca nodded absently. What Sdapezi wanted was the soldier's dream; a plot of land somewhere in Italy where he could live a life of ease and plenty. At the moment, the realisation of that dream was a long way off, and Casca suspected that even if Sdapezi survived his twenty-five years in the army and was granted full citizenship, his reward was more likely to be a patch of mud somewhere in Britannia.

He suspected Sdapezi knew it, too, but Casca, even though he was not particularly interested in Sdapezi's plans, knew his duty as an officer so he said, "That sounds nice. But you'd probably drink all the produce yourself and end up poor."

"Poor but drunk," Sdapezi grinned. "That sounds good to me."

Casca could not help smiling.

"It sounds good to me, too. Maybe I will come and visit you."

"Oh, you'll be too rich and important to be wanting anything like that, Sir," Sdapezi replied.

Casca had a suspicion that Sdapezi was mocking him in some way but the Decurion's face showed only open sincerity. Still, Casca's good humour evaporated.

He grumbled, "Only if our luck changes and we catch these bastards."

It took twenty-two days of fruitless searching before their luck did eventually change.

They found a small settlement, the usual cluster of grubby, stinking roundhouses perched on a low hill, surrounded by a shallow ditch and crude stone palisade that served to keep the livestock inside but would hardly inconvenience any serious attacking force. As he had done at so many of these places, Casca rode to the gate and demanded to see the head man. He was grudgingly welcomed, supplied with some food and drink for the men and fodder for the horses, then was allowed to deliver his usual message, the speech so well rehearsed by now that he could give it almost without thinking.

Casca could barely understand more than a handful of words in the local dialect but young Hortensius, who had been born in Britannia and whose mother tongue was similar to that spoken by the Brigantes, translated for him.

The head man and his companions listened anxiously, nodding vigorously when he had finished. In a mixture of broken

Latin and Brythonic, they promised to keep the peace. Then they assured him that Venutius would do the same because his messengers had told them so.

Casca frowned as Hortensius translated their harsh, incomprehensible words.

"What was that about Venutius?" he asked the young soldier.

After a few babbling exchanges with the savages, Hortensius informed him, "They say that Venutius has reclaimed his fortress in the North."

Casca swore as he realised the implications. Venutius was a known renegade and had proved troublesome in the past. If he had returned, he presented yet another problem for Rome.

"This bloody country is teeming with rebels," Casca complained. "We'll need to go back and tell the Governor. This could be serious."

He almost spat the words, knowing it meant the abandonment of his search for Calgacus and Brennus.

"No, Sir," said Hortensius. "They say Venutius has promised them peace with Rome. Apparently he is sending envoys to the Governor to offer his submission."

"The man's a fool," Casca snorted disparagingly. "The Governor will never trust him."

The Brigantes had obviously understood the tone of Casca's derisory comments because the head man began talking again, his tone urgent and emphatic.

Hortensius' eyebrows rose in surprise when he heard what the man was saying.

Turning to Casca, the young soldier whispered, "Sir, they claim that Venutius has captured Brennus."

"Bloody impressive," Sdapezi whistled when he saw the huge ramparts and wide ditch of Dun Brigantia.

The ditch was deep, the ramparts high and faced with large blocks of stone. The massive wall stretched off to the east as far as they could see.

"It's a bit barbaric," Casca observed.

"Not a place I'd want to storm all the same," said Sdapezi.

"The Legions stormed it a few years back."

Sdapezi spat on the ground.

"That's all the foot-sloggers are good for," he grunted, showing the cavalryman's disdain for the infantry.

Clapping his heels against his horse's sides, Casca called, "Come on, the gates are open. Let's go and find Venutius."

Sdapezi cursed under his breath. He had advised against this mad venture, warning the Centurion that Venutius was a known rebel. Riding into his fortress with only ten men was, in Sdapezi's opinion, a sure way of committing suicide.

Casca, of course, had ignored the Decurion's warnings and insisted that they should be the first to confront Venutius and confirm the rumours about Brennus' capture.

With a deep sigh, Sdapezi signalled to the troop to close up. With his heart pounding, expecting the worst from what he saw as the Centurion's folly, he followed Casca up the wide entrance path to the main gate.

The tall, wooden gates were indeed open but the entrance was guarded by half a dozen long-haired spearmen. Stuck on a pointed stake at the top of the gate was a man's head, the skin rotting and the eyes already gone, food for the crows. Someone, Sdapezi thought, was displaying a message.

Casca stopped short of the gates. He gave his name and demanded to see Venutius. Almost immediately, one of the sentries ran off into the distant settlement to deliver the news of their arrival.

Casca sat on his horse, looking around while he waited for the response. Eventually, the guard returned, waving to them to follow him.

"Look smart now," Casca ordered his men.

He had not seen any evidence that there was a large number of barbarians in this place but with only ten men, he knew that he would need to rely on intimidation if he was to have any chance of leaving alive. He was taking an enormous risk by coming here, he knew, but the prospect of finding Brennus was too much for him to ignore. If the story he had heard was true, the Governor might send some other officer to meet with Venutius. Casca could not afford to let anyone else have the glory of capturing Brennus.

To his surprise and relief, he soon discovered that intimidation would not be necessary. Venutius himself came to meet them, standing on the open ground in front of his roundhouse, with a gaggle of long-haired warriors around him. Women and children gathered to see the Roman soldiers, although they kept a respectful distance.

Casca dismounted, striding to meet the King as if he had no concerns at all at being in the heart of what was technically a hostile settlement. Behind him, Sdapezi and the others remained on horseback, eyes watching warily and lances held tightly in their hands.

Venutius, bedecked in gold jewellery, his long, greying hair neatly combed, his hazel eyes sparkling and with a broad smile of welcome on his face, extended a hand in greeting as Casca walked up to him. To Casca's relief, the King spoke in good, if heavily accented, Latin.

"Greetings, Centurion. You have got here very quickly. I had not expected my messengers to have reached the Governor yet. I am Venutius, King of the Brigantes."

"Quintus Sempronius Casca. Centurion, Third Illyrian Cohort," Casca announced.

There was something about the King's manner that he instinctively distrusted but now was not the time to make quick judgements. He clasped the King's forearm and gripped it firmly as they exchanged the traditional greeting.

Seeing Venutius' jewellery and his well-cut clothing, Casca was all too aware that his own armour and cloak were travel-stained and shabby. Still, he had the advantage, because Venutius, even though he styled himself a King, was only a barbarian.

Casca explained, "My men and I were in the area when we heard you had returned here. I have not yet spoken to the Governor. I thought it best to come and see for myself whether the reports were true."

Venutius gave Casca an appraising look.

"You are a brave man," he observed. "I was under the impression that Rome regarded me as an enemy."

"That depends."

Venutius' eyebrows rose.

"On what?" he asked carefully.

"On whether or not there is any truth in the story that you have Brennus here."

The smile returned to Venutius' face, broader than ever.

"Oh, yes," he beamed. "That is true."

"May I see him?" Casca asked.

Venutius replied, "I had thought we would entertain you and your men first. You must be tired and thirsty after your journey here."

Casca kept a stern look on his face. He had long since learned that it was important to let barbarians know who was in charge.

"I would prefer to see Brennus first," he insisted firmly. "After that, we can eat. And speak of what happens next."

Venutius gave a slight nod, clearly put out but not prepared to argue.

"Of course. Come with me."

Casca signalled to Sdapezi that the troop should remain mounted, then he followed Venutius through the widely scattered houses. Half a dozen warriors fell in behind them. Casca felt his back itching, just between his shoulder blades. If Venutius intended to kill him, he would never have a better chance. Casca did not yet trust the self-proclaimed King of the Brigantes but the man's manner suggested that he was anxious not to offend Rome. Acting as if he had no concerns, as if the notion of anyone trying to harm him was unthinkable, Casca walked alongside Venutius as outwardly relaxed as if he was strolling through the forum of Rome.

The King, too, appeared at ease as he led the way through the settlement.

"This Brennus is a formidable warrior, you know," he said pleasantly.

"I know. That is why the Governor wants him."

"Alive, no doubt?"

"Very much alive. He will be sent to Rome."

"To be ritually strangled?"

"Probably."

Venutius grinned, "It is no more than he deserves. He is brave and strong but he is rather stupid."

"What makes you say that?" Casca enquired.

"Well, perhaps we should say he is naive. Just as well, or I would not have caught him so easily."

Venutius halted outside a roundhouse where two spearmen stood watch at the door.

Turning to Casca, he said, "You do understand that I offer this man to Rome as a token of friendship. There have been misunderstandings between us in the past and I wish them to be

240

resolved. I have no desire to fight Rome. On the contrary, I can be of great help to you."

Casca replied, "I understand. But such things are for the Governor to decide. My task is to take Brennus to him."

He gave Venutius what he hoped was an encouraging smile as he added, "But I will certainly relay your wishes to the Governor."

"Excellent," nodded Venutius.

He signalled to the guards to stand aside, then went in through the low doorway.

Casca followed. Inside, there was no fire, just a plain, earth floor with a pile of furs at one side to serve as a bed, and a wooden pail, stinking of urine, on the opposite side. There were also two more warriors, armed with long spears, standing watch over a man who was huddled in the centre of the floor. The prisoner was shackled with iron manacles around his ankles and wrists, and with another long, iron chain fastening him to a massive wooden log. The chain permitted him some movement but the enormous weight of the log was clearly intended to prevent him moving very far.

Casca immediately recognised the broad-shouldered figure of Brennus.

The recognition was mutual. Brennus' eyes widened when he saw Casca, perhaps hinting at a touch of fear, but he remained seated on the ground, watching the two newcomers with a resentful, sullen expression.

Speaking in the native tongue, Casca said, "Hello, Brennus."

Brennus did not reply.

Betraying a hint of surprise, Venutius asked, "You know him, then?"

"Oh, yes. I know him. That is why the Governor sent me looking for him."

"And now you have found him. Thanks to me."

Casca ignored the Brigante King's obvious satisfaction. Instead, he asked, "What about the others?"

Venutius was momentarily caught off balance but he recovered quickly, asking, "What others? We have his woman. We are keeping her separate to ensure he behaves, but there were no others."

Casca frowned, "Are you sure? He was travelling with several others."

"I am positive," Venutius asserted. "There were only the two of them. This one is yours. I will keep the girl for myself."

Casca waved a hand irritably, chopping it down in an unmistakeable gesture.

"No," he said insistently. "If she is his woman, then she goes to Rome as well. Unharmed."

Venutius shrugged. Casca could see that the King was annoyed at being told what to do but Venutius made a show of conceding graciously.

"Very well," he sighed. "You may have the girl as well."

Casca went on, "But I would like to know what happened to the others they were with. The Governor wants one of them as well."

"Really? Why is that?"

"Because one of Brennus' companions was called Calgacus. He is a famous rebel. Perhaps you have heard of him?"

For a moment, Casca thought that Venutius had been overcome by shock. The blood drained from the King's face and he almost staggered. With an effort, he regained his composure, the blood pumping back to his cheeks, turning them almost red with excitement.

Venutius was breathing quickly and his eyes sparkled with excitement as he asked, "Calgacus is here? In Brigantia?"

"You know him?"

Venutius' hazel eyes took on a faraway look, as if he was staring right through Casca.

"Oh, yes," he breathed. "I know him."

His eyes snapped back into focus and he blurted, "We must find him. We must find him and kill him."

Casca shook his head.

"No. The Governor wants him alive, too."

Venutius stared intently into Casca's eyes. This time, there was no hint of concession in his expression as he said, "Believe me, my friend, that would not be wise. We shall hunt him down together and when we find him, you can have Brennus, you can have the girl, you can have all the others. But Calgacus is far too dangerous to take alive. I want to see him dead. You can take his severed head back to the Governor if you must, but I want him dead."

242

Casca stared back at the King, amazed at the vehemence in the older man's tone. Venutius' desire to see Calgacus die was so fierce that it visibly burned in him.

After a moment's consideration, Casca nodded, "We have a deal."

Predictably, Brennus refused to tell them where Calgacus was. When Venutius threatened to have Tegan beaten and raped if he did not talk, all that Brennus told him was that they had parted somewhere in the hills and that Calgacus was heading north.

Venutius ordered his men to beat Brennus but the big man did not change his story, even after suffering some painful blows and yet more bruising to his battered face. Persuaded that he might be telling the truth, Venutius relayed his words to Casca.

The Centurion had been unable to follow most of what the two men had said but he had witnessed the beating with some satisfaction. When Brennus refused to divulge any more, Casca suggested that there was another way they could verify the truth.

"You should ask the girl," he suggested.

Venutius' face broke into a wolfish grin as he agreed, "Naturally."

They went to another roundhouse, this one also guarded by two spearmen. The girl, young and pretty, with long, dark hair and a slim figure, was hobbled at the ankles and wrists by lengths of rope rather than the iron chains that imprisoned Brennus. She was free to move around although Venutius had set a plump woman to watch over her.

"She is no danger to us," Venutius told Casca. "But I have learned it is as well to have prisoners watched closely."

Casca said nothing. These barbarians had no buildings of stone, with deep cellars and dungeons where prisoners could be locked away behind heavy doors of thick, solid wood. But then, he knew, the Britons were not civilised. They were not at all like the Romans, who knew how to keep their prisoners secure.

Venutius stalked over to Tegan. He gripped her arms, shook her and began rattling out a string of harsh words. She looked terrified, her face deathly pale. Casca saw tears come to her eyes as Venutius slapped her across the cheek. Then the King pushed her down, forcing her to her knees so that he towered over her. His hands clamped around her head as he bent down, putting his face close to hers to snarl a demand. Tearfully, she began to talk.

Venutius kept his hands around Tegan's head until she had finished speaking, then he released his grip and turned to Casca.

"She says the same as Brennus," he announced in disgust.

Casca swore, "Then Calgacus will be long gone by now."

With a wicked smile, Venutius informed him, "No. She said one other thing that Brennus must have forgotten to mention to us. It seems that Calgacus is hurt and can hardly walk. They were holed up in some mountain hut, waiting for his leg to heal."

Casca's heart began to beat faster. He could see the same eagerness on Venutius' face.

"Where?" he asked.

"She does not know. Somewhere in the hills to the south-west."

"Brennus must know."

"I doubt that he would tell us, even if we tortured him," Venutius replied. "I am happy to do that, but your Governor wants him whole, does he not?"

Casca chewed his lip while he considered how much leeway his orders gave him regarding Brennus' state of health when he was presented to Agricola.

He said, "Perhaps we should torture the girl in front of him. That would make him talk. I'd rather have her alive but if it means finding Calgacus, she is expendable."

Venutius laughed, "You are a man after my own heart, Centurion Casca. But, much as I would enjoy watching her suffer, there is no need."

"No need? How will we find him, then? This is a big country."

"Precisely. Which is why torturing either of them may prove fruitless. Brennus might agree to lead us to Calgacus then conveniently forget the way. He could lead us all round the hills for days. He could certainly delay us long enough for Calgacus to make his escape."

"So what do you suggest?"

Venutius explained, "This is indeed a big country. But you forget that it is *my* country. I am the King. I will find him."

After seizing Dun Brigantia, Venutius had sent riders out to all the villages and farms, announcing his return, calling for warriors to join him and demanding tribute. Most of those riders had returned, so the King called them to him and began questioning them.

"There is a man we must find," he told them. "He is an enemy of Brigantia. His name is Calgacus. He is tall, broad-shouldered, like an older version of Brennus. He carries a large sword in a scabbard of silver and gold. And unless his companion is dead, he always has another man with him. A short fellow who carries two Roman swords."

There were blank looks from most of the warriors but one of them, a thin, rangy man with a squat nose, raised a hand.

"My King," he volunteered, "my men and I saw a man with two swords. Up in the hills."

Venutius instantly snapped his gaze to the speaker.

"Where and when?" he demanded.

The warrior rubbed his chin while he searched his memory. After a moment, he recalled, "It must have been three or four days ago. We were on the way back, crossing the hills to make the journey shorter. There was a mountain hut, one of those shelters that the people use in summer, but there was a fire because we saw smoke coming from the roof. Some men were living there. One of them was a short fellow, just as you describe, and he carried a Roman sword at each side."

Venutius sat back on his chair.

"So," he smiled, "the Runt is here. Which means that Calgacus is also here. Did you see him?"

The warrior shook his head.

"I don't think so. But he may have been inside the hut."

The man gave Venutius an apologetic look as he explained, "There were six of them, all armed, and there were only three of us. They claimed to be refugees fleeing from the Roman province. I gave them the news that you had returned and they said they would come here to join you."

Venutius understood that the warrior was afraid in case he had unwittingly done something wrong. Normally, the King would have enjoyed making the man suffer but the thought of finding Calgacus over-rode all other considerations.

"Could you find the place again?" he asked.

"Of course, my King," the man replied, eager to please. "It was in the hills just above Tumnorix's village. On horseback we could be there in three days. Two if we travel fast."

Casca had been bursting with impatience while he listened to the exchange. He could tell that the warrior knew something but he could not understand what was being said. At last, Venutius turned to him and translated the conversation.

Elated by the news, Casca punched his right fist into the palm of his left hand.

"We must go. Quickly."

Venutius smiled manically, his excitement almost matching that of the Centurion.

"Indeed we must," he agreed. "This time, I will see that renegade dead."

Chapter XXIII

Calgacus was always miserable when he was unwell. He spent his days resting his leg, grumbling and cursing at anyone who came near him. Only Runt seemed impervious to his morose mood but, as he explained to the others, he had known Calgacus long enough to know that this was just the big man's way when he was forced to be inactive.

"He'll cheer up once he is able to get up and about," he assured them. Privately, he was not so sure because he knew that Brennus' departure had hit Calgacus hard. With little else to occupy his mind, Calgacus had spent days brooding over his son's decision to leave and Runt was not sure how to pull his friend out of his gloomy mood.

Despite Calgacus' morose humour, the mood among the other men was better once Brennus and Tegan had left. They missed Tegan because she worked hard and was easy on their eyes, but Brennus' constant sniping had been wearing on everyone's nerves. Once he was gone, they all felt the atmosphere lighten.

Knowing that they would be compelled to remain in the hut for some time, they spent a few days carrying out repairs and improvements to make the hut wind and water-tight. The hugely-muscled sailor, Ger, attacked the nearby trees with awesome power, wielding his small axe so ferociously that he was able to fell and strip timber faster than any two of the others.

"He's useful when a ship needs repairing," laughed Risciporus as another sapling fell under Ger's onslaught.

Ger's stolid features barely registered a smile at the compliments. He felled trees, chopped the wood and carried huge bundles back to the hut. When the walls had been patched, he built a stock of firewood that Calgacus reckoned would last all winter. That prospect soured his mood even more, for the thought of being penned in this forlorn place for several months was not one that he relished.

The weather remained dull and overcast although the rain showers were few, if heavy. Whatever the weather, Calgacus insisted that someone kept watch, so they organised a small post high on the summit of the hill above the hut from where they could see in all directions. To provide some shelter for the man on watch, they gathered large stones which they used to build a small, circular wall, using the dry stone construction that farmers had used for generations to keep their livestock penned in. This post was manned at all times, even during the night of Samhain, although Calgacus, understanding the fear that would grip men on that night, suggested that they all stay together on the hilltop.

He hobbled up the slope, using his long stick to help him walk, feeling sharp pains with every step but stubbornly refusing all help.

From their high vantage point, they could see the bonfires in the village far below them and could even make out the dark shapes as people moved around the flames.

"There will be a big feast down there," Adelligus mused wistfully.

"And beer," Cawrdaf added.

"But there is better company up here," Runt pointed out.

They spent the long night talking and joking, studiously avoiding any reference to the evil spirits that they knew would be roaming the land all around them, ghosts that were kept away only by the flames of their small fire. When dawn arrived, they returned to the shelter, laughing and joking, pretending they had not been concerned at spending Samhain night outdoors.

The repair work kept them busy for a few days, after which they sat around, simply talking idly among themselves. Risciporus, accompanied by Ger, visited the village again and obtained some more food, handing over a few silver trinkets from Calgacus' dwindling supply, but when he returned, he had a worried look on his face.

"They are not exactly friendly," he recounted.

"They probably don't have much food to spare," Calgacus commented. "Feeding us will eat into their winter stores."

"They seem to have plenty of food," Risciporus muttered. "They just don't like sharing. Still, perhaps we won't be here much longer."

He gave Calgacus a hopeful look but Calgacus scowled, "That depends. This damned leg seems to be taking forever to heal. I keep thinking it is better but as soon as I start to walk, the damn thing flares up again."

"That's because you're getting old," Runt told him with a happy smile. "Thirty years ago, that sort of thing would have healed itself in a few days."

"Thank you for that thought," muttered Calgacus drily.

Runt grinned back at him. Then, delving inside his tunic, he dug out a long length of braided cord which he folded into two strips. He began twirling it in his hand.

"My old sling," he explained. "I'll see if I can add some things to the cooking pot."

Risciporus seemed amused.

"You can actually hit something with that?" he asked.

"Of course. Come along and watch if you like. Mind you, I am a bit out of practice."

Out of practice or not, Runt went off with Risciporus, returning some hours later with a small, scrawny goat.

"It was injured already," he informed the others. "It must have wandered off from some farm or other."

Calgacus shot his friend a look of suspicion but Runt gave the impression of being entirely innocent and Risciporus backed up his story.

The goat was skinned, cleaned and cooked. Runt scraped the fat from the inner side of the hide, then soaked it in water mixed with ash before stretching it out to dry, pinning its edges with heavy stones so that it would dry more or less flat.

"Not very sophisticated," he complained. "But it will do."

Risciporus said, "Perhaps you should show us all how to use a sling. Maybe we could all do a bit of hunting. At the very least it will help pass the time."

With nothing else to do, Runt took them up on the suggestion. Adelligus had a sling of his own, though he admitted that he could not match his father's skill in its use.

"It's just like throwing a stone," Runt explained to his new pupils. "Everyone can do that. The sling just makes your arm longer, so you can throw further. The trick is to throw accurately."

Risciporus was fascinated and insisted on being allowed to try his hand. Runt passed the sling to him.

"Put your finger through this small loop at the end of this cord," he told the seaman. "Then hold the other cord, place a stone into the cradle and start swinging. When you want to throw, you just let go of the loose cord and the stone flies out. The other cord stays in your hand because of the loop around your finger. It's very simple."

Adelligus gave a demonstration, whirling his own sling to hurl a small stone far across the hillside.

Runt gestured to Risciporus.

"You try," he said encouragingly.

Grinning nervously, Risciporus placed a small stone in the leather cradle. The others stepped back as he began to whirl his arm. He gave a little jump as he released the cord. The stone flew sharply upwards, speeding into the sky before falling to the ground barely ten paces from where Risciporus stood.

His face fell but he endured the mocking laughter with good grace, picked up another stone and tried again. This time he sent the stone more or less across the hill in front of him. Turning to face the others, he beamed at them.

"It's not too difficult once you get the hang of it," he grinned.

"I think you need a bit more practice," Runt cautioned.

Soon, the others had all made a few attempts. Only Calgacus, who sat watching from the doorway of the shelter and Dunnocatus, who was on watch, did not take part. For the next two days, the men made slings of their own and practised hard. They used strips of leather from the goat's hide, although Runt assured them that hemp or wool made better material for the twisted cords.

"Leather will chafe your fingers," he warned them.

Ulcattus and Cawrdaf showed some skill and, after a few days, even Risciporus was able to hit a reasonably large target more often than not. Ger, though, soon gave up as he seemed incapable of releasing the stone at the correct time. The bald-headed sailor could hurl the slingshots a long way but nobody was ever very sure which direction the missiles would take.

"Even standing behind him is not always safe," complained Adelligus when he was forced to duck to avoid one of Ger's misdirected stones.

Ger tossed away his sling in disgust and stalked off to the woods, growling under his breath. When he returned, he was carrying a large chunk of wood which he began trimming with his small axe. He worked in silence, ignoring the questions that the others fired at him while a growing pile of wood chips and splinters gathered at his feet. After a while, he stood up, hefting the wood in his huge fist.

250

It was almost as long as his arm, tapered at the lower end so that he could grip it, but thicker at the top. He had shaped an edge on one side of the upper end, creating what looked like a long-bladed wooden axe.

Ger grinned as he displayed his new weapon.

"Now I've got a club," he growled happily.

Runt looked at the massive weapon, nodding in appreciation.

"It's crude but I wouldn't want to be on the receiving end of a blow from that," he said.

"Try it out," Calgacus encouraged Ger.

The big man swung the club gently, testing its weight.

"Nothing to hit," he grumbled, sounding disappointed.

"You could try it on a shield," Risciporus suggested.

Runt shook his head.

"He'd smash it and we only have three shields between us."

Ger settled for battering some young trees. The massive club gouged great chunks from the trunks, sending splinters flying, and he pronounced himself happy with the results. He was immensely proud of his new club which he carried with him wherever he went.

To keep them busy, Runt organised some mock combats, pitting the three sailors against the three young warriors. The sailors soon discovered that the warriors were able to beat them with ease, their spears and swords moving with astonishing speed. Only Ger was able to hold his own by the simple expedient of ignoring his opponent's weapons and bludgeoning them to the ground with his massive fists. Impressed by the big sailor's power, Runt spent some time showing him how to fight against a man with a spear or a sword. Ger, sweat dripping from his bald head, threw himself into the training sessions with relish until Runt called a halt for fear that someone would suffer a serious injury.

Excusing himself from the trials, Risciporus came to sit beside Calgacus.

The Captain observed, "The way your men go on, you'd think you were preparing for a fight."

"It's always better to be ready for trouble," Calgacus replied. "That way you won't be caught by surprise if it arrives."

Risciporus nodded, "I can understand that. The sea can be a dangerous place and the best sailors are those who are best prepared."

He gave Calgacus a thoughtful look as he continued, "I won't pretend I am enjoying this, but if you can get us safely away from here and beyond the Romans' reach, I'll build myself a new boat. I'd like to go back to what I know best."

Calgacus smiled, "When you have a new boat, I'll even come out to sea with you."

"That sounds like a bargain," Risciporus laughed.

Calgacus rubbed the back of his leg.

"It won't be long now," he promised. "I'll be able to walk normally in a few days."

"We could try to buy some horses from the village," Risciporus suggested.

"Do you think they would sell us any?"

"Probably not. But we could ask."

"All right. Why don't you go down tomorrow and ask them."

Early the following morning Risciporus took all that remained of their silver and gold, hoping to barter them for at least one horse, but Tumnorix, the surly head man, refused to even consider the exchange.

"I have few enough horses," he told Risciporus. "Even to be rid of you and your companions, I will not sell them to you."

He looked pointedly to one side where a young man was holding two long leashes which were attached to the collars of a pair of enormous, shaggy-coated mastiffs with huge jaws and evil, red eyes.

Risciporus understood the message. He knew that the head man was lying about having few horses. Risciporus had seen that the village had several of the beasts, but he also knew that to challenge the lie would be dangerous. Tumnorix eventually sold him some salted meat for an extortionate price, but that was the only trade he would enter into.

Disconsolately, Risciporus climbed back up the high, steep slope without the horses he had hoped to buy.

Calgacus clapped him on the shoulder.

"Don't worry about it. I'll be fine for walking soon. Ten days at the most."

"Never mind that," said Risciporus, trying to make a joke of his failure. "I wanted a horse for myself. I'm not used to walking."

"We'll both need to put up with that soon," Calgacus told him. "We have nothing left to barter, so we'll run out of food in a few days."

"Tumnorix won't help," Risciporus sighed glumly. "He's more likely to set his dogs onto us."

"I'm sure we can manage for a while yet," Calgacus assured him.

To alleviate the worries about food, Runt and Adelligus went off into the hills, seeking the high ground where deer roamed the moorland. Without hunting bows, stalking the alert beasts was not easy, for as soon as Runt stood to begin whirling his sling, the deer would scatter, but on the third attempt, he threw a lucky shot that struck the foreleg of a young hind that had strayed too close to their hiding place.

Leaping from cover, Adelligus hurled his heavy spear at the injured animal and managed to strike its neck. The hind went down in a tangle of long legs. Runt and Adelligus ran towards it, swords already drawn. They finished the animal off quickly, then carried it back in triumph.

"That will last us a while," Runt announced proudly as they presented their trophy to the others.

In truth, the deer was skinny, its ribs showing against its sides, and they all knew that venison had very little fat because deer are built for agility and speed rather than for endurance. But Runt and Adelligus had done well, and the whole group enjoyed a few days of good eating.

Risciporus, still not looking forward to the prospect of the long walk that lay ahead, suggested, "We could stay here all winter if you can keep doing that."

"We were lucky," Runt replied with a shake of his head. "And it took us all day to catch this one. It's not easy to get close to them. If the snow comes, they will be forced down to lower ground and we might have more chance of catching them, but it still won't be easy."

"I don't suppose you saw any horses while you were out there?" the Captain asked hopefully.

"Just the deer and a couple of wolves," Runt replied.

Two days later, they did see horses. Cawrdaf, who had been on watch, hurried down to the shelter to bring warning of three riders approaching from the west.

Runt said, "I'll speak to them."

Signalling to Calgacus, he suggested, "You'd better stay out of sight. If there is trouble, you'll be better off inside."

"You mean you'll be better off not having to watch out for me," Calgacus said.

Runt laughed, then turned away to organise the others. He sent Cawrdaf back up to the hilltop to keep watch in case the three riders were simply a scouting party for a larger group. Then he had the others spread out slightly. They all kept their weapons close. Ger made a point of picking up his massive club and swinging it loosely in his hand.

The horsemen rode up slowly, offering no overt threat. They were well wrapped against the chill and each man held a long spear and a small shield. Their small, shaggy horses were laden with bags of fodder and food supplies.

Runt stepped forwards to meet them, holding up a hand, palm outwards, in greeting.

"Hello, friends. What brings you this way?"

The leading rider, a tall man with a squat nose that looked as if it had been broken at some time in the past, nodded a faint greeting in reply.

"Just passing," he said. "We are on our way back to Dun Brigantia."

"You are a long way from home," Runt observed.

"So are you, to judge by your accent," the horseman replied.

Runt gave a shrug.

"We used to live further south but the Romans have a new Governor and they have been throwing their weight around. We decided to come north, to where there are still some free people."

The Brigante tribesman's eyes roved around suspiciously, taking in the other warriors and the weapons. After a moment, he seemed to reach some sort of decision.

Drawing himself up, he said, "You should come to Dun Brigantia. You will be welcomed there. We can always use more men who know how to use a spear or sword."

"Maybe we will," Runt nodded, feigning interest. "But I don't know Dun Brigantia. Who rules there?"

254

"It is the home of Venutius, King of the Brigantes."

Runt could not hide his surprise.

"Venutius? He is back, then? I had heard he was defeated."

"He is back," the rider confirmed with a hint of pride. "He is King once again."

"Then we shall travel north and join him," said Runt.

The rider nodded. He did not look entirely convinced by Runt's promise but he accepted the words at face value. Giving a small wave, he said farewell, tugged on his reins and led his two companions back down the slope, then continued along the narrow upland valley that led to the north-west.

Runt stood watching until the three Brigantes had vanished from sight, then he went into the hut, calling the others to join him.

"What's wrong?" Calgacus asked.

"How long before your leg will be up to walking?" Runt countered.

"A few more days, I think. Why?"

With a grimace, Runt informed him, "I have some bad news."

Chapter XXIV

Venutius took thirty men on the search for Calgacus, all of them mounted. In his absence, he left Praxus, one of his senior men, in charge at Dun Brigantia.

Einon, who was riding with the King, questioned the wisdom of Venutius leaving so soon after he had reclaimed his position as King.

"You should stay here," he urged Venutius. "Let me find this man Calgacus for you. Messengers and envoys are coming in from all across the Kingdom, bringing promises of loyalty. They expect to see you."

Despite Einon's appeal, Venutius was not to be dissuaded.

"I have heard those promises before," he replied bitterly. "Believe me, they are not worth the effort of listening to. The same chieftains who are sending word of their allegiance to me swore loyalty to Cynwrig only a couple of years ago."

"You still need them," Einon persisted.

"I need the support of Rome more," Venutius pointed out. "Killing Calgacus will ensure that I have that support."

"You have already given them Brennus. Is that not enough?"

Venutius' eyes took on a dangerous sheen as he responded, "No. I want Calgacus dead. He and I are sworn blood foes and he has thwarted me too often in the past. This time, I will finish him."

"And what then?" Einon asked. "Will you return once this Calgacus is dead?"

"No," Venutius frowned. "It will be necessary for me to go to the new Roman Governor. I don't trust this cold-eyed Centurion and I need to be sure that the Governor knows that I was the one who delivered his enemies to him. Besides, I will have to swear loyalty, and probably agree to give hostages."

He saw the flicker of concern in Einon's eyes and added, "Don't worry. You will not be among them."

Acknowledging his favoured status with a nod, Einon said, "You will be putting yourself in danger, my King."

"It is necessary," Venutius insisted. "But it is worth the risk. This Casca wants Calgacus as much as I do, so I can trust him to help me track him down. As for the Governor, the Romans like to see people grovel before them. If I have to, I will crawl on my belly and offer half my wealth in tribute. I will make any promise he cares to ask for, so long as I am counted among his friends and allies."

Einon smiled, "And promises can always be broken later."

"You are learning, my lad," Venutius chuckled.

Lowering his voice to barely more than a whisper, Einon asked, "What of Praxus, lord? Do you trust him to remain loyal if he holds Dun Brigantia?"

Venutius was unconcerned.

"Praxus is a born follower. He will not dare do anything except what I tell him."

Einon smiled as he recalled old Praxus' reaction when he had been told he would be in charge during Venutius' absence. The King, he thought, was correct, for Praxus had appeared worried, constantly asking questions about what he should do and frowning nervously as he had watched Venutius lead the hunters out of the Dun.

Yes, Einon thought, Praxus was a born follower. Not like himself, who held the King's trust despite his youth and relative inexperience. Einon was proud of his new status because he would be Venutius' deputy on this latest mission, the hunt for the King's oldest and most dangerous adversary.

The thirty men in the King's party were all dressed for war. They rode with the ten Romans and, in their midst, their hands tied, were Brennus and Tegan.

Casca rode at the head of his troop, glad to be away from the confines of Dun Brigantia and eager to track down Calgacus. After so many weeks of fruitless effort and missed opportunities, he had begun to believe that his fortune was changing at last. Brennus was already his, now riding with four troopers assigned to guard him. Soon, he would find Calgacus.

Already, Casca was imagining his next meeting with the Governor. He could envisage the surprise on Agricola's face when Casca presented him with a captive Brennus, with the head of Calgacus, and with a new and subservient ally in Venutius. A posting as senior Centurion to the legionary cavalry was the least that Casca expected in exchange for these gifts.

He eased his horse into a faster canter, moving up the long column until he reached Venutius' side. The King wore a fine jerkin of chainmail, the tiny rings of metal gleaming in the bright sunlight. He had long, well made boots of fine leather and a patterned cloak of green, blue and brown. Allied to his habitual gold rings and neck torc, the clothes showed that Venutius was a man of wealth and power. Casca was not sure who the King was trying to impress, but he recognised that Venutius was using this sortie almost as a triumphal procession just as much as a hunting expedition. A hunting expedition with a human quarry, Casca reminded himself.

He said to the King, "Are you sure that you need all these men?"

Venutius replied with a grim nod.

"I would have brought more but I need to leave old Praxus with a strong force of warriors I can trust."

Casca understood. Venutius' hold on Brigantia was still tenuous. Still, forty men to capture one injured rebel seemed extravagant.

"More?" he asked in a light tone. "I would have thought there are already more than enough of us. The girl said there were only eight of them left in Calgacus' party."

"He has won before against worse odds than that," Venutius responded. "Do not underestimate him, Centurion. Calgacus is no ordinary man."

"Perhaps not. But he is old and he is injured. I think we will be able to handle him."

Venutius' face remained stern as he warned, "When we find him, kill him quickly. Do not keep him alive. Do not gloat over his capture. Just kill him."

"Do you not want him to know that it is you who has killed him?"

With a shake of his head, Venutius said, "Not any more. Years ago, I would have wanted nothing better, but I have learned that it is unwise to take chances with Calgacus. I will be content if I see his corpse."

Casca shrugged. Sometimes he thought that he would never understand the attitudes of these barbarians.

Looking beyond Calgacus' inevitable death, he remarked, "Once we have his head, you will accompany me south, to meet the Governor."

Venutius had always intended to do that but he bridled slightly because Casca had framed his words as an instruction, not a request. Masking his annoyance, he gave a thin smile and nodded.

"Of course. Nothing would please me more. It is time that the Brigantes became friends of Rome once more."

Casca kept his thoughts to himself. The Ordovices had been friends of Rome once, until Brennus had become their leader. At least with Brennus, the Romans had known where they stood. Looking at Venutius, Casca could not help but think that the King's friendship would last only as long as it suited him. Casca decided that he would speak to the Governor privately and try to persuade him to have Venutius sent to Rome as a captive along with Brennus. That would be the safest course of action, he reflected.

He smiled to himself as he rode on, turning thoughts over in his mind. Thanks to him, the barbarians would soon be bereft of leadership. Perhaps he should ask for more than a simple posting to a legionary cavalry troop. Perhaps he could join the Governor's own staff. How could Agricola refuse a man who had achieved so much? Casca's career prospects were suddenly looking very good indeed.

The journey to Tumnorix's village was uneventful. Venutius pushed the pace, arriving late on the second day after leaving Dun Brigantia. By the time they rode into the settlement, Casca had only the dimmest notion of where they were, for the journey had followed a convoluted route through the hills. He knew that his men were feeling anxious about being stranded in the midst of the barbarians but Casca was not concerned. He and Venutius had a shared goal. Once they had killed Calgacus, all they had to do was head south, where fame and glory awaited.

The sour-faced, grey-haired Tumnorix welcomed them, although his aged eyes betrayed his concern at being required to feed so many additional mouths in winter. Still, he did not voice those worries but ushered Venutius and Casca into his roundhouse, a dark, gloomy place that smelled of woodsmoke, damp earth and too many people who, in Casca's opinion, were badly in need of a bath.

Tumnorix clapped his hands, snapping at the women to provide a hot meal for the noble Venutius and his Roman allies.

While the food was being hastily prepared, he surprised Casca by producing an amphora of fine wine, although the effect was rather spoiled when it was poured into crudely fashioned pewter beakers.

While Casca sipped the wine, Venutius did not waste any time. He told Tumnorix, "I am seeking some men. They are my enemies. I had heard that they were seen near here, camping in one of your high, summer shelters."

Tumnorix's face twisted in a grimace of distaste as he nodded, "Aye, there are men here. They have been up in the hills for more than a full turning of the moon now."

He gestured with his hand, indicating somewhere high above them as he recounted, "Just up on the other side of that hill."

Venutius looked up eagerly, as if his gaze could penetrate the smoke-shrouded rafters and thatching of the hut to see to the summit of the hill that overlooked the village.

He asked, "How many of them are there?"

Tumnorix shrugged, "I have seen only four. But one of them looked like that big fellow you brought here in chains."

"He was with them some time ago," Venutius acknowledged. "Now he is a prisoner and we are seeking the others. Can you give us guides?"

"Of course," Tumnorix confirmed. "But they will be able to see you coming long before you reach the top of the hill. They have a man on watch all the time."

Casca swore when Venutius translated that news for him.

"Then they probably saw us when we rode in," he observed.

"Very likely," Tumnorix agreed. "But I have not seen any of them for a few days. They stopped coming here to ask for food when I threatened to set my dogs on them."

He looked uncertain as he added, "They may have moved on."

Casca took charge of the discussion. Through Venutius, he asked several questions about the lie of the land. Once he had his answers, he made his decision quickly.

"You should send ten men out this evening," he told Venutius. "They should leave now, before it gets too dark for any sentry to see them. Tell them to ride west, then to approach the shelter from the far side at daybreak tomorrow."

"A diversion?" Venutius asked.

"In a way," Casca agreed. "If there is someone watching then I am hoping that they will not suspect we are looking for them if some of our men ride on. But their main task is simply to cut off any retreat. The rest of us will leave here before dawn and go straight up the hill. If the rebels are still there and if they have a man on watch, he won't see us in the dark until it is too late. Then we can catch the rest of them easily enough. If they do happen to see us coming, your riders will be able to hunt them down. We will trap them between the two groups."

He brought his hands together, closing them tightly as if he was squeezing some unseen object.

"Good enough," said Venutius. "I'll put Einon in charge of the riders. He's reliable and it will do him good to have a command. But what if the rebels have moved on?"

"They will have headed north," Casca replied. "They are on foot. We will hunt them and we will catch them."

He paused, then added, "But they are there. I can feel it. The gods are with us. Tomorrow morning, they will all be dead."

Venutius took a long, savouring sip of his wine.

"I will drink to that," he smiled.

261

Chapter XXV

Casca was roused in pitch darkness. He had been given a roundhouse to himself, the family who normally lived there having been decanted to a neighbour's home. Casca had briefly considered sharing the same quarters as his men but had dismissed that idea. His Centurion's rank entitled him to some privileges.

He had slept in his tunic, wrapped in his long, red cloak, lying on a heap of furs spread over a bed of hay and bracken. It had been a cold, uncomfortable night and he suspected the bedding was infested with fleas, so he was not sorry to be woken early.

As he shivered in the cold air, Hortensius helped him strap on his armour and fasten his cloak.

"The lads have got some warm tisane brewing, Sir," the young trooper told him. "Shall I fetch you some?"

"That would be welcome," Casca replied.

He rubbed the stubble on his chin, deciding that he could shave later, once the rebels had been captured and killed. Hortensius scurried off, returning a few moments later with a clay beaker of steaming liquid. Casca took a sip and pulled a face at the bitter taste.

"What's in it?" he asked.

"Don't know, Sir," Hortensius replied. "Just whatever was available, I suppose."

Casca wondered whether his men were playing some sort of trick on him, using some foul ingredients to mix a drink for him as a petty revenge for having been dragged on this mission. While he would not put such a prank beyond them, Hortensius' face was entirely innocent and Casca decided the soldiers would not play tricks when a fight was imminent. He drained the hot drink as quickly as he could, grimacing slightly at the bitter aftertaste. At least it had warmed him up.

He strapped his long cavalry sword to his waist, rammed his plumed helmet onto his head and went to find his men.

Outside, the night was dark and the air bitingly cold. The ground beneath his feet was as hard as iron, coated in a white film of heavy frost which crackled and crunched beneath his steps.

Casca shivered as he crossed the village, noting with satisfaction that the barbarians were rousing themselves. From one house he could hear the sound of Venutius complaining about something but Casca walked on. There would be time enough to speak to Venutius later.

Sdapezi met him at the roundhouse where the troopers had been billeted for the night. It was one of the larger homes, with a high roof and two doors. The family who lived there had not been happy at being evicted but Casca had insisted that his men should be billeted together, so the barbarians here had also been forced to move into their neighbours' homes for the night.

"It's very comfortable," Sdapezi said in answer to Casca's enquiry about their lodgings. "Warm, too."

"Not so warm out here," Casca grumbled, reflecting on his own cold, uncomfortable night.

"No. It feels like it might snow," the Decurion commented as he rubbed his hands together then blew on them in an attempt to warm them.

Casca glanced upwards but the night sky was dark, no stars showing through the heavy clouds. Even the moon was hidden, its presence revealed only by a faint glimmer off to the east.

"Snow, hail or thunder, we are going," Casca insisted firmly.

"Of course, Sir. I just hope the bloody Brigantes are of the same opinion."

"I'll make sure they are," Casca promised. "How are the prisoners?"

"Behaving."

Sdapezi led Casca inside. A wave of heat from the hearth fire hit Casca as he went through the doorway. Here, he found the troopers finishing their preparations for the night attack, checking one another's armour and testing the blades of their swords for sharpness. Despite the cold and the early start to the day, they appeared to be in good humour, teasing one another and joking among themselves. They fell silent, straightening to attention when Casca entered.

He looked around, forcing a benevolent smile to his lips. Were they laughing about the drink they had given him? No matter.

"Carry on, lads," he told them.

To one side of the hut sat the figures of Brennus and Tegan, each with wrists and ankles chained by heavy, iron shackles. The key to the fetters was tucked under Casca's tunic, hanging from a cord around his neck. He saw Brennus scowl up at him and even the girl seemed unusually defiant. She lifted her head to say something to him, a short string of harsh, angry words that seemed incongruous coming from such a pretty face. He caught a mention of Calgacus' name but that was all he could make any sense of.

Casca called Hortensius over to him.

"What did she say?"

Hortensius spoke to the girl and she repeated her words, almost spitting them out.

Hortensius looked faintly embarrassed as he reported, "She says that Calgacus will kill us all, Sir. Sorry, Sir."

Casca gave a scornful laugh as he replied, "Tell her that I will return just after daybreak and I will show her his head to prove that she is wrong."

Hortensius relayed those words, then translated the girl's harsh response.

"She says he probably left the shelter long ago, Sir. She claims we will not find him."

"In that case he will hardly be able to kill us all, will he?" Casca mocked. "All right, that's enough nonsense. Let's get ready to go."

He turned to Sdapezi and ordered, "I want two men left here to watch the prisoners. They are not to be left unattended and nobody else is to see them."

"Very good, Sir," Sdapezi acknowledged.

"Hamar and Tulban, I think."

"Sir?"

Sdapezi was surprised. The two men Casca had named were probably the most experienced and certainly the most reliable men in the troop. Sdapezi had assumed they would be at the forefront of the day's action.

Casca explained, "The rest of us can take care of the rebels, Decurion. With Venutius and his men, we have more than enough to catch half a dozen old men. But I want no chances taken with these two."

"Very good, Sir," Sdapezi replied.

He turned away to find the two men who had been chosen for the guard duty.

"You're the lucky ones," Sdapezi assured them in a low voice. "The rest of us have to go mountaineering in this weather."

The two soldiers grinned. As veterans, they knew an easy job when they saw it. Remaining in the warmth of the roundhouse was infinitely preferable to climbing a hill in the freezing darkness.

"Keep a close eye on the prisoners," Sdapezi warned. "Best to separate them, too."

He waved a hand towards the opposite side of the house as he went on, "Put the girl over there. That way, if one of them gives you any trouble, the other one is too far away to interfere."

Casca clapped his hands together.

"Time to go, lads," he announced.

They assembled outside, with Sdapezi standing smartly at one end of the line of seven men. Each of them held a lance and a small cavalry shield, their long swords hanging at their waists.

"Look smart now," Sdapezi urged them. "Let's show these savages how proper soldiers behave."

There seemed to be a great number of barbarians gathering in the village, although it was difficult to tell just how many there were because no torches had been lit. Casca had forbidden that for fear that anyone on watch at the top of the hill would see the unusual activity. There was, though, a sense of many bodies gathering in the open space at the centre of the village.

From out of the shadows, Casca saw Venutius striding across to meet him. The Brigante King was wearing a heavy sheepskin jerkin over his chainmail tunic, with thick, woollen leggings and fur-lined boots.

His breath steamed in the night air as he said, "We are ready, Centurion. Tumnorix and his men will accompany us. They are eager to rid themselves of these renegades who have taken so much of their food these past weeks."

"How many do we have in our army now?" Casca asked, barely trying to disguise his sarcasm.

"Thirty seven of us, plus your own men. As well as Einon's ten we sent out yesterday."

"That should be enough to catch eight sleeping men," grunted Casca. "Come on, it is time to go. There are less than two hours till dawn and we need to have secured the summit by then."

265

"You Romans are always impressive to watch," Venutius remarked, doing a slightly better job than Casca had done of masking his mockery. "Sometimes I think you can't even go for a piss without making a plan beforehand."

He turned away before Casca could respond, waving his hands to summon his ragged band of warriors.

Casca watched as the Brigantes headed out into the night towards the dark bulk of the steep hillside.

"Tell them to keep quiet," he hissed at Venutius.

It was, he thought, a forlorn hope. The Brigantes were chattering among themselves as they walked. In their midst, Casca saw old Tumnorix, wrapped in heavy furs, a long spear in his hand.

With a sigh, Casca turned to Sdapezi and the six other troopers.

"Come on. This lot will never make a surprise attack. We need to get to the top first to take care of any sentries."

They followed the mob of Britons, often stumbling in the darkness as they picked their way out of the village, their route determined by the many stone walls that marked out the fields and pastures. Soon the ground began to rise and Casca urged his men on, pushing through the Brigantes to take the lead. Casca had no idea where Venutius was, nor which of the men were supposed to be the guides, but he decided that a guide was not really necessary.

"Just keep going uphill," he told his men.

Their breath billowed around them as they plodded upwards, the grass and bracken of the hillside crackling beneath their feet as they stepped on the frost-coated ground. Often, men would slip, but Casca urged them to keep moving.

He soon found that he was sweating despite the desperate cold, his skin feeling wet and clammy beneath his clothes, the muscles of his legs protesting against the strain of the climb. In the darkness, he could not tell how high they were but the slope kept rising in front of him, so he pressed on.

The Brigantes were still close by. He could hear the rustle of movement and the sounds of men breathing heavily as they climbed but the talking had ceased. To Casca's annoyance, some of the Britons began to pass him, sliding up the hill like ghosts, silent and deadly, and apparently unaffected by the rigours of the climb. In a loud whisper, he told them to wait, but they appeared not to understand him and their dark shapes kept moving ahead of him.

266

Casca halted, taking a few moments to regain his breath. He checked that his men were still with him.

"All here, Sir," Sdapezi whispered.

"How far to go, I wonder?" Casca frowned.

"Hard to say, Sir. A few times I thought we'd reached the top but there always seem to be more of the damn thing. It didn't look so high yesterday."

Casca sighed, "We need to keep moving. These barbarians will get there before us and ruin everything if they attack too soon."

The seemingly endless climb continued. By now, Casca was feeling the strain of wearing his heavy armour. He and his men were cavalry, unused to the rigours of fighting on foot. They gradually slipped further and further behind the Brigantes who passed them with mocking smiles on their faces.

As dawn approached, Casca heard Venutius nearby. In a low whisper, he called to the King to tell his men not to go further than the summit.

"Tell them to take out any sentry and then wait for us," he insisted, swearing softly at the knowledge that his plan was already being altered. He had wanted to reach the summit first but the Brigantes were obviously going to beat him to the top of the hill.

Seething with frustration, he forced himself to keep moving, almost on all fours now as the hill grew even steeper. Under his breath he maintained a steady stream of low curses. He hated it when things started to go wrong.

His fears were compounded when a spot of wetness splashed onto his hand. Another slapped into his face. He could not prevent himself groaning as he recognised the beginnings of a snowfall.

In the space of a few heartbeats, the ground was slippery with white as the first drops quickly developed into a heavy fall. Casca's chilled fingers grew numb with cold and the snow fluttered into his face as the climb became even more difficult. He was tempted to lower the face mask of his helmet but that would restrict his vision even more, so he plodded on.

Unexpectedly, a whispered voice called to him from some distance away to his left as a dark shape materialised through the snowy shadows. It was Venutius.

The King's face was drawn and pale, the exertions of the climb clearly having taken a lot out of him. He looked like Casca felt.

"What is it?" Casca asked.

"There was no sentry," Venutius informed him glumly. "There is a small outpost over that way but it was deserted."

Casca blinked, peering into the darkness.

"We are at the top?" he asked.

"You have come too far to the right, but yes, we are all here. Tumnorix and his men say the hut we are seeking is a little way down the far side."

Venutius waved his hand vaguely northwards as he asked, "What do you want to do now?"

Again Casca looked into the night but all he could see was swirling snow appearing out of the darkness.

"We wait," he decided. "Get everyone together on the summit. We will go down at dawn."

Venutius muttered, "It will be a cold wait."

"It won't be for long. Sunrise can't be too far away and it will be worth it to catch Calgacus."

"Aye, there is that," conceded Venutius. "Come this way, then."

They huddled into the small shelter of stones that had been built on the summit. There was not much room in the tiny outpost so while Casca, Venutius and Tumnorix found shelter behind the crude stone walls, the rest of the soldiers and warriors were forced to cover their heads with their cloaks and sit out on the cold hillside, allowing the snow to cover them in a fine layer of ghostly white. It was, as Venutius had predicted, a cold wait.

Casca was glad to be able to rest, even if he was freezing. He saw that, like him, Venutius was breathing heavily, grateful for a chance to recover his strength. The Brigante King was also worried.

"It is not like Calgacus to leave nobody on watch," he remarked. "Maybe we are too late and he has gone."

"If he has, we will still catch him," Casca said with more confidence than he felt. "The one good thing about this snow is that he will leave tracks we can follow. But he may still be there. He might have decided there would be no point in leaving someone on watch on a night like this."

Venutius asked, "Do you take in your sentries when the weather is bad?"

Casca hesitated, knowing his tired mind and chilled body had almost led him to make a mistake. He knew that Venutius was right but the only response he could truthfully give was that his men were Romans, not barbarians. One could not expect military discipline from savages but to say so would be foolish when he was surrounded by barbarians.

He gave a weak smile and shrugged.

"Perhaps you are right," he admitted.

Venutius stared at him. Casca had the uncomfortable feeling that the Brigante leader knew exactly what he had been thinking but Venutius merely said, "We will soon find out."

It was difficult to tell when dawn arrived. The sky was hidden by the blanket of dark, snow-laden clouds, so the usual gradual lightening of the eastern horizon was lost somewhere in the murk, but soon the gloom was eased and what had been mere dark shapes slowly became more defined as the light revealed their details.

Rubbing his frozen hands together briskly, Casca declared, "Let us do this. There is enough light now."

Gratefully, the men rose, shaking the snow from their cloaks, flexing numbed fingers and stamping their feet as they tried to cast off the worst effects of the freezing temperature.

Tumnorix, his aged features even more wrinkled and surly than usual, pointed with his long spear.

"That way," he informed them.

The small shelter was covered by a layer of snow that concealed its outline but Casca soon made it out in the growing light. He led his troop towards it, signalling to Venutius and Tumnorix to take their men to the flanks. They crunched down the slope, slipping and sliding, the snow covering their feet at every step.

The shelter looked cold and deserted. Casca's heart fell. Despite the signs, he had tried to convince himself that Calgacus would still be here, that the rebels would remain for months rather than try to travel home in winter. Now, he was not so sure.

Far off to his left, he saw a ragged line of horsemen appear as Einon's band of riders rode into the upland valley after their long, night journey. Despite the cold, the hard climb and the snow, Casca's plan had worked. All he needed now was the final result.

Twenty paces from the hut, he signalled to his men. They broke into a run, or as much of a run as they could through the hampering snow. One of them burst through the hut's door, dashing inside with lance at the ready. Others piled in as quickly as they could but by the time Casca arrived, Sdapezi was coming back out with a grim expression on his face.

"It's empty, Sir," the Decurion reported.

Casca pushed through, going inside to see for himself. Getting out of the snow at last was a relief, but that relief was quickly dampened when he saw the cold hearth and the empty hut. Beside him, Sdapezi said nothing, waiting for a reaction.

Venutius came in through the doorway. He looked at Casca with a blank expression.

"What now, Roman?" he asked.

"We go back and fetch our horses. We find him. He can't have gone far on foot, even if he left a few days ago."

Casca tried to sound positive although he knew that the task was not as simple as he made it sound. The chances of finding a small band of fugitives in the wide lands of Brigantia were slim.

While Casca had been talking to Venutius, Sdapezi had squatted down beside the ring of stones that formed the hearth. He touched the ashes, burying his fingers deep within them, then looked back up at Casca.

"There is a trace of warmth here, Sir," he said. "This fire probably only went out late yesterday."

Casca hurried to squat down beside the fire. He smiled as he touched his fingers to the ashes.

Standing up, he said to Venutius, "By Jupiter! We will catch him. He can't be far away."

Chapter XXVI

The heavy shackles that manacled his ankles and wrists were, to Brennus, a symbol of his utter defeat. All his life he had had so many dreams; dreams that had been sown and nurtured by the tales his mother had told him of his great, warrior father. Calgacus himself did not interest Brennus, but his famous deeds did. Everywhere among the free tribes, men sang of the mighty warrior with the magic sword who won victory over the Romans when everyone else suffered defeat after defeat at the hands of the invaders. From a young age, Brennus had been determined to prove that he could surpass the fabled Calgacus, the father who had abandoned him to a life of slavery.

Brennus had begun to turn his boyhood dreams to reality when he had seized his freedom, then fulfilled them when he had taken the rule of the Ordovices from the weak and womanly Cadwallon. He had shown that he could defeat the Romans when he ambushed their patrol and later, when he had destroyed their fortress. That had been a great time, a time when he had basked in the glory of Kingship, in the power of the Ordovices. It had been a time of triumph. He had been Brennus the King, a man worthy of his own songs.

Then, somehow, it had all gone wrong. Brennus had heard the tales of the Roman Legions but the reality was that he had little conception of just how many heavily armoured men the Empire could bring against him. The speed with which they gathered an army to face the Ordovices so late in the season had caught him by surprise. Despite this, he had been confident that his tribe were strong enough to win where others had failed. But then Calgacus had arrived so unexpectedly, with his predictions of defeat. That, Brennus decided, was when something had changed in his fortunes. There had been nothing but bad luck ever since that night.

Now he sat dejectedly with Tegan a few paces from him and two Roman soldiers watching them closely. There was little prospect of escape. He knew what the Roman Centurion, Casca, had planned for him but he could think of no way of avoiding that fate. At every turn, even when he had tried to throw Venutius off Calgacus' trail, Tegan had been used as a weapon against him. A part of him, the part that had made him kill Cadwallon's family, told him that Tegan was doomed anyway and that he should not allow the threats of what the Romans would do to her to influence him. But when he looked at her delicate face, pale and frightened yet still defiant, he remembered his mother and he knew that he could not bear to watch Tegan suffer.

That knowledge caused him to curse himself even more, for a leader should be ruthless. He saw that he was weak because he would not sacrifice Tegan to prevent her from being used against him.

Defeated, despising himself for having been used and trapped by Venutius, he felt despair welling deep inside him. If there was no escape, why not simply force the Romans' hand? Why not make an attempt to escape and ensure that they killed him quickly?

He looked at the two guards. They were sitting on stools, one at each doorway, facing each other across the hut while Brennus and Tegan also sat opposite each other at the sides of the house. Chained as he was, Brennus could move, but not quickly enough to reach either of the guards before they could kill him. The long cavalry lances were held ready, the soldiers watchful. If he moved towards one of them, the other would be able to come up behind him. Unless he threw himself onto the tip of the first man's lance, they would overpower him easily enough. But, for the moment, there were only two of them. Until now, there had been a host of Roman soldiers and Brigante warriors watching him. Would he ever have another chance like this?

He looked across the fire to where Tegan was sitting. She, too, must have realised that this could be their last opportunity. He wondered whether the expression in her eyes was encouragement to do something or a plea to do nothing. He could not ask her, for any word he said would be punished, not by anything happening to him, but by Tegan being beaten.

He knew that if he was going to do anything, he must act soon. He decided that he would stand up. The guards would do the same. They would shout at him, threaten him with their lances and, if he did not sit down, one of them would approach Tegan. That would give Brennus the chance to attack the other man. If he was lucky, very lucky, he could dodge past the point of the lance, bear

272

the soldier to the ground and use the heavy iron shackles to strangle the guard or beat him to death. The other man would probably kill him, would certainly threaten to kill Tegan, but Brennus reasoned that the two of them were dead anyway, sooner or later. A quick death was preferable. He had lost everything else, so why not try this last, desperate gamble? Anything was better than being herded away across the sea to Rome like some sacrificial animal.

He was not sure how long the other soldiers had been gone but it seemed a long time. It would be dawn soon. His mind made up, he tried to warn Tegan by fixing her with a hard stare and widening his eyes. She must have understood because she closed her own eyes, then gave the slightest nod of her head.

Brennus took a deep breath, preparing himself, but a sudden noise from outside distracted him. The guards heard it too, for their heads cocked to the side as they listened. It had sounded like a woman's muffled shriek of alarm. Dogs barked furiously, then yelped and fell ominously silent. Then came a voice, calling a question. Brennus could not understand the words, but he recognised that the language was Latin.

He saw the two soldiers stand up. They were puzzled by the noise but the sound of Latin being spoken had obviously reassured them. He saw their shoulders relax slightly. One of them said something, making the other man laugh.

Brennus watched as the soldier to his left turned to the doorway behind him, from where the voice had called out.

Brennus' hopes of escape faded as he realised that he was too late to make an attempt on the guards. Latin voices from outside could only mean that Casca and the other soldiers were returning. Brennus turned to watch the soldier to his right, trying to gauge whether he could reach the man quickly enough to have any chance of getting away.

As he turned, he saw the door swing open and a dark shape rose up behind the guard. The soldier must have heard the movement because he began to turn but he was too slow. A hand whipped round his face, clamping over his mouth and jerking his head back while another hand slashed a wickedly sharp dagger across his exposed throat. A shocked, rasping gurgle escaped from the Roman as blood gushed from the awful, fatal wound. The soldier sagged, crumpling to the ground to reveal the huge figure

273

of Calgacus, a bloodied knife clasped in his hand and a wild, feral expression on his face.

The second soldier whirled as Calgacus stepped over the body of the man he had killed.

"Come on, then," Calgacus invited, speaking loudly and gesturing an invitation with his dagger.

The soldier lowered his lance, tucked his shield close to his body and stepped forwards, circling towards Brennus so that his shielded left side would be closer to Calgacus when he moved round the central hearth.

Brennus tensed, then pushed himself to his feet in a clank of iron chains. The Roman hesitated, recognising the potential threat.

Before any of them could move, the door behind the soldier burst open and Runt charged in, two short swords held ready. At the same time, Calgacus shouted a challenge and darted towards the soldier. The legionary was caught in two minds, facing two opponents and with Brennus also threatening him. Too late, he decided to face Runt's attack as the little man dashed across the house to confront him.

With a speed that astonished Brennus, Runt leaped forwards, one sword knocking the lance aside, the other stabbing towards the soldier's face.

Frantically, the guard retreated a pace, flinging his shield furiously round to block the blow, but Runt was inside his guard and able to shoulder the shield away.

Runt's two swords sought the exposed places that were not protected by the soldier's armour. One blade slashed his thigh, the other plunged up under the rim of his breastplate, driving into his belly. The soldier screamed, the sound filling the house, then dying away suddenly as a final stab to the throat killed him.

Almost nonchalantly, Runt wiped his swords clean before carefully pushing them back into their scabbards.

"That worked well," he observed casually.

Calgacus had moved to stand in front of Brennus, his blue eyes shining. He did not waste time on pleasantries.

"Where is the key to your chains?" he demanded.

"Casca, the Centurion, has it."

"Damn!"

Calgacus looked at the iron manacles as if trying to judge whether he could tear them apart with his bare hands. After a moment's thought, he said, "All right, we'll need to do something else about them. There is a smithy here."

"We need to be quick, Cal," Runt warned as he went to help Tegan to her feet.

Calgacus countered, "We won't run fast with the two of them chained up like this."

Tegan's face was alive with smiles of relief as she blurted, "The Romans are out looking for you."

"We know," Runt told her. "We saw you arrive yesterday. Now come on, or they'll be back to catch the lot of us."

Brennus' mind was almost numb with confusion as Calgacus ushered him outside. The cold air hit him as he went out into the still dark of early morning. Against a backdrop of falling snow, he saw Calgacus' three young spearmen facing a gaggle of women, children and old men while the three sailors stood to one side, trying to look threatening. Only the massive Ger managed it convincingly, but that was more than enough. The villagers stood in a frightened huddle, the women clutching their children close. In front of them lay the blood-stained bodies of Tumnorix's hounds.

Adelligus cast a quick look back over his shoulder as Calgacus and Runt helped Brennus and Tegan to hobble outside.

"The whole village heard the dogs," the young man explained.

"Just keep them out of our way for a little while," Calgacus told him.

Signalling to Risciporus, he added, "You and Ulcattus go and find horses. Get ten of them saddled if you can. Set the rest loose and scatter them. Cawrdaf, go help them. Ger, you come with me."

Turning to Runt he ordered, "You and the other two watch the crowd. And keep an eye out for Venutius and the others returning."

Runt gently pushed Tegan to follow Calgacus. Manacles clanking, she struggled after the big man while the others hurried to carry out Calgacus' commands. Still gripping Brennus' elbow, Calgacus made straight for the smithy that lay off to one side of the village. Ger, holding his massive, sharpened club in his meaty fist, ambled after him, while Tegan, feeling dwarfed by the three men, shuffled along between them.

Candlelight shone from inside the smithy as the burly figure of the smith stepped out into the night, his breath steaming

275

in the cold air. He carried a long-handled hammer in his hand but Calgacus drew his long sword, kept walking and called, "Stand aside or die. Your choice. I don't much care either way but I don't have time to argue about it."

The smith was a big man and no coward, but he heard the promise of violence in Calgacus' voice. Slowly, he lowered the hammer to the ground and stepped aside. "What do you want?" he asked in a surly tone.

"These chains removed," Calgacus replied, gesturing to Brennus' shackles.

"Do it yourself," the smith rasped scornfully. "I won't help you."

Calgacus smiled, "We will. Ger, find some tools and see what you can do, will you. Be quick."

He waved his sword at the smith, motioning for the man to move to one side. Reluctantly, the smith did so. His eyes showed that he was still considering offering some resistance but Calgacus' sword kept him in check.

Ger, Brennus and Tegan made for the door to the smithy. As they reached it, there was a cry from the darkness as a figure dashed out of the swirling snow, a slim-bladed sword held high in a raised hand.

It was a boy, perhaps thirteen or fourteen years old. He yelled a high-pitched war cry as he charged at Calgacus.

To Brennus, everything appeared to happen in a blur of black night and white snow. The smith cried out in alarm as the boy rushed forwards. Ger whirled, raising his massive club but Brennus could see that he was too far away to block the boy's attack.

As the boy ran at him, ready to strike, Calgacus stepped aside, almost casually, his own sword still held low. He shot out one leg, tripping the boy who fell sprawling onto the snow-covered, iron-hard ground. Calgacus was on him before he could move, kicking the sword out of reach, then grabbing the collar of the boy's thick woollen tunic to haul him upright.

As the dazed boy struggled weakly in Calgacus' grip, the long sword came up.

His voice tinged with panic, the smith yelled, "No!"

In one easy motion, Calgacus hurled his stunned captive at the smith who caught him, wrapping his burly arms protectively around the boy.

Calgacus growled, "If he is yours, make sure he behaves. Next time I will kill him."

Gesturing to Brennus and the others, he barked, "Don't just stand there. Go inside. Get those irons off as quickly as you can."

Even with the huge hammers, chisels, pliers and iron saws, wielded by Ger's prodigious strength, it took a long time to hack away the chains. The big sailor sweated as he cut, hammered, twisted and pulled at the thick metal. While he worked to free them, Calgacus stood in the shelter of the doorway, watching outside, but telling Brennus and Tegan his story while posing questions of his own.

"You fell in with Venutius?" he asked.

Brennus' mind was clearing at last and he was able to reply, "Yes. He told me he was going to fight the Romans, so I helped him take his home back. Then the treacherous bastard had someone hit me on the head. Next thing I know, he's got Roman allies and says he's going to hand me over to them."

"That sounds like Venutius," Calgacus agreed. "Some of his men came by this way and we heard the news that he was back. We were all set to leave when we saw you riding into the village, so we circled round and came in from the other side. We saw them all go off up the hill, so we thought we'd give them enough time to get to the top. Then we came in to get you."

"Casca won't be happy," Tegan smiled as Ger removed the encircling iron from her wrists.

Half turning in the doorway, Calgacus gave her a warm smile of his own.

"Better yet," he grinned, "Venutius will be freezing his arse off up there. By the time he gets back, we'll be gone. That will really annoy him."

Ger finally wrenched the last shackle from Brennus' feet. Free once more, Brennus stood up, rubbing at his wrists and ankles.

"That feels good," he said. "Now, a sword and a horse, and we can be gone."

Calgacus tossed him the slim sword that the smith's son had been carrying. "Use this. It's the only one we have spare. The horses are coming."

They went outside, pulling their cloaks close. The snow was still falling heavily, covering the ground almost to their ankles

277

now. Overhead, the sky was lightening a little, though still grey and blanketed by heavy clouds.

Runt appeared, his bare head white with snow. Behind him came the others, leading a string of horses after them.

"All done?" he asked.

"Perfect timing," Calgacus told him cheerfully. "Let's go."

Runt helped Tegan up into the saddle of a shaggy-coated mare, then had to assist Risciporus. The ship's Captain had been loud in his wishes for a horse but now admitted that he had never actually ridden one. The other two sailors were equally inexperienced.

"We'll team each of you up with someone who knows what they are doing," Runt told them.

While Runt organised the others, Brennus nudged his mount over to stand beside Calgacus. The young warrior asked, "What about the other horses?"

"What about them?"

"You should kill them. They won't go far from home in winter. If you don't get rid of them permanently, Casca and Venutius will be after us as soon as they return. They will be able to follow our trail easily in this snow."

He jerked his head towards the milling figures of the sailors as he continued, "And they will catch us because this lot won't be able to ride properly."

"We'll have to take our chances," Calgacus replied.

"No, we must kill the horses," Brennus insisted.

Calgacus looked him in the eye as he said, "For one thing, we don't have time. For another, horses are sacred to Epona. I will not risk bad luck by incurring the wrath of the Goddess."

Brennus scowled, chewing his lip.

"I do not understand you," he sighed after a few moments. "You killed the dogs easily enough. And you killed those two Romans without a second thought, yet you let the smith's son live and you won't slit the throats of a few horses."

Glancing to where the smith and his son still stood watching them, Calgacus gave a slight shrug.

"There was no need to kill the boy. Anyway, he is not my enemy. Nor are the horses. The Romans are."

Brennus shook his head in frustration.

"The boy would have killed you if he had the chance. And the horses will be the cause of all our deaths before long."

278

His angry glare returned as he warned, "You are not ruthless enough."

"You are not the first to say that," Calgacus conceded.

Mystified, Brennus rolled his eyes. Then he asked the question that had been nagging at him since the rescue.

"Why did you come back for us? You could have got away."

Calgacus jerked a thumb to where Tegan was sitting nervously while Runt eased his horse alongside her, making sure that she was confident enough to ride. Grinning, Calgacus explained, "I like the girl. I couldn't leave her. Besides, it will annoy Venutius, and that is worth a little risk."

Brennus frowned, "You came back for Tegan?"

Calgacus laughed, "Well, maybe not just for her, although I would have if she was the only prisoner. But you were there too, and if you don't know why I came back, then perhaps you still don't understand me."

Brennus' frown did not altogether fade but his lips twitched in a faint smile.

"I am grateful," he admitted. "But I think you were stupid. We are all in danger now. They will come after us."

Calgacus' face took on a hard expression as he nodded, "Let them. If I get into trouble, maybe you can rescue me for a change."

He saw a flicker of resentment spark in Brennus' eye and quickly added, "That was supposed to be a joke, son. Runt is always telling me I am not very good at them."

Brennus relaxed slightly. He said, "No, you are not."

As they shared a brief moment of understanding, Runt trotted up to them, Tegan following close behind.

"All ready," he announced. "We'd best get moving."

Looking up at Brennus, he grinned, "Rescuing you is getting to be a habit, lad."

Brennus gave Runt a wry smile then turned back to Calgacus.

"It is funnier when he says it," he explained, indicating Runt with a sideways nod of his head.

"Story of my life," muttered Calgacus.

He hauled on the reins, kicking his heels against the horse's flanks and urging it into motion.

"Come on, let's get out of here."

As he passed the smith, he leaned out of his saddle to say, "When Venutius returns, tell him that Calgacus was here."

The smith gave a brief nod, then tugged his son back to allow the riders to pass. In moments, they had left the village and disappeared behind a curtain of falling snow.

Chapter XXVII

"I told you he was dangerous," Venutius said as he stood staring down at the lifeless bodies of the two Roman soldiers.

He should have been angry but he was so tired and cold that he could not summon the energy for anger. All he felt was frustration, weariness, and a warped satisfaction at seeing Casca thwarted. Still, however satisfying it was to be proved correct, he knew this was a blow to his own plans.

"What shall we do now?" he asked Casca.

The Centurion stood with icy fury shining from his eyes. Impatiently, he gestured towards the corpses.

"Have them buried," he ordered his men. "And find the horses."

As the soldiers hurried to obey, Casca turned his blazing eyes on Venutius.

"We must go after them," he insisted. "We can follow their trail easily enough."

Venutius gave a tired nod. He was committed to helping Rome and even though it was the Romans who had allowed Brennus to escape, Venutius knew that his attempts to win the friendship of the Governor depended on re-capturing the rebel leader.

Wearily, he suggested, "We should rest a while and have some warm food. The smith said that some of them were inexperienced riders. It will not take long to catch them."

"We will leave as soon as my men are buried and the horses rounded up," Casca replied tersely. "Use that time to get some rest and some food if you want, but be ready."

"As you wish," Venutius agreed, hiding his irritation at the Centurion's haughty manner.

He left the Romans to their task. Taking Einon with him, he returned to Tumnorix's roundhouse where the elderly chieftain was supping some hot broth in an attempt to warm his shivering body after the exertions of the night climb. Gratefully, Venutius and Einon each took a bowl of the steaming soup from the head man's wife. Venutius smacked his lips appreciatively as he felt its warmth sliding down his throat into his belly.

"This is good," he said approvingly.

Lifting his bowl, Tumnorix slurped as he spooned his own soup into his mouth. He peered over the rim of the bowl, his eyes questioning.

"What will you do now?" he asked.

"We must go after them."

Tumnorix hesitated, uncertain whether to put his next question. Eventually, he asked cautiously, "Is it truly Calgacus the Swordsman?"

"It is," Venutius confirmed reluctantly.

Tumnorix sighed, "I can give you six men. We do not have enough horses for any more to go with you. Also, I need to keep some men here in case he returns while you are away."

Venutius sensed that Tumnorix was saying more than just the spoken words. He recalled that the old chieftain had joined the previous rebellions against Cartimandua, which meant that he had seen Calgacus in action. Venutius understood the old man's reluctance to face the swordsman again.

He said, "Your men will be welcome, but you should stay here."

Tumnorix acknowledged the words with a slight bow and an expression that did little to hide his relief.

"So should you, my King," he advised softly.

Venutius took a deep breath, exhaling slowly before admitting, "Sadly, I must go with the Roman Centurion. I would rather not, but I have no choice in this."

"Calgacus will seek to kill you," warned Tumnorix.

"Yes, he will. But I will ensure that I have my best men around me at all times. I do not intend to blunder into any traps."

A wicked smile flashed across Tumnorix's wrinkled face as he guessed, "Let the Romans do that, eh?"

Venutius permitted himself a smile of his own as he nodded, "Indeed. Calgacus will set a trap for us. I am sure of that. He does not have enough men to face us in an open fight and he will not be able to travel quickly enough to escape us. Therefore, he will try to ambush us in some way. If he kills me and the Centurion, he knows that our men will probably give up the chase."

282

"But if the Romans are caught in his trap, you will be able to mop up the pieces."

Venutius finished his soup with a flourish of his spoon.

"Exactly so," he agreed.

Mercifully, the snow had stopped falling by the time they were ready to depart. Heavy clouds still obscured the sky and the air remained bitingly cold but Casca was pleased by the conditions.

"Their tracks will remain visible for hours," he declared. "Fresh snowfall will not cover them and the snow that has fallen will not melt. They cannot escape us now."

The Centurion, now with only seven troopers following him, set off at a fast pace. He was glad to be back in the saddle once more rather than tramping through the hills although, despite his outward optimism, the weather was far from ideal. His fingers were numb with the cold, his lips dry and cracked and he could not stop shivering. He was also tired from lack of sleep and the exhausting night climb up the steep hill. Looking round at his men, he could see that none of them were in much better shape than he was, but he pushed them on, knowing that he must find the rebels. He could not return to the Governor with the news that he had captured Brennus then lost him again.

Deep inside, Casca burned with a cold fury. He had failed to find Calgacus, had lost two men and, worse, his prisoners had escaped. The Gods, he thought, were mocking him.

Damn the Gods, he decided. He would not return to the Governor as a failure. He would go after the rebels and he would catch them.

He glanced back over his shoulder to check that Venutius and his warriors were following the small troop of Roman horsemen. They were there but he could not make out the figure of the King because the Brigantes were all dressed alike in heavy furs against the cold and Venutius was riding in the middle of the group.

Casca dismissed the King from his thoughts. He did not much like the man anyway and it suited him to be left to lead the expedition. Turning his attention back to the terrain ahead of him, he concentrated on the task in hand.

The trampled slush left by the fugitives was an easy trail to follow, leading away from the village to the south, then curving slowly westwards into the thickly wooded hills. It was ideal country for an ambush, so Casca sent two of his men ahead to scout the way.

The first few hours were cold and uneventful. The rebels had made no attempt to conceal their flight, ploughing up into the high country through snow that covered the ground in a thick carpet. Casca and his men followed the trail doggedly but their progress was slow as the horses slipped and stumbled through the wintry drifts. Then the scouts returned with the news that the rebels had ridden into a forest where their trail vanished.

Casca called a halt at the edge of the trees. It was a mass of densely packed pine trees, typical of British woodland. Dark and brooding, the snow-laden branches still green despite the late season. Such woods, Casca knew, were often regarded as holy places by the Britons for the trees were green all year round, a sign that they were favoured by the Gods.

Casca, though, was more concerned with the practicalities of pursuit than the superstitions of the barbarians. The branches of the trees were so low that it was difficult to ride in such a place and even more difficult to see in the gloom. What Casca could see was that the snow lay heavily on the branches of the trees, leaving the forest floor virtually clear. He could see where the renegades had entered the forest but then the trail vanished. Under the intertwined branches of the pines, the forest floor was as dark as a moonless night.

"What now?" Sdapezi asked.

"Fetch Venutius. If he has any woodsmen, they might be able to pick up a trail."

The King, when he arrived, soon dispelled Casca's idea.

"They could easily slip round us if we go in there," he said. "I have men who could follow a trail but it would be slow work. There is a faster way."

"What is that?" Casca demanded.

"We should ride round the woods. They won't have stopped in there with half the day still to go. We can pick up their trail where they left the woods. It will be much faster than trying to follow them through it."

Casca rubbed his chin thoughtfully.

"What if they are hiding in there?"

"Then we lose nothing by circling the woods. They will still be in there. But I doubt they will do that. They have little food and will soon starve if they try to remain hidden."

Casca knew he must make a decision. His men were horsemen, soldiers who needed open ground to operate properly. Tramping through a forest handed all the advantages to the enemy and increased the chances of walking into a trap. After the effort of climbing the hill in the early morning, he had no wish to spend any more time on foot.

"All right," he decided. "Let's try it. You lead half of your men round to the left. I'll go take my men and the other half of yours to the right and we will meet on the far side. How far does this forest extend?"

Venutius exchanged a few words with some of Tumnorix's warriors, then reported, "They say it is large. It would take a whole day for a man to walk around it."

"It is just as well that we are not walking, then," remarked Casca. "Let's move."

From high in a tree, his dark clothing blending in with the shadowy browns and greens of the forest, Adelligus peered through a curtain of foliage, watching the Romans and Brigantes as they split into two groups and rode off. He waited for a count of three hundred heartbeats then, when he was sure they were not returning, swung off the thick branch and dropped lightly to the ground.

Moving in a low crouch, he ran deeper into the forest, his heart almost bursting with excitement. This, he thought, was why he had always longed to be a warrior like his father and Calgacus. When they had first set out on this journey he had imagined it would be an interesting enough trip, but one that would provide little excitement. Instead, there had been more danger and adventure than he could ever have imagined.

Once again, they had outwitted the enemy. Adelligus had grown up regarding Calgacus as little more than a rather gruff old man who governed the village with a stern manner and an almost obsessive attention to ensuring that his people were capable of defending themselves. Adelligus had listened to the tales his father told of battles and raids, of long rides and longer marches through the territory of the Romans. His father had always downplayed his own part in the stories but Adelligus could remember Calgacus telling him once that Liscus was the best warrior he knew, and the best friend a man could have. Adelligus had been proud when he heard that. Now that he had seen how the two old men had effortlessly slipped back into their role as warriors, he began to

285

understand why the other men of the village spoke in awed tones when they recounted Calgacus' deeds. The seemingly endless practice bouts with spear and sword now made perfect sense to Adelligus.

Yet he was still not a warrior and would not be until he had killed an enemy. That was the one thing this adventure had lacked. He understood why they were hiding rather than fighting, but Adelligus wanted to prove himself in battle and, so far, he had not been given the opportunity. He enjoyed outwitting the Romans but, despite the overwhelming odds against them, he could not help feeling disappointed that he had not yet faced the ultimate test of bravery.

Deep in the forest, he found the others hiding in a low dip in the ground behind a rocky outcrop.

Wanting to practise his woodcraft, he tried to approach unseen but Calgacus suddenly materialised from behind a tree, startling him.

"Where are they?" the big man asked.

Quickly, Adelligus explained what he had seen.

Calgacus gave a satisfied nod when he heard the young man's report.

"Even better than I'd hoped," he smiled. "Now we don't need to worry about trying to get past them without being seen."

Quickly, Calgacus roused the group and told them to get moving once again. With Adelligus scouting ahead, the party led their horses through the dark forest, ducking low beneath the overhanging branches as they went. Nobody spoke except to softly reassure the horses which were skittish at being in such a dark, confined place as the deep woods. Nobody complained about the cold or about their tiredness. Ever watchful, they followed Calgacus back to the place where they had first entered the woods.

Adelligus crept back to collect his horse from Cawrdaf who had been holding it for him.

"All clear," the young man announced in a low whisper.

"Mount up," Calgacus ordered. "We will ride back along the track they left. Keep in single file and make sure your horses stay on the snow that has already been trampled."

He lifted his heels to nudge his horse into movement, then led the way out of the trees.

It was slow going, for the passage of so many horses had turned the pristine whiteness of the snow to a churned morass of dirty, slippery slush.

After only a few moments, Brennus rode to the front to come alongside Calgacus.

"Where are we going?" he wanted to know. "This will just take us back to the village. If we turn off, they will see our tracks."

"No they won't," Calgacus replied. "Now get behind me or you'll leave hoofprints that are going in the wrong direction."

Scowling darkly, Brennus grudgingly fell back into line behind Calgacus, muttering under his breath while obeying the command.

A little further back, Tegan turned in her saddle to look at Runt.

"Brennus is right," she frowned. "How can we leave this trail without the Romans seeing where we have gone?"

Runt smiled back happily.

"Wait and see," he told her.

She had to wait until mid-afternoon, although it was hard to tell the time precisely because the sun was concealed behind a thick blanket of dull, grey clouds that stretched from horizon to horizon, hovering low over the hills and carrying the promise of more snow.

Calgacus called an unexpected halt as they reached a shallow stream that bubbled icily down the gentle slope, crossing their path from left to right.

"This way," he told them, pointing uphill. "Be careful. Go slowly because we can't afford any accidents."

So saying, he urged his horse into the water, turning to walk it upstream.

Tegan twisted round once again, smiling broadly at Runt who gave a gentle laugh.

"They won't see our tracks now," he chuckled.

Following in a long line, the ten riders eased their horses into the chilly water and made their way up the slope. When they were far above the lower trail, Calgacus splashed back out of the water, then led them up into the hills.

Beyond the first crest, they found another woodland of tall trees, thick with undergrowth, though much of it was sharp, brittle twigs that were waiting for spring before turning green again. They pushed their way through, heading into the depths of the woods.

287

They stopped near the stream, now a mere trickle of water that lay in a deep groove in the soft earth that it had gouged out for itself over countless years.

"Time for a short rest and some hot food," Calgacus announced.

They lit small fires, trusting to the canopy of branches to disperse the faint wisps of smoke. Using platters of tree bark, they heated some water, mixed in a handful of the salted meat and dried vegetables that they had taken from Tumnorix's village, then squatted down to eat. The food was thin, watery and bland, but its warmth revived them. Nearby, the horses were able to crop the damp grass.

"This is a better place to hide than that last forest," Risciporus observed. "Do you think we will be safe here for a while?"

"I'd rather push on," Calgacus replied. "I know it will be dark in a few hours but we need to put as much distance as possible between us and the tracks we left. As soon as the horses are rested, we'll move on."

"You think they will find us here?" Risciporus asked nervously.

"I'd rather not take the chance," Calgacus explained. "If we are lucky, it will take them all day to figure out that we are not in the other wood. After that they will send out patrols to try to pick up our trail. Sooner or later, they will spot where we came out of the stream. We have gained a day, I think. We need to use that time to get as far away as we can. So, a short break to get some warmth and to rest the horses, is all we can afford."

Brennus, still brooding and impatient, asked, "Where are we going? Venutius will call out all his tribe to find us."

"Yes, but they will be looking for us to the north because that is the way they think we will go."

"Venutius is not stupid," Brennus argued. "He will send men south as well, in case we have tried to double back."

"He will send men in every direction," Calgacus agreed. "Which is why we must use the time we have gained. But we will not go north or south. We will go west."

"West?" Brennus enquired.

"We will cross the hills and head for the far coast. There we will buy or steal a boat and Risciporus will sail us back up to Iova."

Risciporus' craggy face broke into a smile as he said, "Even in winter, that sounds better than walking all the way."

Brennus was unconvinced.

"It is dangerous to cross the hills in winter," he objected. "We don't have much food and we will need shelter at night."

Calgacus gave a slight shrug of one shoulder.

"West is the safest direction. eastwards, the land is flatter and more populated. I am hoping they won't expect us to go west because even if they reckon we are trying to get a boat, Venutius knows our home is on the east coast. He can't possibly know that we are heading for Iova."

Shuffling restlessly, Brennus muttered, "We will probably all die from the cold long before we reach the coast."

"It is the best chance we have," Calgacus insisted. "Or would you rather fight fifty armed men?"

Brennus stared back at him, his eyes hard and unyielding "Yes, I would."

Calgacus held his son's gaze. Taking a deep breath, he sighed, "You and I need to talk."

"What about?"

Calgacus did not answer. Instead, he rose to his feet and gestured for Brennus to follow him as he walked away from the fire, into the woods beyond their camp site.

Brennus looked around at the faces of the others who were making a poor show of appearing not to be watching him. Only Tegan looked him in the eye. She gave him a brief nod of encouragement. With a sigh of resignation, he pushed himself to his feet and followed his father.

Moving to the edge of the trees, Calgacus found Ger, who was on watch.

"Go and get something to eat," he told the big sailor. "I'll stand watch for a while."

Ger nodded his thanks, moving wordlessly back into the trees. When he was gone, Calgacus waited until Brennus arrived.

"What is it?" the young warrior asked, angry tension radiating from every fibre of his body.

After a brief moment's hesitation, Calgacus said, "I am not good at this sort of thing. It is especially difficult with you. You don't make it easy for me."

"Why should I?" Brennus demanded. "I am grateful that you rescued me from the Romans but that does not outweigh what you did before."

His eyes were filled with resentful accusation as he added, "What you did to my mother."

Calgacus knew that he must remain calm in the face of his son's anger. It was not easy because his own temper was notoriously short and Brennus was so volatile that the slightest wrong word might cause him to erupt.

Taking a deep breath, Calgacus spread his hands in a gesture of openness. "Look, I know you have reason to hate me for what happened to your mother and for how you grew up. But those things are past. I cannot change them. We must work together now. We both want the Romans gone from our lands, so we have much in common. You have seen how hard it is to defeat them. I can show you how we can do it. If you come back with me, you can become a War Leader of the northern tribes. I told you, we are building an alliance. You can help me do that."

Brennus pursed his lips, his eyes still seething.

"I hear that you already have a son," he said in a harsh voice. "He must be a prince, not a bastard ex-slave like me. Will he not dispute my position?"

Calgacus took another deep breath before responding, "Togodumnus is not a warrior. He is a good lad but we do not see eye to eye on some things. As for you, your birth does not define you. You are who you have made yourself. You can be a great War Leader. Togodumnus will not dispute your right to that. In fact, he will probably welcome it."

Brennus snorted a short laugh.

"It is just as well you don't have any other sons," he grunted. "You don't seem to be able to get on with the ones you do have."

With a rueful smile, Calgacus admitted, "I told you I am not good at this sort of thing. There are many things I am not good at. But what I am good at is fighting."

"We have done precious little of that so far," Brennus accused, though his tone was less hostile than it had been. Calgacus' admissions appeared to have relaxed him a little. Now he seemed to be merely irritated rather than angry.

"That is the point," Calgacus persisted. "I told you before that you should only fight when you are sure of winning."

290

"That is not the way a warrior should behave," Brennus argued. "Only cowards do not face their enemies."

"Only fools fight when they are sure to be defeated," Calgacus retorted. "If you fight and die, who is left to protect the women and children? The point of war is to win, not to show how brave you are. Can you not see that?"

For a moment, Calgacus thought he had gone too far, that Brennus would react angrily again but something he had said or done must have struck home because Brennus paused and rubbed at his bruised head.

"It does not sound right," the younger man sighed.

"Then at least give me a chance to show you that it is right," Calgacus pleaded.

He put his hands inside his cloak, tugging underneath his tunic. After a few moments of fumbling with frozen fingers, he pulled out a leather thong that hung around his neck. On the end, the thong passing through a small hole in its centre, was a golden coin. He lifted it to show Brennus.

"This is a coin of my father's," he explained. "It was given to my brother, Caratacus. He passed it to me on the day he was taken prisoner. When he handed it to me, he made me promise to continue the fight. I have done my best to keep that promise. One day, I will pass it to you. When you are ready to lead the war against Rome."

Brennus reached out slowly, touching the shining coin with his fingertips. His eyes studied it carefully, seeing the design of the horse on one side, the wheatsheaf on the other, the markings around the edges that he recognised as writing although he could not read them.

"It is very fine," he acknowledged before withdrawing his hand. "But I do not want it. I am of the Ordovices, not the Catuvellauni. It has no meaning to me other than what it could buy."

Shaking his head, Calgacus tucked the coin back under his tunic.

"I hope you will come to change your mind about that," he sighed, unable to conceal his disappointment. "You may have forged your own path but you have the blood of Catuvellauni Kings in your veins and this coin is a link to your ancestors. They were great men, just as you could be."

291

"Blood ties mean nothing," Brennus stated flatly. Then he gave a faint smile as he said, "I would rather have your magic sword."

"It has no magic," Calgacus told him.

"That is not what the songs say."

"The songs are wrong," Calgacus said adamantly. "It is a fine sword, another heirloom of my family, but there is no magic in it."

"You should tell people that there is," Brennus advised. "If men believe you have a magic sword, they will be more likely to follow you into battle and your enemies will fear you."

Calgacus gave a weak smile.

"Perhaps you are right. Maybe with your help and a little magic, we can throw the Romans back. What do you say?"

For the first time that Calgacus could remember, the fire inside Brennus appeared to dim as the young man gave him a broad grin.

"I say we should give it a try," Brennus agreed.

Chapter XXVIII

Casca swore under his breath when he saw Venutius and his men approaching. His frustration and anger kept mounting as one thing after another seemed to conspire against him. He had circled the forest, paying close attention to the snow-covered ground but had seen no break in the smooth covering, no sign that anyone or any creature had left the shelter of the dark trees. As he rode, he had tried to convince himself that if he failed to find the tracks, Venutius and his men would surely see something on their half-circuit. When he saw the King cantering towards him he knew that hope had been dashed. The Gods, Casca reflected grimly, were still mocking him.

He was certain that he had missed nothing on the long ride around the irregular borders of the forest. Now Venutius shook his head to confirm what Casca already knew.

"No sign of anything," the Brigante King reported.

"Then they are hiding in the woods somewhere."

"We don't have enough men to search the whole forest," Venutius pointed out.

"We must try," Casca insisted. "We know they went in and they haven't come out, so they must be in there somewhere."

"Then we should go back to the place they entered and see if we can find some tracks. That would be better than blundering through the woods in the hope of catching them."

Casca exhaled loudly, releasing a cloud of steam into the frosty air. He bit back the retort that he had suggested that very thing in the first place.

"All right, let's do that," he agreed. "But we should continue our circuit. Just in case either of us missed anything."

Venutius did not rise to the barely disguised hint of distrust in Casca's words. He simply nodded and said, "Very well. But we won't have time to search the forest today. It will be dark soon. We'll need to make camp somewhere tonight."

"Then that is what we will do," Casca told him testily. "Now, let's hurry. They may have been watching and slipped out after we passed them."

The two parties of searchers separated once again, riding off to complete their circuits of the wide forest. They forced their tired horses through the snow, ignoring their own hunger and the biting chill of the winter air. Somewhere in the trees their enemies were hiding and Casca was more determined than ever that they would be caught. They must be caught.

Riding alongside him, Sdapezi commented sourly, "That bastard is laughing at us."

"Who? Calgacus?"

"No. Venutius. He's all smooth and polite on the outside but the bastard's grinning inside because we can't find the rebels."

Casca said, "He needs to catch them as much as we do."

"Maybe, but he's enjoying seeing us struggle all the same."

"I don't care," Casca rasped bitterly. "As long as we find them, he can laugh as much as he likes. He won't be laughing when we hand him over to the Governor along with Brennus."

Sdapezi shot his commander a startled look.

"I thought he was going to be our ally," he said.

"Do you trust him?" Casca asked.

Sdapezi's craggy face broke into a grin as he replied, "About as much as I'd trust a Syrian whore not to rob me."

Casca nodded, "Exactly. We may need him just now but once we get back to civilisation, I'll make sure he is put in his place."

"Very good, Sir," Sdapezi said in a satisfied tone. "Let's hope we get back soon, though."

Casca could not agree more.

Night was falling by the time they arrived at the point where they had first followed the rebels' tracks to the forest. They had completed the long trek round the woodland with the same lack of success as the first part of their search. Venutius was already there, his men sitting disconsolately on their horses, surrounded by rising clouds of steam from the breath and warm bodies of their tired mounts.

Venutius was on foot, standing beside the young warrior, Einon, at the edge of the trees. He waved Casca over.

"There seem to be a few tracks," he informed the Roman, "but not enough to follow a trail."

Leaving his horse, Casca ducked under the low branches of the trees, stepping into the gloom of the forest. When his eyes had adjusted to the dim light, he looked down to where one of the barbarians was squatting low, running his fingers over a faint line on a patch of frozen mud. The tribesman looked back over his shoulder and spoke to Venutius.

"What did he say?" Casca asked.

"He says it was definitely made by a horse," the King replied. Then he frowned as he added, "But it was coming out of the trees, not going into them."

Casca's brow furrowed. The faint mark on the ground was too vague and indistinct for him to be certain that it had been left by the imprint of a horse's hoof.

"Is he sure?" he challenged.

Hearing his doubt, the barbarian stood to face him. The man's conviction was plain, even if Casca could not follow his babbling explanation.

Venutius translated, "He is absolutely certain."

Casca rubbed his chilled hands together while he considered the implications.

"Are there any other tracks?" he asked.

"Apparently not. A few shallow imprints that might be the traces of men or horses, but the ground is still frozen hard."

"One hoofprint does not make a trail," Casca mused.

"No, but if we were tracking deer or boar, we would take that spoor as a sign of which way to go."

Casca turned, peering into the almost impenetrable darkness beneath the low branches of the pines. He tried to imagine what it would be like to search this forbidding forest, shuddering slightly when he visualised edging between the trunks, never able to see more than a few paces ahead, never knowing when a spear or a sword might strike out from the shadows. It was a daunting prospect and not one that he wanted to dare.

He turned back, moving to the edge of the wood, staring at the ploughed tracks which showed where he and Venutius had followed the rebels from the village to this forlorn place. He signalled to Venutius to join him.

"For the sake of argument," he said to the King, "what would those tracks look like if the rebels had gone back down the same trail?"

"May Brigantia preserve us," breathed Venutius. "That would be just like Calgacus. He's a sneaky bastard."

Casca nodded slowly but another thought had occurred to him.

"Then again," he suggested, "he might have left that track deliberately to send us back that way while he stays safe and warm in the forest somewhere."

Venutius gave a bark of a laugh.

"Yes, he might have done that. So, Roman, what will we do next? You had better guess correctly."

Casca looked skywards, chewing his frozen lips as he studied the overcast gloom.

"It is nearly dark," he sighed. "We will camp here under the trees tonight. While there is still a little light, send your best trackers deeper into the trees to see if they can find any more signs of where the rebels might have gone."

"And tomorrow?" Venutius asked.

"I will decide in the morning," Casca replied.

Inwardly, he knew that his decision would be, as Venutius had said, no more than a guess.

The tired soldiers and warriors gratefully hauled themselves into the shelter of the trees. There was little for the horses to eat so fodder was taken from the bulging sacks that had been tied to the saddles. Fires were lit and food cooked.

Casca sat with his back against the knotted trunk of a tree, doing his best to ignore the clumps of wet snow that occasionally dripped from the branches that swished just above his head. He removed his helmet, laying it on the ground beside him, then pulled his cloak tightly around his shoulders. Now that he had stopped moving, the cold seemed to be leaching into his bones and he found it difficult to prevent his body from shivering.

Hortensius brought him a small mug of hot, watery broth and a hunk of stale, honeyed bread which he accepted with a curt nod of thanks. As he sipped at the liquid, he realised that the strain of searching for the rebels was wearing him down. He was not only physically tired, he was mentally drained, so weary that he felt he could sleep for days, even in this harsh place.

Despite his exhaustion, his tired brain whirled with thoughts. He cursed himself for allowing Brennus to escape. He should have returned to the Governor with his captives, handed them over, placed Venutius in Agricola's hands and let Calgacus go. Whatever Venutius said about his old adversary, Calgacus was not important. His name was famous but he had done nothing for years. Ruefully, Casca told himself that he had allowed his ambition to blind him to the risks of trying to catch one extra rebel.

The Governor had asked for Calgacus as well as Brennus, but to have delivered one would have been better than losing both.

Angrily, Casca swallowed the last dregs of his broth and bit off a chunk of the stale bread. Tomorrow, he vowed. Tomorrow he would catch them.

The night was cold and uncomfortable but mercifully uneventful. Casca woke in the early hours just before dawn when Sdapezi brought him some warm barley gruel. Casca grimaced as he swallowed the lumpy mush. Civilised people knew that barley was for horses but the ignorant Britons ate it as a staple of their appallingly bland diet.

Sdapezi sat on a rock nearby and apologised, "Sorry, Sir. That's all there is."

"Any of the lads got some wine?"

Sdapezi grinned, "I'll see what I can do."

"Make sure it's well watered," Casca told him. "I don't want anyone getting drunk."

Sdapezi wandered off, returning a few moments later with a small wooden beaker of dark wine which he passed to the Centurion.

"That's just about the last of it, Sir. Five parts water."

Casca sipped the wine. It was poor stuff, and heavily diluted, but it was better than the dark, frothing beer that the barbarians drank in such quantities.

"Thank you," he said as he washed down the last of the awful gruel.

"So what are we going to do, Sir? I don't much fancy tramping through these trees for days on end."

"Neither do I," Casca agreed.

Venutius approached, looking refreshed and clean-shaven as if he had spent the night in a warm, comfortable house. He asked the same question as Sdapezi. "Well, Roman, what do you suggest we do?"

Casca rubbed his stubbled chin as he answered, "First, I am going to shave."

"And what then?" Venutius persisted.

"I don't suppose your trackers found anything?"

Venutius spread his hands in a gesture of defeat

"Alas, no. Nothing they would follow with any certainty. If it were not for the trail in the snow, there would be no reason to think the renegades are in here at all."

Casca nodded thoughtfully. He suspected that Venutius' men would have said that even if they had found tracks. None of them wanted to venture into such a dark and dangerous place in search of men who might be ready to spring an ambush from behind any rock or tree.

Casca stood up, stretching his muscles.

"We must split up and search for them," he announced. "Send half your men into the forest. They must search as much of the place as they can. Send the rest on another circuit of the woods in case the rebels left during the night. I will take my men back towards the village in case they did double back on us."

"We are spreading ourselves thin," Venutius observed.

"If you have any better ideas, perhaps you would tell me!" snapped Casca irritably.

Venutius gave a slight shrug.

"It will be as you say," he conceded ungraciously. "But I will stay here with some of my men. If any of the groups find a sign of them, they can send word back here so that we can call all our forces together."

Casca nodded, "Very well. Now, I will shave and then we shall find these rebels."

The pale light of the winter sun was edging above the hills as they set off. The weather had changed again, Casca noted, with the wind now coming from the west, gusting across the rugged hills, bearing clouds that threatened rain rather than snow. The temperature seemed to have risen slightly, for already the snow was becoming soft and wet.

"Bloody miserable country," Sdapezi muttered as he held a palm upwards, testing for rain.

Casca did not disagree but he was more concerned at the prospect of losing the trail.

"Keep your eyes on the ground to either side of the track," he ordered his men. "If the rebels came back this way, they won't have gone all the way back to the village. Watch for their tracks."

Aware that his search for Brennus and Calgacus was floundering, both literally and figuratively, he set off back along the churned morass of brown, wet slush which was all that remained to mark their previous day's journey.

Standing at the edge of the woods, Venutius watched the small Roman patrol ride off to the west. He was in two minds as to whether he should wish them success or not. He knew that his own position was still precarious and that finding the fugitives would enhance his chances of being welcomed by the Governor but riding around the wilds in winter was not his idea of what a King should be doing. He felt as if he was adrift on a wide sea, being pushed and pulled this way and that, unable to steer a straight course, but at the mercy of the elements. Even during the long years as a fugitive King, he had not felt so unsure of what to do. The only thing he was certain of was that he was not going to blunder through the forest in search of Calgacus.

To make a show of following Casca's instructions, he sent ten men into the woods with orders to search for any signs of the rebels, and another group of five to ride the circuit around the borders of the forest, but he told the rest of his men to build fires at the edge of the woodland and settle down for a day of rest.

Venutius sat under the shelter of a tree with ten men posted nearby. Einon lit a small fire and sat opposite the King, holding his hands out to the meagre flames for warmth. After a few moments' silence, he gave Venutius a questioning look.

"You do not think Calgacus is in the forest?" he asked.

"I have a feeling that he would have attacked us last night if he was. Calgacus is not one to miss a chance like that."

"We had plenty of men on watch. Perhaps he was afraid, or perhaps he is just waiting for us to split up," Einon suggested. "He may be hiding and watching for opportunities to pick us off one by one."

Venutius shrugged, "Perhaps. That is why most of our men are here. If we lose a few scouts in the woods, we will know where Calgacus is."

He rubbed his hands together for warmth as he continued, "I'm afraid that trying to second-guess Calgacus is pointless."

Einon shifted slightly, as if trying to gauge whether he should ask his next question. After some indecision, he plucked up the courage.

"Lord, some of the men say that Calgacus cannot be defeated."

A dark shadow crossed Venutius' brow as he retorted, "He can be beaten. I have defeated him before. I just wasn't able to kill him."

Einon gave the slightest of nods.

"That is good to hear. But there are stories that he has a magic sword. Is that true?"

Venutius hesitated for an instant before replying, "No, it is just a sword. A beautiful thing, to be sure, but it has no magical properties that I know of."

Einon still appeared unconvinced. The King's hesitation suggested that there was more to the story than he was prepared to divulge. Einon was tempted to press the matter but he reckoned he had pushed things as far as he dared. He had spoken to some of the older warriors who had told him how Calgacus had once marched into a Brigante camp, facing an army of thirty thousand men on his own to reclaim his sword from Venutius. Einon knew that storytellers always exaggerated events but more than one man knew the tale and it seemed to Einon that no man would do anything as foolish as that unless the sword in question had some special powers.

The fact that Calgacus had somehow slipped past them in the night, killed two Roman soldiers and freed the prisoners, added to the aura of invincibility that his name attracted. Einon knew that many of the men were nervous and he was beginning to share their anxiety.

Venutius said, "Tell the men that Calgacus is an old man now. His sword is famous, but not magical. When we find him, we will kill him."

"Yes, Lord," Einon acknowledged.

Venutius sighed as he watched the young man go. Damn those songs, he thought. Everyone knew that Calgacus had a magical sword because the songs said so. The sword had once been in Venutius' hands and he knew it was a fine weapon, an heirloom of the royal house of the Catuvellauni, wielded by Caratacus himself. Venutius tried to recall whether he had felt its powers when he held it but he was certain that there was nothing special about it except its resonance as a symbol of the resistance to Rome.

Doubt momentarily swept through him as he realised that he may not have felt its power because he had not truly wanted to fight against the Romans. Perhaps it only gave its aid to those who fought against the empire? He recalled how his Captain, Corlus, had used the famous sword in his single combat against Calgacus and how easily Corlus had been defeated. Was that because Corlus, too, was not an enemy of Rome? Had the sword withheld its power from him? Was it now providing magical assistance to Calgacus, allowing him to slip, unseen, past Venutius' men?

Venutius shivered. Damn those songs.

Chapter XXIX

"Things all sorted between you, then?" Runt asked.

Calgacus nodded, "We have come to an understanding."

Runt peered ahead to where Brennus and Ulcattus were taking their turn to scout the way.

"That's good," he commented. "Have you thought about what happens when we get home?"

"What do you mean? Brennus is my son. He will be welcomed."

"You have another son who expects to be head man some day."

"He will be. But Brennus will be War Leader of the alliance after me."

"I'm glad you've got it all worked out," Runt said. "At least you have a reason to want to get home now."

Calgacus heard the regret in Runt's voice and felt a pang of guilt. For his friend, there was little to look forward to. In his younger days, Runt had been a notorious womaniser but once he had met Elaris, he had changed. Now she was gone, leaving a void in Runt's life. Calgacus knew that the danger they had encountered on this journey had sparked some recovery in his friend but the hurt of loss was plainly still there.

Unsure what to say, he replied, "I'm sorry, Liscus. I've been too wrapped up in my own plans to think of much else. But you know there are plenty of people who still need you. Adelligus for one. And me, of course. My plans for a great alliance will come to nothing if you aren't around to watch my back."

Runt turned a sniff into a laugh as he insisted, "I'm all right, Cal. I just miss her sometimes. But don't worry about me. I'll keep watching your back."

"Then what can go wrong?" smiled Calgacus.

Casca knew that he had lost the trail. They had followed the melting track of slush more than half way back to Tumnorix's village without finding any sign that the rebels had split away from the path. He was beginning to doubt whether they had doubled back at all because he had seen no signs that anyone had retraced their steps along the trail.

Tired, cold and frustrated, Casca was running out of ideas. He sent Hortensius and one other man ahead to check with the village head man that the rebels had not been seen, while he and the others rested beside a small stream that crossed their path. The horses pawed at the melting snow, seeking out the grass beneath while the men filled their waterskins from the icy water of the stream and chewed on strips of tough, salted beef.

Sdapezi and Casca moved a little way uphill to a spot where they could talk without being overheard by the men.

"They must still be in that forest after all," Sdapezi offered.

"I suppose so. But why?"

Sdapezi shrugged, "Why not? It keeps them out of the snow and it's a damn good place to hide. We'll need an army to find them in there."

"It doesn't feel right," Casca sighed softly.

"Nothing about this whole thing feels right," Sdapezi muttered. Then he saw the spark in Casca's eye and hurriedly added, "Sorry, Sir."

Casca removed his helmet and ran his fingers through his matted hair.

"This Calgacus is a clever one," he commented, half to himself. "Remember how he bluffed us after the battle with the Ordovices, when he stood in that pass and dared us to walk into a trap?"

"You weren't to know how few men he had," Sdapezi said reassuringly, although his words let Casca know that the Decurion was not prepared to count himself as the person who had been tricked.

Casca let Sdapezi's correction pass.

"We are playing his game," he muttered. "He tricked us once more when he rescued Brennus. Now he's doing it again. He wants us to think he is hiding but I'll wager he's long gone from that woodland."

"But how? We'd have seen the tracks in the snow. Unless they all grew wings and flew away."

Casca admitted, "I don't know how, but I feel it."

He gazed up into the snow-decked hills as he went on, "He is out there somewhere."

Sdapezi said nothing. If Casca was correct, there was very little hope of finding the rebels. As far as Sdapezi was concerned, they had had their chance and they had lost it. All he wanted was to rejoin the army and settle into winter quarters for the next few months. Like all the troopers, he was sick and tired of trudging through the bitter cold, always hungry, never warm. He longed for the chance to visit a bath house and relax in hot, steaming water, and to fill his belly with hot food.

That seemed like an impossible dream. Glancing at Casca, he knew that the Centurion would not give in so easily. The man's career depended on finding these rebels and Sdapezi knew Casca well enough to understand that he would not stop searching, no matter how long it took.

The two riders who had been sent to the village returned, their horses weighed down by some additional fodder and a small supply of grain. Dismounting, young Hortensius clambered up the slope to report to Casca, his feet slipping on the melting snow as he picked his way up the side of the stream.

He saluted.

"They haven't been to the village, Sir. The head man is sure of that. We brought some extra supplies, Sir, though the barbarian wasn't too happy about handing it over. I said you'd pay him later."

"Well done, lad," Casca nodded approvingly. "Have a short rest, then we'll be off."

"Thank you, Sir," Hortensius beamed.

The young soldier turned to go but lost his footing on the treacherous surface as he turned. He stumbled, almost fell, then, with his arms flailing wildly, slipped again and splashed into the icy waters of the stream. He cursed loudly as his feet went into the fast-flowing, bitterly cold water.

Laughing, Sdapezi stepped close, holding out a hand to steady the young soldier.

"Come on, lad, this is no time for paddling."

Hortensius clambered out, shaking his head in annoyance. He stamped his feet on the soggy bank, turning the thinning snow to dark slush. With his cheeks faintly blushing and his waterlogged leather boots squelching, he walked carefully back down the slope to join his comrades who greeted him with mocking laughter.

Sdapezi watched him for a moment then turned back to Casca who was staring down at the noisily babbling stream.

304

"Sir?" Sdapezi asked.

In response, Casca nodded towards the water.

"It's getting deeper and faster because of the snow melt," he observed. "What will happen if it bursts its banks?"

"We'll all get our feet wet," Sdapezi replied glumly.

Casca shot him a dark look.

"I meant what will happen to the snow?"

Frowning at the seriousness in Casca's tone, Sdapezi said, "The snow will wash away. Same thing will happen if it rains hard."

Casca's eyes lit up as he declared, "And the tracks will also disappear."

With a determined gleam in his eye, he grasped his helmet, ramming it back onto his head. He was all eagerness and excitement again.

"We must be quick," he announced. "Split into two groups. You take three men downstream and I'll take the others up the hill."

The Centurion's sudden animation perplexed Sdapezi.

"Yes, Sir. May I ask why?"

"To look for tracks coming out of the water, Decurion," Casca explained sharply.

Understanding dawned on Sdapezi's face as he gazed down at the fast-flowing stream.

"You think they used the water to hide their tracks?"

"I don't know for certain," Casca replied briskly. "But it would explain why we can't find their trail. If they did, we will need to be quick if we are to find them before the snow melts completely. Get the men mounted up."

Casca hurried to his own horse, using a convenient rock as a mounting stool while Sdapezi barked at the troop until they were all ready to depart.

Bursting with impatience, Casca led the way up the slope, waving to Sdapezi to head downstream. He could tell that the Decurion thought this was a desperate idea, a frantic gamble that defied logic but Casca felt that he was beginning to understand Calgacus. Venutius may have known the renegade for years but the Brigante King was no warrior. He thought like a politician, not like a soldier. Casca was a soldier to his core and he knew he was right. Calgacus had tried to trick them again. Casca was convinced of it. All he had to do was prove it.

He found the tracks within half an hour, a muddy, trampled trail that left the stream and led towards yet another dark patch of woodland which covered the upper slopes of the hill ahead of him. With relief surging through him, he turned to the three troopers with him. He jabbed his fingers at them as he rattled out his orders.

"You two go back to Venutius and tell him to bring all his men here as quickly as he can."

Pointing to the third man, he instructed, "You go down and fetch the rest of the lads."

The first two riders tapped their lances to their helmets in salute, wheeled their mounts and set off down the slope, but the remaining trooper, a veteran named Daszdius, hesitated. He gave Casca an enquiring look.

"What about you, Sir?" he asked.

The Centurion replied, "I'm going to see where the trail leads."

"Yes, Sir," Daszdius acknowledged uncertainly. "On your own?"

"Don't worry," Casca assured him. "They will not be waiting for me. They are trying to escape from us. Now go and fetch the others. Join me as soon as you can."

"Yes, Sir."

Daszdius obediently tugged on the reins, turning his mount to begin the treacherous descent.

Alone on the wintry, wind-swept hill, Casca gave a short laugh of delight. He knew he had been right. He understood his enemy now and because of that understanding, he would catch them. They would not escape him this time.

The hunt was on once more.

Chapter XXX

Heavy, grey clouds masked the sky, occasionally spitting droplets of icy rain on the steep-sided hills. Most of the snow that had covered the ground had vanished, melting away to swell the mountain streams, although the highest peaks were still shrouded by white caps, a constant reminder of the dangers of travelling in winter.

Calgacus and his companions forged on, heading ever westwards across the hills. There was no shortage of water but their food was running low, forcing them to ration what little remained.

Runt and Calgacus rode at the rear of the column, making sure that nobody lagged behind.

"How long will this take, do you think?" Runt asked as they reached an upland plateau, a wide expanse of grass and heather which offered no shelter from the blustery west wind that clawed at the exposed skin of their hands and faces.

Calgacus shrugged, "I don't know this part of the country at all. Probably another two or three days until we reach the coast."

"That's what I reckoned," sniffed Runt.

He twisted in the saddle, looking back over his shoulder for signs of pursuit. "We'll run out of food before then," he observed as he turned back.

"I know. Maybe we will find a farmstead."

"Maybe."

"You're growing miserable in your old age," Calgacus chided.

Runt gave his friend a weak smile as he admitted, "I just have a bad feeling." He twisted again to check the trail behind them, relaxing slightly when he saw nothing except the grey hills and a solitary crow wheeling high above their heads.

"I don't like the thought of Venutius hunting us," he explained. "If they find our trail we won't stand much chance of escaping again."

"You *are* in a happy mood today," Calgacus observed.

"Someone has to do the worrying," said Runt.

"That's usually me," Calgacus pointed out.

"Yes, but you've cheered up since you and Brennus settled your differences, so I'd better do the worrying for you."

"Worry about it if it happens," Calgacus told him.

Runt twisted round again and swore as he stiffened in the saddle.

"It's happened!" he hissed.

Calgacus reined in, turning his horse to one side. When he peered back through the overcast afternoon, he echoed Runt's swearing. Three riders had appeared, several hundred paces back, edging over the summit of the last crest they had crossed. As Calgacus watched, one of the riders turned and galloped away, disappearing over the hill while the other two horsemen moved cautiously forwards.

"He's gone to fetch the rest of them," observed Runt.

"How in Andraste's name did they find us so quickly?" Calgacus wondered.

Runt declared, "Never mind that, we need to ride fast now."

"We should kill those two," Calgacus said, nodding towards the distant riders.

"How? There is nowhere to hide and we can't waste time going back there. They'll just ride away. Anyway, the others could be right behind them."

Calgacus nodded, realising that his friend was correct.

"Let's give them a chase, then," he decided.

He yanked on the reins, bringing a whinny of protest from his mount as he turned. Clapping his heels to the beast's flanks, he urged it into a gallop. In moments they had caught up with Risciporus and Ger who were bringing up the rear of the long train.

"Move!" Calgacus yelled. "They have found us!"

A flicker of momentary panic rippled along the file of riders as they all turned back to see the two Brigante horsemen who were silhouetted against the dull horizon.

Brennus came galloping back to meet Calgacus.

"What do we do?" he asked.

"We run. You lead the way."

"Do you want to find somewhere to face them?"

Calgacus shook his head emphatically.

"Not unless this is only a small group. If the main force is on our trail, there are at least forty of them. We can't fight that many. We need to try to lose them again."

Brennus gave a grim smile. In a low voice, he said, "We won't outrun them. We have too many inexperienced riders."

Calgacus held his son's gaze, acknowledging the truth of his statement.

"We have to try," he said.

Brennus did not argue. He gave a curt nod, wheeled his horse and rode off, signalling to Adelligus to join him.

Calgacus waved at the rest of the group.

"Go!" he roared.

Obediently, with fear etched on their faces, they coaxed their tired horses into a run, thundering across the high moor after Brennus.

Still bringing up the rear, Runt eyed the sky with a sour expression.

"Not a good day to die," he muttered.

"No day is a good day to die," Calgacus replied. "But we've faced worse odds than this before."

"Brennus is right. We'll have to fight them sooner or later."

"If we do, we'll need somewhere better than up here. But let's hope it won't come to that."

Now that uncertainty had been replaced by the knowledge of their discovery, Runt's face broke into a weak smile.

"I hope you are working on a plan," he said.

"Yes. We run."

"That'll do for a start."

They galloped after the rest of their companions, twisting from time to time to check on their pursuers. The two Brigantes maintained a good distance but were never out of sight as Brennus led the way down steep slopes, across small streams, then up the next hillside. They skirted small clumps of trees, avoided patches of jumbled rocks, riding as fast as they dared but always the small figures of their hunters kept pace with them.

"We could do with a thunderstorm," Calgacus called to Runt as they galloped along a narrow valley.

"Have you sent a prayer to Taranis?"

"Of course. But I don't think he is listening to me today."

"You can't trust the Gods," Runt shouted back.

309

Calgacus nodded. The god of thunder had often sent storms to aid him, storms that had come at times when he needed help. Today, though, Taranis seemed to be busy elsewhere. The sky remained determinedly dull, cloudy and sullen for as far as he could see. The weather would not save them today.

Up ahead, Brennus was leading the way across a broad but shallow stream. The horses splashed through the chilly water, scrambled up onto the far bank, then turned to follow the course of the river along the narrow floor of the valley. Then, without warning, Brennus waved his arm urgently, pointing to the right as he and Adelligus made for the steep, open hillside. The others followed, urging the horses on but the animals were tired now, their breathing laboured, their legs faltering as they tackled the slope.

"Something's wrong," Calgacus observed as he made for the hillside. "We should stick to the low ground."

In response, Runt pointed to the left, to the hill on the other side of the valley. At the crest, a group of riders had appeared, spearpoints glinting dully against the drab sky.

"They must have split up. Those two behind us have been herding us."

Calgacus turned, wishing now that he had taken the chance of attacking the two riders who had been following them. Then, glancing back over his shoulder, he saw that there were no longer two pursuers, but nearly twenty. And they were closing. Already, they were approaching the foot of the valley, heading towards the river. On the far hill, the other group of riders were picking their way down the slope. He could make out the crested helmet of the Roman, Casca, among them.

Cursing, knowing they were trapped, he urged his horse to climb the hillside.

The hill was not high but it was steep. The horses were barely walking by the time they reached the long, flat, rock-strewn ridge that formed its summit. Here, Brennus had stopped and the others were clustered around him, their faces pale and anxious.

As Calgacus reached them, he called, "Why have you stopped?"

Dismounting, Brennus gave him a helpless look.

"I'm sorry. There is nowhere to go."

Calgacus looked over the heads of the men in front of him. Climbing down from the saddle, he pushed his way through, picking a course across a jumble of large boulders to the far side of the ridge where he came to a sudden stop.

Runt came alongside him, uttering a low whistle as he saw what lay ahead of them.

"That's a bastard and no mistake," the little warrior whispered.

At their feet, the ridge came to an abrupt halt as it fell away in an almost vertical cliff on the north and west sides. Calgacus felt a momentary vertigo as he gazed down over a hundred paces of sheer rock. He took a step back, away from the edge, then turned to look along the ridge to the east.

The descent at the far end was less steep than the climb they had just made but there was no hope of taking that route because Brigante warriors, having dismounted, were already scrambling up the slope to block off the eastern end of the plateau.

Moving back to the southern side of the escarpment, he looked down to see that the pursuers had left their horses at the foot of the slope, where a group of ten warriors had formed a loose cordon along the base of the hill.

He watched the climbing men, seeking out Venutius. The Romans were there, still wearing their armour and carrying their long lances. Then, in the midst of a group of warriors, he saw the grey haired man who wore the dull bronze of a chainmail tunic under a sheepskin jerkin.

Calgacus clenched his fists as he watched his nemesis slowly climb the hill, closing the trap.

"What now?" Runt asked.

Calgacus thought for a moment, letting the chill breeze cool his burning face. "If we mount up, we could ride down and smash through that cordon at the foot of the hill," he suggested.

Brennus looked sceptical.

"The horses are exhausted," he pointed out.

Runt added, "By the time we got down there, it wouldn't be a cordon. They would get together and block us easily enough. We might break through but we'd lose more than a few doing so."

"We could wait until nightfall," Brennus offered.

Softly, Calgacus said, "I don't think they will allow us until nightfall."

"So we fight them," Runt stated calmly. "This is as good a place as any. They can only come at us from one direction and the ridge is so narrow they can't all attack at once. Six of us could hold this ridge."

"Not for long," Calgacus frowned. "There are only nine of us and they'll soon have more than thirty at the other end of the ridge, with another ten down at the foot of the hill."

"We've faced worse odds," Runt reminded him.

Brennus' eyebrows arched as he asked, "When?"

Runt told him, "Your father and I once tackled a Brigante army of thirty thousand. Just the two of us. We sent them packing that day, so this should be easy."

Brennus looked from one man to the other, clearly unwilling to believe Runt's boast. After a moment, he asked, "So how do we do it?"

Calgacus' blue eyes had been studying the terrain intently. He did not answer for a long time but looked along the ridge to where the Romans and Brigantes were gathering. Then he turned back to the rest of the group who were watching anxiously. He smiled.

"I'll tell you how," he declared. "But we need to work quickly."

Venutius had scarcely had time to recover his breath when Casca stalked towards him, cloak flapping in the wind.

"We have them now," the Centurion beamed.

Sweating profusely and still breathing heavily, Venutius gave the Roman a pensive look.

"The stag is most dangerous when he is cornered," he warned, his voice still trembling from the exertion of the climb.

Casca clucked his tongue.

"Perhaps. But I am not going to just sit here and wait for them to starve to death. Get your men ready."

"Give us a short time to rest," Venutius pleaded. "It has been a long ride and a steep climb."

Casca gave the King a look of disdain. He could practically see the fear in the man's eyes. Glancing around at the other Brigantes, he could sense their reluctance as well. They had hunted their quarry for two days but, now that they had trapped them, the Brigantes seemed apprehensive about making the final assault.

"We outnumber them nearly four to one," he pointed out with a mocking sneer.

312

"In which case there is no rush to attack them," Venutius replied.

"You are afraid of Calgacus!" Casca realised.

"He is a man to be feared," Venutius admitted. "But let us rest and then we will join you in the attack."

Casca snorted, "Very well. But while you are resting, perhaps I should go and see if I can resolve this without a fight. Would that suit you?"

Venutius was surprised.

"You intend to talk to them?"

"Why not? I will make them an offer. All I want is Brennus and Calgacus. The rest can go if those two surrender to us."

Venutius shook his head.

"Calgacus won't surrender," he asserted.

"Not even to save the others? Perhaps not, but we lose nothing by making the offer and it might create some tension among them if the rest of them realise they don't need to die."

Venutius straightened his back, stretching the muscles. He glanced along the desolate ridge to the rocky promontory where he could see the rebels were hurriedly clearing rocks from the flat section of the escarpment and piling them in a crude barricade to guard the southern side of their position.

Nodding, he advised, "You should also kill the little man. The one with two swords. He won't stand by and watch Calgacus be executed."

Casca gave a thin smile as he admitted, "Oh, I intend to kill them all. Just because I make them an offer does not mean I have to keep to it once they have surrendered."

"You are a devious man, Centurion," accused Venutius. "I thought you Romans were men of your word."

"That depends on who it is we give our word to," Casca replied.

The Brigante King forced a smile to his lips as he shrugged, "Go and speak to them, then. We will be ready to attack by the time you get back."

Casca gave a slight, almost insolent, bow, then turned and set off along the narrow ridge towards the renegades.

Venutius watched him go, a grim thought forming in his mind. The King called Einon to him.

"Lord?" the young man asked.

313

"It seems likely there will be a fight," Venutius told him.

"You should stay out of harm's way," Einon advised. "I will have six men watch over you."

"Thank you. Calgacus is likely to try to kill me if he can. But there is more."

"More?"

Venutius put an arm around Einon's shoulder, pulling him close so that he could speak without his words carrying to the small group of Roman troopers who were gathered nearby.

"I do not trust this Roman," he explained in a low, urgent whisper. "He gave me his word that he would help me gain the Governor's favour but he just admitted that his promises mean nothing if given to a non-Roman."

Einon glanced at Casca's distant figure, nodding his head slowly.

"What do you intend to do?" he asked.

Venutius gave the young man a wicked smile as he revealed, "When faced with a threat, the best thing to do is eliminate it."

Einon's eyebrows arched in startled surprise.

"You wish to kill the Romans?" he breathed in astonishment.

Venutius nodded slowly and very deliberately.

"Precisely. Let them lead the fight. Let them suffer casualties. When the fighting is over and the rebels are all dead, then we will dispose of any who are left. But we must make sure to kill them all. There can be no survivors."

Are you sure this is necessary?" Einon frowned.

"I am not prepared to take the risk that I am wrong," Venutius informed him. "Believe me, I am no stranger to making promises to my enemies in order to deceive them. I can recognise the trait. Casca intends to betray me."

"And once they are all dead?" Einon asked.

"Then I shall go to the Governor with a tale of his soldiers' heroic death and my own display of devotion in killing the two renegades. That will accomplish everything I need."

Einon nodded as the scale of Venutius' thinking became clear to him.

"I will pass the word quietly to men I can trust," he promised.

314

"Good. But do not act too soon. Await my signal. Is that clear?"

"Yes, Lord. We will be ready."

Venutius rubbed his chin as he watched Einon move among the warriors. There were only eight Romans. One or two would probably die in the fighting because Calgacus was no easy opponent. If Venutius and his men made sure that the Romans bore the brunt of the fighting, perhaps they would lose three or four men. Then, when the rebels were finally overwhelmed, it would be simple enough to kill the rest of the unsuspecting troopers. When that was done, all that he would need to do would be to take the heads of Calgacus and Brennus to the Governor, along with a tale of Casca's glorious last fight. If things went to plan, Venutius would be welcomed as an ally of Rome, his position as King confirmed.

It was a bold step and not one that Venutius would normally consider but Casca had more or less admitted that his word could not be relied upon. Having spent the past few days in the Centurion's company, Venutius was under no illusions that Casca regarded all barbarians as little better than beasts. No, the Roman was definitely not to be trusted.

"Someone wants to talk to us," said Runt, jerking his thumb in the direction of the advancing Centurion.

Calgacus straightened up from placing another boulder along the edge of the ridge. The wall was low, scarcely more than knee height, but he knew that any sort of barrier would deter men from trying to cross it and the wall should act as some protection for their right flank. With the wall on their right and the precipice on their left, the only avenue for the attack would be straight at them, along the narrow, uneven ridge.

He wiped dust from his hands and arched his spine, rubbing life back into the muscles as he turned to watch the approaching Roman.

"All right, let's see what he wants."

He turned to Risciporus, Ulcattus, Ger and Tegan who were still piling rocks on the crude wall.

"Keep going," he told them.

Tegan gave him a tired, nervous smile. She was trying to hide it, but the strain of the past days was plainly wearing her down.

"What does he want?" she asked.

"I'll tell you when I get back," he replied.

Flanked by Brennus and Runt, Calgacus walked to meet the Centurion.

The Roman stopped several paces from the Britons, far enough away to avoid any attack.

In a formal voice, he announced, "I am Centurion Casca of the Fifth Illyrian Cohort."

Calgacus kept his face expressionless as he replied, "We know who you are. What is it that you want?"

Casca, his face shaded by the raised face mask of his helmet, stared back at the tall warrior. His formal greeting had been rebuffed but what could you expect from barbarians? His gaze flickered over Runt, then settled on Brennus. Finally, he turned his eyes back to Calgacus.

Disdainfully, he said, "So, we meet again, at last. But you can't trick me here. There are no trees for you to hide behind. This time I can see how many men you have. Or should I say, how few? You know that you cannot defeat me."

"Then why are we talking?" Calgacus responded brusquely. "If you want to fight, go and fetch your men. We'll soon see how good they are. And we outnumber you. There are only eight of you."

Casca frowned, "I did not think you were blind. Have you failed to see that King Venutius has brought his men with him?"

Waving one hand dismissively, Calgacus gave a snort of derision.

"I did not think you were stupid," he retorted, "but if you trust that snake, you must be. Venutius will let you and your men do all the fighting, you know. Then, when I have killed you, he will turn tail and run away like he always does. I know him, you see. Much better than you do, obviously."

Casca tried to conceal his discomfiture. This was not how the conversation was supposed to go. Angrily, he jabbed a finger at Calgacus.

"You are a dead man!" he snapped. "Nothing can change that."

His finger stabbed towards Brennus as he continued, "As are you."

Then he lowered his hand, making an expansive gesture of conciliation as he went on, "But I am in a generous mood today.

316

There is no need for the rest of your companions to die. I have no interest in them."

His eyes held Calgacus' gaze as he said, "If you two surrender to me, I will ensure your deaths are quick and painless. The rest of your friends will be free to go."

"I have a better idea," Calgacus replied as if he had not heard Casca's words. "I will fight you in single combat. If I win, we all go free. If you win, then I will be dead and Brennus will give himself up to you."

"I am not a fool, Barbarian," Casca retorted. "We both know that I have nothing to gain by accepting such a challenge. I am a soldier. I fight to win. I have all the advantages here. You have heard my offer. I will give you a little time to consider it, then we will attack and you will all die."

"I don't think so," Calgacus said. "Did Venutius forget to tell you about my magic sword?"

Casca frowned uncertainly.

"What are you talking about?" he demanded.

Calgacus reached back to tap the hilt of the great longsword that hung at his back.

"It must have slipped his mind. But his men know about it. That is why they are afraid of me. They know I cannot be defeated while I carry this sword. Why don't you ask them?"

Casca shook his head, apparently dismissing the suggestion.

"You have heard my offer," he rasped. "I suggest you accept it. If you do not surrender, you will all die."

"Then give us time to discuss it," Calgacus replied. "I don't think you and I have anything more to say to one another."

Casca backed away, his eyes never leaving Calgacus. Then he turned and quickly walked back along the ridge.

"He's made us an offer," Calgacus explained to the others once Casca had gone.

After telling them what the Centurion had said, he asked for their opinions.

"Can we trust him?" Risciporus asked nervously.

"I doubt it," Calgacus replied. "We certainly can't trust Venutius.

"I can vouch for that," Brennus agreed.

317

"On the other hand," Calgacus put in, "the rest of you mean little to either Venutius or the Romans. I don't expect they will let you go free but they might be content to take you as slaves."

"They won't do that to me," Runt vowed. "I have been a slave once and I'm never going back to that life."

"But can we defeat that many of them?" Risciporus asked.

"Anything is possible," Calgacus told him. "I won't lie to you. Some of us won't survive but this ridge is only wide enough for around a dozen of them to come at us at once. If we can kill their leaders, the others might give up. I've seen it happen before." Giving them a wide grin, he added, "And these are only Brigantes, after all."

He studied their faces, mostly pale and determined. Risciporus and Ulcattus were clearly afraid but the others seemed determined enough.

He went on, "But there is no need for everyone to fight. In fact, I want some of you to climb down that cliff and try to get away. Risciporus, you should go because you can sail a ship to get back home. Take Tegan with you. And Adelligus. Anyone else who wants to go may do so."

Adelligus' young face darkened as he bristled angrily, "I will not leave while there is fighting to be done. I am a warrior."

Calgacus waved a hand to calm the young man as he explained, "I need you to protect Tegan and Risciporus."

"I am not afraid to die here," Adelligus insisted proudly.

He looked at his father and asked, "If you stay, what is there for me to go back to?"

Runt gave his son a weak smile as he replied, "I would rather that you lived."

"I am staying," Adelligus declared.

He slammed the butt end of his spear into the damp turf, signalling his determination.

Before Calgacus could argue, Tegan moved to stand beside Adelligus and said, "So am I."

Risciporus' face bore an appalled expression as he stared at the girl. After a moment, he looked at Adelligus, swallowed, then turned to Calgacus and said, "Well, there is no point in me going on my own, so I suppose I shall stay too."

318

He cast a glance towards the cliff behind them and shrugged, "Anyway, I don't have a head for heights. I don't think I could climb all the way down there."

Calgacus looked at the others, his eyebrows raised in question.

Hefting his massive club of sharp wood, Ger rumbled, "I will fight. I'd like to try this out for real."

Cawrdaf and Dunnocatus nodded grimly.

"We are your men," said Cawrdaf. "If you fight, we fight."

Ulcattus gave a frightened smile but managed to say, "If everyone else is staying, I will, too, although I don't know what use I will be in a fight."

Looking around the group, Calgacus felt pride swelling within him.

He said, "Thank you, my friends. Well, if we are to fight, let's try to make sure we win. Here's what I want you to do."

Chapter XXXI

Calgacus surveyed the tiny space where they would fight. Between the crude, hastily-built wall on the south side and the precipitous northern edge of the ridge was an open area of relatively flat ground no more than fifteen paces wide. This was where they would make their stand.

He had made the best use of their slim resources that he could. The low wall was now several paces long, enough to slow anyone attempting to encircle them from that side. He had placed Runt and Dunnocatus on the right of their line and instructed Risiporus and Ulcattus to stand further back and use their slings to dissuade any Brigantes who might try to clamber over the wall.

On the left, Adelligus and Cawrdaf also had their slings ready, with their spears laid on the ground within easy reach while, in the centre, he, Brennus and Ger would form the main defence. They would be protected by the only three shields available because he expected them to face the most determined attack.

"Casca wants Brennus and me," he told them. "So use your spears to drive them towards us. Don't let them get close to you. You don't need to kill them, just stop them from getting round behind us."

Tegan had gathered a supply of small stones which she distributed to each of the men who would use slings. This was the surprise Calgacus hoped would give them a slight advantage. Neither the Romans nor the Brigantes had any archers so would only be able to inflict damage at close quarters. Calgacus hoped that the slingshots might disrupt their attack before they were able to close the gap.

"I'll see if I can hit Venutius," Runt promised. "Although I expect he'll be skulking at the back as usual."

Risiporus, regarding his sling with a bemused expression, forced a smile as he said, "The one good thing is that there are so many of them that even I won't be able to miss."

Calgacus' final instructions were for Tegan. Pulling her aside, he offered her his dagger.

"Thank you," she nodded. "But I don't think it will be much use against a spear or sword."

"It's not for fighting with," he told her gently.

As understanding dawned on her young face, he went on, "If they break through our line, I want you to take one of the horses and try to escape. It won't be easy but you might be able to dodge past the men at the foot of the hill. If not, use the knife as you think best."

She gave him a grim, determined nod.

"Thank you for everything you have done for us," she whispered, reaching up to kiss his cheek.

He smiled at her, then turned back to rejoin the others, picking up his borrowed shield and drawing his long sword.

"They're getting ready at last," Brennus informed him. "They must have realised we're not going to surrender."

At the far end of the ridge, some one hundred paces away, the Romans and Brigantes were indeed preparing to advance. They were not in any hurry, it seemed, and Calgacus was grateful that they had not attacked immediately. The time Casca and Venutius had given them had been enough to allow them to prepare.

Yet when he saw the numbers arrayed against them he knew there was little prospect of surviving. For a moment, his sword felt heavy in his hand as his mind filled with memories of the past. Visions of faces and names flashed past his inner eye, reminding him of just how many people had died during the long years of war.

His brother, Togodumnus, after whom his own son was named; Senuala, who had loved him and betrayed him and given her life for him; Tannattos, who had died when the Silures smashed the Second Legion; Gutyn, who had fallen in that same battle, young and brave and always laughing; broad-shouldered Garathus who had been shield-bearer to Cartimandua and had died protecting the Queen from Venutius' rebel army; Donnus and the other men of the Catuvellauni who had followed Calgacus into the wilds rather than serve Rome and who had been killed because of that fateful decision. And Bonduca, his sister, who had died after leading the great revolt that had almost ended the Roman occupation.

There were others, too many to count them all, but Calgacus remembered their faces. So many of them dead while he had survived. The memories flooded him, threatening to distract

321

him from what he needed to do. Angrily, he gathered the memories together and he used them to fuel the fire within him. All those people had died resisting the Romans and he had led most of them to their deaths. He was determined not to lead any more friends to that fate. Not here. Not on this barren, windswept hilltop. Not today.

A small voice inside his head told him he could not prevent his friends from being massacred but he stilled that doubt because he knew he could not afford to give in to such thoughts.

As he sought inspiration, another face appeared in his mind's eye, the face of his brother, the great King, Caratacus, who had been captured and sent to Rome as a captive. Almost the last thing Caratacus had said to him was that he should never give up the fight against Rome and Calgacus was proud that he had held to the promise he had given that day.

The memory of Caratacus gave him strength. Slowly, deliberately, he raised the sword high, the sword that had once belonged to his famous brother.

"Time to taste blood," he said to the blade.

"You should give that thing a name," Brennus told him.

"What?" Calgacus frowned. "It's got a name. It's called a sword."

"No," grinned Brennus. "A proper name. Something like *Foe-Killer* or *Blood-Spiller*."

Calgacus shook his head. The idea of giving a sword a name was as absurd as naming a plough or a shovel but Brennus' suggestion sparked a reminder of another old companion.

"You'd get on well with Annwyl the Bard," he told his son. "If he was here, he'd give every one of our swords a name and sing about our great victory."

"That sounds good," Brennus agreed.

"He'd make most of it up, of course," Calgacus assured him. "Bards always do."

"Men need songs," Brennus replied. "I think today would make a great song."

Runt promised, "If we survive this, I'll make up a song for you and sing it every day."

Some of the others gave nervous laughs and Calgacus shot his friend a grateful look. He had been worried by Runt's air of fatalistic resignation, as if the little man no longer cared whether he lived or died, but the joke he had made sounded much more like his old self.

Calgacus followed his friend's lead by calling to Adelligus and Cawrdaf, "You young lads remember to hold your position. I don't want you killing them all. Leave some for the rest of us."

Another ripple of nervous laughter ran along the line and he knew it was time to instil yet more confidence in the less experienced men.

Raising his sword again, he called, "All right! We are here and we will hold this ground. Don't be worried by their numbers. They can't all come at us at once. And remember, the men we face are either cavalrymen who aren't used to fighting on foot or cowardly Brigantes led by a man who always gets others to do his fighting for him. So let's make them fear us!"

He thrust his sword arm high, pointing the massive blade towards the dull, grey clouds.

"Camulos!" he bellowed, invoking the name of the ancient War God of the Catuvellauni.

"Camulos!" came a ragged echo.

"Louder!" he shouted. "Camulos!"

"Camulos!"

This time they turned the cry into a roar. The sound rolled along the ridge, a sound of defiance and promised death that told their enemies they would not surrender.

Even Brennus was yelling at the top of his voice, calling on the God of his father's lost tribe. He grinned at Calgacus as he did so and the older man felt a surge of pride.

"I am glad you are here with me," he told his son.

Brennus gave him a puzzled look, then smiled.

"So am I," he replied. "Although I wish you'd kept to your rule of only fighting when you know you can win."

"We are going to win," Calgacus assured him. "They are afraid of us. That is half the battle."

"What's the other half?" Brennus asked.

"Having good comrades around you," Calgacus replied. "That's why we can't lose."

The words were spoken with bravado and he knew Brennus could see them for what they were but the young warrior laughed aloud.

"How can we lose?" he grinned.

323

Then there was no more time for talking because the enemy were advancing at last.

They came hesitantly, picking a cautious way along the rock-strewn plateau. The Romans were in the front rank but they were spaced a few paces apart because their long cavalry swords, ideal for hacking down from the back of a horse, needed room to swing, so Casca's men could not stand close together as the heavily armed legionaries did. This, combined with their smaller shields, made them more vulnerable than the Roman soldiers Calgacus usually faced.

Behind Casca and his troopers came the Brigantes, clustered together as if seeking shelter behind the armoured men. They were huddled in a tight group, their spears protruding above their heads like the spines of a hedgehog.

"Let them get close!" Calgacus called. "And keep cheering!"

"Camulos!"

There were no chants from the enemy. Roman soldiers never shouted war cries and the Brigantes seemed almost cowed by what they intended to do. That, Calgacus knew, stemmed from their leader. Concealed somewhere in the midst of his warriors was Venutius, a man who could inspire fear but who never gained true loyalty and who would never lead a war band from the front.

The advance crept towards them, slowly closing the distance.

"Be ready!" Calgacus called.

He raised his sword high in the air again. Then, when the Romans had reached to within thirty paces, he swept it down.

"Now!"

The six men with slings whirled their long cords in rapid circling motions and released a volley of stones. Normally, such an attack was virtually useless against a Roman advance but this small volley did some damage. One stone rang loudly as it smashed off Casca's ornate helmet, forcing the Centurion to stagger and stop for a moment. Another clattered loudly from a shield but two others smashed into the unprotected Brigantes, sending one man to the ground with his skull broken and another reeling back with a shattered arm.

"Again!"

A second volley swept out in response to Calgacus' command, downing two more Brigantes and disarming one Roman who was forced to drop his sword when a slingshot caught his right arm.

"One more!" Calgacus yelled, seeing Casca shouting at his men to resume their advance.

The third volley of stones flew across the narrowing distance and created more havoc among the Brigantes. Calgacus saw one man crumple, his hands clamped to his leg, while another reeled from side to side, his vision blinded by a stream of blood running from a nasty gash on his forehead.

"Spears!" Calgacus yelled.

Adelligus and the other young men dropped their slings and picked up their spears, and Runt drew his twin swords, clashing the blades together to send a ringing warning to his foes that he was ready for them. Only Risciporus and Ulcattus retained their slings, each hurling another stone at the densely packed warriors who were now barely fifteen paces away.

Calgacus braced himself for what he knew must come next. The Romans would charge at them, trusting to their superior numbers to add weight to their attack and overrun the thin line of defenders like a tidal wave crashing over rocks.

But Casca was a horse soldier, not an infantryman, and Venutius was no warrior. Instead of running, the Romans and Brigantes resumed their plodding advance and Calgacus saw, in that moment, that he really did have a chance to win this fight. It was a slim chance, a crazy chance, but he had been a warrior all his life and he could read a battle as well as any man alive. He could sense the mood of combat, could tell when men were ready to break and when they were capable of heroics.

Surprise could win battles, he knew, and he had an opportunity to surprise his enemies.

Once the fight was joined, he knew the superior numbers of the enemy would win the day. It would only take one of his comrades to be cut down and a gap would appear which would lead to them being surrounded and slaughtered.

But the Romans were reluctant to charge because there were so few of them and they were unsure of their allies, while the Brigantes seemed content to let the Romans take the lead. Neither group, it seemed, were in a hurry to engage in close combat.

325

Instinctively, Calgacus knew what he must do. It was a desperate gamble but he knew it might be their only real chance. Even then, he would need to rely on his friends following his lead.

It took half a heartbeat for the idea to form and for him to make the decision.

He charged.

With a roar, Calgacus hurtled into the Romans. As he ran at them, he felt as if he was watching himself, not really there, but the old habits of battle were never forgotten and the burning desire to win gave strength to his limbs. He did not need time to think about what he needed to do, he simply did it.

Time seemed to slow but he did not. He was as fast as lightning while, in his eyes, the enemy moved at a snail's pace. He was on them before they could react.

He wanted to get at Casca, but the Centurion was to his left, intent on reaching Brennus, so Calgacus struck the man who faced him.

Their shields smashed together. The Roman staggered, forced backwards by the ferocious power of Calgacus' onslaught. Calgacus' sword lashed out, catching the hand of the Roman to his right, cutting through flesh and bone to slice off two fingers. The soldier screamed, dropped his sword and lurched away.

The Roman who faced Calgacus was also falling, tumbling backwards to the damp earth. Calgacus aimed a kick at him, catching him between the legs. The man gasped a silent scream, writhing in pain at Calgacus' feet.

Then the Brigantes were around him. Calgacus looked for Venutius but the King was too far away. Other warriors were close by, sharp spears and bright swords ready. Without hesitation, Calgacus swept into them.

A spear jabbed for his face but he blocked with his shield, danced inside the reach of the long weapon and rammed his sword into the Brigante's belly. Twisting, he frantically blocked a thrust from another warrior who had made a clumsy and tentative attack. Dispassionately, Calgacus recognised that the warrior was frightened, his eyes wide and startled even as he stabbed his spear forwards. A swift swing of Calgacus' sword sent him away with blood pouring from a half-severed arm.

He roared at them, daring them to attack him.

"Camulos!"

326

The cry was repeated from behind him and suddenly, where there had been only enemies, Ger appeared, swinging his massive, sharpened club with awesome power and using his borrowed shield as a battering ram to flatten anyone who stood against him. The sailor's bald head glistened with sweat as he bludgeoned down a Roman trooper, the heavy club beating so hard that the Roman's iron-bossed shield cracked and splintered under the power of the onslaught. After clubbing the Roman to the ground, Ger turned to smash the skulls of two Brigantes who tried to cut him down.

Two more Brigantes came at Calgacus. He caught one of them with a blow to the thigh which felled the man in a welter of pain and blood. The second man thrust with his spear. Calgacus saw the strike flashing towards him. It still seemed ludicrously slow yet he knew it must have been fast because he had no time to bring his sword or shield up to block it. He let it come and felt the tip of the spearpoint ram into his breastplate. Without consciously thinking about it, he had braced himself for the impact. He rode the blow, twisting his body slightly so that the iron spear scraped along the front of his bronze armour, then he swept his sword up to knock the spear away to his left. He reversed his swing, the heavy sword moving as if it weighed nothing in his hands. The Brigante let out an involuntary yell of fright as the blade arced towards his face. He jumped away but the tip raked down his forehead to the bridge of his nose, drawing a spray of bright blood. The man dropped his spear and fell to the ground, his hands clasped to his face.

Calgacus ignored the fallen men. He turned to see Runt, dealing death with his two short swords, with Dunnocatus beside him, ramming his spear into the chest of a Brigante warrior.

Slashing at one Brigante with his sword while barging another tribesman aside with his shield, Calgacus was still aware of what was happening around him. He yelled a warning as a Roman swept in behind Dunnocatus. The young warrior tried to turn but the Roman swung his heavy sword, catching Dunnocatus on the back of the neck, felling him instantly.

Runt spun, stabbing out, but the Roman dodged away, ducking behind two Brigante warriors who converged on the little man.

327

Disdaining all thoughts of defending himself, Runt leaped furiously to the attack, driving the two tribesmen back with a blisteringly fast series of thrusts and swings.

Calgacus recognised that the fight was at a critical stage. His unexpected attack had created confusion and fear among the Brigantes. They had expected that the Romans would reach him first but he had smashed through the thin Roman line and the Brigantes had been shaken. But there were still more than enough of them to win this fight if someone were to rally them.

He took a glance to his left and saw that Casca was indeed rallying the right flank of the attack. Here, Brennus had followed Calgacus into the fight and was furiously hacking at the Centurion who blocked and parried, while shouting to his men to surround Brennus and cut him down. Beyond the cluster of struggling men, Adelligus and Cawrdaf were battling against four Brigantes but were being pushed slowly back. Faced with swords, the two young spearmen knew that they could not allow their opponents to get inside the reach of their longer weapons, so they were forced to retreat whenever a Brigante dodged past the tips of the spears. Yet every step they took left Brennus more exposed to the encircling Romans and Brigantes.

Calgacus roared a challenge as he darted for Casca. He batted aside another Brigante, saw Brennus fell a Roman trooper with a savage cut to the man's leg, then leaped at Casca, attacking the Centurion from behind.

Casca still wore his face mask, fighting like some impassive God of War. The mask impaired his vision but he must have heard Calgacus' shout, for he turned, swinging his shield out to block Calgacus' blow. Brennus tried to cut at the Centurion but was forced to defend himself from another Roman who was joined by a young Brigante warrior wielding a long sword. Calgacus was left to face Casca alone.

He was horribly aware that his back was exposed to anyone who cared to attack him but Brennus had been in desperate need of help and now that he had attracted Casca's attention, Calgacus had no option but to fight the Centurion. He could only hope that Ger and Runt would be able to protect him from any other attack.

Most individual combats are over quickly. Within a few moments of trading the first blows, both men know which of them is the better or stronger fighter. Calgacus' first blow rang off the polished, iron boss of Casca's oval shield. The blade gouged into the wood before Calgacus tugged it free in time to block a swipe from Casca's own sword. Those two blows told Calgacus that he had the Centurion's measure.

Casca may have known it, too, but he did not shirk the fight. He raised his sword arm again, preparing to strike. It was a cavalryman's move, a blow Casca must have practised thousands of times, but always on horseback when he had time to prepare before hacking at his target. Calgacus had spent a lifetime fighting on foot at close quarters. Time still seemed to run at a different pace for him. He saw his opening as soon as Casca raised his sword and he knew that he had won this fight even before he struck the decisive blow.

He lunged forwards, using the brief moment when the Centurion's arm was drawn back. The tip of Calgacus' blade found the gap unerringly. It caught Casca's forearm, drawing a spurt of dark blood. With a roar of pain and defiance, Casca flung his shield arm forwards, trying to force Calgacus back. Calgacus retreated one step, then twisted, lashing out his left leg to smash the heel of his boot into the Centurion's exposed leg just above the bronze greave that protected the cavalryman's shin.

Quickly regaining his footing, he blocked Casca's swinging sword with his shield, then heaved, knowing that the Roman's injured leg would hinder his movements. Dashing forwards again, he smashed his shoulder into the Centurion, pushing him away, then dropped low to sweep his sword at the man's legs.

Off balance and unable to dodge, Casca screamed as the deadly blade hacked into the side of his left leg. The edge of his greave crumpled under the impact and Calgacus' blade sank home, smashing the Centurion's bones. He toppled, unable to defend himself, falling face down on the ground.

Without hesitation, Calgacus stepped over him and rammed his sword into the small of Casca's back, just below his armour. A grotesque spasm seized the Centurion's body, then he lay still.

Calgacus turned, prepared to defend himself from another assault but on the right of the battle Ger and Runt had driven off the attackers. Only one Roman still stood, the man who had killed Dunnocatus, and he was backing away, knowing that the fight was lost because the Brigantes had lost heart and were falling back.

329

Calgacus turned back to his left in time to see Brennus hack down the young Brigante swordsman with a ferocious sweep of his blade, driving the tribesman to the ground.

Beyond Brennus, near the edge of the cliff, Adelligus and Cawrdaf had been joined by Ulcattus and Risciporus. They had charged their opponents, downing two and driving the others off but Ulcattus, inexperienced in war, lay on the ground, bleeding from an awful wound to his belly.

The two Romans who still faced Brennus fell back, one of them bleeding profusely from a wound on his leg. They had seen Casca fall, had seen the Brigantes retreat and they knew that, against all the odds, they had lost. A shouted command in Latin from the solitary Roman on the far side of the ridge urged them to fall back. Abandoned by their allies, the soldiers backed hurriedly away.

Calgacus could scarcely believe it. He looked around for more enemies to fight. A gaggle of Brigante warriors still stood, some fifteen paces away, gathered around Venutius but they showed no inclination to attack. They had lost half their number either dead or wounded and Calgacus could see that they had no wish to add to that.

Standing above a cluster of dead and wounded foes, Brennus roared in triumph, spreading his arms wide, raising his sword and shield and tilting his head back as he screamed his triumph to the heavens.

"Camulos!"

Calgacus whirled back to face their enemies. Despite Brennus' roar of victory, he knew the fight was not yet over and that they must press home their advantage now. The Brigantes were shaken and demoralised but they still outnumbered Calgacus' small band. He glared at them, knowing that Venutius was among them, knowing that he at last had a chance to end their old feud. He pointed his sword at the small band of Brigantes.

"Kill them all!" he bellowed.

Then it happened.

Even while Calgacus was shouting his command and the Brigantes were taking a pace backwards, ready to flee, a figure pushed forwards from their midst, grabbing a long spear from one of the warriors. Grey-haired, dressed in a coat of mail topped by a sheepskin jerkin, Venutius screamed in rage as he hurled the spear.

Whether it was skill or luck that guided Venutius' aim, the spear flashed towards Calgacus with astonishing speed. Yet still he was able to watch it dispassionately, knowing that he had time to move. He ducked low, allowing the long shaft to whistle over his head. He grinned as he stood straight once more, then turned when he heard a strangled gasp from behind him, a sound that was cut off almost before it had begun, to be followed by a wail of horror from Tegan that echoed across the hill and sent a shiver like ice through Calgacus' veins.

He turned to see that the spear had flown on, much further than he would have thought Venutius could possibly throw. It had missed Calgacus but it had struck Brennus, catching him in the throat while he still gazed to the sky, thanking the gods for granting him victory.

Calgacus watched in horror as blood sprayed, Brennus fell, and an awful silence covered the tiny battlefield like a shroud.

Chapter XXXII

For a long, horrible moment, nobody moved. Across the narrow ridge, everyone stood transfixed by the sight of Brennus toppling to the ground.

Venutius appeared to be as appalled as anyone by what he had done but his shock lasted only until Calgacus broke the spell by turning to face him. Venutius saw the dark fury in Calgacus' expression and he turned to run, scrambling down the steep hillside as fast as he dared go.

Calgacus leaped in pursuit but a burly Brigante stepped in front of him, sword in hand, ready to defend his fleeing King.

Without thought for his own safety, Calgacus discarded his shield, tossing it to one side and then gripping the hilt of his massive sword in both hands. With a furious yell, he leaped at the Brigante, delivering a flurry of blows with such ferocity that the man's sword was knocked aside as if it were a toy. Calgacus' next blow smashed down on the man's collar bone and drove down through his ribs until it lodged deep within his chest. The Brigante collapsed to the ground but Calgacus' sword was wedged so deeply that it took him a moment to yank it free. By the time he had done so, the rest of the Brigantes had turned tail and, like a flock of startled sheep, had run after Venutius.

Yelling incoherently, Calgacus chased after them but Runt darted to intercept him.

Calling Ger to help stop Calgacus' mad charge, Runt shouted, "Leave it, Cal! They are gone."

Ger pushed his massive bulk in front of Calgacus, preventing him from pursuing Venutius. Runt dropped his swords, stooped to grab a stone and quickly loaded it into his sling. He took a few paces, whirled the sling, then hurled the stone down the hill after the fleeing tribesmen. The stone vanished into the crowd without any apparent effect. The Brigantes continued to leap and stumble down the steep slope, heading towards the foot of the hill where their horses were tethered.

"The bastard killed my son!" Calgacus roared.

He stood, arms lowered, still holding his sword, but as he watched Venutius escape, the fury drained from him, ebbing away as he saw the Brigantes reach their horses. With the men who had remained at the foot of the hill, Venutius still had enough warriors to attack again but the Brigante King had lost all interest in the fight. Near panic, the tribesmen gathered their mounts and galloped away.

Runt retrieved his swords, wiping them clean on the rag he kept for that purpose. He sheathed them, then said, "Come on, we need to get away before they come back."

"The Romans are still here," Ger rumbled.

He pointed with his massive club, its edge now splintered and dark with blood. Three Roman troopers remained at the far end of the ridge. One was lying down while another tended him. The third stood, sword drawn, watching the tribesmen warily.

Runt gave Calgacus a questioning look.

"Do you want them dead?" he asked.

Wearily, Calgacus replied, "Leave them. There is no point. They are beaten already."

Runt nodded. Telling Ger to keep an eye on the Romans, he ushered Calgacus back up to the narrow end of the ridge.

By the time they reached their friends, Calgacus felt more tired than he could ever remember. His body ached from exertion and from a bruise on his thigh. He could not remember receiving the blow but it throbbed and was tender to the touch. He also had cuts on his sword arm, small nicks that had trickled blood down to his wrists. He winced as he felt his newly-healed calf muscle protesting again, and when he breathed hard, he could feel his ribs aching where he had allowed the spear thrust to strike his breastplate. The pain and weariness drained him but the physical pain was as nothing compared to the awful emptiness he felt.

The others were standing in a knot around the spot where Brennus had fallen. Calgacus was dimly aware of Adelligus, his cheek bleeding from a long cut that would leave a livid scar when it healed. The boy's face was a confused contradiction of elation and hurt as he saw them approach. Then the small crowd parted to reveal Tegan on her knees, cradling Brennus' lifeless head in her lap. The spear that had killed him lay discarded to one side but the awful wound it had inflicted could not be hidden.

Calgacus knelt, gently reaching out to touch Brennus' cheek. Tears stung his eyes.

Tegan looked at him and he saw that she was sad but not tearful.

"He died as he would have wanted it," she said. "In victory, with you beside him."

"The spear was meant for me," he whispered hoarsely. "I should have let it hit me."

Tegan shook her head.

"No. If you had died, the Brigantes would have kept fighting. We would all be dead."

"You don't know that."

"I know he would not want you dead," she insisted.

Calgacus could not find any words. The thought drummed through his mind that Brennus had joined the long, long list of people who had died following him into battle while, yet again, he had somehow managed to survive. Looking at his son's dead face, he felt as much guilt as sadness. He had known Brennus for only a few, short weeks and now he was gone. Gone because Calgacus had dodged Venutius' spear throw.

When he closed his eyes he could see the long, iron-tipped shaft coming for him. He wondered why he had ducked instead of trying to knock it aside with his shield. That would have been dangerous but he could have done it. If he had, Brennus would still be alive. Guilt gnawed at his heart.

While the others waited uncertainly for Calgacus to say something, Tegan gently laid Brennus' head aside, rose to her feet and announced, "We must bury him. And the others. Down by the river. The ground will be softer there."

She laid her hand on Calgacus' shoulder as she continued, "Come, we will need your help."

Calgacus stood up and took a deep breath.

"This is not over," he whispered, although nobody was quite sure who he was speaking to. "I will have vengeance one day."

Sdapezi waited while the two barbarians walked slowly along the ridge towards him. The men approached casually, their swords still in their scabbards but Sdapezi kept his own sword ready. He had seen the two of them fight and he knew that, despite the apparent lack of threat, these men were deadly. If he had not seen it for himself, he would not have believed that such a small band of barbarians could smash a Roman line and rout a much larger war band. It should not have been possible and yet it had happened. And now the big man, Calgacus, was coming towards him.

Calgacus halted a few paces away. When he spoke, it was in coarse, accented Latin, his voice thick with suffused anger.

"Your allies have deserted you," he said. "And your commander is dead."

"So what happens now?" Sdapezi asked.

He heard Daszdius rise to his feet behind him. Daszdius was a reliable soldier but he suspected that even the two of them together would probably be unable to kill these two barbarians. The promise of death hung in the air, making Sdapezi swallowed nervously.

Still Calgacus made no threatening move. With a casual, almost weary wave of his hand, he said, "Nothing. We will be going soon. We will leave you a couple of horses so that you can return home."

Sdapezi relaxed slightly, but only slightly. He knew it was unwise to trust the word of a barbarian.

"Why would you do that?" he asked.

"Your friend is wounded. You cannot carry him all the way back."

Sdapezi nodded. Hortensius' leg was badly gashed and the boy was moaning in pain. Without a horse to carry him, there was no way of getting him back to the legions. Even with a horse, the boy's chances were slim. Infection or loss of blood would probably kill him.

Sdapezi looked into the barbarian's eyes as he nodded, "I think there has been enough killing today."

Calgacus informed him, "One of your other men is still alive although I don't think he will last long. We will leave him for you."

"Thank you," Sdapezi acknowledged, wondering who else had survived.

"When you get back to your Governor," Calgacus went on, "tell him what has happened here. Tell him also that if he comes to the North, I will be waiting for him. The tribes will be ready for you."

"I will tell him," Sdapezi promised.

Calgacus held his gaze, then turned to go.

"Stay here until we have gone," he warned. "Then you can do whatever you think best."

He paused, then turned back and added, "There is one other thing you must tell your Governor."

335

"What is that?"

"Venutius of the Brigantes is not to be trusted. Whatever he says, he will lie to you. You would be well advised to kill him."

"I will be sure the Governor gets that message," promised Sdapezi.

Runt and Calgacus made their way back up the ridge to where their companions were gathering the horses and preparing to take the bodies of their dead comrades down to the river. There was one other problem because Ulcattus, although fatally wounded, would probably endure a long, slow, painful death and Calgacus had been wondering what to do for the best. Carrying him would be futile yet abandoning him was unthinkable.

Tegan had promised to tend to the sailor but now, as Calgacus walked over to her, she came to meet him with a sad expression on her young face.

"He is dead," she informed him flatly.

"Already?"

Tegan shrugged.

"It's probably just as well," Runt commented.

"What do we do with the wounded?" Tegan asked, gesturing to the fallen Brigantes and the one Roman who were lying among the dead, moaning and calling weakly for help.

"Leave them," Calgacus replied tersely.

Tegan fixed him with a hard stare.

"You can be a cruel man," she said accusingly. "It would be kinder to kill them quickly."

He replied, "I am not feeling particularly kind today. Leave them. Their friends may return for them."

Tegan's lips set in a thin line but she caught sight of Runt signalling surreptitiously to her. She decided not to argue. Besides, there was something else she needed to show Calgacus.

Motioning for him to follow her, she said, "You must see this one."

She led him to where Brennus had fallen, where the bloody spear still lay on the damp grass as a reminder of its last, fateful act. Nearby, the dead and wounded were piled in a narrow strip where the fighting had been fiercest. Here, a young Brigante warrior, his face clean-shaven and deathly pale, was lying on his back, a dreadful wound gashed down his chest. Beneath his blood-soaked tunic they could see his ribs. His eyes were open but barely registered their presence as they stood over him.

Tegan explained, "This man is called Einon. One of the women in Venutius' band told me that he is Venutius' son."

Calgacus looked down at the dying man. He knew that Tegan was waiting for some sort of reaction from him but he felt no emotion. Brennus' death had drained everything from him, leaving him empty and cold.

"I did not know Venutius had a son," he eventually managed to say.

"Not an official one," she told him. "But he favoured Einon above other men."

"So what do you expect me to do?" he asked her.

"You should kill him," Tegan urged. "It would avenge Brennus."

"No. He is dying anyway. I will take my revenge on Venutius, not on a wounded man who cannot fight back."

Tegan frowned. She chewed her lower lip, regarding Einon whose laboured breathing was rasping in his throat.

"Perhaps you are right," she sighed softly.

"Come on," Runt put in. "We must go before Venutius finds enough courage to come back."

Tugging Calgacus' sleeve, he turned away, heading for the downward slope to the river. Calgacus followed without a backward glance but Runt looked back and gave Tegan a slight nod of his head.

Tegan waited for a few moments. When she saw that Calgacus was busy speaking to Risciporus, she knelt on the ground beside Einon.

The young man's eyes flickered towards her, recognition flaring through his agony.

Swiftly, Tegan drew out the dagger Calgacus had given her.

Leaning close to Einon, she whispered, "This is for Brennus."

A tear trickled from Einon's eye as Tegan's knife took her revenge. She could not tell whether he was grateful or afraid, but she ended his life swiftly, just as she had ended Ulcattus' suffering when the sailor had begged for death.

Wiping the blade clean, she tucked it into her belt, stood and walked away.

Chapter XXXIII

Agricola sat in his office, leaning forwards, his elbows on the large desk, his chin resting on his clasped hands while he listened intently to the man standing in front of him.

The small room was illuminated by oil lamps set in brackets on the wall, casting guttering shadows that could not hide the exhaustion in the soldier's face. He had been given a new cloak and shoes, his armour had been cleaned and polished, he had been fed, had washed and shaved, but the red-lined, hollow eyes showed the toll that his journey had taken. Still, he spoke calmly and clearly, missing out nothing of importance as he gave his report. When he finished, he gave the Governor a smart salute.

Agricola leaned back in his chair.

"Centurion Casca is definitely dead, then?" he asked.

"Yes, Sir," Sdapezi replied.

"But the barbarian, Brennus, is also dead?"

"Yes, Sir."

"Then Casca did his duty."

Agricola paused for a moment before continuing solicitously, "But only three of you survived?"

Sdapezi swallowed.

"That's right, Sir," he croaked.

It had been a long, arduous and miserable journey through rain and fog, with scarcely any food to eat, yet somehow they had reached the army and young Hortensius was, miraculously, still alive by the time they had handed him into the care of the surgeons. The doctors had fussed and clucked their tongues but they had admitted that Hortensius had every chance of making a full recovery. That, at least, was something Sdapezi could be proud of. His report to the Governor, no matter how much he tried to flower it up, was a tale of one failure after another. Fortunately for Sdapezi, they were Casca's failures although he was cynical enough to expect that might not prevent some share of the blame being cast in his direction.

Agricola leaned forwards again, his dark eyes boring into Sdapezi.

"And what else can you tell me of this fellow, Venutius? He has come to me seeking friendship. You tell me that his claim to have killed Brennus himself is true?"

"Yes, Sir," Sdapezi confirmed non-commitally.

He had heard that Venutius had arrived at the fort several days earlier. It had taken a conscious effort for the Decurion not to seek the man out and kill him on the spot.

"But Centurion Casca did not trust him?" the Governor pressed.

"No, Sir. Rightly as it turned out. The bast— ... the barbarian ran and left us."

"Quite. And it seems the other barbarians did not trust him either."

Agricola seemed amused at the Decurion's report of what Calgacus had said about Venutius.

"No, Sir."

Sdapezi was uncomfortable being so close to the Governor and under such intense scrutiny. He had told the man everything but Agricola seemed determined to go over it all twice. Sdapezi felt so tired that it was an effort to remain upright.

Agricola's face betrayed nothing as he nodded, "I see."

He tapped a pensive finger on the table, then his face brightened into a friendly smile as he said, "You did well, Decurion. Now, you should go and get some rest. Tomorrow, I will decide what is to become of you."

He noticed the brief spark of concern in Sdapezi's eyes and quickly added, "Don't worry, man. I always have need of resourceful soldiers. I will think of something that is less hazardous than your recent assignment."

"Thank you, Sir."

Agricola gave a gesture of dismissal and Sdapezi saluted, spun on his heel and marched from the room.

When the door had been closed, Agricola turned to Tacitus who had been standing to one side, listening to the Decurion's report.

"Well, Publius? What do you think?"

Tacitus considered his reply carefully. He began with the obvious.

"Brennus is dead. So is Casca. That removes two problems for you, I think. Casca hardly covered himself in glory and it would have been difficult to reward him had he returned alive."

"Indeed," Agricola agreed.

He raised an eyebrow, indicating that he expected more.

"But these are small concerns," Tacitus continued. "That Venutius claims to be King of the Brigantes and wishes to be an ally means, I suppose, that next year's campaign is made much simpler. We can march north with no opposition. If we can trust him."

Agricola smiled. It was a smile Tacitus had seen before and he knew that it presaged a correction to his forecast.

"The Brigantes," Agricola informed him, "are notoriously fickle. Whatever Venutius may say, some of them will oppose us. That is their way. So, we shall proceed on the basis that the entire tribe will be hostile."

"I bow to your greater experience, Sir," Tacitus conceded smoothly. "But what of Venutius himself?"

Agricola ran a hand through his close-cropped hair as he mused, "Yes, that is something to ponder, isn't it? It seems that nobody trusts the man. Having met him myself, I am not surprised."

"Shall I have him executed?"

Agricola waved a hand, dismissing the suggestion.

"No, I think not. We shall invite him to be my guest. Permanently. He will accompany us on the campaign. You never know, he may prove useful. If he does, perhaps I will install him as a puppet King one day. Or perhaps not."

"And if he does not prove useful?" Tacitus asked.

Agricola merely gave a thin smile which told Tacitus the answer. Hostages who were not useful did not generally grow old.

"He will need to be closely guarded," observed Tacitus.

"Of course. I shall allocate a squadron of auxiliary cavalry to watch over him. And I think I shall appoint that fellow Sdapezi as its commander. He deserves some reward. See to that, will you?"

"Centurion rank, Sir?"

"Yes," Agricola confirmed.

"Very good, Sir."

Tacitus knew that his father-in-law was quick to promote men who had shown some ability. Unlike some generals, Agricola never bothered himself with anyone's background. All that mattered was that a man could do the job required of him. Sdapezi had indeed shown remarkable resourcefulness. Promotion to

Centurion would also mean he would be in the Governor's debt. A commander could never have enough soldiers who were indebted to him. It helped to keep them loyal.

Agricola observed, "I can tell by your tone that something is bothering you, Publius. What is it?"

"I am sorry, Sir. You know more about these barbarians than I do, but I do think it would be better to dispose of Venutius permanently."

"Perhaps," Agricola smiled. "But there is one thing you are forgetting, Publius."

"What is that, Sir?"

"Sdapezi tells us that Calgacus suggested we should kill Venutius."

Frowning in puzzlement, Tacitus agreed, "That is what he said. But you yourself told me that these Britons often squabble among themselves. The two men are obviously enemies."

"Precisely. But Calgacus is also *our* enemy. From what we have heard, it seems that age has not diminished his capacity to cause trouble. We shall have to face him one day."

"If what he says is true," Tacitus pointed out.

"Oh, he will fight us," said Agricola airily. "Have no doubt about that. But the point is that if he wants Venutius dead, then that is a good reason for us to keep the wretched man alive. You should never do what your enemy wants you to do, Publius. Remember that."

"Yes, Sir."

"Now, I think I will retire for the evening. Tomorrow will be another busy day."

Tacitus nodded. That, at least, was true. Every day was a busy day when you worked for Agricola. Even with winter upon them there was much that the Governor wanted done. There were roads to be built, forts to be sited, rivers to be bridged. There were supplies to be gathered, weapons to be manufactured and soldiers to be drilled until they were exhausted. In the springtime, the army would march north and the Brigantes would be incorporated into the province. They might resist or they might not. In the end, it would make no difference, for they would be conquered and they would be civilised.

And after that?

The island stretched for many more miles to the north, all the way to the rugged mountains where the Caledonians and Picts waited.

Tacitus had a mental image of masses of barbarians lining the hilltops, brandishing spears as they yelled defiance at Rome. It would be a glorious victory for the Governor when they were crushed. It may take a few years but it was inevitable. Nobody could stand against the Legions. Not even Calgacus.

Chapter XXXIV

"It is good to be home," Beatha said happily.

"Yes."

"It is a shame Fulvia and the children cannot come back here."

Calgacus shrugged, "They have their own life now."

They had stayed on Iova for a few weeks, celebrating the Midwinter solstice with Cadwgan and the druids and enjoying being with Fulvia and her family. But Iova was not their home, so they had eventually set off on the long trek across the wide northern lands. It had been a wrench to leave, and Calgacus had been touched to see that his grandchildren were sorry to see him go.

He had also been sorry to say farewell to Risciporus and Ger but the sea Captain was adamant that he would find a new crew and resume his old life, so they had embraced as friends, then Calgacus had led his small party home.

Smoke curled into the overcast sky from the rooftops of the roundhouses as the riders approached the village. Recognising them, the watchmen called the people out to greet them. By the time they reached the first homes, an excited crowd had congregated.

Pushing aside his weariness, Calgacus gave orders for a feast to be held to celebrate their return, an announcement which brought shouts of approval from the villagers.

Beatha smiled and waved as she rode up the gentle slope to their hilltop homestead, while Fallar, radiant despite the heavy, hooded cloak that concealed much of her face, drew admiring glances from some of the young men who had clearly missed having her around. Calgacus thought to himself that they would be even more disappointed if her marriage to Coel's grandson, Tuathal, became a reality.

They had stopped at Coel's broch on the way home and Beatha had spoken to the young man, reluctantly conceding that he seemed, as she put it, nice enough.

343

Old Coel had pushed the idea of a marriage but Calgacus had been too weary and full of grieving, so he had put the matter off and had managed to escape without making a firm promise. Still, he had been forced to agree to return the following year to discuss the tribal alliance and he knew that he would not be able to avoid the question of Fallar's betrothal for much longer.

As they passed through the village, the people clustered around, calling out questions. Among them were Dunnocatus' mother and brothers. Calgacus reined in his horse, dismounting to speak to them but the tears were flowing before he was able to say a word. They knew from his expression that Dunnocatus would not be returning.

"He died a warrior's death," he told them. "You should be proud of him."

The mother was sobbing, clinging to her two remaining sons for support. Feeling helpless, Calgacus promised, "I will come back and speak to you later."

He turned away before his voice could betray his own sorrow.

They rode out of the village, through the fields and up to the wooden wall that surrounded Calgacus' home. Another small crowd had gathered at the gates to welcome them back.

Garco was there, grey-haired and slightly round-shouldered now, but still alert and dependable. Beside him was Togodumnus, Calgacus' son.

Calgacus stopped dead when he saw him, for Togodumnus was wearing a red, Roman cloak, fastened at the shoulder by an ornate, Roman-style brooch.

Beatha turned to Calgacus. As always, she had instantly understood his reaction.

"Cal, do not be angry," she warned. "Remember, he is your son."

"My son died," Calgacus hissed. "Venutius killed him. Now the Romans are taking my other son."

"Do not judge before you have heard the tale," Beatha told him under her breath. "You are too hard on him."

But the tale was as bad as Calgacus had feared. More Roman ships had sailed up the coast. This time, they had distributed gifts of silver coins, fine jewellery and other trinkets. They had promised peace to all who welcomed them and explained the benefits of friendship with Rome.

344

"They really are wonderful people," Togodumnus declared as they sat round the fire exchanging their stories. "They can teach us so much."

His words cut Calgacus deeper than any knife, casting the accusation that his whole life had been wasted in fighting men who wanted to be his friends.

Calgacus saw Beatha's warning look. He held his tongue but he could not stay to listen to Togodumnus extol the virtues of Rome. Angrily, he stalked out of the house into the night.

With nowhere to go, he tramped to the stockade's south wall. Standing at the parapet, looking down the steep, wooded hillside to the dark waters of the broad river far below, he took a deep breath of the chill air.

"What is a man without sons?" he asked the night sky.

"He is himself," came Runt's answering voice from behind him.

Calgacus turned, grateful, as always, for Runt's company.

"What are you doing out here?" he asked. "You should be with Tegan."

That had been the greatest surprise of the entire journey. Once they had reached the coast, they had stolen a small boat which Risciporus had steered north. During the voyage, Runt and Tegan had sat together, heads close in whispered conversation. Calgacus had assumed they were sharing stories of their respective losses but it had obviously been much more than that. When they had reached Iova, Tegan had stayed with Runt, sharing his bed on the first night and rarely leaving his side since then.

Calgacus had been almost struck dumb with amazement. He recalled how Beatha had laughed at him.

"You are blind sometimes," she had chided. "I saw it as soon as they stepped off the boat."

"I just thought she was more likely to go with one of the younger men," Calgacus had said.

"Liscus is not old," Beatha had smiled. "At least, you keep telling me that the two of you are still young."

She had linked her arm in his, leaned close and whispered into his ear, "Now, why don't you show me how young you still are. I have missed you and we have a small house to ourselves, too, you know."

Being with Beatha always calmed Calgacus but even she was not able to soothe the loss he felt at Brennus' death. Tegan, it seemed, had coped with that loss far better and had found comfort in being with Runt. The relationship seemed to be good for both of them and Calgacus was forced to admit that his friend was more like his old self again, laughing and joking more than he had done at any time in the past year.

Now, standing under the cold stars that shone like tiny sparks of ice against the night sky, Runt said, "I just wanted to make sure you were all right."

Calgacus sighed, "I am still myself, at least. I just feel that I have lost something precious."

"We have all lost something precious," Runt reminded him. "That is what happens in life. But if you keep looking, you'll find other things that are just as precious."

"You sound like a philosopher," Calgacus scolded. "How is Tegan anyway?"

"She is well. Very well."

Runt paused, causing Calgacus to turn an expectant gaze on him.

Runt went on, "She thinks she is pregnant."

"Already?"

Runt shrugged, "Maybe. It's too soon to be certain."

A thought came to Calgacus as he realised the implications of what Runt was telling him.

"Is it yours? Or ...?"

"I don't know, Cal. Neither does she."

"So if she has a son, he could be my grandson?"

Runt tried to stifle what sounded like a soft laugh.

"Could be," he admitted.

Unable to maintain a stern expression in the face of Runt's laughter, Calgacus sighed, "Well, with a father like you and a grandfather like me, he should turn out to be a fine warrior."

"If it's a boy," Runt cautioned.

"If it's a girl, I hope she takes after her mother."

"Either way, I'll be happy. Children are precious. You should be happy, too. Togodumnus is a good lad."

Calgacus tensed slightly. He knew this was the real reason Runt had followed him outside.

"He's not a warrior," he said flatly.

"We have enough warriors," Runt told him. "Perhaps it is a good thing he is different. At least he had the good sense to tell the Romans he was the head man here. He never mentioned you to them."

"I suspect that was Garco's idea," Calgacus muttered. "But we can never have enough warriors."

Pointing out into the dark night, he went on, "Out there, the Romans are gathering, Liscus. One day they will come here, not in a ship bearing gifts but with the Legions. You know that."

"I'm not worried," Runt replied, sounding genuinely unconcerned.

"You're not? You should be."

Runt chuckled, "The only thing I have to worry about is keeping you alive. If the Romans ever get this far north, you'll beat them."

"What makes you so confident? However often we beat them, they keep coming."

Runt laughed softly again as he explained, "I know you, Cal. You're angry. You are angry because Brennus is dead and you are angry because Togodumnus has been dazzled by the Romans. But if you are angry, the Romans had better be careful. They've never beaten you yet."

"So why do all my victories end up feeling like defeats?"

"That's the stuff," Runt smiled encouragingly. "Stay angry."

Calgacus lifted his hands in the air in a gesture of mock despair.

"So all you are going to do is keep me angry?" he asked.

"It's worked for the past thirty-five years," Runt grinned happily.

Calgacus shook his head. This was the old Runt, back from the blackness of grief that had held his spirit chained all year. Calgacus' own grief was still sharp, still close to the surface, but he knew he would gain nothing by allowing it to rule him.

"I suppose I'd better go back inside," he sighed.

"Yes, you should."

"All right. You go ahead. I'll just be a moment or two."

Runt wandered back to the roundhouse, leaving Calgacus alone beside the wooden palisade. Still staring southwards, he could make out the flickering, orange light of a fire from the far side of the river, a tiny spark in the distance, no bigger than the stars above his head. Idly, he wondered who would be out on a cold, winter's night like this. Only a fool, he thought to himself. A fool like me.

Digging under his cloak and tunic, he pulled out the golden coin that hung around his neck. Under the pale starlight it was too dim to make out the detail but he ran his thumb over the familiar surface, feeling the contours of the horse that was etched on the obverse side.

He had wanted to give this coin to Brennus but that would not happen now. It was still his. He was still the War Leader, son of the great Cunobelinos. When the Romans came, it would be up to him to face them. It would be his burden and nobody else's.

He put the coin to his lips, kissing it gently before tucking it back out of sight beneath his clothes where it held his memories close to his heart. All of his memories.

Taking a deep breath, he turned back to the roundhouse. Tonight was a night for feasting and getting drunk. Tomorrow, they would make their plans.

When the Romans came, he would be ready.

Author's Note and Acknowledgements

Most of what we know about the life and campaigns of Agricola comes from the writings of his son-in-law, Tacitus, who is probably the most famous and certainly the most quoted of Roman historians. He wrote a biography of Agricola, extolling the general's virtues and recording his campaigns in Britain. Some modern historians have questioned the strict accuracy of Tacitus' claims, suggesting that some of the things he says Agricola achieved were actually accomplished by Agricola's predecessors as Governor. However, we must remember that the term, "historian" had a slightly different meaning to the Romans. Like other writers, Tacitus intended that his writing should not only record events, but should entertain and make political points relevant to his own day. It was also his duty as son-in-law, to paint a positive picture of his famous relative.

As for Tacitus himself, very little is actually known about his life. In fact, it is not even certain what his correct praenomen was. It is recorded both as Publius, as I have used in this story, but also as Gaius. How such a famous writer can be so shrouded in mystery is a quirk of history.

Whether Tacitus did actually ever visit Britain is not known. He certainly mentions Britain frequently in his other writings, although whether the information he provides comes from personal experience or from speaking to his father-in-law, is debatable. Tacitus never claims to have visited the province and there is no evidence that he ever did so, but it was not unknown for senior Roman officials to employ members of their family on their staff, so it is not impossible that Tacitus may have done a spell of military service under Agricola. At least one modern author has claimed that the descriptions of Britain that Tacitus gives are so vivid that they must come from personal experience. Admirers of Tacitus' writing style would probably claim that he is renowned for memorable descriptions, irrespective of whether he had seen the things he describes. With no conclusive evidence either way, I decided to bring him to Britain in this fictional work on the grounds that there is no proof that he did not visit these shores.

As for the new Governor, Agricola's first action on his arrival in Britannia was to subdue the Ordovices who lived in what is now central Wales. Tacitus does not name the leaders of the revolt and the character of Brennus in this story is entirely fictional. Tacitus claims that the reward for rebellion was for the Ordovices to be wiped out. No doubt this is an exaggeration, although the Ordovices are not mentioned again in Roman writings.

After his rapid and conclusive victory, the recording of which smacks of Tacitus talking up his father-in-law's actions, Agricola re-conquered the island of Anglesey which had previously been devastated by Governor Paulinus some eighteen years earlier. That Agricola had to return there is a sign, perhaps, that the druids had not been completely destroyed by the first attack.

Agricola's next task will be to complete the conquest of the Brigantes. This famous tribe had, according to Tacitus, been subdued a few years earlier by Governor Cerialis, with Agricola, then commander of the Twentieth Legion, allegedly playing a prominent role in those campaigns. However, Tacitus records that Agricola had to fight his way north, so it is possible that Cerialis' campaigns had not been entirely successful. Equally, it can be argued that Tacitus merely wanted to give Agricola credit for finally conquering a tribe who had, in reality, already been defeated. As is so often the case when dealing with First Century Britain, the precise details of what actually happened remain shrouded by the passage of time.

I should point out that the historical Venutius had vanished from the records by this time. However, my fictional character is so necessary to Calgacus' story that I could not simply kill him off. He is far too much fun to write about to permit that.

Venutius' home, as described in this story, is based on the Iron Age fortifications at Stanwick, near Scotch Corner. These were excavated by Sir Mortimer Wheeler, who claimed they may have been the home of Venutius, although others have claimed that they could equally have been the home of Queen Cartimandua who has featured prominently in my earlier Calgacus stories. Readers of the Calgacus adventures will know that I placed Cartimandua's home much further south, principally because I wanted the northern base to be Venutius' home.

Whoever lived at Stanwick in reality, they had connections with Rome because roof tiles and other Roman luxury items have been found on the site. I have given this place the fictional name of Dun Brigantia as I have been unable to find any reliable source for its original name. The name "Stanwick" is from Anglo-Saxon or Old Norse and simply refers to the stone walls that can still be seen there today.

I should also briefly mention the palace attributed in this story to King Cogidubnus of the Regni where Agricola and Tacitus were entertained at a banquet. This description is based on the magnificent remains of an enormous complex at Fishbourne. This has been associated with Cogidubnus (sometimes confusingly also referred to as Togidubnus) since the first excavations in 1960 although there is no positive evidence linking him with the site except the fact that the palace or, more correctly, extremely large villa, was built on such a grand scale that it must have been the home of some wealthy and important person. Some historians argue that it could have been the residence of a Roman Governor but I make no apology for giving it to Cogidubnus, a character who has often been mentioned in the Calgacus stories but has never appeared in person. I thought it was time to give him a cameo role and Agricola's arrival was the ideal opportunity because the new Governor made a point of trying to convert the leading British families to Roman ways. There is an often-cited passage in Tacitus which describes how, at Agricola's urging, the Britons adopted the toga, spoke Latin and enjoyed theatres, baths and amphitheatres. Tacitus often seems to have a regard for what later British imperialists would term the "noble savage" and, in a manner typical of his writing, he says that the Britons thought that behaving like Romans made them civilised although it was, in reality, merely another sign of their slavery. Whether Cogidubnus would have agreed with that assessment is something about which we can only speculate.

I should also put in a brief word about the sailing ship captained by the fictional Risciporus. This is based on a type of vessel usually referred to as a Birlinn but which is only known through carved representations on gravestones and other monuments. It is often claimed that this type of boat has Nordic origins but there are clues suggesting it is much older than the Viking era and, indeed, the Birlinns seem to have had a flat stern

351

rather than the pointed one of the Viking longships, with its rudder placed centrally.

A replica Birlinn has been built and has proved extremely seaworthy, nimble and fast, thus providing the basis for Risciporus' outmanoeuvring of a Roman galley. This is not implausible since Julius Caesar himself recorded that the Celtic tribes of what is now northern France possessed extremely nimble sailing ships which his own navy struggled to overcome.

As for Calgacus, he will find that the greatest tests of his life will soon be upon him. Some may consider him past his prime as a warrior, but he will need all of his experience if he is to face the advancing Roman army because Agricola is absolutely determined to conquer the whole island. There are many battles still to be fought.

As always, I owe thanks to several people for assistance with this story. Moira and Stuart Anthony for reviewing and commenting on the drafts, and my son Philip for designing the cover. Connor Stables did some excellent work researching the Birlinns and the works of several modern historians, especially Alistair Moffat, provided some excellent background. Many other friends and family provided encouragement which enabled me to press on with this work even when I struggled with some aspects of the story. My thanks to all of them.

GA
April, 2015

Other Books by Gordon Anthony.

All titles are available in e-book format. Titles marked with an asterisk are also available in paperback.

In the Shadow of the Wall*
An Eye For An Eye
Hunting Icarus*

The Calgacus Series:
World's End*
The Centurions*
Queen of Victory*
Druids' Gold*

The Constantine Investigates Series:
The Man in the Ironic Mask
The Lady of Shall Not
Gawain and the Green Nightshirt

A Walk in the Dark (Charity booklet)

ABOUT THE AUTHOR

Born in Watford, Hertfordshire, in 1957, Gordon's family moved to Broughty Ferry in the early 1960s. Gordon attended Grove Academy, leaving in 1974 to work for Bank of Scotland. After a long but undistinguished career, he retired on medical grounds in 2008 without having received any huge bankers' bonuses.

Registered blind, Gordon had more time on his hands after retiring so, with the aid of special computer software, he returned to his hobby of writing and had his debut novel, "In the Shadow of the Wall" published in 2010. Gordon's books are now being read by a world-wide audience. As well as his historical adventure stories, he has ventured into crime fiction with some spoof murder mysteries in the "Constantine Investigates" series. He is also kept busy with speaking engagements, visiting libraries, schools and community groups to talk about his books.

In addition to his novels, Gordon devotes some of his time to raising funds for the RNIB. As well as visiting schools and social clubs to talk about his sight loss, he has self-published a charity booklet titled, "A Walk in the Dark", a humorous account of his experiences since losing his eyesight. The booklet is available free from Gordon's website www.gordonanthony.net

All Gordon asks is that readers make a donation to RNIB. This booklet can also be purchased from the Amazon Kindle Store. Gordon will donate all author royalties to RNIB.

Now almost completely blind, Gordon continues to write stories and, in his spare time, attempts to play the guitar and keyboard with varying degrees of success.

Gordon is married to Alaine. They have three children. The family lives in Livingston, West Lothian.

You can contact Gordon via his website or by sending an email to ga.author@sky.com

10960617R00200

Printed in Great Britain
by Amazon.co.uk, Ltd.,
Marston Gate.